Climb of the Heart

Paperback ISBN: 978-1-967628-03-2
Hardcover ISBN: 978-1-967628-09-4

Catalog data:
FIC027020 – Fiction / Romance / Action & Adventure
FIC027010 – Fiction / Romance / Contemporary
FIC002000 – Fiction / Action & Adventure
FIC044000 – Fiction / Women
FIC019000 – Fiction / Literary

 Emerald Books

Bend, Oregon
printed in the United States
Library of Congress control data has been applied for

Climb of the Heart

by Bart Sobel

1. Dr. Audrey Ferrington

Audrey Ferrington is a societal hybrid. The offspring of socially prominent Boston Brahmin stock, she moved with her family to northern New Mexico at age thirteen. Jonathan Reed Ferrington, Audrey's father, opted for a career in education, achieving a full professorship at Harvard before he was thirty-five. Subsequent national recognition as an innovative humanities teacher, as a Reconstructionist philosopher and a modern day disciple of John Dewey, propelled him as a guest lecturer throughout the country. Her mother, Abigail Hinckley, a direct descendant of the first governor of the Massachusetts Bay Colony, was a professional fundraiser for liberal causes. During her early childhood, both parents were occupants of innumerable foundation board seats. Eventually tiring of the limelight and the burdens of social privilege and distressed by a perceived superficiality in their professional lives, the family shocked the elite East Coast aristocracy when they abruptly dropped titles and prestige to pursue a simpler life by moving to a modest ranch near Albuquerque, New Mexico, so that Jonathan could accept a position as Director of State

Educational Services. Their drastic lifestyle move made the front page of the *Boston Globe* and was even recorded by the *New York Times* and *Time* magazine, but, in time, the press and its public found new idols to worship and the Ferringtons, leaving behind the socially prominent world of Back Bay, were forgotten, though not abandoned by the social register. For a while the rumor mills circulated—a family plagued by dark hidden secrets—but soon, unearthing nothing, they were left alone to make their most unusual journey.

Audrey was a unique amalgam—a Northeastern, privileged, liberal intellectual transplanted to a Western, egalitarian, conservative, physically-oriented environment. While her upbringing had instilled the love of all things academic, her new environment taught her to equally cherish physical pursuits. Jonathan and Abigail encouraged her propensity for independent free-thinking. As a result, her politics were unadulterated liberal and her lifestyle highly eccentric. As Audrey grew to womanhood, her personality combined a bold and adventurous playfulness with hard-bitten intellectual discipline. Concern for the underprivileged had been indelibly ingrained into her subconscious by her father. Perhaps he had gone overboard, but once arriving in New Mexico, Jonathan Ferrington faced each day believing his efforts could and would make a difference. This legacy left its mark on Audrey.

Beginning in high school, she had worked for and with underprivileged Chicanos against the Anglo-dominated mining and energy companies that controlled the resources of the northern part of the state. Audrey was neither a fanatic nor an idealist, she simply had principles. But unlike her father, Audrey felt no alienation from established, white, upper-class society. She moved easily from the sophistication of Albuquerque's private tennis club to the raucous environment of a local Chicano bar. When in the company of her peers, Audrey never failed to criticize herself and her white friends for their needless lavishness, on the other hand, she didn't hesitate to scold the Chicanos for their lack of industriousness and discipline. Though she spoke with conviction, she pursued a path of rational discourse, and never failed to employ her natural charm or her sex appeal to win a point. It was this sense of contradictory balance that allowed Audrey to move so easily and gracefully through life. Formal rules had no meaning; life's path was fraught with inconsistencies. In high school the young Ferrington gained notoriety as both a scholar and an athlete. Valedictorian of her high school class, she opted for a small, prestigious liberal arts college in the East. Accomplished as a tennis player, skier, and middle-distance runner, Audrey knew from an early age that she wanted a stimulating career enriched by recreational sports, as opposed to the life of a professional athlete. Her enthusiasm for science was kindled by a freshman chemistry professor. A career as a physician offered the ability to merge her love for the rationality of science and her need to serve humanity; this professional path proved to be the perfect goal.

Ever since her late adolescence, Audrey viewed sex as a healthy release from tension, as well as just plain enjoyable. At age sixteen, she lost her virginity. From then on, Audrey ensured she was connected to a man who was capable of fulfilling her sexual desires. In comparison to her tumultuous adolescence, her mid-twenties taught her to choose her romantic liaisons more selectively, but that was not always the case. Her first high school boyfriend was, as was the dream of any sophomore cheerleader, the quarterback of the football team, Johnny Blackwell. In the backseat of a beat-up Chevrolet, evenings were spent spreading a blanket under starlit nights; Audrey, for a year, reveled in their exploring every inch of each other. By the end of her sophomore year of high school, her parents confronted her—they had become aware that she was using birth control pills. Without even a hint of embarrassment, Audrey confirmed their accusations. But her quarterback was soon leaving to attend a southern California university. Amidst a deluge of tears, but much to her parents' delight, Johnny Blackwell left for college. Audrey cried and, as much as she missed him, it was the return to celibacy that proved most upsetting. This predicament did not last long. Like a butterfly opening its wings for the first time, she discovered the physical exhilaration found in sex and could think of no valid reason to deny herself the pleasure. Even though she lacked emotional connections with the boys after Johnny's departure, she experimented. Never sacrificing her pre-occupation with attaining superior grades, knowing from an early age that pursuing a career in medicine was her destiny, Audrey would put in the mandatory rigorous hours of study and then find herself exploring the wrong side of the tracks, rather than enjoying the traditional Friday and Saturday night high school events with friends. Cheerleading was forgotten once a fake ID gained her access into smoky bars. Standing with a beer in her hand, a cigarette dangling from her lips, listening to country Western music blaring from a jukebox, she'd watch as ranchers and pot-bellied truck drivers played endless hours of pool. Audrey's new style included skintight jeans and a cropped top; she obviously preferred going braless now too. Guzzling alcohol dulled her senses, coaxing her into losing her inhibitions; she began experimenting for experiment's sake, hardly remembering their names—first there was Ralph, a bearded high school drop-out, then Don Macky who smelled from working long days as a cattle feeder. Sex on impulse, accepting dares, flirting and teasing; during the year since Johnny Blackwell's departure, she lost count of the number of men she'd slept with.

Her parents, bewildered and distraught, were aghast at her behavior. A light would flicker in the kitchen when she'd arrive home, often past two or three in the morning. To gain entrance to her bedroom, she had to pass by her mother who, thoroughly exhausted, sat at the kitchen table with her eyes closed, her fingers cradling her face. Abigail would awaken, her pained eyes pleading to understand, but Audrey remained unfazed and unwilling to explain her behavior. The next morning, in the middle of history class, Audrey was summoned to the guidance department. Her parents, the school principal, the guidance counselor, Louise Fetcher, and a child psychologist, Dr. Amos Appleby, stood waiting for her. As if on a distant planet, she listened as the adolescent therapist instructed the group that Audrey needed therapy and, equally important, constructive hobbies to occupy her time. Her father insisted on violin lessons; her mother heard that the racquet club recently hired a tennis professional. "Given Audrey's natural athletic ability, tennis would be an ideal outlet to channel her physical needs." And, Dr. Appleby, to no one's surprise, accepted the confused adolescent as a patient. After an hour, the meeting ended and all were satisfied that Audrey would redirect herself from a freight train running amuck. With Dr. Appleby's assistance, she would be reprogrammed into a positive, healthy direction. Passively Audrey sat listening, nodding while her elders sermonized.

During the spring of her senior year of high school, at least on the surface, it appeared that Audrey abandoned her wildly destructive side, and with Dr. Appleby's able guidance, and to her parents' delight, she voraciously channeled her energies into three areas—academics, music lessons, and honing her tennis skills. Academics required minimal effort and college acceptances came in droves, both Stanford and Northwestern universities accepted her into a special combined six-year undergraduate and medical school program. Although Audrey's choice was the Palo Alto campus, her parents were emphatic that a traditional four-year liberal arts curriculum was the more judicious choice. Harvard, Princeton, Wellesley, and Swarthmore were the four finalists and, after a family conference with Dr. Appleby, Swarthmore, a prestigious liberal arts campus on the outskirts of Philadelphia, was selected. Never once did her parents bring up her outrageous ways of the previous year; they accepted that adolescence took strange twists and incidents from the past were conveniently not discussed.

Abigail and Jonathan Ferrington reveled in their daughter's interest in the violin and tennis. On weekends, she spent endless hours with her violin instructor, Harold Mitchell. Listening to music, playing concertos together, and studying composition, the violin instructor remained an enigma. Why Mitchell, a tall, lanky man in his late twenties, chose Albuquerque as his home base perplexed her. Raised in Chicago, an undergraduate degree in music from Yale University, a master's from the prestigious Juilliard School in New York City, Mitchell committed himself to a career devoted to musical composition. Mitchell lived the life of a hermit, earning barely enough to survive by taking on an occasional tutoring job. Opportunities for income were few and far between as people in Albuquerque didn't exactly queue up to take violin lessons. Much to his surprise, Mitchell grew to look forward to his daily lessons working with his only serious protégée, Audrey Ferrington. The two maintained one strict rule—their conversations, either directly or indirectly, only in-volved music. As the months progressed, the hours spent with her instrument became a release; she found peace in both playing and listening to the violin. She sat for hours listening while Mitchell played pieces by Chopin and Haydn, marveling at her tutor's dexterity, his passion, his mastery, as his fingers deftly plucked the strings. Toward the end of their first year to-gether, Audrey's progress was so swift that the duo played compositions together from diverse works spanning Franz Lizst to Johann Sebastian Bach. Her parents, listening from an adjoining room as the two played the finale from a Claude Debussy waltz, spontaneously, at the conclusion of the piece, entered the room and clapped. Her mother even went so far as to inquire if they'd be willing to have a formal public recital, but Audrey refused.

As the violin became her private vocation, the mastery of the game of tennis evolved into a full-fledged passion. Running, grace, agility, Ferrington combined the raw power of a wild colt interspersed with the delicate hands of a veteran Murano glass blower. Tennis was transformed into a well-choreographed ballet. Her body, straining to its maximum, pushed herself into realms once thought impossible. Mastering a stroke meant learning the proper technique, but also included precise execution to elevate the game to its rightful art form. Her parents' choice for an instructor, a blond Australian journeyman, Hans Belderstein, was a former touring professional. Belderstein, in his time, played in the qualifying rounds to gain admittance to the main draw in Wimbledon, the French and Italian championships. At his best, Belderstein once reached the second round of the Australian championships. But, more than a player, Belderstein was the consummate coach. Schooled by some of the greats of Australian tennis, Belderstein possessed a magnificently crafted assortment of shots. Relishing the challenge of working with Audrey, Belderstein demanded that before moving from a topspin cross court backhand to an underspin backhand approach, Audrey needed to properly master the shot before progressing. It was sometime during their third or fourth month of his tutelage that Belderstein casually remarked that Audrey, drenched in sweat, looked particularly beautiful. She scolded him and demanded he concentrate on tennis. Never again did Belderstein make any remark that could be interpreted as having even the remotest shade of sexual overtones. Their relationship had a mission, a well-defined task; like a tiger stalking its prey, Audrey set out to become technically proficient.

Preoccupied with her hobbies, Audrey seemingly lost interest in prioritizing her sexual explorations. By the end of senior year, she was already playing number one singles on her high school team. Much to everyone's surprise, she was crowned champion of the New Mexico State Girls High School Tournament. Accompanied by her mother and coach, she subsequently traveled around the Southwest and was victorious in three United States Tennis Association tournaments. A month after her graduation, she played and lost in the finals of the prestigious United States eighteen-year-old hard court championships held at Kalamazoo, Michigan. Tennis scholarships poured in, but she stayed the course, Swarthmore remained her choice, and a career as a doctor, decided at age eight, remained the focus. Early in August, Dr. Appleby, after almost two years of twice weekly therapy, summoned Audrey's parents for a farewell meeting. He proudly proclaimed Audrey was prepared to psychologically meet the world; Abigail and Jonathan were delighted, no one dared mention that it had been but a brief eighteen months since she had mistakenly ventured onto a disastrous path.

The remaining two weeks prior to her departure for college were extremely busy with packing and saying her goodbyes. On her last day at home, she met Hans Belderstein for lunch and they ended up in bed. Her departure from Albuquerque brought tears to her parents' eyes but Audrey felt determined she would meet and conquer whatever challenges lay ahead.

Audrey entered Swarthmore College at age eighteen. It was in the spring of her sophomore year that she first met Philip. As with most meetings, their initial acquaintance was happenstance. She had been persuaded by her friend, Amanda

McCracken, to attend an art exhibit for a group of young, aspiring French sculptors. A man, somewhat older but dashingly handsome, came over and asked her opinion of the pieces they were viewing. The two talked for a few moments. Audrey, fascinated by Philip's expansive knowledge of art, stood mesmerized. She felt an unmistakable desire to work her charms; but before being given the opportunity to kindle his interests, Philip turned, excused himself and abruptly left. Audrey would not cross paths with this handsome man for three years.

2. Mr. Philip Hornsby

Philip is the only son of Wilton Ainsley Hornsby, one of the richest men in America with family holdings conservatively estimated to exceed half a billion dollars. The Hornsby family was engaged in a multitude of businesses through the auspices of an industrial conglomerate, Hornsby Enterprises, Inc., and via the investment banking firm of W.A. Hornsby. Philip was raised in the time-honored tradition of any young prince and heir to a fortune. Reared in a magnificent, white palatial estate in mainline Philadelphia, the Hornsbys also had homes on three continents—a villa at Tryall in Jamaica, an estate in the south of France, and a ski house nestled beside the Little Nell lift in Aspen, Colorado.

Philip attended Exeter Academy, an exclusive preparatory school, and was groomed from an early age to assume his preordained and rightful place in society and business. Summers were spent on the shores of Lake Winnipesaukee honing his athletic skills at Camp Tecumseh. From his earliest memories, and rightfully so, as Wilton Ainsley Hornsby's only son, Philip was destined to head Hornsby Enterprises, but only when his father thought he was ready to assume command. After the proper tutelage in financial matters, the chairmanship would eventually be his. Stepping stones were mandatory; he would work his way up the corporate ladder and secure a suitable marriage for the purpose of fathering a male heir. This was all part of the pre-ordained scenario.

Wilton Hornsby, known by friends and foes alike as W.A., was something of a dinosaur, a mogul in the old style, left over from the last century. Powerful, strong, opinionated, he didn't entertain what others thought. Business was like a roller coaster: One had to ride the highs, extract every inch of the thrills, and when the lows came, as they inevitably did, tightly grip the rails and plow through. Over the years, W.A. chiseled a reputation as a domineering, self-confident giant who believed in the divine right of the rich to their station in life. In his early business career, W.A. allowed nothing to interfere with building his empire—ruthless, straightforward, honest, although most called it arrogant. The method didn't matter, results were all that counted. By the time W.A. passed his sixtieth birthday, he was acknowledged as a titan of the business community, and seldom a day passed that his name didn't appear in the *Wall Street Journal*.

In his later years, he felt safe being magnanimous and in complete control. W.A. became respected, listened to, often feared, but as times changed, his outright ruthlessness was no longer required to protect and enhance the Hornsby interests. Instead, W.A.'s empire became so vast and diverse that a diligent stewardship brought optimal results. W.A. developed a social conscience; the notion of sharing his wealth was regularly honored through the auspices of the Hornsby Foundation, a charitable institution in which he ensured the coffers were always full.

Raising his only son proved far more troublesome than even the most complex hostile business takeover. It was this belief—that the cream rose to the top—that guided the rearing of his son. When Philip reached his mid-teens, W.A. subscribed to the belief that a young man deserved a certain period of time to indulge in youthful indiscretions, but no pregnancies please. The development of athletic prowess was also recognized, though an essentially unproductive necessity of manly energy. W.A. knew that men had to go through this stage, as evidenced by his own Olympic medal for equestrian accomplishments that proudly adorned his mahogany library wall. Not unlike pledging a fraternity, W.A. tolerated and understood the rocky road of passage from adolescence to adulthood. During his teenage, college, and business school years, W.A. silently but tactfully encouraged Philip to pursue and master both women and sports. With reference to the former, W.A. sternly advised Philip to keep it brief and casual and avoid embarrassing complications. With reference to the latter, W.A. offered little advice, although he did not attempt to conceal his lack of enthusiasm for the path chosen by Philip to express his zeal—scaling foreboding rock walls.

Philip, after leaving the cloistered protectiveness of the Phillips Exeter Academy, followed his ordained path and attended Harvard University to study finance; it was there that Philip began experimenting with dangerous sports. There were encounters with scuba diving, auto racing, whitewater kayaking, even skydiving. Each fling lasted barely a few weeks or months before Philip moved on to something else. W.A. considered these adventures as Philip's way of lashing out and establishing himself; yet, he controlled himself and said nothing. Philip continued his search for an appropriate challenge, something that he could sink his teeth into, until finally a European friend and fellow undergraduate from Salzburg, Austria, introduced him to mountain climbing. In this sport he found what he was seeking. By applying his physical strength and his compulsion for control and command, Philip achieved success and became world-renowned. Approaching a climb as he would a corporate takeover, Philip became the master of marshaling resources, plotting a carefully honed assault and harnessing fear, all essential to scaling a foreboding, natural obstacle. Even during his apprentice stage, Phillip enlisted America's most accomplished climbing legends as instructors. To Phillip, the climbing of mountains was the equivalent of chivalrous warfare for young lords from an earlier age. Though he reveled in the challenge and the conquest, he felt a surge of pleasure when his will overcame dangers. Philip never attempted a major climb without meticulous planning, proper preparation, and state-of-the-art technology. Nor did Philip ever attack any mountain without an army of helpers waiting in the wings. In his one noted failure, a wintertime assault on a technically difficult pitch on Cathedral Ledge in New Hampshire's White Mountains, he was heralded by both critics and supporters for his discipline and acute judgment in abandoning the climb when the weather turned ominously gray and nasty, even though he was but a hundred feet away from the summit.

A verbal minimalist, as a youth Philip's conversations were short and to the point. Carefully choosing words, he seemed more than satisfied with his destiny. To the extent that he rebelled against the future plotted for him by W.A., he programmed each adventure so as to minimize risks. Perhaps Philip abandoned the other dangerous sports he had experimented with because the odds could not be adequately tipped in his favor, or perhaps because he knew that W.A. would not have tolerated an extended fling with something as foolhardy as hang gliding. But there was an element that was intrinsically regal about mountain climbing, with its majesty, its grandeur, its reliance on technical expertise; climbing combined skill and risk that befitted an individual of his privileged lineage.

W.A. tolerated his son's climbing years because he was wise enough to know that he could not simply forbid Philip from pursuing his passion. However, upon his graduation from the University of Pennsylvania's Wharton School of Business with a master's degree, W.A. cleverly restricted Philip's ability to partake by increasing time needed to tend to his responsibilities with Hornsby Enterprises. Thus, without the issuance of an ultimatum and the accompanying risk of revolt, W.A. was able to slowly but confidently control and eventually terminate his son's mountaineering career. The rock climbing was, as W.A. predicted, a passing fancy of his son's youth. Philip had climbed many major peaks of North and South America and Europe, as well as an aborted attempt on the South Col route to Everest that left him, because of a sudden storm, less than a thousand feet from the summit. Phillip resigned himself to abandoning his goal of standing atop Everest when his father announced that his son would, within the next decade, assume his rightful place as the company's chief executive officer. Philip would be responsible for guiding the path of an empire of over 150,000 workers, seventeen companies whose total financial resources exceeded $675 billion. Strangely enough, while all Philip had to do to march up the corporate ladder was be a loyal foot soldier, from the moment he embarked on a business career, he was a born superstar. Philip surpassed W.A.'s acumen with a knack for a deal. Success after success marked his entry to the world of high finance. W.A., after a trying period of having to put up with Philip's adolescent extravaganzas, within a couple years of Philip's joining the workplace, was duly satisfied that his son sufficiently matured and was ready to assume his rightful seat at the helm of the Hornsby Empire. With his business career fully launched, Philip sacrificed the free time to pursue hobbies, hence the exploration of his past was laid to rest.

3. *Audrey & Philip*

In her senior year of college while representing Swarthmore in the NCAA tennis tournament, Audrey again encountered Philip, a few years after their initial interaction. Philip, though already an executive at Hornsby Enterprises, was at the tail end of his youthful exploration and mountaineering phase, vacillating between adventurer, entrepreneur, socialite, and eligible bachelor. On this particular day, he served as the umpire for a third round match in an NCAA Eastern Regional Championship and, as coincidence would have it, Audrey was one of the contestants. Philip simply could not keep his eyes from wandering over to her perfect body. He knew she looked familiar, but it took him most of the match to place her. This beauty first graced his presence at the French sculptor exhibit he attended a couple of years ago. She was hard to forget. Phillip officiated the match as he sat mesmerized watching her every move. Audrey was a superb tennis player, ranked among the top twenty in the NCAA. She easily won her match and captured Philip's attention. Perhaps it was the sweat glistening from her body or her natural beauty, but he sat on the edge of the umpire's chair, smitten. In the clubhouse after the match, as much as he disliked small talk, Philip approached the victor and re-introduced himself, even admitting that they had previously met. No games and no mystery, Phillip was not coy about pursuing this second chance encounter. They easily chatted about tennis, schooling, and endless other subjects. He was specifically amazed that she had declined various potentially lucrative offers to join the ranks of touring tennis pros and, instead, had her heart set on a career in medicine. Their conversation flowed so naturally, they hardly noticed that most of the clubhouse had emptied out around them. Fascinated by this woman, Philip asked her to go out, inviting Audrey to join him for some tennis at the prestigious Philadelphia Club. She quickly accepted the invitation, and later that week spent a Saturday afternoon beating Philip on the tennis court and then, with sweat coating their bodies, making love in one of the club's guest rooms. There was a connection there; that afternoon was most definitely about passion, but admiration and awe in both directions too. Phillip and Audrey saw each other a few more times before the summer recess but, curiously, none of the encounters led to a romantic liaison. Such busy schedules resulted in them drifting apart. Philip, fully occupied in the family's investment banking business, made no effort to pursue the free spirit who momentarily crossed his path. Ferrington was equally willing to leave the liaison for what it was, an impulsive fling, as her time was consumed with professional commitments.

A few years later their paths inadvertently crossed again; this time in one of the corridors of Hornsby Pavilion at the Children's Hospital of Pennsylvania. Seeing Philip in the hall, Audrey confidently approached him and without hesitation embraced him warmly. Dressed in his three-piece, deep blue, pin-striped banker's suit, Philip was stunned by Audrey's display of public affection. The ease with which she so naturally handled their meeting by leaning over and nonchalantly kissing him served to embarrass him. He remembered the soaring passion that had accompanied their brief tryst at the club, and how surprised he was that she never pursued him. Chatting, catching up on the time that had passed, Audrey informed Philip that she was presently a medical student at the University of Pennsylvania. In turn, he conveyed that he was a trustee of the school, as well as the heir to the Hornsby fortune, the one that built Hornsby Pavilion, the same ward in which she would be conducting her upcoming residency. The string of coincidences made them both laugh.

Finding Audrey intriguing, Philip exercised his influence, entered the dean's office, and read her medical college file. He was more than pleased to discover her exalted roots. The offbeat, liberal side of the Ferrington family could be overlooked because they cared for Native Americans. Nevertheless, the family had solid roots. While her father had strangely and seemingly inexcusably left the Boston area, Audrey's mother maintained her heritage and was a recognized leader of a major foundation dedicated to enhancing educational opportunities of the economically disadvantaged. Ever infatuated, he read on. When he added to the equation Audrey's good looks, brains, and athletic abilities, Philip knew her equal would be difficult to find. So, sitting in the registrar's office reading her file, he determined the appropriate next step meant embarking on a campaign to court Audrey as his bride.

Gaining Audrey's attention proved to be much simpler than Phillip anticipated. She was attracted to him and opted to skip playing games and accept his frequent requests to see her. Their romantic escapades were even better than their brief interlude a few years prior. But, like a wild horse, Audrey had little interest in being tamed. As his thoughts turned serious, much to his surprise, Audrey resisted. While she enjoyed dating Philip and had no hesitation about sharing a lusty hour, night, or weekend with him, she rejected every suggestion of a more permanent relationship. Marriage was not something she thought about seriously; she was clearly not ready to settle down until the completion of her medical internship and residency. Additionally, as Mrs. Philip Hornsby, she would have to live in the glare of the public spotlight. Saddled with vague memories of her father's unhappiness at being a recognized public figure as a lecturer at Harvard's School of Education, his desire for privacy and his ultimate choice to return to a simple uncomplicated life plagued her thoughts. Audrey accepted his requests for dates, but anything that smacked of a more permanent relationship was emphatically rebuffed. And, once again, their newly rekindled relationship ultimately fizzled. Philip, rather than protesting or bullying his way with her, instinctively knew he needed to be patient; bucking broncos could be broken. Recognizing Audrey's circumstances, Philip concluded that this particular moment was inopportune but time was on his side; he could afford to withdraw, keep his eye on Audrey through his connections at the university, and then resume the chase when her studies became less demanding. It might take time, but he felt confident she would eventually see the light. Much like stalking a company, patience was a virtue. Philip's predatory nature told him that timing was everything; the right moment would come, but for now, wait. Since the ultimate objective was everything, Philip believed that his goal would be more easily attained if, for a year or two, there was separation. Having spent two decades at boarding schools, college, and graduate school, "absence makes the heart grow fonder" was an adage Philip subscribed to with religious fervor. Enabling Audrey to enjoy her independence, Phillip stepped back with grace and good humor, never considering the possibility that a rival might usurp Audrey's affections.

Fate intervened, even without Phillip's manipulation, and their paths crossed once again. During the summer of her third year of medical school, Audrey was employed as a part-time teaching pro at the Philadelphia Country Club. It was not the income that drew her to the tennis courts, but rather the respite that the club afforded from the rigors of her demanding studies. Though she had anticipated the possibility of seeing Philip, the prospect of such an encounter did not deter her from taking the position. Perhaps her subconscious was leading her to temptation. About two weeks into the summer, the inevitable confrontation occurred at the annual July Fourth Dance. The entire Hornsby clan was in attendance. Philip escorted a tall brunette who wore a spectacular tiara and a glittering emerald necklace. Audrey attended as an employee, with orders to mix drinks and amuse the unattached males standing beside the bar. He tried not to show it, but throughout the cocktail hour she felt Philip's eyes staring at her. As soon as his date left for the restroom, fueled by a couple of cocktails, Philip began his assault, asking her to join him as the band played a slow, romantic Cole Porter melody. Audrey questioned her resolve to resist long-range plans; after all, by every traditional factor used by women over the ages to size up potential mates, Philip topped the scale—charming, intelligent, strikingly handsome, considerate, and filthy rich. His conduct, as evidenced by his willingness to wait, made it appear that he respected her. Suddenly, the differences between them did not seem all that important. Philip accepted Audrey's liberal political views, and even though she did not agree with his conservatively adamant pro-business stance, she found it surprisingly easy to acquiesce to his reserved and undemonstrative demeanor. Philip was strong and ultimately, whether she agreed with his particular point of view or not, she respected his towering strength.

After exchanging the usual pleasantries and compliments, Philip managed to lead Audrey from the ballroom without being observed before his bejeweled escort returned. Taking Audrey to the farthest reaches of the grounds, the footbridge over the pond guarding the thirteenth green, Philip broke the ice.

"So how have you been, stranger?"

"Considering that I've not heard from you in almost two years, I'm surprised to hear you ask that question," Audrey playfully teased.

"You know I care about you," Philip responded very earnestly.

"So, why the disappearing act? Even though I wasn't able to make a commitment, we could have gone out, had fun, or just kept in touch."

"Look, Audrey, I thought you preferred that I back away; no pressure. If I was mistaken, I apologize," Philip explained in a diplomatic tone.

"Philip Hornsby, you are a deceitful bastard. I don't believe for a minute that you casually gave up the quest. Aren't you the guy who never gives up until he reaches the summit?" Audrey's tone was sarcastic. "You probably had your spies in the Foundation and on the Medical College Board keep track of my every move. All you rich guys are the same—think you own the world and all of its female inhabitants. Well, Philip Hornsby, you don't own me!"

"Am I about to be the beneficiary of a personal rant? In honor of the Fourth, should I prepare myself to endure a political diatribe against the male members of the rich, wicked Hornsby clan?" queried Philip, mocking Audrey's sarcastic tone.

"Part of me despises your power and wealth. Hornsby Enterprises has a dreadful record on environmental matters, a long history of doing extensive business with suspect governments, supports right-wing politicians, fuels the coffers of conservative pro-life zealots, and what you and your family support runs contrary to my beliefs. Even when the Hornsbys are charitable and donate millions to the hospital, it comes with strings; the Hornsby Pavilion is nothing more than a monument to your father's corruption and through his self-serving generosity, his plea for heavenly forgiveness."

Philip let her carry on, finally interjecting. "What the hell does that have to do with 'How've you been?'" asked a bemused Philip. After an awkwardly long pause, he asked the obvious question: "Why so hostile?"

Audrey knew that she was making no sense; she was simply wrestling with her own indecision. It was obvious that Philip had not lost interest in her, but she sensed a battle raging within her psyche—submit, fight, cling to her independence. It was that part of her which opposed a permanent affiliation. Not unaware of the conflict that plagued Audrey and perceiving a lack of conviction and hesitancy in her voice, Philip turned calculatingly aggressive. "Is it fair to blame me for the sins of my father and my family? I have never asked you to approve of my political or social views. Do you only go out with men who replicate your own political philosophies? Hell, I thought you were an independent, free thinker. Perceive me as an opportunity, not a threat. Go ahead, try to convert me, you might succeed in redirecting Hornsby money towards something you believe in."

The idea embodied in Philip's response was appealing but she was hardly naïve or easily manipulated. Besides, long ago she realized the best defense is a strong offense. "I doubt that you have the freedom to redirect anything, including your own life."

He brushed off her comment. "Don't tell me that you're afraid to do battle with the establishment?"

"I have enough causes in my life," was Audrey's trite response. Her resistance was fading before Philip's arguments.

"Am I so loathsome that I'm to be avoided like a Montague?"

"Philip, you're a real bastard. You're taking advantage of my hormones." Audrey knew that all was about to be lost. She didn't want to weaken, but was afraid that she was about to commit a grievous error. Her inner self was filled with passion; her heart overriding logic, "If I'm a Capulet and you're a Montague, the ending is likely to be depressing."

"Audrey, I haven't yet asked you to marry me, so we are not talking about a union of two warring families, just whether you will once again agree to go out with me, if I decide, upon reflection, to ask for the pleasure of your company."

"As your lordship wishes," mocked Audrey as she deeply curtsied toward Philip. Rising from her bow, and yelling, "Piss off, your arrogance!" Audrey surprised Philip with a swift charge that sent him reeling off-balance over the bridge railing into the pond. Audrey felt a great surge of joy and relief rush through her body as she saw the head of the Hornsby heir emerge through the tangle of water lilies. She laughed triumphantly as a tadpole fell from his dripping tuxedo. For better or worse, the Rubicon had been crossed, and Audrey had leaped from the balance beam of her life, even though it was Philip who plunged into the deep.

"Holy Christ, Audrey! How will I ever explain this to Cynthia?"

"Tell her the truth. Tell her you made a play for another woman and got pitched into the pond. I'll bet she turns as green as her emeralds. While you're at it, tell her about years ago in guest room C."

"You can't do this! I've been working on Cynthia for six months. Now that you have ruined my summer plans, you had better be ready to take her place." With those words, Philip splashed from the pond and started after Audrey. Watching Philip rid himself of the lily pads as he emerged from the water, Audrey kicked off her shoes and dashed toward the clubhouse, Philip slowed by his sopping foot gear and the clinging wetness of his clothes. However, knowing the golf course and taking shortcuts, he managed to catch Audrey as she raced past a clump of trees protecting the approach to the eighteenth green. Grabbing her, he hoisted her over his shoulders in a fireman's carry. Before she could put up a struggle, he lugged her to the cabana area of the swimming pool. Finding the hidden key outside the entrance to the Hornsby cabana, Philip took the laughing Audrey inside, where they spent the rest of the night alternating between fits of passion and blissful serenity. The jilted Cynthia returned home alone, a mystery surfaced when the groundskeeper turned in a pair of abandoned shoes to the club's lost and found.

Audrey and Philip dated steadily for the next year. Though the relationship flourished, it never again reached the level of spontaneity and excitement of July Fourth. It was a comfortable arrangement; Audrey was happy that thus far little of the Hornsby side of his life interfered with their relationship. Actual time spent together did not amount to much and business and politics rarely came up, but when they did, Philip was ready to listen to Audrey's point of view, and he even recognized the validity of some of her positions. On the basis of her arguments, he interceded with the Hornsby Foundation and arranged for a research grant to support a study of the effects of pollutants on the water supply for the indigenous living on reservations in northern New Mexico.

Philip knew to be patient and, ever so slowly, Audrey came to regard her feeling of comfort as a sign of love and accepted the idea of Philip as a permanent partner. Philip shared the same point of view, and they began talking about marriage. The

Hornsby family was apprised of the likely prospect of the addition of a Ferrington, the news not greeted with a standing ovation because the young doctor wasn't from a suitably prestigious family, but W.A. had no choice but to make the best of the situation. Audrey's background was unblemished; she had a splendid personal résumé combined with smashingly classy looks, and knowing full well that any mate his only son would choose would in some respects be a compromise, this girl was probably about the best that W.A. could reasonably demand. W.A.'s trump card was his belief that Audrey would mellow with age as she came to appreciate the advantages of being a Hornsby. Besides, all through his life he witnessed person after person whose liberal politics were compromised by the advantages of untold wealth. Though W.A. would have preferred the neatly packaged Cynthia, and personally enjoyed the connection of her parents—the sole owners of one of the nation's largest electrical distributors—W.A. was wise enough to know that he had no real grounds for active opposition to Audrey. Much like a young colt, he felt that if properly harnessed, her exuberance would age well. He had no doubt that Philip possessed the wherewithal to transform her into an ally.

Life marched on; Audrey finished medical school, graduating with the highest honors. Accepted for postgraduate study at facilities all over the country, Audrey chose the hospital of the University of Pennsylvania for a year of internship and, after finishing, in a move that surprised all, she stayed in Philadelphia to do her residency and fellowship in pediatric oncology. As Audrey prepared to start her residency she came to realize that emotionally she was either in a rut or simply, to her great surprise, happily settled. Her life was in perfect balance; there were no drastic ups or downs; no monumental highs or sinking lows; no peaks or valleys; Philip was there, her needs were cared for, her wishes met. After a candlelit dinner Hornsby proposed marriage. Ferrington accepted and although no date was set for either an engagement party or wedding, an inevitable progression was taking its due course.

Sweat glistened off her body. As Audrey prepared to return serve, she whispered to her doubles partner, "Philip, the cabana right after and throw away the key!" He knew what she wanted, the thought intoxicating, but he had to deal with the match at hand. Philip was competing fiercely, but less effectively than usual. His errors cost them two games as he strained to hold his serve, hitting an overhead long and netting a center court volley. He watched Audrey masterfully hit a backhand winner and then disguise a drop volley that both opponents lunged for but neither came within a racquet's length of the ball.

"Advantage Ms. Ferrington," announced Morton Wyman after Monica netted a service return. Settling down, Philip's game improved; the score was 6-2 and 5-0 with Audrey serving for the match. Point one was a clear winner as Audrey's first serve, a high, kicking topspin blasted over Monica's outstretched backhand. This victory would be their third consecutive club championship against their usual opponents, the Beales. Audrey played beautifully, intermixing a balance of power, grace, and finesse. She was in a class by herself. In reality, she was competing against herself, carrying Philip by making almost no errors, and, hitting penetrating approach shots, setting Philip up to hit easy winners.

"Fault," called the umpire.

"Bear down, Audrey," Philip shouted over his left shoulder. She laughed.

Her second serve landed in the far corner of the service box, but Peter returned it to Audrey's backhand. Her two-handed response was deep down the middle, Peter managing a weak lob over Philip.

"Switch," called Audrey as she moved to her right to take the lob on the bounce. But Philip moved back under the shot and struck the ball short to the backhand court. Peter, moving in, propelled the weak return deep behind Philip's lunging reach.

"Deuce," said the umpire, as a scattering of applause emanated from the gallery of club members.

"Audrey, concentrate, you were out of position. Don't give it away!" said Philip in hushed tones that nonetheless struck Audrey as Vince Lombardi-ish in vehemence. Audrey was confused by Philip's pep talk. She had beaten the Beales almost single-handedly and had carried Philip in the process. She had played with superb skill, yet it was Philip who was urging her to greater heights.

"Philip, sweetie, next time I say 'switch' move your ass," ordered Audrey. She was not angry at Philip, as his concentration was so intense it made him miss the message. Changing tone, Audrey tried to calm Philip. "Relax, we're doing just fine. Enjoy yourself; I don't want you to have a stroke on the court as I have big plans for tonight."

Even Philip had to smile at Audrey's audacious enthusiasm and good humor.

"Sorry, I'll save myself for later; perhaps I was getting a bit overenthusiastic."

"Now you're talking," said Audrey, grinning broadly.

Her first serve to Monica was powerful and deep, the return long by three feet. Her next serve to Peter spun away from his backhand, but he managed a cross court rally. Audrey pounded a return deep to Monica's forehand. Facing match point, Monica's return was about two feet above the net and down the middle. Philip moved easily into the path of the ball and punched a clear winning backhand to the court.

"Okay! Super tennis," cheered Philip as Audrey jogged forward to embrace him. "Congratulations, champ. Now wasn't that fun!"

Knowledgeable tennis aficionados in the crowd applauded Audrey's masterful display of dominance. Some suggested that the Hornsby-Ferrington team should be excluded from the annual tournament, but recanted saying W.A. would probably buy the club and change that rule. The four players moved toward the net. "Congratulations, Peter. Sorry Monica dear, but it was a rough day at the hospital, and I had to get my aggressions out," apologized Audrey.

"Hey, you were great," responded Monica. "I'll bet you'd give Serena a real tough go."

"Good show," was all Peter said as he shook his opponents' hands.

"Thanks, Morton," called Philip as he led Audrey to the annual trophy ceremony. Hand in hand, they moved to the winner's circle. As they waited for the presentation to begin, Audrey leaned toward Philip and whispered in his ear, "The real fun begins soon!" He remembered and smiled.

Immediately following the presentation of trophies, W.A. approached from the sideline and warmly congratulated the champions. "Excellent tennis! Philip, I've seen you play better, but you're lucky your partner was at the top of her game. Thanks to you, Audrey, I won another wager from Mr. Beale. And, I would be happy to donate my winnings to a cause of your choice." W.A. then turned to his son. "Philip, you must see me immediately after the ceremony concludes. It is essential that we review the details of that Swiss project this evening, as I have a full day of commitments tomorrow."

Without saying a word to Audrey, Philip dutifully turned and followed his father. Silently, Audrey cursed the Swiss, the Hornsby business, and W.A.'s interference. So, she suggested

W.A. donate his winnings to a militantly radical group, hoping to pain him a bit. As the day's sweat dripped between her breasts, she watched the two men walk away deep in business discussion; Audrey stood alone, furious she no longer had the opportunity to celebrate her victory with some naughty fun.

4. A Moment of Reflection

A black beeper sat visibly atop the pile of clothes they had passionately ripped off the night before; fortunately the intrusive device had been silent all night. Audrey glanced at the muscular body beside her, marveling that Phillip could be so supple and lean, considering it had been over two years since he last seriously trained. She wanted to wake him but she knew Philip cherished his rest—one of his few indulgences—and, in less than an hour, both would have to leave—Philip to work and she back to the arduous routine of the hospital. Her residency was the termination of a long academic ordeal, but she knew the ensuing results would be worth the present sacrifices. Inching upward on the fluffy pillows, Audrey propped her back against the cold plaster wall. Peering through the musty windows, she watched as a drizzle fell. Unable to sleep, Audrey questioned her decision to do her residency in Philadelphia. After four dreary, dark winters at Swarthmore, she had sworn to attend either Stanford or UCLA Medical School; but involved, or rather infatuated, with Philip, and neither of them wanting to commute, she turned down the sunny warm skies of California for the gray, drab wetness of this godforsaken state. Enjoying a rare indulgence, Audrey took a deep drag and let smoke from the cigarette ooze through her nostrils. Her small breasts slipped free of the covers, she nestled her soft skin against his and ran her hand upward over her well-defined deltoid muscles. Even though four years of medical school and a year of internship required enormous amounts of her time, somehow she still managed to stay in shape. Running a minimum of five miles three times a week, engaging in a rigorous daily workout regimen that included weights and playing tennis three times a week, she molded her body into a magnificent physical specimen. Never permitting herself to put on an ounce of extra weight, the word *no* was a prominent part of her vocabulary at the dining table. She would have possibly indulged herself a bit more, but she knew Philip demanded perfection; Philip thought of a woman's body as if it were a temple—a treasure to be molded and crafted. Each line of her agile figure flowed; she moved with the grace of a maestro producing a harmonic sound from a two hundred-piece orchestra. Philip took pride in people noticing the couple as they entered a room.

She examined her sleeping bed partner—the undulating waves of his jet-black hair were tinted with minute specks of white; his deep-cut brown eyes were crowned with bushy, dark brows, sculpted muscles graced his six-foot frame. Not only was he strikingly handsome, but Philip carried himself with an unmistakable air of superiority. His precise intellect dominated conversations; his mere presence, nurtured by his quiet confidence, exuded charisma. Audrey admired that Philip never openly flaunted his accomplishments—self-assured, articulate, worldly and a renowned sportsman, he possessed an uncanny acumen for maintaining a carefully constructed public veneer. Philip, at age thirty-two, possessed a catalog of accomplishments that most men wouldn't achieve in a lifetime; awarded the prestigious Explorers' Club Badge of Recognition for his effort in the Himalayas, considered by social circles as one of the most desirable bachelors in the city, Chief Operations Officer of a worldwide financial empire, and, even without a formal doctoral degree, in demand as a lecturer in both economics and Renaissance art at prestigious universities throughout the country.

Audrey cherished that their careers evolved independently. Their courtship grew slowly, during the initial years Audrey wanted a relationship with no long-term commitment. Often, for periods lasting nearly a month, they didn't even see each other; then, suddenly, they would resume with an incredible weekend celebration at the Plaza. Their conversations ranged from psychoanalysis to neo-impressionism; they shared gourmet dinners of delicately seasoned French food, both had similar tastes for extremely dry, aged champagne accompanied by caviar—but only the finest Beluga or Segruva. Although time together was extremely limited, in their few opportunities, traveling with Philip opened doors—Paris, Nice, Zermatt, Acapulco—together they shared the excitement of exploring the world, whether snow skiing in the Alps, whitewater rafting in Utah, or sailing in the Caribbean.

The fact that neither Philip nor Audrey was an avid conversationalist allowed each to exist independently and their relationship seemed to be nourished by the exoticness of their shared journeys. The term *minimalist* would aptly describe them individually, when together everything was well-conceived and details meticulously planned. Although she found Philip a bit stringent and compulsively disciplined, a vast departure from her experiences in Albuquerque, he opened doors to the world. A die had been cast; both were settled, comfortable, and marching headlong into their relationship and careers.

5. *The First Compromise*

Audrey's schedule consisted of forty-eight hours continuously on and twenty-four hours off; in moments when she wasn't busy, she slipped into the doctors lounge, closing her weary eyes while lying on the sofa. In spite of her hectic schedule and the ungodly demands of her medical career, her relationship with Philip persevered. Philip proved to be accommodating and considerate. The time they spent together became symbiotic; he understood her constraints and she his. A phone ringing in the waiting room woke her.

"Another unexpected night out of town, Philip?" Audrey spoke into the telephone receiver.

"Chicago, New York, then on to Zurich."

Hornsby spoke with precision. "But I'll return by next Friday; if I remember correctly, you're not on rotation that weekend."

"Should I expect another business emergency to appear?" Audrey teased.

"What are you driving at?"

"Philip!" her raised voice registered her mounting frustration. "It's been over two weeks since we were together. As long as I have anything to do with it, the cornerstone of our relationship is not going to be steeped in celibacy."

Philip laughed. "I've always been attracted to the tiger in you!"

"Then why don't you spend a little more time prying open the door and exploring the hospitality of the tempest?"

"I'll work on that . . . for now, hold that thought until I'm back on Friday!"

Audrey, stubbing her cigarette in the ashtray, balanced the pros and cons of their relationship. Naïve she wasn't, everything had a degree of compromise, but Philip's lack of spontaneity was the one Achilles heel that she found especially irritating. Even their sexual life followed a set script with few deviations permitted. Although she craved making love to begin a day, Philip despised sex in the morning, and, according to Philip, appropriate times for lustful liaisons were best suited for weekends, late afternoons, or before sleep; at other times he was armed with excuses.

Audrey showered as Philip continued to sleep. She returned to the room to towel off water dripping from her body. The amber glow of the streetlamp allowed her to dress without turning on a light. Bending over, she lightly kissed Philip's forehead. Unexpectedly he awakened and was surprised that Audrey was up.

"Why so early?" he inquired.

"This morning I'm beginning my residency. After four years of medical school and a year of internship, I'm finally working in a discipline of medicine that interests me, pediatric oncology. Besides, this rotation promises to be intriguing. The doctor in charge of the unit has an unconventional reputation as well as a notoriously unforgiving temper."

Philip's eyes remained glazed as she slid her robe to the side of her shoulder.

Begrudgingly he sat up. "A number of decisions are pressing."

"You mean your father is again questioning our marriage? He'll never approve. I can hear him questioning the value of a cowgirl from New Mexico. 'Does she have anything to say? Why marry beneath you?' It's only a matter of time before he confronts you."

Philip responded confidently and objectively. "W.A. will go along with whatever I want."

Audrey chided him. "Then I suppose it's your mother, the self-proclaimed expert of modern art? Is she putting on her usual airs? And by the way, except for being acquainted with a few names, your mother doesn't know a Seurat from a Pollock."

"As a matter of fact she called last night. Instead of the country club, our engagement party will be held at their mansion; invitations went out yesterday. She made reservations for your parents to stay at a suite in the Park Plaza Hotel."

Shock spread across Audrey's face. "You must be kidding?"

"Everything is set." His voice carried with it the finality of a completed business deal.

"Why wasn't I consulted? Every time I enter their estate, they make me feel like a pagan is invading!"

"There's no sense getting upset!" Philip's answer was emotionless. "Engagement parties are for parents."

"Philip, I'm not someone you wind up and magically I do what's expected." Defiance tinged her voice as she slipped into her white lace panties.

"Come on, Audrey, at this moment I don't need complications."

Hands on hips she confronted her fiancé. "We'll make a deal. I'll go along with the engagement party, but all details concerning our wedding are my choice. I want to be married outdoors on an early fall day with the mountains in the background; the burnt leaves of autumn tumbling to the ground. Freshly gathered bouquets will decorate the altar." Her eyes stared into the morning haze, "surrounded by only a few intimate friends. And no grandiose party!"

Philip began to dress. "Just go through with an engagement party that will satisfy my father and we'll marry in the fall; location, setting, the choices are yours. If it'll please you, I'll even marry in New Mexico. You have a promise; my parents and I will not offer a word in protest. I trust we've reached a reasonable compromise."

6. *Meet the Magician*

Exiting the elevator in the hallway, clad in starched white coats, a new group of medical residents, before being permitted entrance to the ward, were pushed into a closet which contained a one-way mirror so they could spy inside the ward. The white and chrome antiseptic corridor was bathed by fluorescent lights. Every bed was filled by an adolescent. Only the flesh tones of their faces and hands and the color of their hair and eyes disturbed the blandness of the hospital ward.

"The pathology exam was not as bad as I thought it might be," said a boyish-looking, six foot four inch specimen whose blue-eyed, blond good looks attracted the attention of three of the five women in the group.

"For sure, Doug. Dr. Thompson was a real sweetheart."

"I think he took pity on us," responded Beverly Watson. "But are you ready for this?"

"I guess so," Doug sarcastically replied.

"Well, I'm not," hissed Beverly. "The pediatric cancer ward is supposed to be the worst part of this residency. The chief, Dr. Nicholas Kalamatra, is known to be a real tough taskmaster."

Jill Predergast joined in the dialogue. "I've heard he's such an oddball that residents give up on this rotation."

"What about the kids?" asked Doug.

"They're all classified as critical," said Jill. "Dr. Kalamatra is their last hope. I guess that is why he's so tough and demanding; it's a life-and-death struggle in there."

"Have any of you guys ever met him?" asked Beverly.

"Not me," said Willard Brennan, "but I hear he's beyond eccentric."

The door behind them was slammed shut; impatiently they waited. The desperate faces of children screamed in silent agony. Pain etched in the withered cheekbones of the girl at the far end of the ward was recorded instantly in the pit of Doug Herman's stomach. A boy lying across from the window had tubes penetrating his nose, arm, and groin. Next to the boy lay the oldest-looking of the group, a girl about 13 years old. Her cold icy eyes peered listlessly into the fluorescent lights. A petite girl, perhaps five, lay vegetable-like beside the mute girl, her body plugged into numerous machines.

"It's ghastly," murmured Wendy Morgan.

David LeThou glared at his peers and observed in his usual manner. "It's a hospital and we're here to treat sick people."

Fifteen minutes went by while they waited. The ward was silent, except for the beep and hum of the various medical machines. A half dozen nurses moved about in orderly, business-like fashion, attending to their chores. Examining the anguished faces of the children, Dr. Ferrington audibly gasped. Perhaps three dozen children, ranging in age from three to thirteen, occupied the spacious but sterile accommodations. Surrounding each bed was a battery of electronic monitors and devices. Every child had a plasma regulator hanging from the right- hand corner of a steel bed. Most of the children had plastic cords that pumped glucose, medication, or life-supporting blood into bodies. Faces were pale. This ghastly sight reminded Audrey of pictures she had seen of Nazi concentration camp victims; she wanted to turn her head but her professional training forced her to keep looking. Groomed not to show emotion while on emergency room duty, even when patients had died in her arms, Audrey never shed a tear. Arriving ambulances brought in patients barely clinging to life, and when her life-saving efforts failed and victims died, Audrey and the attending resident would return to the doctors' lounge and devour unfinished sandwiches. Medical training taught her to be thorough, to avoid being swayed by emotional appeals, to treat abnormalities as a science, to test and retest before diagnosing. Though she regularly proclaimed herself immune to the normal emotional response to illness, something about the sight of these slowly dying children profoundly moved her.

Seconds turned into minutes. The waiting continued; the doctor, or rather, the magician, or whatever he called himself, had not yet made his entrance. Audrey, her face almost pressed against the glass, could not take her eyes off the two girls in adjoining beds situated nearest the nurses' station. The youngster in the bed adjoining the station looked almost healthy, rosy cheeks, wavy curly blond hair, large dimples, and a ready smile. Audrey watched, fascinated as the bubbling girl kept flashing the adjoining patient pictures from a comic book. The girl being shown the pictures did not emit even the slightest response, her head lying motionless on a pillow. Tubes inserted into her body rendered her unable to move.

Suddenly the door separating the ward from the nurses' station crashed open and an apparition in black burst into the room. As Dr. Nicholas Giovanni Batiste Kalamatra sped past the group of stunned medical residents, he nodded in their direction but did not say a word. With his magic wand swinging wildly, top hat placed on a moving cart being pushed before him, the chief of the service went prancing about the ward. As the doctor swept from bed to bed, his black flowing cape whirled and billowed. For an instant Audrey feared that the sudden entrance of the practitioner of the black arts would frighten the children. Much to her amazement, the ward burst into a rising chorus of giggles, laughs, and howls of delight. The magician positioned himself in the middle of the ward, bowing to the juvenile audience with a graceful circular movement, and announced his presence in a voice that parodied a circus ringmaster.

"Ladies and germs—I mean liberated female characters and gentlemen! It is my pleasure to announce that the incomparable, the stupendous, the sensational, the world's greatest magician, Harry Blackstone, has canceled his scheduled appearance in the Hornsby Pavilion for this afternoon." A chorus of boos filled the room, but the speaker, undaunted, continued. "It is thus possible for the management of this establishment to afford you the opportunity to preview the magically marvelous machinations of the brightest young star in the world of illusion. The Children's Hospital of Pennsylvania is proud to present the one and only— me, Nicholas Giovanni Batiste Kalamatra."

More boos filled the air as Nurse Gwendolyn interjected her prepared line: "The initials stand for 'Not Good But Krazy.'"

"Tell it like it is, Gwendolyn," a young male patient called out from the end of the room as the other children cheered, booed, or applauded.

In the observation booth, the residents were dumbfounded that the creature in black was their newly designated mentor.

Clapping his hands to alert the children to the commencement of his first trick, Dr. Kalamatra took a crystal ball from the metal cart and, to the command of "Presto," with one hand covering the ball and the other clumsily digging beneath his cloak, he produced a fake pigeon. Employing an identical routine, he next produced a frog, two giraffes, and lavender ribbons, which turned colors when swirled in the air. Except for the unresponsive girl, whose glassy eyes appeared to take no notice of the doctor's shenanigans, the other children squealed in delight.

Unnoticed by the children and most of the residents, as pandemonium reigned, the self-proclaimed Houdini journeyed from bed to bed doing magic tricks, the doctor, masquerading as magician, glanced at each chart, concentrating on developments during the past twenty-four hours. Each child was examined as coins and flowers appeared from various parts of Kalamatra's cape. Adjusting tubes, ordering medications, barking instructions, the oncologist finished each examination by digging into his vest and popping lollipops into waiting mouths.

Inside the observation booth, the doctor's antics offended most of the interns, while others, Audrey included, spellbound, nudged closer to the glass partition.

"He's a raving lunatic!"

"I've never seen anything like it!"

"The guy must have gotten loose from the psychiatric ward."

David LeThou summarized the collective shock and dismay of the anti-Kalamatra faction; shaking his head, he lamented, "And we're supposed to study with him for the next few years. Doesn't medicine demand some degree of dignity? If any of us had any fortitude, we'd formally complain to the hospital director."

As their collective stares remained peeled to the one-way glass, Dr. Kalamatra, after completing rounds, stood in the center aisle for his grand finale. Holding his hands high in the air, he tried unsuccessfully to silence the children.

"I know where the pigeon comes from!" yelled the youngest patient. "Just look under his coat!"

As he fumbled his way through another trick, Audrey cringed at the doctor's ineptitude. It didn't take a critic to realize that Dr. Kalamatra was a miserable magician. His tricks were done sloppily, cards were fumbled, and he invariably hesitated at inappropriate moments. After years of practice, his entire repertoire numbered less than fifty tricks.

"Do the train," a boy yelled.

"Don't get over-excited," Nurse Gwendolyn warned a small boy seated in a wheelchair.

"Oh, please." The boy, trying to get up to see better, accidentally pulled out an intravenous line.

"Be careful . . ." the voice behind the starched coat menaced. Nurse Wilson hated it when excited children caused unnecessary extra work.

"No! No! Basta! Let 'em have fun," Kalamatra robustly answered, his voice resonating in a fake Italian accent.

Other children yelled as the doctor began a card trick.

"You're not fooling us!" children began screaming from various parts of the ward.

"Now-a you see-a da card, then-a you don't," Kalamatra announced. "Then-a you blink-a . . ."

"Go on, close your eyes, do as he says," droned Nurse Gwendolyn, without the slightest enthusiasm.

". . . da eyes and when-a you open . . ." Children peered at Kalamatra between spread fingers. ". . . da eyes, presto, no card-a!"

The trick brought forth a chorus of boos and taunts. Abruptly, Kalamatra pushed the rolling cart of magic tricks down the center aisle and propelled it toward one of the nurses who barely stopped its momentum before it collided with her. Mocking a locomotive, Kalamatra, pumping his arms, imitated the sound of a steam engine. "Train to Allentown on Track four. All aboard that are coming aboard!" Slipping on an engineer's cap which he magically produced from his cape, the head of pediatric oncology resumed his chugging and churning. "This train stops at …"

"Philadelphia," a boy screamed.

"Washington."

"Miami."

"Disney World." This destination brought forth a general cheer.

Kalamatra journeyed to each bed so that every child could pick a destination. After each command, Kalamatra blew a horn and hit the top of his hat with his hand. Each time he struck the cap, which was filled with talcum powder, puffs of white "smoke" billowed skyward. Everyone except the oldest girl, who seemed completely disinterested, registered his or her choice, Kalamatra's arms and legs then churned, imitating starting an engine. Signaling Nurse Wilson with a wink of his eye, Kalamatra began chugging down the aisle, gradually gaining speed. Those children who could walk on their own formed a line behind him, the first child having taken hold of his cape. Where possible, the nurses, against their will, stuffed other children into wheelchairs or momentarily moved their beds into the line of the train. After those capable got on board, Kalamatra waved goodbye and headed toward the exit as children raucously cheered and booed, screaming for the magician to continue.

"Dr. Kalamatra, let me off in Hollywood," one of the older girls screamed.

"Please do a new trick for us next time," a boy pleaded.

"Fool us," a boy yelled. "Make Gwendolyn disappear, or saw Nurse Wilson in half." Cheering for the latter remark was unanimous.

"How about the magician flies through the air next time?" Kalamatra asked. As in a preview of coming attractions, he spread his arms wide and extending the cape he circled the ward like a giant bat before disappearing through the swinging doors.

Audrey, unable to take her eyes from the children, kept staring through the one-way glass. As soon as Kalamatra departed, Nurse Wilson seized control of the ward. Calm and order were immediately reinstated, beds and patients returned to where they belonged. The staff then attended to necessary chores—charts were checked, catheter bags emptied, intravenous tubes adjusted. Two attendants wheeled a stretcher next to the bed of one of the girls, before being taken away she was lifted onto a cart and a strap was secured around her midsection.

A moment later, still stunned, before any of the medical interns had digested what they had just witnessed, the door to their cramped chamber swung open. "Well, what did you learn?" the magician suddenly turned into a stern taskmaster.

No one answered.

"Speak up!" the doctor ordered. Still dressed in his magician's outfit, hands on his hips, his penetrating eyes interrogated the neophyte doctors. Residents either looked at Kalamatra's feet or, averting his brown eyes, feigned studying the blank wall, the floor, or the ceiling.

The doctor's voice turned crisp and analytical. "Look at the little girl with the full, blond hair sharing her comic book. She's about to have chemotherapy twice a day, supported by a regimen of radiation therapy," Kalamatra volunteered. "We fight like hell but almost always are defeated, that child has a couple months left, maybe less." Kalamatra's remark brought home the grim reality of what was going on in the ward, the realization bringing a lump to Audrey's throat and a knot to her stomach.

Panning the room, the oncologist repeated his earlier question. "I'm waiting. I asked you what you learned. Remember, you're doctors, you've finished your formal medical training and you're here to gain practical experience. Well, I'm waiting . . ." Kalamatra challenged, "Speak your mind!"

LeThou glanced at his colleagues. Noticing the downcast heads and averted eyes, he concluded that no one was likely to confront the crazed doctor. Deciding to be true to his convictions, LeThou calmly and firmly spoke. "We came here," he summoned the courage, "to study medicine, not to critique a magic show."

"I have no idea what you were doing," Carla Adams was less forthright. "As a magician, you're not getting a job with the Ringling Brothers Circus!"

Once Pandora's Box was opened, insults flew. Kalamatra listened in bemused silence. He had heard the protestations of shock and outrage many times before from medical students, interns, residents, as well as a growing chorus of his colleagues.

When the criticism subsided, Audrey Ferrington spoke. "I was both surprised and embarrassed. Never in our years of training have any of us experienced anything like this. But, as to the quality of the medical care the patients were receiving, none of us are in a position to judge."

After a moment of silence which told Kalamatra that his new students had nothing more to say, the doctor moved toward the hallway and then abruptly turned to face his charges. "Medically, you have been groomed in the administration of tests, reading results, analyzing charts; your training has taught you well. But unfortunately, most of you have no idea what medicine is about—sympathy, caring, sensitivity, insightful judgments. Most of those children are dying. Look at their faces. Within the next six months, I'll be lucky if a dozen are still alive." Pain and ethos marked Kalamatra's words. "In the brief time they have left, we, as doctors, have an obligation to make their lives a little less painful. That is the meaning of medicine; those kids are human beings, and, however sick they may be, they deserve to smile." The doctor's voice, rising to a crescendo, bellowed, "Injections, chemotherapy, radioactive cobalt, is that all those children represent to you? Perhaps some of you think of those patients as guinea pigs primed for yet another medical experimentation." After a brief pause, his voice modulating, he began again in an almost pleading fashion. "Will any of the myriad devices of modern medicine bring those children pleasure before they die?" He shook his head. "I seriously doubt it." Rhetorically he asked, "Is the practice of medicine limited to the clinical treatment of disease? Isn't laughter and pleasure a part of the health-restoring process? The children feel better when they laugh, when they take their minds off their terrible sickness." Launching into yet another rage, Kalamatra's tone turned menacing. "Obviously most of you have either forgotten or don't care to remember that human beings have feelings while being ravaged by disease. We as doctors are not robots and, as long as you are assigned to my service, you will act like human beings, and you will work just as hard at making patients laugh as you will at diagnosing their illnesses and prescribing treatment."

Taking his top hat and tipping it toward the group, Kalamatra, mimicking his departure from the ward, rushed out of the room, cape flying behind him, and quickly disappeared down the hallway.

A moment after Kalamatra's departure, David LeThou whispered, "His reputation as a weirdo doesn't begin to do him justice!"

With the ice broken for a second time, other students joined the attack. "The man's a lunatic!"

"This promises to be quite an experience," Carla said in resignation.

"An outright disgrace!"

"Provisions should be taken to censure this outlandish behavior," LeThou spat.

"Look, I don't pretend to understand his behavior or his methods," Jill Prendergast said, "but there is no sense prejudging him. He is supposed to be a brilliant doctor. There are only a handful of physicians in this hospital who have obtained an international reputation, and Dr. Kalamatra is one of them. I, for one, intend to learn what I can from him. Besides, he made children laugh, perhaps some diversity from our standard rounds will do us all some good."

"It's obvious," Doug interjected, "Jill is balling Kalamatra." Amidst general laughter and grumbling, the group left the observation room to continue their day's activities. Leaving the room, Audrey looked over her shoulder, back into the ward, staring through the glass wall at the now expressionless children.

For the remainder of the day Audrey was upset. She had heard rumors about his antics, but she was not prepared for what had occurred that morning. The zest, energy, and conviction were all obvious. The caring, passion, and emotion appeared very human, but terribly unscientific. Yet, sandwiched in the confusion she witnessed, the eccentric doctor was clearly practicing the art of healing. Her curiosity piqued, late in the afternoon she entered the dark, five-story medical library building. An hour's research unveiled three highly acclaimed books written by Dr. Kalamatra and scores of articles printed in the most prestigious of journals; his research was published in five languages. A librarian informed her that physicians from all over the world came to the hospital to consult with the oncologist. More perplexed than ever, Audrey concluded that Kalamatra's passion, his eccentricities, bespoke a man of great triumphs and enormous failures. Though Audrey couldn't get a handle on her precise feelings, she felt some sort of weird unexplainable camaraderie with the passionate genius.

7. *Game, Set, Match, Audrey*

After leaving the hospital Audrey was still thinking about Dr. Kalamatra's antics. As she walked through the archway and colonnade to the Hornsby Pavilion, Audrey spotted a dark blue Mercedes Benz convertible parked in the doctors lot. Philip Hornsby sat across the driver's seat with legs propped on the passenger's side. As Audrey excitedly ran over to the car, she noticed, as usual, Philip was engaged in yet another one of his standard, endless telephone conversations. Before Philip knew she was there, Audrey had her hands on his shoulders. Though momentarily startled, Philip enjoyed the surprise and affection; he knew it was Audrey before his brain actually recorded a visual image of her strawberry-blond hair cascading over her forehead, covering her pale, blue-green eyes as she leaned forward and gave him a kiss on the cheek.

Clasping a hand over the mouthpiece of the telephone he said, "Hi, doc! W.A. is on the phone, we're discussing the fluctuating conversion rates of Deutsche Marks." Sounding very matter-of-fact, Philip said, "I understand, Dad. The plan makes good fiscal sense, and I'm sure I can convince the Swiss bankers to convert, reconvert, leaving us with a minute part of a percentage point as a commission." He listened for a few moments then said, "Dealing with volume, a sixteenth of a point's spread, even for less than a twenty-four-hour period, adds up." Audrey started massaging his neck, fingers were teasing his left earlobe when Philip impatiently retorted, "Please, love, this is serious business. Later, there will be time."

"You're no fun," teased Audrey. She whispered, as her tongue flicked in his ear. "All you and W.A. ever do is talk about money. Isn't it boring when you already have so much? Go ahead," she chided, "tell your dad you need to choose, make more money or allow your woman to seduce you. I know he'll opt for wealth, it's your reaction that interests me."

Philip frowned at Audrey, his eyes telling her to behave. "Look, Dad, Audrey just arrived, and we're going to the club. Tomorrow, before my trip to Germany, I'll be at the office and we'll have ample time to review details of a financing vehicle."

Audrey's hand edged past his knee. She was neither annoyed nor serious, merely playful. Whenever she saw Philip after being apart from him for a few days, she inevitably acted like a frisky puppy at the sight of its master. She pranced and played with him, full of energy and mischief, seeking to provoke a similar response. Her methods varied; sometimes they were mental, other times physical. Philip understood the game, even if he did not play it as well. Although his response was usually cool, though never cold, there was something about Audrey that managed to penetrate his veneer and bring a smile to his face. Perhaps it was her spark, her vitality.

They had reserved a court to play singles. It was a disaster in the making; although everything Philip did was done well, he did not play tennis as well as his fiancée, even though he refused to admit it. Surprisingly to coaches and sportswriters, she opted for a lifestyle involving more than the tennis circuit. However, she had kept up her game, and while not good enough to compete against the top women in the world, she could occasionally beat second-echelon satellite tournament players. On the rare instances when time would permit an extended period of smashing tennis ball after tennis ball, ranked pros fell before her with a substantial degree of consistency. Even during medical school, she managed to play at least five hours of tennis each week. It was her personal form of therapy, and as the tensions of her career mounted, the fuzzy balls were smacked with increasing velocity. Audrey had no intention of giving up the game; one, because she cherished the feeling of being in shape, and two, because she loved to bang the hell out of those yellow tennis balls. Tennis was a necessary cathartic release; sweat glistening off her sculpted body kept raw physical fury alive. Philip, in his own right, was also a fine athlete. His lanky, six-foot-three-inch frame showcased his well-defined muscles; he prided himself in staying in excellent physical shape. Current time constraints limited him to tennis, running, and swimming to maintain good muscle tone, but his youth and mid-twenties were defined by life as a mountain climber, a sport which he'd achieved international prominence with his impressive string of high-altitude technical rock-climbing successes. As a tennis player he was a naturally gifted, good-to-excellent club amateur with an unquenchable drive to win, but no match for his fiancée. In Philip's youth he was too busy mastering the technical expertise necessary to scale untouched peaks, never having the time to work on the fine points of his tennis game. Yet, his lack of polish played second fiddle to his insatiable desire to succeed. He had a killer instinct and played with a fierce intensity that rattled opponents. Ironically, Philip easily secured triumphs, but never seemed to have any fun on the court. Smiles and laughter were nonexistent. His approach to the game was similar to a researcher painstakingly dissecting a frog; each move was deliberate and calculated. The joy he derived from the game came after a match was over, when he could savor the exhilaration of victory, basking in the glory of beating his opponent. At the very beginning of their relationship, Philip enjoyed hitting tennis balls with Audrey. While she was technically far more proficient, the few times when they played matches against each other, Audrey won each time, although not without difficulty. Philip grunting, straining, imploring himself, launched into every match as if defeat carried with it a permanent scar. Audrey and Philip both realized at a point when their relationship became serious that it would be better for them if they no longer competed against each other. Their matches were too frustrating for Philip and simply no fun for Audrey. Today they'd practice; Audrey was adamant that the days of keeping score against each other were over. But as a mixed doubles team, they were unbeatable in tennis club circles. They were so good that Philip suggested exploring entering serious tournaments. He even fantasized about them trying to qualify for the U.S. Open, but Audrey declined. Her excuse was that with the burden of her medical studies, she simply couldn't allocate the time. However, she secretly feared that Philip's mediocre serve and weak backhand would be systematically destroyed by quality male players. Why expose the explosive Philip to surefire frustration, Audrey reasoned. Besides, if she ever really felt the urge for serious tennis competition, she could someday find the time to properly train for the Open as a singles player and then go as far as she could.

Her fingers slid under his shirt and ever-so-slightly brushed against his chest. Audrey warmed to the goal of chipping away at Philip's aristocratic facade. When alone with her, Philip let down his guard; but placed in society, Philip acted in the manner expected of him. Audrey loved prying open the private Philip, his dignity, determination, quiet assurance, and dry wit. She became determined to expose this person, successfully stripping away his stuffy, formal persona.

Audrey Ferrington could have been handed life on a silver platter but she took pride in earning what she had. Undergraduate and medical school were successfully navigated with highest honors; nothing, and nobody, stood in her way. Hard work and grueling hours, and a few accepted roadblocks as bumps in the road, but no obstacle proved onerous enough to derail her. Medical school was a grind, but her resolve remained steadfast. Audrey would take a few knocks, but her determination landed her squarely on her feet. Her life's path was clearly marked, defined by a noble profession and a male companion, both worthy of sharing and enhancing her journey.

With the weekend in sight, one of Audrey's colleagues was sick, so she was called on to do two successive rounds. After nearly forty continuous hours of work, she was exhausted, both physically and mentally. As hard as Audrey worked, the patients under her care seemed to drift deeper into a bottomless abyss; and, to compound matters, her supervisor, Dr. Kalamatra, proved a rigorous taskmaster who worked equally hard or harder and never once admitted tiring. Although she'd expected it, after all she'd heard torturous stories, but now that she was going through the process, Audrey was experiencing firsthand that a medical residency was akin to an endless road to hell. Frustrations mounted and demands on her time kept piling up, but Audrey instinctively knew she needed a weekend away to pamper herself. But her career, like an oil rig repeatedly hammering into the earth, kept up its incessant pounding. As if the merciless grueling pace of her job was not enough, Audrey craved a release from her mounting physical frustration. She was determined that her charm would make Philip begin to rethink his hasty decisions to attend business meetings, leaving her alone. Audrey, ever the pragmatist, knew only too well that the demands of her work, of her limited time for intimacy, and their repeated self-inflicted physical isolation was causing her undue tension, a situation she was determined to remedy.

8. *Introducing Senator Hornsby*

A who's who of Pennsylvania Republicans arrived at W.A. Hornsby's estate for a political luncheon. All sensed it was more than a casual chit-chat when none other than W.A. stood at the door greeting guests. Escorting Mr. Harry Arndael into the parlor, he asked, "Will you, if the occasion should arise and our esteemed senior Senator chooses not to seek reelection, be in a position to support Philip's candidacy?"

W.A. Hornsby believed in confrontations. Harry Arndael, a successful industrialist whose business was largely dependent on construction subcontracts, removed his glasses. Thirty years in the masonry business taught him the importance of trading favors. Acquiescing too quickly meant he'd lose any advantage, be considered easy prey, and be unable to extract an endorsement to sweeten his pie; and, if he acted too slowly, he'd antagonize, become too abrasive and again lose. "Perhaps . . ." he slowly began, "we can talk about that later. As I told you, next month I have some pressing concerns, contracts terminate, two hundred, maybe three hundred, employees will soon be available. As soon as I can clear up this practical matter, I'll have more time to be able to give full consideration to upcoming political matters."

"If it's an impending contract that's causing you concern, I just might be in a position to assist." W.A. lit his cigar.

"It doesn't work that way." Ellis Shakelford, a young lawyer recently elected President of the School Board, quickly responded. "W.A., this is a new age in politics, the public expects and demands transparency. Republicans are straight above board; we're not a party that trades favors."

"Progress never waited for purity," W.A. shot back.

Shakelford's lips tensed, but seeing the tenor of the group solidly behind W.A., the upstart lawyer relented.

W.A. addressed the gathering. "This informal exploratory meeting of our steering committee is designed to help determine the future of the G.O.P. from the state of Pennsylvania." He surveyed the room, pleased that matters were going as planned. Horse trading, exchanging favors, all were designed to produce the desired results, but, with W.A. choosing the invited guests, and, more importantly, dominating the conversation, he hadn't left room for surprises. W.A. eyed the men seated around the mahogany table. Billy Alveni, the head of Capital City Technologies, a corporation that relied on miniature ball bearings, manufactured at W.A.'s Allentown plant, was solidly in his corner. So was Aaron Bergley, the heir apparent to the city's municipal union, who, through Hornsby's financial assistance, catapulted into a power icon representing city employers. Also solidly in favor of Philip's candidacy were His Right Reverend Joseph Maloney, the prelate of Philadelphia; Harold Curtis, Chairman of the Board of American Textile; and Representative Holden Cartwell, an eleven-term congressman stalwart who, through the generous donation of W.A., won by simply out financing every other candidate. Potential politicians became intimidated by the financial burden of entering a race against him. Harry Arndael would go along so long as he threw him some bones. W.A. slightly worried about Barry Tutworth, a lawyer fresh from five years with Common Concern; Wilbur Holden, the crusty, old Republican City Planning Chairman who chose to remain noncommittal, and especially Ellis Shakelford who represented the new upcoming breed of politicians, the altruistic do-gooders who took themselves too damn seriously.

"Of course," W.A.'s tone was measured, "our esteemed Senator Perkins deserves the courtesy of feeling no pressure from within his own party. But if he chooses not to seek re-election, I want a united front." W.A. eyed the room; no one voiced an objection. "Now, perhaps, a little lunch is in order." W.A. rang a delicate Chinese bell. Large, double-panel, oak doors opened, and three butlers, dressed in starched cream-colored tuxedos, entered. Within a couple of minutes, the mahogany conference table was covered with an Irish linen tablecloth, white bone china decorated with hand-painted fox hunts laid next to the ornate settings of King Richard's silverware. Distinctive *WAH* engraved, heavy crystal glasses were soon brimming with a French 1966 Bordeaux. The conversation flowed from one frivolous matter to another, most of the guests concentrating their efforts on a luncheon comprised of eggs Benedict, poached pink salmon, flaky thin croissants, and complemented by a Syrian salad; the luncheon finished with a light, but delicate, chocolate mousse accompanied by cappuccino or espresso.

Before escorting his guests to the barns for a tour, a dessert wine and then vintage port were opened to celebrate the occasion. After drinks were poured, W.A. stood, raised his glass and toasted: "To the Republican Party, to its revitalization and, I might add, if the opportunity arises, to the political rise of a man capable of rejuvenating this great party—Philip Hornsby."

After tipping glasses, Harry Arndael took his cue and spoke. "Perhaps an infusion of new blood makes sense. I feel that in good conscience, if our esteemed Senator decides not to run, I will throw my weight behind Mr. Hornsby's candidacy."

The reverend spoke, "If the opportunity arises, I think we can rest assured that the people of my congregation will solidly stand by young Hornsby."

Holden added his opinion, "A primary battle must be avoided. Let the five Democratic hopefuls fight it out, they never have enough sense to keep their dirty linen to themselves. No need to drag in derogatory information; the self-defeating Democrats do it for us."

W.A. then summed up his feelings. "At all costs, the Republican candidate must stay impeccably clean. He must remain clear of any hint of a scandal; his public image must be beyond reproach. What this country cries for today is a bona fide hero, someone with zest, clear vision, and vitality for life!"

Frivolous laughter echoed from the chamber, the dense aroma of cigar smoke permeating the room. W.A., enjoying these behind-the-scenes manipulations, informed the group that his son Philip, who was presently traveling between Paris and Geneva representing the Hornsby Foundation's investment banking interests, had no notion that his name was being held in the wings pending next week's announcement of Senator Perkins' future political plans. W.A. assured the assembly that the news that this august group even considered Philip would pleasantly shock his son. "But," W.A. continued, "with Philip's impeccable background, it seems logical he'd eventually run for public office. Philip has crafted a meticulous reputation—prep school at the prestigious Exeter Academy, a Phi Beta Kappa degree from Harvard, five years of working at major brokerage houses, and, for the past four years, top-level managerial experience with one of the largest privately owned investment entities in the country." W.A. ended by informing the group, "Philip is considered to be one of the country's premier authorities on tax-free, short-term securities . . ." No one seemed to care.

"I've never met Philip so tell me more about the man I've supposedly endorsed." The party quieted as Ellis Shakelford questioned W.A.

The elder Hornsby, sipping on a drink, puffed his cigar. "He's six-foot, three inches, broad shoulders, jet-black, flowing hair, ruddy accented cheekbones, kind of looks like me." Strained laughter greeted this remark. W.A. continued. "Philip is both an expert in Egyptian art and French Impressionism, a collector of rare Chinese stamps, master of five languages, dresses conservatively and speaks well."

Billy Alveni voiced, "Perhaps he'll come across as too chic? The electorate wants dynamism and charisma. Mind you, I have no personal agenda regarding your son, but my concern is that the son of a wealthy man might not ring true to blue-collar workers."

W.A. seized the moment. "Back in his youth he was a wild colt, even I couldn't control him." The elder Hornsby laughed, "If a public relations firm handles him properly, Philip can be portrayed as a person who can relate. It's all a matter of how he's promoted; smart marketers will be able to capitalize on one of Philip's few peculiarities—a desire to dare the unknown." The room went dark, a large-scale movie screen slid down and a slideshow supporting W.A.'s narration began. "I don't know if you're aware of his extensive mountaineering background, he used to be one of America's best. In his early twenties, Philip crisscrossed the globe with his climbing feats." Pictured on the screen were lions and tigers with snowcapped mountains far in the background. "In Africa, to his credit is Kilimanjaro; Europe, both the Matterhorn and the North Face of the Eiger; a resounding first in the Himalayas on Nanda Davi; he was on the

South Col a thousand feet from Everest's summit, when circumstances beyond his control forced him to halt."

"Does he still climb?" the monsignor asked.

"Heavens no! After years of worrying, the boy finally came to his senses. Pressure of work and rapid promotions caused an end to these adventures. Even though I wasn't overly happy with these journeys, I made sure his efforts were well chronicled. During this stage of his career, Philip's name even appeared on the cover of *Outdoor* magazine. If promoted intelligently, Philip can be transformed into an individual who makes dreams a reality." All sat back as the screen showed pictures of Philip standing triumphant, flag in hand, on majestic summits.

As W.A.'s guests were preparing to leave, Shakelford cornered W.A. "I didn't appreciate the comment about my naïveté, nor did I appreciate the pushing of your son. You manhandled that group, it wasn't a discussion, we came to hear a proclamation!"

"You're shrewd, and I admire that," W.A. deliberately chose his words. "You'll probably go far if a Republican wins!"

"I'm not here to argue. I want a Republican to be victorious in November and your son, purely from what you've said, certainly stands as good a chance as any. I just don't want you to think you can bully me!"

W.A. stood, knowing when to back off, and escorted his guest to the door.

9. *Fate Intervenes*

The strong smell of wildflowers permeated the warm spring air. May in Colorado's Rockies was Harry Birdwein's favorite time of year. It was a time of renaissance and hope. And it looked so damn pretty. No matter what his emotional state was in March, by May, Harry was in good spirits. The promise of spring always revitalized his soul. Indeed, even when his wife, Emma, died more than twenty winters ago, Harry emerged from the depth of despair as the wildflowers bloomed in the high mountain valleys.

The student bearing the telegram found Harry in his customary morning locale—tending to his hybrids in the fields a short distance behind the buildings that housed the university's botany department.

"Professor Birdwein! Professor! I have a telegram for you from London!"

"Shirley, are you calling me? Over here, come through the gate and take the path on the right, but mind the seedlings."

"Professor Birdwein, a FedEx just arrived! I thought it must be super-important, so I decided to bring it to you here."

"Thanks, Shirley. You're very thoughtful."

Birdwein knew that Shirley, the undergraduate assigned by the financial aid office to work with him as a part-time secretary, tried too hard to please and would have brought him a note from his barber canceling an appointment. As his fingers opened the envelope, Harry Birdwein tried to guess what was inside—an announcement of a new hybrid, an invitation to speak at a conference on plant genetics, perhaps even a nomination for an international scientific prize? Harry unfolded the paper and, to his great surprise and joy, read the most exciting message of his life:

London May 15

Birdwein: Japanese expedition planned for next spring canceled. Mountain open. The Nepalese Government must fill the gap promptly. Have put hold on the slot. Can you do it? Shall I confirm the American expedition to Mount Everest next spring? Advise! If affirmative, we must go and observe the mountain as soon as possible.

Austin Morley

"Well, I'll be! Eureka! Fantastic!" The exclamations bubbled from Harry's lips with a glee and exuberance that was contagious. His eyes gleamed; raw energy burst through the pores of his skin and charged the surrounding air with a palpable feeling of excitement.

"What is it?" Shirley asked, bemused but almost frightened by the energy radiating from the usually measured Professor Birdwein. "Are you okay?" Recalling her presence and wanting to share the thrill of the moment with someone, Harry grabbed Shirley by the shoulders. Fearing, yet welcoming, an imminent embrace, Shirley prepared herself for a tumble into newly sprouted corn stalks.

Lifting and moving her to within inches of his face, Harry jubilantly explained the reason for his passion: "I am going to Mount Everest! Morley got it for me. I thought my chance would never come. It's the wildflowers, Shirley, the wildflowers. Fantastic!" While spewing forth his emotions, Birdwein twirled Shirley, then bringing her close, placed an exuberant fatherly kiss on her right cheek.

"Shirley, this is a day I'll never forget!" Birdwein abruptly released her and without pausing, began running toward the gate. As he moved, he called back to the startled undergraduate, "Come on, Shirley, we've got to respond to Morley!"

"Sure, I'm right behind you, Professor."

Harry Birdwein had been climbing mountains ever since he entered high school. He was still in gradeschool when his uncle, Austin Morley, ten years his senior, dragged him to a nearby hill, but once on an incline, he found a home. In junior high school, he stared at topographical maps during the week and on weekends he'd climb. At age fourteen, he went to Mount Katahdin in Baxter State Park in Maine's Allagash Wilderness. It had been a fantastic three days—warm and clear, and from the summit it looked as if all of New England was within his grasp. Though he had accepted his uncle's invitation, the climb would entail hard work for a lazy teenager sleeping under the stars on a surface far different from his warm mattress. Yet the experience opened a door that would never close and now propelled him toward the top of the world. Harry came into his own during those three days on Katahdin. For the first time in his life he appreciated his own unique capacities—physical strength, stamina, patience, an unusual ability for conquering the most dangerous and taxing route up a hill. Ascending to a summit proved exhilarating; reaching the pinnacle, his feelings of accomplishment and unmitigated pride were almost ethereal. The sense of power, dominance, and oneness with the sweeping landscape was overwhelming. A self-knowledge of true accomplishment put a smile on his face. To young Harry, who had recently completed a ninth grade course in European history, the only adjective that came to mind that properly characterized his feelings as he stood atop Maine's highest point was Napoleonic. From that moment on, he shared the drive and ambition to conquer new and greater worlds.

In a neverending series of battles, Harry Birdwein and Austin Morley bested many mountains in the Rockies and the Andes. Though both showed great promise as world-class Alpine climbers, Morley increasingly paced himself ever more slowly and grew extremely apprehensive when attempting major peaks. While his uncle didn't relish dangling from a rock wall, Austin Morley did find joy reveling in the behind-the-scenes preparation. He took delight in organizing the endless details—analyzing the necessary technical equipment, determining the proper amounts of food, obtaining the necessary permits. His passion for making other peoples' dreams a reality so overwhelmed him that he resigned from his accounting practice, left America, set up shop in Kathmandu, and devoted his full energies to launching a Himalayan trekking company.

But that was not the case for the young Birdwein. At age twenty, during a summer vacation from Bates College, where he was studying botany in order to enhance his appreciation of what he saw on innumerable treks and climbs, Harry was invited by a Swiss friend to join an assault on the Eigerwand—the northern wall of the Eiger, a foreboding monstrous sheer rock. With little knowledge of what was involved, Harry, who had almost no experience on rock faces, enlisted as a team member. He vividly remembered Morley coming with him, observing the mountain and helping him secure the necessary gear. From that moment on, their roles became etched in stone, Harry Birdwein the climber and Austin Morley, the behind-the-scenes supporter. When Harry first assessed the Eiger he was both breathless and frozen with fright. He was sure he would never survive the climb; the ominous wall stood perched like a giant exposed sword. But after a few days of practice, he quickly learned the essential techniques of rock climbing, and rather than work his way to the Eiger's summit by curling around the mountain, thus avoiding the wall, he started a career as a rock climber by a direct attack on the formidable face. Through three incredible days, Harry thrived on the sureness of his new skills. Austin Morley perched, binoculars in hand, following his daring young nephew's every move. As he clawed his way up the wall, Harry, stumbling into his passion, became increasingly confident in his ability to overcome one of nature's most formidable obstacles. The challenge of rock climbing, when compared to alpine trekking, was far greater, but so were the rewards. Sweat dripped like a cascading waterfall, muscles pulsated, but the feeling of accomplishment as he stood atop the Eigerwand was, for Harry, far more intense than the end of any of his previous alpine treks. Having taken on a new challenge and having proven to himself that he was more than its equal, Harry Birdwein, from that moment on, could never turn back.

Over the following two decades, he took on any and every rock climb of substance. If climbers dared contemplate it, Austin Morley would accomplish the logistics of aligning the necessary supplies, thus affording Harry his opportunities. Harry Birdwein's reputation grew in direct proportion to his triumphs and now, some thirty years later, the entire mountaineering world knew the name and accomplishments of Harry Birdwein—not because he bragged or publicized his exploits via films, magazine articles, or other forms of mass communication, but, rather, because his colleagues unabashedly sang his praises.

But even more surprisingly, Austin Morley turned his passion into a world renowned Nepalese trekking company. From his Kathmandu offices, any objective, however remote, however implausible, could be accomplished through his wizardry.

Though success and fame were his, and so many of the world's rock faces had fallen to his strength and skill, Harry retired as an active climber at age forty unfulfilled. Even though the memories he left were enough to fill a bookcase of scrapbooks, there was always one more peak, one more mountain, a different variation that would tax both his ingenuity and ability. Most glaring in his omissions was a successful ascent of the granddaddy of all—Everest. No mountain climber worth his salt doesn't dream of locking horns with the world's highest pinnacle; Harry Birdwein was no exception. Shortly after he teamed with Austin Morley, Harry began reading about Mount Everest and the successful assault of the Kiwi beekeeper Sir Edmund Hillary and the Nepali sherpa Tenzing Norgay. The fascination, or rather preoccupation, had begun. "Everest . . . Everest . . . Everest . . ." pounded within his psyche. Over the years he meticulously studied the mountain and the attempts of all who followed the 1952 British team. In the course of those studies, Harry's attention was constantly drawn to the Southwest Face, the most difficult approach to the summit. There, sitting some 26,000 feet above sea level, Harry's eyes remained riveted on the penultimate rock climb—a sheer rock wall, some 1,000 feet high, guarding the approach to the 29,000-foot summit. No one had ever contemplated, let alone attempted, to scale this foreboding yellow band. Rather, the Bonnington expedition and the Japanese attempt employed the southwest approach only to the point where the rock band bisected the face. From there the attacking parties either veered south or west, not only eschewing the direct approach but never even considering setting a foot on the wall. For years, Harry found himself preoccupied with a dream of matching his courage with his abilities against this virgin rock face. Whenever he dared voice those dreams, his uncle, Austin Morley, quickly became his harshest critic. Morley badgered him incessantly with a host of valid reasons why his idea was pure folly; if rarified air wasn't enough, the need to cart bulky cylinders of life-giving oxygen apparatus would be like telling a marathon runner to embark on the twenty-six-mile journey with lead sinkers tied around their ankles. Added to these obvious hindrances were the problems of bitter cold, unpredictable weather, howling winds, and the virtual impossibility of a rescue attempt in the event of a mishap. Though Harry knew Morley's criticism had merit, his dreams adhered to the belief that with proper planning and the advent of new products featuring space-age strength, but ultra-lightweight climbing aids, the yellow rock band could be scaled delivering the conqueror direct access to Everest's summit.

Harry Birdwein was a man of simple pleasures, his son, mountains, and botany. Ever since his wife's passing, his efforts centered on raising Peter. He was mother, father, friend, helper, coach, diaper-changer, and valet all rolled into one. His son was his extension, his appendage. When Peter took ill, he shivered; when the toddler spiked a fever, he would sit by his side, wishing only that he could bear his suffering. Twelve years after Emma's death, when Peter was beginning his adolescence, tragedy again reared its ugly head. Harry's best friend at the university, Elmer Johnson, and his wife, Eleanor, journeyed to Estes Park, Colorado, for a day of cross-country skiing in early April. Their tracks indicated they made it to the summit, but sometime during the late afternoon, as they neared their car, a massive avalanche swept them away, suffocating the couple in ice tombs. It was left for Harry to inform Elmer and Eleanor's eleven-year-old son, Clayton, of his parents' demise. Harry remembers the child helplessly weeping; he pledged on his best friends' graves that, from that day on, he would raise Clayton Johnson as his son. During the ensuing years, Peter, Clayton, and Harry became bonded as if stuck together with glue; to the outside world, their climbs and exploits painted a picture of daredevils, but, amongst the three, their relationship was marked with caring and empathy. Few outsiders were ever invited to enter their house; their lives intricately intertwined, they neither needed nor sought outside support. Balancing life's three pillars—an academic career, mountains, and rearing his sons—proved difficult but not impossible. Although it left time for virtually nothing else, for Harry Birdwein, the adage "less is more" not only made his passions acceptable, it added clarity. Years marched by and he stayed committed. But advancing years, while not dampening his unbridled enthusiasm, have a way of humbling even the most ardent climber. A few months shy of his fiftieth birthday, Harry no longer dreamt that he could ever scale Everest's yellow band; his coordination had lost the razor's edge of perfection that it once enjoyed. Leg and arm muscles lacked the staying power, the surefire glue they once knew. While Harry no longer saw himself climbing the rock band, that made no difference, because his alter egos, his sons Peter and Clayton Johnson, could and would climb for him. Harry would be the climbing coordinator, the quarterback, the mastermind; Austin Morley the expedition planner, and Peter and Clayton would do the conquering.

Until Austin Morley's surprise message, Harry Birdwein had given up the dream of his youth, an ascent to the top pillar of the world. In the interim years, numerous groups clawed their way atop Everest. During the climbing seasons, pre-and-post monsoon, spring and fall, minute dots plodded up the traditional South Col route. But for Harry Birdwein, simply reaching the summit would not be enough; every time he looked at the stack of pictures before him, the menacing rock band at 26,000 feet played havoc with his imagination. The botanist was intoxicated by what it represented—an opportunity to push the human spirit to a new dimension. Harry Birdwein fervently believed his sons possessed the skills, the determination, and the courage to translate his dreams into a reality. Emailing Morley: *Tentative go! My boys and I will join you and go to Everest and see firsthand obstacles that must be overcome.*

Harry vividly remembered the March night when Clayton and Peter returned from a highly successful South American ascent and, to their surprise, he left a message that he was in Denver on unexpected business and would be home late but wanted them to wait so they could join him for coffee. Later that evening he excitedly barged through the door and, without even shaking the film of snow from his wool sweater, spread topographical maps over the table, pointed to a rock wall, and, bubbling with enthusiasm, stated, "You deserve this opportunity! It's been arranged. Peter, open the pantry and bring out a decanter of sherry. Tonight we celebrate." He pounded his son's back. Harry laughed; Clayton and Peter, trying to become oriented with what was happening, blankly stared at the crowded topographic maps. "You don't understand, do you?" Birdwein's laugh was infectious. "What you're looking at is an enlarged blowup of the southwest wall of Everest, Austin Morley wired from Kathmandu that he's arranged approval to launch an expedition up this previously untouched wall."

From that winter evening to this spring reconnaissance mission, their waking hours were filled with the intoxication of this journey. They talked, slept, and were consumed by tackling Everest. They continued with the business of maintaining their lives; Harry as a botany professor at the University of Colorado; Clayton, a member of a specialized avalanche patrol; and Peter, who apprenticed himself in building log cabins while avoiding having the pressures of using his engineering degree which would force him into full-time employment. But as the weeks dragged on, optimism could only take them into the realm of dreaming. Saddled with their collective Himalayan inexperience, they knew their task in organizing and financing an expedition was a mammoth undertaking; yet all were convinced that any and all obstacles, regardless how onerous, would not stop them. Problems continued to surface, yet Harry kept his quiet resolve. His preliminary attempt at arranging funding, securing and organizing equipment, and negotiating for official American geographic approval was met with rejection. Refusals were all similar—when a potential sponsor found that the objective was Everest's yellow rock band, acknowledged leaders in American mountaineering wouldn't dare associate themselves with a mission involving such great risk. While the climbers' reputations were impeccable, knowledgeable outside observers considered pioneering a route up the wall to be an impossibility. All politely noted that while the younger Birdwein and Johnson made their reputation as rock climbers, none had been on a major alpine climb and, most importantly, were Himalayan novices. Harry Birdwein feverishly worked through the details, and although there were many gaps to be filled and numerous rejections piled on his desk, late fall found them, as scheduled, leaving to survey their intended spring conquest of Everest. For Harry Birdwein, this trip was a needed relief; actually climbing the mountain seemed like a minor task when compared to the massive bureaucracy and red tape of launching this undertaking. Proud to a fault, Harry Birdwein was desperate to raise the funds enabling the three of them to travel to Kathmandu to meet with Austin Morley and then on to Everest Base Camp, the launching pad. This exploratory endeavor required Harry to take out a second mortgage on his small two-bedroom home.

The four men spent nearly two weeks trekking to Everest Base Camp to face, firsthand, their proposed objective: the yellow rock band protecting Everest's summit. A decision could not be made to either go ahead or abandon the mission until his sons confronted their obstacle with their very own eyes. Ultimately, it was Peter and Clayton's decision if the proposed route was within the realm of human possibility.

Arriving at Base Camp just as the sun was setting, they watched as darkness settled into the crevices of the foreboding peaks. After a meager dinner consisting of hot tea and dehydrated peas and beans, Harry sat by the dwindling fire, staring at the surrounding giants as a full moon illuminated the mountains.

"Get some sleep!" Morley yelled.

"It's just so goddamn big!" Harry mused.

Morley, wrapped in his sleeping bag, joined him by the smoldering embers.

"Your idea is bloody crazy," Morley said as he emphatically offered his unsolicited opinion. "In 1975, Bonnington was foolish enough to try the gully before the Southwest Face of Everest."

"And?" Harry questioned.

"Two were lost, but miraculously he succeeded." Austin Morley's eyes scanned the wall. "But Harry, what you're proposing is utterly ludicrous. No one can possibly scale almost a thousand feet of exposed rock at an elevation of 26,000 feet!"

"The scope, it's awesome." Harry Birdwein's words were slow and measured, his enthusiasm guarded, his eyes remaining peeled on the glistening moonlit rock face.

"I never could have imagined you were taking this foolhardy idea seriously. Bloody fool I am, how could I have been talked into this reconnaissance mission?"

Birdwein disregarded Morley's mutterings, his eyes fixed on the yellow-stained granite through the telephoto lens. "What attracts you is the height, isn't it?" Morley droned. "You're no different. Simply because it looms the highest, you feel compelled to wrestle with Everest. Harry, what you're proposing is suicidal. Success should be our ability to add Clayton and Peter to an already growing list of people who have made a summit assault.

Morley shook his head. "My dear nephew, so many years together, so many campfires, always the same; in the beginning, unbridled enthusiasm, an unquenchable will, a vocabulary that doesn't contain the word no. I'm sorry for you, and all of the other self-possessed pioneers. Why must one do what one has never done before? Is the mountain anything less now that the assault up the South Col is becoming commonplace, the publicity minimal, the notoriety obscure? Has Everest lost its luster because in the spring of 2003, thirty, maybe fifty, people scaled Everest's summit in one single day?"

"Publicity doesn't interest me," Harry interjected.

"Is it unadulterated purity? Oh, please!" Morley chided.

"We will combine the logistics of an alpine assault with the technicalities of scaling a rock face." Birdwein uttered his words with a quiet but forceful refrain. "The wall can be conquered."

"Simply reaching the top by the conventional route, won't that suffice?" Morley asked.

"That's not why we came!"

"How about the West Ridge?" the veteran mountaineering guide questioned.

"Tom Hornbein and Willie Unsoeld successfully pioneered that route in the American sixty-three expedition."

"First ascents are finished on this mountain. When Chris Bonnington led a party up the supposedly unclimbable Southwest Ridge in seventy-three, the mountain had been violated by all routes."

"That's not so. After they reached 26,000, they cut under the wall and shimmied their way through the lefthand gully and then traversed the upper snow field to the summit."

"What they accomplished was momentous." Morley gave homage. "Their expedition will go down as one of the major firsts in all of mountaineering."

The botanist spoke without conceit. "I'm not taking anything away from the enormity of their achievement. But, over the years, the art of mountaineering has become more sophisticated; advances in technical equipment and skills have opened new horizons. What was previously thought impossible is now being scaled; climbers are breaking new ground, setting foot on walls once thought unapproachable. Memorable firsts, that's the essence of pure mountaineering. Nobody can doubt Nick Estcourt's pioneering venture, without technical support or oxygen, up the gully adjoining the Rock Band to the Upper Snow Field. Even today that ranks as the pinnacle of pushing human abilities to the brink. But, taking nothing away from Estcourt's efforts, nor from those that followed, Doug Scott, Dougal Haston, and Hamish MacInnes, is for Peter and Clayton to reach the base of the Rock Band at 26,000 feet and instead of skirting under and scampering up a crack either left or right of the face, to directly tackle the thousand foot monster. No going around, or under, or to a side, my boys will do what's never before been accomplished, climb the blasted yellow barrier."

Morley assessed. "No one, no matter how good, can, in a single day, hammer sufficient pitons on that wall."

"Finally, my friend, we agree!" Morley couldn't believe what then came from Harry's mouth. "They'll have to bivouac for a night suspended by a sling."

"Dangle for a night unprotected on that wall . . ." Astonishment tinged the expedition coordinator's words.

"You heard me!"

"Absolute insanity! You're either a complete fool or just plain suicidal!" Austin Morley gathered himself to his feet and re-entered the tent.

All night Harry Birdwein sat beside the glowing embers. At the first hint of morning light, Austin Morley again came out to join him. "Bloody couldn't sleep!" he bitched. "Closed my eyes and my chest felt like it was caving in. I almost forgot how much my body detests this god-forsaken, oxygen-deprived altitude." He stared upward as the morning sun bathed Everest's crest before digging metal supports into the snow and attaching a telephoto lens, Birdwein steadied himself as he meticulously studied the yellow rock face. Over their thirty-year relationship, Austin Morley couldn't believe how little his nephew had changed. Birdwein, now a stocky but muscular professor of botany at the University of Colorado, was still the zealot, the purist, a no-nonsense individual, a man of few words. The massiveness of his calloused hands emitted comfort; the barrel chest poured strength; the curly, disheveled hair over his rugged, bearded face shielded eyes that gleamed with tenderness. When he spoke, his words were clear; his actions conveyed a simple, but direct intent of purpose. Morley, in his three decades of equipping expeditions, had seen many brave, some foolhardy, some courageous men and women willing to dare, but few adventurers passed before him who exuded the quiet confidence chiseled into Harry Birdwein's rugged face. It was his nephew's youthful exuberance that launched his career and now, thirty years later, both in the backend of their careers, strange circumstances again brought them to dare the unknown.

Harry looked toward Morley. "Is there any way we can reach the mountain by avoiding the Solo-Khumbu Ice Field?"

"All routes on the mountain require passage through the glacier."

Morely pointed to a series of rock piles topped with wooden crosses. "They're tombstones, monuments to all those who have died trying to conquer Everest. One of those crosses belongs to Jake Breitenbach, who died due to a collapsing ice wall. You just don't seem to realize."

Birdwein, annoyed at the constant jabber, but realizing the key role Morley would play, looked up. "After all our years together, don't think I'm naïve. Those of us who climb knowingly take a chance. Climbing tests human vulnerability, I'd be a fool if I wasn't aware that death is a possibility."

"Harry, quite the bravado. You can't tell me you're not afraid of dying," Morley declared.

"It's impossible to be insulated from the dangers. Fear incapacitates," Mallory said. "Dreams live in those shadows. Only here do I live fully, pushing life's limits. Austin, our success won't spoil this mountain, lessen its magnitude, or change this peak. Everest will remain, reigning supreme, fighting the savage battle of wind and snow. But the human spirit gains only so far as one dares to tempt limits, the mountain is nothing but the staging for a grand Broadway production. What I'm proposing is facing risks armed with precision and skill." Harry pointed to two figures slipping into harnesses. "My son and Clayton Johnson are two of America's best. They personify the new breed. If the yellow band can be climbed, they've earned the right!" Harry admiringly stared at Peter and Clayton. "At my advanced age, those two sons are all I have; I'm not about to go back to the drawing board."

"I don't think the bloody climb can be done, Harry. A damn fool's adventure it is!"

"Austin, when did you become so cautious and conservative? Hell, in our younger days when we climbed together, you did the daring while I was typically the doubtful American."

"Look, Harry, there are lives at stake, and your plan could easily cost a fortune in human flesh. Furthermore, there is my business and my reputation to be preserved."

"It's not your position or mine to deny them!"

As the sun set, lavenders and purples bathed Everest's upper flanks. Peter, Clayton, and Austin were busy lighting lanterns and preparing dinner but Harry's eyes remained peeled to the oculars of the telescope. "Stop what you're doing! Look! Finally I know why the smooth slab of rock between the gully at 26,000 feet and the Upper Snow Field is referred to as the yellow band.'" Grabbing binoculars, all stared high above as the departing sun left the mountain in a blaze of colors.

Austin Morley broke the silence. "A geologist explained conditions have to be perfect. When there is no wind and usually high temperatures during the day, a thin film of moisture is created, then at sunset, with the sun still blazing, a chilling cold turns the thousand-foot face yellow. Mesmerized, the four sat transfixed. For Harry, Clayton and Peter the dream of setting foot on the yellow band was intoxicating.

The next morning, the four men moved the telescope to different vantage points to survey the yellow band. But sheer distance precluded a sufficiently close inspection to reveal cracks to claw their way up. In order to make a definite decision, Peter Birdwein and Clayton Johnson set off to cross the feared Solo-Khumbu Ice Field. Glistening ice shimmered off the expansive field as Clayton Johnson, pulling on the rope, muscled his slender six-foot-three frame onto a narrow mantle beside Peter Birdwein. "Clamp into this halter, the pitons didn't bite so I secured an expansion bolt into the ice."

"Perhaps a little overly cautious," Johnson chided his adopted brother and climbing partner.

"Perhaps."

Perspiration poured over Peter's forehead, the tiny beads freezing on his bushy eyebrows. Four hours later, maintaining the lead rope and pointing ahead his fingers motioned to a rocky knoll, he noted, "If we follow the crack another two hundred yards, we'll be through the glacier and can set up a camera for a more detailed inspection."

Johnson, brushing his wavy black hair from his eyes, hoisted the trailing duffel bag and clamped the loose end to Peter's belt.

"What do you think you're doing?" Peter protested.

"After all, we're partners. I was feeling you were going to deprive me of the taste of being out in front," Johnson laughed. "I've followed diligently, never uttering a word of complaint, carrying equipment while you've led. And stop being so damn serious, traversing this ice field is nothing when compared to our ascent of El Capitan. If this wasn't the feared Solo-Khumbu Ice Field, we wouldn't even be roped together." Sharing a candy bar, the two laughed. Peter Birdwein's memory flashed to an incident six years ago soon after they first paired as a team. The winter day was cold and overcast, they were climbing on an unknown wall in western Utah; it was technical, but not overly difficult. All morning, Clayton complained about their ponderously slow progress, their overemphasis, or more precisely, Peter's preoccupation with securing every conceivable safety measure. Then, the unexpected happened. Birdwein, as the lead climber, clumsily left his entire bag of hardware unfastened. Without warning, the bag of technical gear became dislodged and plunged nearly a thousand feet to a desert valley floor. Johnson became irate, screaming at Peter that they would now have to unnecessarily risk their lives minus technical support. Peter was apologetic, but both knew they had no alternative but to scale, without aid, the remaining five hundred feet. Peter had never seen Johnson unnerved; their previous climbs usually found Clayton in the front, but Peter's careless mishap caused havoc with his climbing partner. Bracing himself, Peter assumed the lead and forcefully attacked the rock. Johnson followed, mute, disconsolate. After they reached the top, Clayton Johnson, never once complimenting Peter for his magnificent effort, again chastised him for his clumsiness. It wasn't until later that night after a beer that Johnson let it slip that he had intentionally unclasped the clamp holding the hardware. Laughing, he confessed, "It's about time someone helped convince you just how good you are!" From that moment on, Peter climbed with renewed self-assurance using technical aids only when mandatory.

Their friendship, seldom based on words, solidified as they became recognized as America's premier rock climbers. Theirs was an unlikely pairing; Clayton was prone to emotional outbursts, and Peter was known as reserved and quiet, but both were fiercely independent, driven by a thirst for wandering and a passion for venturing into the unknown. Most of all, they shared a rather unique simplicity in the way they viewed life: it was to be enjoyed, nothing more, nothing less. Johnson, more boisterous and extroverted, always kept up a steady banter; he constantly mumbled, barely loud enough to be audible, poking good-natured fun and wondering if Birdwein possessed the requisite energy to catch him in the event of an untimely fall. Peter never joked about accidents and rarely displayed humor. The more raucous Clayton became, the more Peter cringed. The two Birdweins bristled at Johnson's antics; their temperaments were stoic and quite contrary to Clayton's exuberance and playfulness. Yet, Clayton was accepted as a brother and as a son.

"Harry, give me those binoculars." Morley intently watched as Clayton and Peter scaled the final face on the far side of the glacier.Morley peered at the scampering figures, his concentration sharpening. "They're not even tied together. Raving mad is what they are!"

"The ice field doesn't test their ability." Harry Birdwein's eyes never left the scope. "My boys are two of the best in the business!"

Austin Morley shook his head. "Look, Harry," he muttered, "I've been all over the world, to every continent with an assortment of some of the most peculiar men and women on this planet, but this venture stands apart because it reeks of danger. Since my name is listed on the trekking permit with the Nepalese government as the official sponsor, before this fiasco continues, I'm contemplating withdrawing my support."

"You're just nervous," Harry shot back. "Calm down and relax. Have faith in us."

"Harry, let me be frank. You've never led a Himalayan expedition. You don't know of the difficulties, the inaccessibility, and the debilitating effects of the altitude. Besides, you haven't even told me who else you've recruited for the summit push."

"Just those two."

Morley shook his head in utter disbelief. "You're even crazier than I thought." The expedition planner then paused. "Don't be naïve. Clayton and Peter will need help, three hundred sherpas will have to haul gear from Kathmandu, the team will need a doctor, a communications network, and at least a dozen high altitude sherpas."

Harry Birdwein boiled. He despised Morley's defeatist attitude; his constant barrage of negatives was wearing thin. "Stop focusing on all of the obstacles!"

Morley was equally frustrated. "I have been wanting to tell you, but I thought eyeing the wall would speak for itself, the addition of another climber is mandatory!"

The botanist cut him off. "My boys are better alone!"

"That might be . . . but not so fast. If you took the time to carefully read the expedition's permit, which you obviously haven't, the king's permission is granted only if two conditions are met. One, I'm responsible for coordinating all details. And two, in a section regarding conditions, one of four designated climbers must be part of the summit attempt."

"You've negotiated what?" Harry screamed. "Why didn't you tell me these stipulations before now?"

"Because after seeing the wall, I thought for sure that you and your sons would give up. I never expected you'd want to continue."

Harry turned away, staring at the rock band.

Austin Morley became apologetic. "All along I've harbored serious doubts about the feasibility of the plan. No doubt your sons are excellent climbers." Morley peered at the two dots clawing up the mountain. "But unless a miracle strikes, they'll fail. Nevertheless, your unbridled enthusiasm is contagious. Mind you, I'm not happy, but you initially brought me into this business so I owe you. Reluctantly I'll help, but only if you can meet the conditions of the permit, employ the resources of my offices in Kathmandu, and convince one of the four mentioned climbers to join you. If that is all achieved, I agree to arrange the necessary permits and staff for the expedition."

That night, seated around a campfire, Harry challenged the Scotsman. "Tell them! Share the provisions of the permit with my sons."

Morley fumbled. "Securing a permit from the Nepalese government to attempt Everest is in itself quite an undertaking. The mountain is already booked, both pre- and post-monsoon season, through the next decade at least." An opportunity presented itself because the Italian Army Expedition was postponed. Suddenly a vacancy opened and, knowing your father has always voiced an interest, I managed to turn their disappointment into our advantage."

"Get on with it." Clayton Johnson's tone was firm.

"Go ahead!" Anger marked Harry Birdwein's voice.

Johnson, broken from his trance, took notice of the brewing confrontation. Since his parents tragically died in a car accident almost nine years ago, he could only recall a few instances when the botanist became irritable.

Peter, impatiently staring at Morley, propped himself in his sleeping bag. "My father asked you to speak!"

"The permit," Morley tentatively began, "was difficult to obtain. Outside the United States, none of you are known and the route you're proposing is outrageous. Frankly, officials in the Nepalese home office laughed; a night hanging on an exposed rock wall just below Everest's summit, sleeping in harnesses, unprotected from buffeting winds, officials thought I was certifiably crazy to be associated with such a bizarre plan."

Peter, never a man for unnecessary words, interrupted. "Get to the point!"

"I had to make a deal." Morley's voice was apologetic.

"A what?" Johnson burst forth.

"My name is attached to the permit!"

"You've made that point," Peter countered.

"Besides you two, I guaranteed the Minister of the Home Panchayath Affairs that either Barry Surate, Jack Meldlem, Philip Hornsby or Jimmy Buschkof would be one of the three lead climbers on the assault team."

Johnson exploded, "I've never climbed with any of the four, and now you're telling me I'm going to put my life in their hands!"

"Come now," Morley tried to placate Clayton, "certainly you are familiar with those names! You want a chance at the wall, then you're going to have to compromise. Without an experienced alpine climber, one who's been on Himalayan assaults, one who either has been to the summit or near the summit, the Nepalese government wouldn't even consider your plan."

"Why wait until now to tell us?" Peter fumed.

"I felt after this exploratory mission, after you had faced the wall, you'd come to your senses and give up this expedition. But I guessed wrong!"

An awkward silence followed. Johnson's anger burned in his glaring eyes, his foot kicked the smoldering fire, sparks danced into the night. So many aspirations and hopes were tied to this endeavor, now another stumbling block could derail their path to success. Peter was more accepting of the news; if a compromise was mandatory, he'd adjust. The names filtered through his mind: Barry Bear Surate, manager of Western Equipment and Mountaineering Corporation, ascents of Annapurna, Chamabang, member 1972 Patagonia Expedition, famed for reaching 28,000 feet on Everest's South Col without oxygen; Jack Meldlem, head of a mountaineering school in the Grand Tetons, numerous assaults on Mount McKinley, previously a Peace Corps volunteer in Nepal; Philip Hornsby, presently located on the East Coast, heir to the Hornsby Foundation, a major name in mountaineering in the early seventies, successful member of a United States team on the world's second largest peak, K-2, a near miss on Everest; and Jimmy Buschkof—Nanda Devi, Chomo Uno, and Everest to his credit, professor of geophysics at the University of Washington, arrogant, a loner but an acknowledged leader of American Himalayan climbers.

Peter broke the silence. "I'm not happy with Buschkof or Hornsby. Buschkof will try to take over; Hornsby, to my knowledge, hasn't climbed recently." He turned to his father. "You're leading this expedition, what do you think?"

"Certain decisions can't be mine. It's you who will have to trust your lives to a stranger. If either of you wish to call off the expedition, I understand."

10. Keeping the Dream Alive

Harry Birdwein's office in the botany department at the University of Colorado was cramped as Peter and Clayton arrived for their scheduled briefing. It had been a month since their return from Nepal. Harry, compulsively busy, seemingly ate, slept, and worked around the clock trying to put the pieces together to launch the expedition. Tired, his eyes swollen, deep bags drooping, he motioned for his sons to enter.

"Buschkof informed me two weeks ago that he was committed to a federal research project, I pressed him into asking his dean and reluctantly he did." Peter and Clayton waited. "The old warrior was correct. There was no way the administration at the University of Washington would give him another leave of absence. He wishes us well, but regretfully must decline."

"Have you heard from Bear Surate?" Peter questioned.

Harry's eyes never left his cluttered desk. "Judging from our conversation, the mountaineering cooperative business must be booming. They're doing close to three million dollars in gross volume this year, no way he can leave!"

Peter became edgy as Harry hedged. He'd grown accustomed to his father's directness, but because of the bureaucratic hassles of the past couple weeks, seeing his father hesitate made him uncomfortable. "That leaves either Meldlem or Hornsby."

"Jack will be here in less than an hour for an informal, preliminary discussion. That's why I want you both here; it's as much your decision as mine. I've promised him nothing, nor has he committed himself."

"Any early indications?" Clayton asked.

"Meldlem's a quiet man, but I noticed a definite surprise in his voice when I mentioned our proposed route."

"And Hornsby?"

"Definitely a last resort. Since Clayton registered doubt when Morley originally mentioned his name, I haven't even contacted him."

"Didn't Hornsby pioneer a route up Nada Davi?" Peter countered.

Clayton broke in, "With massive support from below, fifteen accomplished mountaineers waited while he and a sherpa scaled the summit. Others later complained the mountain was handed to him, waltzing up to a fully stocked Camp V, and then, with the aid of oxygen, pushing to the summit. Weather closed, no one else had a go. Ensuing published reports hinted of dissent within the ranks of the support team, Philip Hornsby doesn't have a reputation as a purist."

"But he did make it to the top," Peter countered.

Harry summed up the group's collective thoughts. "Without even knowing him, I tend to agree with Johnson. With the co-operation that would be required in our endeavor, Hornsby's reputation of being a questionable team player leaves me suspect."

They waited quietly. All knew the importance of the impending meeting with Meldlem. An incoming fax diverted their attention. Harry's bulging forearm banged against the oak table. Angrily he threw the communication onto his desk. "Damn International Explorers Club. Just who do they think they are?" Birdwein bellowed. "Won't even allow me to make a formal presentation, says our prospectus does not fall within their guidelines. Listen to this. 'We only sanction expeditions that will advance man's appreciation of the geographic world. Your intended trip, according to our standards, does not qualify on two accounts: one, there appears little provision for accomplishing specific scientific research; and, two, we do not sanction expeditions that are too risky.'"

Harry shoved the letter onto an already large heap of rejections. "Look at this stack—Amstel Corporation, American Mountaineering Club, Matterhorn Alpine Products, United Textiles, Northeast Snowshoe Company—it's less than three months until our intended departure and we still have no sponsorship for stoves, lanterns, altimeters, compasses, goggles, sunglasses, plastic bags, crampons, climbing ropes, tents, thermal suits, computers, binoculars, radios, recorders, rescue sleds, medical emergency kit, oxygen regulator, pitons, carbines, drugs, signal flares, aluminum snow ladders, anchors . . . the list goes on and on. Perhaps," Harry hesitated, his words choked, "I'm not the right man for this job?"

"Haven't there been some positives?" Peter tried to lessen the tension.

"We can probably bathe in food, voluminous quantities have been offered. Everybody wants us to try out their products. We have excessive amounts of protein concentrated, freeze-dried recipes, everything from pancake mix to fish, peanut butter, sesame bars, vegetables, wheat germ, natural jam and preserves; seems like every natural or organically oriented firm on the market wants to be included, even a sour mash whiskey firm has offered to specially package spirits so long as the product is photographed at the summit. Success sells, people want their products to be associated with winners. Tackling Everest doesn't permit a climber obscurity; it's naïve to think otherwise. When we picked this objective, I should have known better. Nobody believes we're climbing simply because of the excitement of testing human strength against one of the world's last formidable untouched obstacles. Their thinking is that we crave 'fame,' how far from the truth!" Frustration marked his voice as he continued. "Organizing this expedition is far more involved than I imagined. In the past few months, I've been consumed with stocking an alien world with the necessary amenities of twentieth-century adventurers," Harry Birdwein laughed. "And mind you," his head turned downward, his eyes suddenly sullen, "doing a terrible job."

Peter knew to let his father talk. Harry was not asking for advice, or encouragement; merely, on this rare moment, his self-directed criticism served as a mechanism to relieve his simmering tension. Self-contained, impeccably precise, and strong willed, Harry sculpted a veneer of impenetrability. Furrows lined his face, showing unmistakable signs of crumbling. The uncertainty, the constant rebuffs, the closed doors, all took a toll on this once impermeable botanist. Only a few times in his life had Harry opened up; once, many years ago, he talked about the untimely death of his wife, Emma, the richness of their eight years together, their yearning for an infant, and her tragic depression after childbirth.

Months after the arrival of their first baby, Harry stayed by Emma's side, clasping her hand. Even the slightest movement of an eyelid would rejuvenate Harry's hopes, but Emma, even with his constant care, less than a year after their son's birth, closed her eyes forever. After her death, Harry devoted his life to his son, botany, and mountains. Time was divided between his teaching and writing responsibilities and the demand of being both mother and father, nurturer, housekeeper, and cook. The only other passion in life was exploring mountains; his life was dutiful, predictable, and guided by a strict routine.

As a toddler, Peter remembers being toted on his father's back deep into some unexplored trails in the Rockies. Days were spent hiking and exploring. In his early adolescence, Clayton Johnson moved into their home and the two youths would sit at the base of rock walls while Harry, a master at ropes, would hammer pitons into rocks and, without showing the slightest concern, repel downward. When Harry returned to the campsite, his mood was light and carefree, leisurely kidding Peter and Clayton about the hidden comfort of being suspended on a rock wall. It wasn't until his sons were past their seventh birthdays that the elder Birdwein permitted his boys to climb with ropes. After that, their youth was spent shimmying between minute sleeves gutting bellies of boulders. Strong and agile, the two became comfortable dangling from cliffs. There was no fear, only raw excitement, the rope became an appendage. Father and sons spent virtually all available free time scaling rock faces in the mountains outside Boulder. Both Peter and Clayton developed an intuitive feel, a natural balance, both knew when a pressure point would hold and grew to anticipate and maximize the few moments a hand or foot held firm. Seldom did they climb with an object in mind, the elder Birdwein labeled excursions as rock explorations, but for his sons, these were moments to be cherished, times when the grayish texture of granite were their adored toys.

Peter broke the silence. "What do you know of Meldlem?"

"His record is impeccable. A first on northeast ridge on Mount Kennedy in the Yukon, a member of a Dhaulagiri Expedition, extensive climbs in the Andes and East Africa."

"But does he seem receptive?" Clayton asked anxiously.

Harry was hesitant. "Meldlem's a crusty veteran; he's interested enough to want to hear more, but he gives no initial indication."

"After this recent series of setbacks," Peter pointed to the stacks of sponsor rejections, "our luck is bound to change. I'm not sure why, but I feel Meldlem is our man. Morley is right; details will pull together once we have an acknowledged Himalayan name as part of our team."

Their conversation halted as the slight frame of Jack Meldlem was ushered into Birdwein's cluttered office. One hundred forty pounds, short-cropped graying hair, protruding cheekbones, a face accented by long, sharp, pointed nostrils. Meldlem's dress epitomized a composite of the West; cowboy in the wide-brimmed hat, Cherokee in the braided belt and hand-laced leather moccasins, and typical Westerner dude in blue jeans and denim work shirt. Harry, getting straight to the business at hand, dispensed with formalities and launched into a detailed explanation. Pointing when necessary to an enlarged topographic map, employing slides and illustrations, Harry traced the proposed route of attack from the origin in Kathmandu, through the one-hundred-fifty-mile march to Everest Base Camp, across the treacherous Solu Khumbu Glacier, up the southwest snow gully pioneered by the Japanese and British, and finally, to the yellow band. Meldlem, clasping his hands and wincing, stared intently as he viewed the slides, not asking questions, volunteering information, or giving any indication of his leanings. He was stoic. Harry, not hearing any rebuttals, interpreted the silence as tacit approval and, for a solid hour, explained a plan of attack once on the wall. For the first time in months, the expedition leader's voice hinted a gleam of optimism. "Jack, needless to say, I didn't ask you over so you'd have to listen to an old man rant and rave. You're a masterful climber, that's why I want you to be a member of our expedition." Harry, propping his feet on the table, delighted with his presentation, waited for the forthcoming affirmative response.

Meldlem sat pensively, his eyes staring at the photographs, his muscular fingers kneading his chin. "Harry, tell me," Meldlem began slowly, "only one team plans to make the summit assault?"

"Precisely."

"And where will you be?"

"I'm too old to venture onto the rock wall."

"You're definitely not climbing?" Meldlem seemed relieved.

"I haven't weathered quite as well as you. The accident on the Ruth Amphitheater on Mount McKinley still plagues me. I'll leave the heroics to you men. My satisfaction will come from being part of a team scaling a wall once thought untouchable."

"Well?" Clayton demanded.

"Give him time to answer," Peter interrupted.

Johnson stood. "Let's get to the point. Are you going to join us?"

"No way Jack Meldlem will set foot on that route. A night spent dangling on a rock wall at 26,000 feet is ludicrous!"

Clayton stared out the open window as Meldlem unloaded. "It's actually suicide! Can't be done! Wind, lack of oxygen, exposure, all will launch a deadly counterattack. You're pressing your luck, exposing yourself for an hour or two is rolling the dice, but to dangle unprotected for over twenty-four hours is sheer folly. Instead of squeezing through a gulley and gaining some protection, you're leaving yourself at the mercy of the world's most unpredictable weather. Everest is unforgiving!"

Stung by the severity of Meldlem's rejection, Harry replied, "It can be done!"

"All say that! In the confines of this office, it's easy to utter. Harry, you neither have the experience in leading such a venture, nor do either of these boys have the battle-incurred scars to dampen their enthusiasm. Not that I'm not doubting their abilities; both are highly qualified rock climbers. But imagine taking a neophyte art student and telling him to put the final details on an unfinished Picasso; you'd end up with a mess. Your plan is nothing more than a romantic pipe dream. Harry, believe me, leave it that way." Meldlem forced a laugh. "The mountain can turn monstrous; Everest is not to be toyed with." Meldlem stood and walked out of the office without another word.

"Our choice has been narrowed." Clayton tried to lighten the moment. "And I thought people would wait in line for this chance."

"The way things are going, perhaps we should cancel." Not a drop of enthusiasm could be found in Harry's voice.

"There's still Hornsby," Peter countered.

"His lineage precedes him; mainline Philadelphian currently being touted as the new up-and-coming star of Pennsylvania politics. Petulant and opinionated, no doubt he's successful. It's hard to imagine him joining us, what he'd want with us and what we'd want with him is a mystery; he'll neither accept nor fit in."

"We don't have much of a choice. Morley's list has dwindled to one. Either we try or give up," Peter countered.

Harry Birdwein reluctantly opened the file labeled Philip Hornsby. Since his personal phone number was unlisted, he dialed the corporate offices of the legendary business tycoon, Wilton A. Hornsby.

Speaking with the privileged elite wasn't just a matter of picking up the phone, dialing, and, unlike the pagan 99.9% of Americans who answer their own phones, Harry first started with a receptionist, then a personal assistant, each time pleading to speak directly with Philip Hornsby.

The woman's voice was brusque. "You'll have two minutes, not a second more, to speak with Philip's father, W.A."

"Why the call?" W.A. believed in getting to the point.

The botanist began, "Your son was one of the best climbers ever . . ."

"Was . . ." W.A. interrupted, "is the past!"

"History could be made . . ." Harry Birdwein fumbled for the appropriate words. ". . . The human spirit faces boundaries by challenging the unknown."

"This sounds like a sales pitch, and I am not interested!"

"Your son has a rare chance of being part of a team, doing what others thought was unimaginable." Harry continued to try to find the right words.

"Look, Professor, I'm a busy man, as is my son. And frankly, mountains have never piqued my interest. Whatever captured Philip's attention years ago remains a mystery . . ."

Sensing he was losing ground, Harry interrupted the tycoon. "Please let me at least speak with Philip directly."

"Presently he's about to leave for Europe to pursue a business deal."

"When will he return?"

"Philip's days of daring are over. Youthful indulgences are best left as adolescent bouts with immaturity. Responsibilities change people."

"Please at least give him the message."

W.A.'s response was the buzz of a phone ringing in the botanist's ear.

11. *A Day at Hornsby Enterprises*

As soon as Philip's business on the Continent finished, he proceeded to Charles De Gaulle airport where a corporate jet waited to whisk him back to Philadelphia. His father would be surprised since Philip had no intention of telling him that he was arriving back in town earlier than expected.

When not publicly in view, W.A. took extreme measures to ensure his privacy; a guard was permanently posted by the door protecting W.A.'s private entrance of the Miles Van der Rue—designed, glass-sculptured Hornsby Foundation building located in downtown Philadelphia. Thick metal gates protected the entrance, and the massive front door lined in strips of matching Nicaraguan walnut made it impossible for anyone other than an invited guest to enter. Seeing Philip, the guard held the door open. Once inside the concrete fortress, Philip strode across a pearl-white Indian marble floor accented by an octagonal-tiled mirrored ceiling. A second doorman nodded as Philip walked down the aisle. Although operation of the elevator merely required pushing a button, another attendant tended to this chore. As the elevator took Philip directly to the penthouse suite, the younger Hornsby smiled in anticipation of the astonishment that would be registered in W.A.'s face. The European trip went smoothly, beyond expectations. Philip finished his business days ahead of schedule and since Audrey was unable to free her schedule to vacation in St. Tropez, he headed back to the States. His decision would win on two accounts; his father would be pleased and Dr. Ferrington would be waiting. Dressed in a dark gray three-piece Italian-designed suit, Philip strode through the opening elevator doors, past a battery of surprised secretaries, through a room armed with telecommunication machines before strolling unannounced into an inner office.

W.A.'s bifocals slipped from his forehead. "Can't believe my eyes!" Motioning for Philip to be seated, the younger Hornsby chose to stand instead. In the midst of a conference call among subsidiary offices in Tokyo, London, Frankfurt, and Istanbul, W.A. barked a series of opening quotes on gold bullion then issued sell orders if his positions reached designated goals.

"Don't let me distract you," Philip jested.

"How'd you get back so early?" W.A. rose and pushed a button and a remote control television monitor zoomed in on them. He then wrapped his arms around his son, whispering, "You do realize our greeting is being broadcast across the world." W.A. had a peculiar habit. Each morning he beamed his picture into television monitors worldwide, wanting his employees to see him, visualize his commitment, and witness his vigor. "All stations remain on hold," W.A. bellowed. "I'll get back in a few minutes." W.A. then cut off the switch to the television monitors, ensuring their privacy. He then walked over and securely gripped Philip's extended hand. "Well?"

"Putting the deal together proved far easier than we imagined. The Saudi government gave us one tenth of a percent gross override; the French persuaded the Moroccans to use our equipment to drill wells, and the Italians, as desperate as they are for petroleum, proved amenable to pay a quarter point over the existing crude prices upon refined oil delivery. A more detailed report bears investigation." A discussion for the next fifteen minutes involved a new business venture, bartering goods from the West with the Russian Commonwealth; the Hornsby Company would offer cigarettes, flour, and sugar and in return receive vodka and petroleum. Philip listened attentively as W.A. outlined the managerial tasks. "The key ingredient leading to the success of this venture," W.A. maintained, "is that everybody will be amenable because everybody will gain. We've just touched the surface," W.A. beamed, "Yankee ingenuity, Arab resources, Russia's inexhaustible needs." His father clasped his son's hands, "There is nobody better than you to make this work!"

Philip stood, apparently to leave. "You're busy and I'm a bit tired."

"No, wait." W.A. suddenly sounded tentative. "Have your three weeks away changed anything?"

Philip appeared perplexed.

W.A. drove directly to the point. "Have you reconsidered your commitment to the girl?"

"Her name is Audrey Ferrington."

"You know who I mean."

"We're going to marry. You and mother can plan an engagement party, a date and place for the wedding is her choice."

"Isn't she from Utah?"

"No. Albuquerque, New Mexico," W.A. mumbled his next words.

Philip looked his father directly in the eye. "Go ahead, get it off your chest."

"Quite frankly, I am unsure if she's right for you. Don't misinterpret my comments, she seems like a fine girl, strikingly beautiful, and her intended professional career is most honorable, but her background . . . you need . . . how should I say it . . . ?"

". . . a more conventional wife?"

"Yes, exactly."

Philip interrupted. "W.A., I've considered that."

"And?"

"We're still getting married. Audrey's smart, beautiful, vital, a perfect mate. She's currently doing her medical residency, and yes, she's more than a homemaker and socialite. Audrey intends to have an active medical practice."

"She needs to be available," W.A. protested.

Philip cut him off. "W.A., in the realm of business you have few equals, but with regard to contemporary values, you're woefully out of touch. Today's women are emancipated, the *crème de la crème* refuse to be classified as second-rate citizens. If anything, Audrey's professional career will counteract what many refer to as the arch-conservative Hornsby way."

W.A. was equally abrupt. "Now is not a time to let anything tarnish your reputation."

"My what?" Philip seemed perplexed at the flow of the conversation.

"Before you go, we must talk." Philip listened attentively as W.A. informed him that in his absence their good friend, Senator Perkins, announced his decision, after three terms, to retire from the U.S. Senate. W.A. then began a lengthy discourse over the practicality of having someone who supported their cause in Washington, the numerous bills in the offering that affected their current and future operation, as well as the impending effects of governmental tariffs on forthcoming international business transactions. Suddenly W.A. switched gears and launched into a tirade over a citizen's civic responsibility, the need for good government, noting that he had been in discussion with politicians trying to locate an appropriate individual to replace the retiring Senator. Summing up his oration, he concluded, "The overwhelming consensus of select party leaders favors your candidacy; you have the education, the business acumen, the *savoir faire*, and keen judgment essential to make prudent decisions." After presenting his case, W.A. waited for his son's response.

Philip, surprised, spoke in a whisper. "Indeed, though I hadn't thought of it, being a United States senator might interest me."

"Precisely my thinking." W.A. extended his hand. "Provided you win!" Simultaneously both men laughed.

Their fifteen minutes alone caused a colossal business backup; a multitude of lights blinked on W.A.'s private line. As his father laid out a campaign strategy, Philip realized W.A. had not simply casually mentioned his entering the political arena. In all Hornsby endeavors, time, research, and planning were all ingredients carefully melded into an already stewing pot. As Philip stood and excused himself, W.A. asked him to stay but Philip responded that he wanted to surprise Audrey. As he was leaving, the younger Hornsby asked his father if there had been any personal messages of importance during his European trip.

"I've managed to hold the enterprise together in your absence." W.A. laughed.

"I'm sure of that."

"Your secretary has scheduled your appointments. A couple days ago, I glanced over the list, nothing appeared out of the ordinary," W.A. reported.

As Philip exited the inner office, W.A., returning to his desk, suddenly remembered, "Someone did call you while you were gone, bit of a disjointed conversation . . . demanded to speak with you, told me his name but I seem to have forgotten it."

"And?" Philip questioned.

"I do remember he mentioned he was associated with a science department at the University of Colorado at Boulder." W.A. paused. "A professor . . . said it was urgent . . . something about an intended trip. Obviously, I told him you were well past that stage of your life."

Philip turned. "Where did he say it was going?"

"Maybe the Andes, perhaps the Alps. I didn't pay attention."

"Why call me?"

"The fellow said something to the effect that your climbs are chronicled in mountaineering journals."

"Did you give him my private number?"

"No, I would not let him bother you."

12. Eat, Sleep, Breathe, Everest

The three ate their main course in silence. Peter Birdwein and Clayton Johnson repeatedly caught each other's eyes, each wondering how they could lessen their father's burden. Preoccupied, Harry's every waking hour was consumed with the thought of Everest. But the reality of seeing a multitude of rejections piled on their father's desk was becoming hard to ignore. Peter and Clayton knew that dagger after dagger of "I want no part of this scheme" was systematically destroying their father's dreams. Dinner finished, they did the dishes, then sat demoralized staring at glowing embers in the fireplace. As splintering logs burned to coals, the elder Birdwein went into a long soliloquy—his dissatisfaction of currently leading a settled, sedentary life, a lifelong desire to challenge the unknown, his fervent hope that he could leave some personal mark, however small, on the world. "I wish it could be only us, without complications, without outside influences. Perhaps it is the sheer size of this expedition that necessitates these complex logistics, but my leadership has failed."

Peter saw the tears in his father's eyes. "Perhaps I should have never attempted this. This venture is beyond my capabilities and my control."

"But it has always been your dream!" Clayton stood by his father with his arms outstretched and his hand lightly touching Harry's shoulder.

Peter spoke in a whisper. "You've always stood behind us. In the Grand Tetons, you were at the base of the mountain cheering us on. When I became ill at the Eiger, who sat by my bed for days forcing liquids into my dehydrated body? You have dedicated your life to us."

Clayton threw an arm around his father's shoulders. "Don't for a moment think we're naïve. Success on Everest, even on the traditional South Col route, is a monumental task; the three of us know the difficulty of what you're proposing. Our surveillance last October was an eye-opener. Harry, you've turned that granite wall into the holy grail. Since the thought entered your mind, you've become obsessed, but at what point," Clayton wondered, "does an obsession become its own worst enemy?"

"But if we stick together, if we help each other, just perhaps . . ."

Peter refused to face his father.

Harry Birdwein's dream of Everest, once so pure, was now tarnished with the grim reality that time was slipping away and the conditions of their permit had not been met.

The hour was barely past seven in the morning when the phone rang, Harry hoped it was Morley from Kathmandu informing him that the Minister of Home Affairs reconsidered and allowed additional names to be substituted as the third climber.

"This is Philip Hornsby returning your call. Sorry about the delay; I was out of the country. Your original message was a bit unclear, so please start from the beginning."

Harry sat up and began discussing the proposed expedition.

Philip gave no outward sign of surprise so Harry continued, "You have been highly recommended by Austin Morley as having the technical skills necessary to be helpful in this endeavor."

Philip asked numerous, detailed questions: climbing accomplishments of the other two lead climbers, and what, if any, corporate firms were committed to support the expedition. He asked if a public relations firm was chosen to publicize the mission and, most importantly, if official sanctions had been ascertained from the Nepalese government. As Philip pressed for details, Harry's original burst of enthusiasm was tempered as he chronicled the expedition's problems. Reluctantly admitting snags, answering no after no, Harry struggled to maintain enthusiasm in his voice.

"The government's approval—why hasn't it been satisfactorily worked out?" Philip didn't ask a question; rather, he had an irritating habit of demanding an answer.

"It all happened quickly, an Italian army expedition that was reserved for this spring abruptly canceled. Morley, knowing I've always been interested, put in an application for the slot. Conditions were present. I've been pressing ahead but time is at a premium." Harry, burdened by the month of rejections, annoyed at being the subject of Hornsby's interrogation, felt the dam burst. "Let me be forthright. Given the tight time constraints, I have doubts whether I'll be able to meet the deadlines."

"Why did you call me?" Philip drove to the heart of the matter.

"Austin Morley promised the Nepalese government that one of four climbers would be a part of the assault team and your name was included." Harry tried to be tactful. "We feel your expertise would be essential."

"If, and I'm not committing myself, I chose to go," Philip's tone was calculated, "it would only be under the following conditions: I'm appointed deputy expedition leader as well as head of the summit team. While the expedition would remain in your name, I'd relieve you of the brunt of the preparations. From the little you've told me, equipment, financing, and sanctions have hit roadblocks. At present, your expedition is now nothing more than a pipe dream; transferring ideas into reality involves bona fide commitments replacing hopes and aspirations, current frustrations mean you've tapped the wrong channels. Let me be blunt, if I choose to be a part of this climb, I would involve myself only if I thought we'd succeed. Now tell me in detail about the other climbers—their strengths, weaknesses, eccentricities."

Harry talked about Clayton and Peter. Philip repeatedly asked pressing questions and, unsatisfied with some of Harry's answers, demanded that a dossier of each climber be forwarded to his Philadelphia office. Philip then pressed Birdwein for specifics regarding his climbing experience, his record as an expedition leader, and his administrative abilities. Harry's curt responses reflected his simmering anger. At what point would he explode and tell this impudent bastard where he could go?

Philip abruptly ended the conversation. "What interests me is that your proposed venture touches something within me that I abandoned long ago; yet, I must admit, the aura of the Himalayas still intrigues me."

Harry, enraged, could no longer control himself. "What makes you think I'd acquiesce to your demands?"

"Dr. Birdwein, from what you've told me, you need me, you're backed against a wall; if you want to succeed badly enough, either do what's necessary or give up!"

Harry bristled. "My call was simply exploratory."

Philip measured his words. "Anemic egos have no place on Everest. If I accept, there will be other battles. Perhaps we can get along, perhaps not. But let me tell you, warm fuzzy relations on a mountain like Everest is not the priority. Success boils down to skill, determination, and technical preparedness. Tomorrow, send me a full packet of material and include topographic maps." The line went dead. If Harry could convince the International Explorers Club to back the mission he'd tell the Philadelphian to get lost. Proceeding with the hope Morley would convince the Nepalese authorities to add names, Harry boarded a plane to Washington, D.C. As the time neared for his meeting with the executive chairman of the International Explorers Club, Harry Birdwein was excited but cautious. Both sons were left in Boulder to handle incoming phone calls while he journeyed to the nation's capital to plead for needed support.

Before leaving the hotel, he called Boulder. "A preliminary hearing with Mr. William Marshall is scheduled later this morning. Telex Morley in Kathmandu to negotiate and buy time. Tell him we'll definitely add a third member to our assault team but," Harry hesitated, "the list he gave us is insufficient. His choices are unavailable, unwilling or, in Philip Hornsby's case, seemingly impossible to work with. Surely Morley can persuade the Nepalese government to be a bit more flexible."

"Should we volunteer suggestions?" Peter inquired.

"Morley is a wily veteran, he'll insist on adding someone familiar with Everest. Let him choose in consultation with the Nepalese government; it's more diplomatic that way. Is anything else happening?"

"An hour ago, Jason McCafferty, the president of Synco Oxygen Regulators said his research department has designed a prototype of a lightweight oxygen unit that will work on the wall. As soon as we get an official sanction, he'll announce he's behind us."

Before hanging up, Peter said, "Dad, call us as soon as your presentation is over. No doubt you'll succeed."

Harry Birdwein hung the receiver back onto its cradle and walked to the offices of the International Explorer's Club. Previously denied sanctioning by the American Geographic Society, this presentation was Harry Birdwein's final hope. It was essential that a prestigious adventure club formally sanction this expedition. Without official approval, corporations and manufacturers would abandon the project. After anxiously waiting, he was ushered into a conference room and, with the aid of slides and topographic maps, Harry Birdwein spoke to the executive council, meticulously detailing the plans for the proposed Everest assault. In an accompanying catalog, every meal, all medicines, foods, backpacks, ropes, pitons, were analyzed and labeled, and, pending the necessary funding, could be ready within the month to ship to Kathmandu. Pausing from his lengthy discourse, Birdwein panned the stone faces at the opposite end of the long table, eyeing the solemn William Marshall, the executive director of the Club. Grim and emotionless, the staid bureaucrat sat blankly giving Harry no indication as to his leanings. Harry finished, "Without your formal support this expedition will never set foot on the rock."

Mr. Marshall politely queried, "Who in the assault team has experience on Everest?"

Birdwein didn't respond.

"You do realize that a Himalayan assault and a technical rock climb are two entirely different endeavors?"

Harry interrupted. "What we're attempting is a first . . ."

Marshall slowly rose from his chair. "I think we've heard enough."

"But I haven't finished." Harry seemed flustered. "There are still pictures and routes to discuss."

"Thank you, Professor Birdwein. Please step into the lobby while I confer with the committee."

Tensely waiting while the committee deliberated, Harry Birdwein anxiously paced the oak-paneled corridor. Marshall's decision was crucial, the prestige of an official International Explorer's Club sanction would also bring with it financial backing that was presently woefully insufficient. Prospective sponsors were a peculiar group, they'd frown at requests from solitary individuals or small groups, but if the group had "official" recognition, they'd queue in line. Harry, pacing, felt sure the actual climb would be easy when compared to these nerve-wracking preparations. He despised the complexity of organizing this expedition, annoyed that an opportunity to achieve his life's dream was now being determined by a bunch of crotchety old men. After less than a fifteen-minute wait the paneled doors creaked open, Marshall motioning for Harry to re-enter. As the botanist took his seat, a disquieting hush crept over the room. Marshall spoke without emotion. "I'm sorry, but in good conscience, we cannot recommend bringing this request to a formal board meeting."

"You can't?" Bitterness stung Birdwein's mouth.

"Your plan is too brash, the proposed route too dangerous, and besides, we see neither the necessary available monies nor the aligned corporate support to bring this expedition to a successful conclusion. That's not the sole reason your application is being denied; the proposed expedition pushes human vulnerabilities past safe boundaries. Dr. Birdwein, it's pointless for me to raise your hopes, our board of directors will not sanction a mission that courts disaster." As Marshall continued, Harry fought to conceal his disappointment, he dreaded telling his sons that their hopes, once so euphoric, would be shattered. Since the moment he received Morley's call, roadblock after roadblock stood in their path; the reality of abandoning their shared dream now seemed unavoidable.

Harry passed through the revolving doors and walked coatless into a blustery overcast November evening. A frigid wind blanketing the streets kept all but a few of the most daring pedestrians locked inside. After the thirty minutes it took to walk to his hotel, he placed a call to the headquarters of the Hornsby investment firm. A secretary icily responded that Philip Hornsby was in a meeting and presently unavailable. Harry demanded the meeting be interrupted, but the secretary was adamant, business meetings are not disrupted. So, Birdwein left a message that he would be in Philadelphia the next evening, dining alone, at the SeaFarer Restaurant at eight o'clock. Harry, with little time to spare, rushed to the train station to catch the express metroliner. The following evening, much to Harry's surprise, Philip appeared.

13. The Deal

Philip interrupted W.A.'s mutterings. "During my recent European trip, do you remember a call I received from the botany professor in Colorado?"

"Yes, so?" W.A. asked.

"Father, I've been asked to be the deputy leader of an impending Everest expedition."

"Utterly preposterous," W.A. quipped. "You can't be serious?"

"I am!"

W.A., knowing not to interrupt his son, fidgeted as Philip rattled through a series of intricate details. His blood pressure rising, W.A. interjected, "Philip, the entire idea is ludicrous. Besides being dangerous, you haven't climbed in years. A time commitment for this type of journey could span months; the trip could interfere with impending political plans, and I, for one," W.A., confident he had rebuked his son's foolhardy notion, "am opposed to this folly."

Philip countered. "I've been close to the summit, but denied because of the mistakes of others. Now, while I'm still physically able, a rare opportunity presents itself!"

"Philip, you're talking like a child. We all grow older. Long ago, I learned to accept each of life's stages with dignity. Youth is wonderful; may its memories burn bright; but Philip, leave the heroics of adolescence to those who are naïve enough not to know better."

"W.A., you talk of climbing as if it's some crazy adventure. Tackling a mountain the size of Everest requires immense planning and precision. With adequate preparation, potential dangers can be reduced. Let's be realistic, this adventure could be the perfect platform to launch a budding political career. If publicized properly, the trip could generate a heroic public image. Right now I'm perceived as being aloof, cold, detached, the privileged son of a rich and powerful man."

W.A. spat, "The whole idea is preposterous!"

"Today's public admires a person willing to dare the unknown. Outdoor magazines crowd newsstands, requests for adventure travel is the craze of travel agencies. Many believe if they don't go out and dirty their hands in good old Mother Earth, they haven't lived. This expedition, with proper publicity, will create an adventure that will capitalize on people's natural wanderlust. Those bogged down in the mundane daily routine of the work world will vicariously follow the expedition; the public will be glued to either blogs or television screens watching intently as a group of heroic Americans dares one of the world's last insurmountable barriers. The public will share our disappointments, exalt in our triumphs, and feel our pain. W.A., it can't be denied, a hero's image is indelible to American politics: Eisenhower marching through Germany. JFK swimming in the Pacific, Carter rafting Bull Sluice on Georgia's Chattanooga River. Issues are secondary; people admire charisma, vitality, and courage. Pennsylvania could have the distinction of sending the first man to scale the previously untouched, foreboding wall of

Everest to Washington. Imagine pictures in the Enquirer—senatorial hopeful Hornsby hanging on at 26,700 feet!"

W.A. moved toward the bar. Philip could tell that his impassioned commentary struck a responsive note. Although his father had a long history of having difficulty accepting new ideas, particularly if they were not his from the inception, Philip knew that if W.A. was included in the planning stages, given an opportunity to be of service, allowed to marshal resources, Philip could win over his father and W.A. would be his staunchest ally.

"Haven't you forgotten you're to be married this fall?"

"I'll postpone the wedding until December."

"Does the girl know?"

"Not yet."

For the next twenty minutes, the two men stayed sealed behind the closed mahogany doors. W.A. grilled Philip. Questions were raised regarding sponsorship, appropriate media coverage, proper financial support. W.A. centered the discussion on Harry Birdwein's credentials, his background, his sons' experience, and how they could incorporate publicity for the entire team, yet highlight Philip without shunning the others. "An opportunity to paint you as daring," W.A. laughed, "mirrored after the Olympics, vignettes of your past, human interest tidbits to soften your tough, aloof veneer." By the end of the discussion, W.A.'s position changed; if properly promoted, his son could be portrayed as combining a mixture of skill and, for Auld Lang Syne's sake, driven by good old American simplicity of purpose, a commitment to succeed, and a willingness to dare the unknown. The fact that the expedition was presently bogged down in both logistics and financial chaos caused neither Hornsby any concern; both knew if the Hornsbys lent their name, the expedition would attract appropriate sponsors.

Elrod Jones knocked at the door. "The missus says people are waiting."

"We'll be just another moment." W.A. stood beside his son. "Philip, I only have one son, you must promise to be careful!" Not a man overly fond of being mushy and sentimental, he then said, "And don't you dare come back exhausted. Remember, this journey is supposed to be a vacation." W.A. poured another round of drinks. "Within a year after you return, you'll be on your way to Washington and." He paused, his finger swirling his drink—"And who knows what else." The two hugged, another joint mission had been launched.

14. A Stolen Moment

Both were so busy that the month leading to the day of their engagement party sped by without Philip mentioning a word of his impending trip to his fiancée. Besides, until details were secured, why initiate a battle that didn't yet exist? A gala party at the Hornsbys' mansion was planned for Saturday night to announce their upcoming wedding and Audrey's parents were flying in for the event. Philip booked a suite at Philadelphia's most exclusive hotel, but Jonathan insisted on making their own hotel reservations. Since her choices would dominate the wedding, without causing a fuss, Audrey didn't protest Philip and W.A.'s plan for their engagement party. The week leading up to the party passed like a blur. Ferrington, immersed in her residency under the supervision of Dr. Kalamatra, worked for endless hours, ran home to eat, shower, get a few hours of sleep, then would return to the hospital to do it all over again. Only occasionally nights were spent with her fiancé, but Philip didn't protest. Even when together, both sensed each other's preoccupation. But, each being so engrossed in their own private worlds, neither probed. Sex was quick and to the point; neither was satisfied but both, because neither had the time or energy to devote to each other, promised themselves that when their personal pressures lessened, the other would be the beneficiary.

Nestled in Philip's arms the night before the engagement party, Ferrington went to sleep with a smile on her face. When she awoke, she was surprised to find Philip seated atop the antique brass bed. Nude to the waist, her lips pursed in an infectious grin, Audrey slid her hand across his exposed shoulder. "Why so low?" she chided as her fingertips swept across his chest. Her fingers worked their way to his underwear, teasingly lowering his pants. Her fingertips found their way beneath his underwear and fondled his penis. Within minutes, her talents were undeniable. Sex with Philip made her feel powerful—the seducer. No woman possessed the cunning ability to intoxicate him the way she did. Every ounce of her sexiness was necessary to loosen him up; when preoccupied, which was typical, Philip was a miserable partner; however, she had her unique way of making him surrender to her powers. While Philip tried to dominate most areas, sexual matters were her domain.

"Your public personality is frightening." She ran her fingers through the hair covering his chest. "Why appear so cold?"

Philip's eyes closed as her hands tenderly massaged his thighs and calves. "Don't go to sleep," she complained. "I need attention." Audrey leaned back, the pleasure turned out to be hers as she had developed Philip Hornsby into a remarkably skilled lover. Both satisfied, they hugged and, for one of the few times either could remember, drifted back to sleep.

15. *An Evening to Remember*

Early that evening, they left his apartment and rode to his parents' house. Philip nodded at the guard posted at the front gate of the Hornsby mansion, seconds passed before an ornate metal gate protecting the driveway swung open. Philip eased the Italian sportscar onto the gravel path then passed under a half-mile of leafless elms that formed an overhead canopy. Nearing the mansion, rows of stained-white cedar horse railing framed the entrance. "Understated grandeur has a certain appeal." Philip didn't expect an answer. "Do you want me to review the names of tonight's guest list?"

"No. I just want it over."

Philip said nothing as he drove his car into the large circular driveway. A fleet of caterers' trucks crammed the maintenance area, the path to the main house cluttered as a small army of workmen hauled tables and chairs inside. Philip inched his car between the workers, giving Audrey a chance to scan the two hundred year old white colonial home. Far from her dream, this wouldn't be a low-key, intimate engagement celebration. Fronting the thirty-room mansion was a series of pillars, tucked to the left side of the mansion, a carriage house used for servants' quarters, and to the right, horse stables and a five-stall garage dominated the landscape. As their car pulled to a stop, Elrod Jones, an eighty-year-old wiry butler who had been under the employment of the Hornsbys for over sixty consecutive years, came forward and promptly opened Audrey's door. W.A., leisurely attired in a deep brown, velour shirt over jodhpurs, stood waiting by the front door.

Audrey, seeing the elderly Hornsby standing by the barn garbed in riding attire, commented, "How, with three hundred guests coming this evening, did you have time for a ride?" The three moved from the mammoth wooden doors as musical instruments were pushed through the open doorway. W.A.'s wife, Eleanor, appeared and after the proper cordial and necessary informal banter, the petite, gray-haired woman asked Audrey if she'd like to settle herself in her room, change clothes, and refresh herself. W.A. suggested that a masseuse be summoned; Audrey thanked him for the offer but said she had to go to a motel in Valley Forge to pick up her parents. W.A. volunteered he had a driver waiting but Audrey was adamant, insisting she would personally fetch her parents.

"She's a little tense. The magnitude of tonight's party has her upset," Philip explained, excusing Audrey's abrupt departure.

"I can understand," Eleanor reminisced, "I remember back when your father and I married—"

"If you don't mind, dear," W.A. interrupted, "Philip and I have certain issues to discuss."

They retreated to the privacy of W.A.'s study, the only room on the main floor not being converted to accommodate the guests expected for the evening's engagement party. W.A. poured himself a vodka martini and brought out a decanter of Philip's favorite vintage port.

"A cigar?"

"No," Philip declined.

W.A. struck a match; the aroma of tobacco soon filled the room. "While Audrey is not exactly what I thought you'd choose, she does have certain qualities …"

"You mean someone who's not of the correct vintage?"

"Well," W.A. sipped his drink, "there's a certain polish that comes with proper heritage."

"Dad, we've been through that."

"Yes, we have," W.A. laughed, "but I'm a persistent bastard."

Audrey drove to a nondescript motel in Valley Forge to retrieve her parents. Driving back, an awkward silence fell over the car.

"Tell me," her father looked at his daughter, "do you love him?" Audrey admired her father's directness.

"He's opened up doors; I couldn't imagine this could happen to a girl from New Mexico."

"You haven't answered my question," her father persisted.

"He's bright and worldly."

"And extremely lavish," Jonathan Ferrington remarked.

"It goes with the territory."

"You mean," Jonathan said, "the Hornsby tradition."

Audrey said nothing.

"The wedding?" her father asked.

"My choice."

Jonathan continued. "Audrey, your mother and I insist your wedding be held at our home."

Abigail interjected, "We have a beautiful backyard; I've already talked to Reverend Douglas, he has reserved August twenty-sixth. We'll have an old-fashioned celebration, dancing, singing, and a barbecue."

"I'll even buy cowboy boots for all the Hornsbys." Jonathan Ferrington's boisterous laughter filled the balcony. "We'll treat the Hornsby clan to some good old Western hospitality."

"Audrey," Abigail interjected, "both your brothers were sorry they couldn't come to the engagement party. You couldn't believe how big David has grown—he's over six feet, two inches and weighs close to 180 pounds. Next year he'll be a freshman at Rice University." Abigail lamented the universal cry of the overprotective mother parting with the youngest of her brood. "Although he's graduating high school, I can't imagine shipping him off. And George wishes he could have come to this party but baseball practice has already started, the coach at the University of Oklahoma wouldn't excuse him."

Audrey nodded. "Of course, I understand." She grabbed her father's calloused hand. "Give Philip a chance. You've only met him twice, each time briefly; sometimes he comes across as stiff, but once you get to know him, he's fascinating. While you might not always agree with his positions, he's a man of integrity, but give him a chance and you'll find common ground."

"So long as we don't talk about politics," Jonathan rendered. "I listened to his highbrow ideas about increased military spending, closing borders to stop the flow of illegal immigrants, making welfare recipients work, stopping the monopoly of public education by giving parents vouchers to allow them to choose between public, private, or parochial schools. Philip's certainly not gunshy when it comes to expressing himself. The man's full of pie in the sky, high-brow economic theory; it basically boils down to if the rich get richer, others will benefit."

Her mother intervened. "Audrey, don't worry about your father, Jonathan will be tolerant. We're glad we came, aren't we, Jonathan?"

"Abigail, don't hush me." Jonathan paused, bitterness hanging on his tongue. "Audrey, you, your mother, me, none of us need to make excuses, we're as good as any of them."

Abigail exclaimed, "Ever since you stepped onto the plane in Albuquerque, you've been brooding!"

Audrey interrupted. "Leave him be. Better his feelings be in the open; remember my decision to come east to college, then to stay in Philadelphia to attend medical school?" Audrey wrapped her arms around her father, and while he didn't return the hug, before they walked into the party, Jonathan kissed his daughter's forehead.

Hundreds of guests, men in tuxedos, women in flowing gowns with glittering diamonds and rubies, patiently waited in the lobby to pass through the receiving line. A twelve-piece orchestra of women dressed in tuxedos stood on the ornate stairway playing the dulcet tones of a Viennese waltz. Butlers and maids holding trays of hors d'oeuvres circulated throughout the milling assembly. Waiters ensured that Krystal champagne graced every glass. On the receiving line an Arab dressed in a flowing caftan wished Philip well then extended his hand toward Audrey. "Good evening Miss or is it doctor?" Without waiting for her reply he continued, "My most gracious congratulations, it is indeed an honor."

"You are?" Audrey asked.

"The ambassador from Kuwait."

After pleasantries were exchanged, the ambassador proceeded to move down the reception party. Audrey glanced toward the rear; her father, after some degree of persuasion, reluctantly stood at the end. W.A. and Eleanor stood at the front, Philip and Audrey came next, her parents last. The guest list read like a Who's Who in the World; everyone had a title, all identified themselves either by their professions or careers, guests were introduced as presidents, chairman of the board, the honorable governor, judge, or the chief neurosurgeon at John Hopkins Hospital in Baltimore. A plethora of ambassadors and high-ranking government officials also were in attendance. Reports circulated that the Vice President of the United States was to arrive, but then W.A. announced that due to a scheduling conflict, he had to decline.

At the conclusion of the formal reception and before commencing with the sit-down dinner, another stream of waitstaff emerged from the kitchen stocked with more champagne, Beluga caviar, smoked salmon, and petite lamb chops adorned with bows. Audrey found herself surrounded by women laden with glittering jewels, fingers extending toward her sparkled with diamonds, necklines had broaches the size of fishing anchors dangling between exposed breasts. One woman, for lack of anything better to say, kept remarking that Audrey looked absolutely scrumptious. "My dear," the woman kept chiming, "so natural looking. I do adore your skin; how, dear, can you keep it so natural?" Audrey tried to excuse herself but the woman kept bantering. "Someone told me you have a profession. How interesting. I once thought of pursuing a career in either insurance or real estate, but that was before my children came along." The incessantly chatty woman laughed at her own joke. "Indeed, those little rascals change things."

"Where are they now?" Audrey's response was as inane as the question. In her peripheral vision she saw her mother engaged in conversation. Although still in the midst of a stupid conversation with the bimbo standing before her, she saw her father push through the crowd toward the veranda; Audrey abruptly excused herself and went outside.

"I agree it's a bit stuffy," she said to her father.

"Too much nonsensical chatter," Jonathan gruffly barked.

She held her father's hand.

"You'd better get back, you'll be missed. I wouldn't want to monopolize half the reason for this party."

Audrey countered, "I hardly know a soul. The party's in W.A.'s honor. They're his guests."

Jonathan turned and faced his daughter.

"Why are you marrying him?"

"I'll be happy."

"Are you in love with him?"

"We'll have a full life!"

"And your medical career?"

"Philip encourages me."

"Too much wealth, it just isn't right!"

"Father, stop being so critical. Now come back inside, dinner is about to be served."

At the conclusion of the meal, Elrod Jones stood and banged a knife lightly against an intricately hand-carved, crystal Waterford glass. "Ladies and gentlemen, your attention," the butler implored.

W.A. cleared his throat, then, waiting until the audience quieted, he began. "I'm a bit hesitant to address such a large gathering; precise words are somewhat difficult; therefore, you'll have to bear with me." W.A. surveyed the crowd, his hand caressing a fresh martini. He took a sip and then explained, "A little extra fortitude for such a momentous occasion." Canned laughter followed. W.A. looked pleased. Rambling, he spoke in platitudes about the joys of marriage; solicitously thanking Philip for his patience in helping him understand a new breed of liberated women. He then joked, "Perhaps it is best to keep my words brief, as I know I am treading on treacherous grounds." Yet he continued his remarks ranging from the state of economic affairs in the United States and ending with a plea for strong political leadership from the state of Pennsylvania.

Audrey, seated next to Philip, whispered how she couldn't believe that W.A.'s meanderings were keeping everybody's attention. "Why now on this occasion?" But her remarks were curtailed seeing her father, seated at the opposite end of the table, wet his cloth napkin to remove a stain from the middle of his ruffled shirt. Jonathan alternated between dipping his napkin in his water glass and staring at his watch.

W.A., coming to the end of his remarks, gestured for everyone to stand. "Now we come to the reason for the party—a toast to the engaged. Ladies and gentlemen, I'm pleased to announce that my son Philip will wed Dr. Audrey Ferrington. To their happiness I offer the following toast: May the good Lord bless and keep them, may they enjoy health and wealth, may my offspring proudly march to the beat of the Hornsby heritage!" The ensemble played a refrain from *Chariots of Fire* as W.A. settled back to his seat. After the ceremonial clanging of glasses and polite applause, the crowd chattered like scurrying ants after being pent up. W.A. held up his hand, but the audience, thinking he was done and their patience wearing thin, was slow to hush. But the elder Hornsby, banging his fist against the podium, demanded silence. "Now for a surprise announcement. Originally, an August date was planned in Albuquerque for the marriage, but an unexpected event has intervened that will necessitate a postponement." The crowd quieted. "Ladies and Gentlemen, Philip has been invited and has accepted to be a member of an impending American expedition that will tackle Mount Everest. My son has been chosen deputy leader of an expedition that will attempt Everest's previously unscaled yellow rock wall." A screen dropped behind the dais, pictures of the intended route plastered on the wall. "Another surprise announcement, Ms., or rather, Dr. Ferrington will also be joining the expedition as the team physician." As the crowd simultaneously rose to its feet in recognition of the requisite courage needed to tackle such a difficult objective, Audrey was dumbfounded. The crowd's response was beyond W.A.'s wildest expectations; an ensuing throng of well-wishers besieged the dais. Hearty congratulations poured in, hands shot forward wishing Philip well. In the confusion, Jonathan and Abigail

Ferrington, without anyone taking notice or offense, slipped into the crowd and departed.

"Philip," Audrey's voice steamed with anger. "I must speak with you!"

"Excuse us." Philip stood and escorted his fiancée onto the patio. Harshly he whispered, "Get a hold of yourself. Don't make an unnecessary scene. Privately we can resolve whatever's bothering you."

Audrey lashed back. "How could your father publicly announce I'm joining you on some mountain extravaganza, especially when I wasn't even consulted?" Her lips pursed, the anger spewing out.

"Perhaps it was a bit presumptuous, but think of it as a gala pre-wedding trip."

"A what?"

"I took it for granted you'd be delighted. You grew up in the wilds of New Mexico; you're strong, in good shape, adventuresome."

"It's ludicrous! I have a career; we plan to marry in August!" Even though secluded on the veranda, Audrey's raised voice attracted stares from those on the other side of the glass. Philip, despising people looking at them, grabbed Audrey's arm and escorted her into the gardens. The frigid night air only fueled her anger. "Your father . . . I can't believe he's going along with this ridiculous idea. And you certainly, without my say so, don't have the right to include me!"

Philip's tone was measured. "You can always say no."

"And my residency in pediatric oncology, did you just forget about my career?"

"It will be arranged. The hospital will cooperate as the Hornsby Foundation has a history of being generous. They'll grant us a small favor; besides, all you'd be asking for is a four-month postponement, a temporary leave of absence."

Audrey's rage boiled. "Philip, do you think I'm nothing more than a mannequin, wind me up and expect me to be at the right places, mouth appropriate words? Am I supposed to stand and clap when a moment ago I hear my wedding is to be postponed until winter? Then I'm told I'm going to head a medical team on an Everest expedition. Don't dare think I'm only an appendage that goes along with your whims and fancies."

"Quit bitching." Philip's tone was measured. "You talk as if you're oppressed, anyone else would be ecstatic. Has your imagination deserted you? You're the one who's always craving romance and adventure. It's you who says that you don't want a mundane life; well, delivered on a silver platter, here's an opportunity."

She stood glaring.

"Frankly, I'm disappointed with your reaction. I imagined you'd be excited. Arrangements will be made for you to do experimental medical studies on the effects of exposure to high altitudes and hypothermia."

"His highness speaks and all are expected to listen?"

"I know it takes you by surprise but isn't it you who's always saying to me, 'Open up, experiment, take a few chances.'"

"No way the hospital will permit this."

"Exceptions have a way of being made . . ."

"What about the risks?"

Philip responded, "I have no intention of killing myself before having the opportunity to marry you."

16. The Kalamatra Bandwagon

One of you needs to join me," the oncologist said as he eyed the eight interns. Not one volunteered to accompany the eccentric doctor in entertaining the patients; instead, all suspiciously stared back at the physician as he strapped on his black magician's cape over his hospital whites. "I said, I need help!"

Reluctantly Audrey Ferrington came forward.

"Wait in the hallway for my cue."

While her fellow students took their positions inside the observatory booth, Audrey, with her stethoscope draped around her neck, a cape draped over her shoulders, hands clutching a tablet in preparation to write notes, stood in the hallway outside the pediatric oncology ward. A voice inside screamed, outfitted in this costume is making a mockery of her training. Medical school taught her to be thorough before rendering a diagnosis, avoid being swayed by emotions, dissect physical abnormalities, then test, retest, then test again. The first commandment of medical school was solidly ingrained in her psyche; in today's society, a doctor could never be too careful. While waiting for

Dr. Kalamatra's entrance, Audrey scanned the room, forced to witness the desperate faces, the silent agony. Pain was etched in the withered, hollow cheekbones of the girl at the far end of the corridor. A cancerous bulbous tumor obliterated the vision of the boy lying in the bed directly in front of her. In an adjoining bed lay a girl about thirteen, her cold icy eyes peered listlessly into the fluorescent lights. Directly across the way a petite girl, perhaps five, lay as a vegetable and, beside her, the most gruesome of all was the soulful eyes of a seven-year-old boy missing an arm, severed by surgery. Nurses coldly went about their business, tending to necessary chores, spoon-feeding the children who were disabled, removing bedpans and piles of excrement.

Suddenly the door swung open and the oncologist swept from bed to bed, his black flowing cape whirled and billowed from the floor. Clapping his hands to gain the children's attention, he took out a crystal ball and, to the command of "Presto!" Kalamatra produced a straw pigeon. Repeatedly digging into his sleeve, he next produced a frog, two giraffes, then lavender ribbons that turned colors when swirled in the air. Except for the oldest girl whose glassy eyes appeared oblivious to the doctor's shenanigans, the other children squealed with delight. Pandemonium reigned as raucous laughter reverberated throughout the room. All the nurses, except Gwendolyn, retreated en masse behind their station, staring stone-faced in obvious disdain to these antics as the self-proclaimed Houdini journeyed from chart to chart. Dr. Kalamatra, after completing rounds, stood in the center aisle for his grand finale. "With so much noise, the crystal ball will not talk."

"I know where it is!" yelled one of the patients.

His outstretched hands fumbled under his cloak, and Audrey cringed at this ineptitude. Kalamatra was a miserable magician; his tricks done sloppily, cards fumbled, invariably he hesitated at inappropriate moments. After years of these legendary performances, his repertoire was minimal, and since some of the children had been on the floor more than a month, a few youngsters recognized the tricks before he began. Announcing that this was his final trick, the doctor growled, "Ciao . . . Ciao!" before signaling for Dr. Ferrington to enter and jump aboard an imaginary caboose. Awkwardly entering, she stumbled down the aisle. Bypassing the speechless Ferrington, Dr. Kalamatra bellowed, "All aboard who's getting aboard!" With his arms chugging, the doctor led the locomotive down the aisle before the two disappeared into the hallway.

Bursting into their conference room, Kalamatra confronted the residents. "Tell me about the girl at the far end, the last one we examined. What did you learn? Speak up!" Trying to remember the child, Audrey peered through the window. Kalamatra was referring to the patient who, except for saliva dribbling from her mouth, looked fine.

"Well?" he demanded. Ferrington watched as nurses seized control of the ward. They methodically attended to details, beds were changed, catheters removed, intravenous checked. Four attendants brought a stretcher next to the bed of the girl with the protruding tumor, lifted her, put a strap around her midsection, then carted her away.

"Chemotherapy twice a day, supported with a regimen of steroids and radiation," Kalamatra volunteered. "But cancer of the throat is a killer, once it spreads to the surrounding muscles and lymph glands, loss of control of her mouth signals metastasis. Dr. Ferrington, you were on the ward, tell the others what you learned."

Audrey glanced at her colleagues for support. Their heads were down, their eyes trained on the shiny vinyl floor, no one willing to confront the crazed doctor. Kalamatra, his bushy eyebrows and full mustache poised and bristling, waited, and Audrey faced the short, barrel-chested, stocky doctor. "As to a precise diagnosis, I'm not in a position to judge. Factual information is needed."

His hands clenched, jaw set, eyes glaring, Kalamatra's facial muscles tensed as his hand lashed forward, fingertips banging on the table. "As I expected, Dr. Ferrington, you personify the breed. I don't doubt that you're well-versed in academics, but where is your sympathy, caring, and sensitivity? Those children are dying. Look at their faces. Within six months we will be lucky if two are still alive." Pain and ethos marked Kalamatra's words. "And in the brief time they have left, we, as doctors, need to make their lives a little less painful. Yes, they are sick patients, but they are also kids." The Greek paused, running his hand through his disheveled hair. "Injections, chemotherapy, drugs, is that all those children represent to you? Are those children only guinea pigs for medical experimentation?" Kalamatra's explosion silenced Audrey, but his tirade continued. "Will any of the devices of modern medicine give those children pleasure by their life's end? I doubt it. Is the practice of medicine limited to merely prescribing drugs and procedures? Why not joy and laughter?" Angrily he faced the residents, "Now that you're assigned to my ward, act like a human being, not a demigod or a rigid test-tube scientist." Rushing out of the room, his cape flying, he slammed the door behind him.

Dr. LeThou led the revolt. "What kind of medicine is he practicing? A guessing game? Kalamatra's unscientific approach ended with the Dark Ages."

Another physician voiced his annoyance. "Perhaps that's how they practice medicine in Greece, but in this country we follow procedures. From what I can see, Dr. Kalamatra is a cross between a self-proclaimed iconoclast and a buffoon. This isn't what we need!" The rebellion continued as the residents, en masse, marched with their grievances to the hospital director's office. Within minutes, they were ushered into the private office of Dr. Reginald Roberts, a well-respected gastrointestinal specialist.

"He's a disgrace to the hospital."

"His childishness knows no boundaries."

"Professionalism has its place."

"It's not necessary to be insulted."

Saying little, acknowledging that he heard their words, the hospital director waited while the assembled residents vented their anger. After the last of the tirade was over, Dr. Roberts spoke. "I've known Kal for the past twelve years; understanding his background sheds light. Nicholas is a first-generation Greek immigrant. After his father passed away, his mother immigrated to America and baked pita for a local grocery store until her death. Eccentric, I'd be the first to concur; abrasive, yes; arrogant, temperamental, yes, but he is not without a redeeming side. Kalamatra's research into the chemical effects of hormonal stimulation in the pituitary gland has been widely publicized and brought great acclaim to this hospital. Outside our facility, he's widely respected. Year after year Kalamatra leads our faculty in attracting outside grants. Currently he's finishing the final months of a National Biological Endowment Award, and while it hasn't been officially announced, he was just appointed the primary investigator of a new Department of Health grant worth at a minimum $2,370,000 over a three-year duration. That carries with it sufficient clout to pay a sizable amount of the salaries, equipment, secretaries, laboratory assistants, and nurses for his department. While I agree that my colleague has more than his share of problems with fellow physicians and students, nevertheless, his patients adore him."

Theodore LeThou chose to be their spokesman. "But what good are all his awards if physicians, nurses, and medical students detest working with him? Kalamatra does not exist in a vacuum, his insane behavior leaves us no alternative but to come to you and seek relief. However distasteful this meeting is, we want to learn. His methods must be brought under control. Dr. Roberts, we, beg . . . implore you to intercede!"

Roberts silenced the remainder of the sentence. "Kalamatra is a brilliant doctor. If you were willing to listen, nobody in the hospital could teach you more, the man has a lot to offer, don't just be lackeys jumping on the anti-Kalamatra bandwagon. Have the courage to evaluate for yourselves. If any of you want to speak with me on an individual basis, I'll listen, but I won't be party to mob psychology."

Afternoon rounds found Dr. Kalamatra dressed in his hospital whites; the only reminder of his morning Harry Houdini routine was a wand he carried in his right hand. The Greek summoned the residents to crowd beside a patient's bed. "Notice the slight dilation in Jennie's right eye." The residents followed Dr. Kalamatra's instructions. "After an examination, Dr. LeThou will inform the group of any other distinguishing physical ab-normalities that are crucial in making a differential diagnosis." The blond resident eyed the seemingly vibrant, curly-haired, nine-year-old girl as she excitedly clapped her hands. The on-cologist then ran through results from a thick notebook containing laboratory results before banging the wand on the bed's metal frame and launching a trick that widened the smile across Jennie's freckled face. As the doctor produced a fluffy, white straw pigeon from his vest pocket, LeThou, eyeing the girl's chart resting at the bed's end, opened the metal cover, his eyes digesting the voluminous laboratory reports.

The doctor's burly hand slammed the girl's medical records closed. "You're not to rely on tests!"

"But . . ."

"Excuse me, Jennie." Kalamatra took out his wand and graced the girl's forehead. "All of you, in here." Seven students meekly followed him into a vacant X-ray room.

"Factual information," LeThou protested. "What can I say without examining hard data?"

"I didn't say read from clinical studies," Kalamatra bellowed. "LeThou's tunnel vision does not stand alone. Open your eyes! Medicine involves seeing and feeling; stop being trained to be prisoners to clinical records. Understand patients are people, they smile, cry, and more than most, since cancer is systematically robbing them of their life, they hurt. The state of modern medicine is pitiful when residents grasp onto charts documenting blood analysis, sugar levels, liver functioning, urine cultures. Now, any of you, tell me what visual abnormalities were evident in Jennifer Quinn?"

"An erratic blinking of the left eye, listlessness in her lower lip, no fluids present in the left nostril," Audrey responded.

"And?" Kalamatra paused.

"Swelling behind the left lymph node."

Staring incredulously at Dr. Ferrington, his beckoning fingers motioned for her to continue.

"Even though hair follicles camouflage the skull, there's an erratic bulge on her forehead. But to make a definite diagnosis, a caliper is needed to measure the radius," Audrey hesitated, "but probably . . ."

"Go ahead," Kalamatra urged.

"The patient . . ."

"Call her Jennie," he corrected.

"Suffers from a rampant spreading carcinoma centered in the left cranial lobe."

"Dr. Ferrington, you are indeed observant. My compliments. Now back to Dr. LeThou. What course of action would you pursue for our patient?"

"A full blood work-up, a transfusion, detailed X-rays, chemotherapy."

Kalamatra shook his head in disgust. "Unnecessary tests create unreasonable hopes, unnecessary worry, needless stress. Jennie, no matter what we do, will be dead within the month. The best medicine is to make the end easier."

Kalamatra then opened the door and with his wand extended, tiptoed over to her. Even before he began a trick, Jennie was laughing. That precise moment made Audrey jump ship from the anti-Kalamatra bandwagon.

Once willing to learn, Audrey had never been so challenged. Hidden within Kalamatra's buffoonery was a physician with the touch of a maestro. The following weeks on the cancer ward proved exhilarating. Audrey marveled at Dr. Kalamatra's keenness. Any physical abnormality, however minute, proved a clue. The Greek possessed an intuitive feel found in a finely tuned violin; his inquiring eyes analytically delved without losing their vivacious glimmer; his exuberance, no matter how outlandish, was contagious. His performances confirmed his mastery in the act of fumbling, but caged within his antics was a willingness to poke fun at himself, thereby allowing children to laugh at his expense. In a ward where depression was commonplace, Kalamatra, even for only a few brief moments, brought laughter.

Audrey, realizing he was a master diagnostician, hounded the oncologist, badgering him to share medical insights. After the other students left, she would follow Kalamatra into his laboratory and together they would study blood sample after blood sample, analyzing slides, reviewing microscopic cell changes due to radioactive X-ray treatments. Hour after hour beside him allowed Audrey to see a side of Kalamatra that few took the time to understand; the arrogant, flamboyant, erratic doctor, when sequestered in his laboratory, diligently pored over minute scientific studies. The Greek had an unwavering commitment to unchaining cancer's crippling effects. Laboring far into the night, tenderness often appeared in the bushy furrows protecting his eyes. So used to being alone, so wrapped in his work, he often forgot that Audrey was there. Constantly experimenting with drugs that might inhibit cell divisions, devising different chemical combinations, adjusting dosages; he'd try anything to halt a disease's lethal destructive path. During times when his experiments brought unsatisfactory results, his hand would lash at the table, the anger welling in his rigid fingers, an outpouring of sorrow for those cursed with cancer. Yet, despite the setbacks, frustration fueled his enthusiasm. His spirit, especially in front of the children, executed courage. Kalamatra was a chameleon; the more Dr. Ferrington spent time with her boss, the more she realized his baffling complexity. Look, see, open your eyes. Kalamatra constantly reiterated that if a cancer in an adolescent is to be mitigated, it must be diagnosed in its most formative stages. Once the disease metastasized, almost always the cause was lost. Demanding early detection, he forced students to take note of any and all observable signs and, under the charades erected by his shenanigans, he veiled the ongoing life and death struggle. Decisiveness was a trademark, if there was a reasonable chance at curative help, he'd order, without hesitation, an operation. If the cancer was inoperable, but if there was a remote chance for a cure, either a regimen of steroids, massive X-ray treatments, radiation, or chemotherapy was prescribed; but if the cause was hopelessly lost, his gift to a child would be to elicit a smile.

Training with the eccentric doctor continued, in the process, Audrey's respect and frustration only expanded for the iconoclastic physician. His every waking moment was dedicated to finding ways to help a child. On a couple of occasions, Audrey repressed tears as she watched Kalamatra hug a small boy even as the youth died in his arms. Yet, conducting rounds, the same man who tenderly cradled the dying boy would turn and mercilessly attack residents with penetrating questions. Residents dreaded examining patients with Kalamatra, feeling as if they were a part of an inquisition. Never knowing what to expect, the Dr. Jekyll and Mr. Hyde personalities would abruptly stop a magic show and demand a resident provide a detailed medical analysis and offer a precise course of medical intervention that should be followed.

While others cowered and dreaded their time with the abrasive doctor, Audrey grew to relish the mental combat. She found herself constantly thinking, her senses sharpening, mind questioning, never had she learned more or been so challenged. Each morning, after rounds and clinic, she burrowed herself into the library, tempering her mental exhaustion with the exhilaration of fusing symptoms with factual information. Patient history was dissected; every nugget of evidence analyzed and scrutinized. Medicine, through the brilliance of Dr. Nicholas Batiste Kalamatra, transformed science into a realm of creativity, but her fascination was not shared by her fellow residents. Theodore LeThou, despising every moment spent in his presence, labeled the forty-year-old doctor angry and insensitive; behind his back, LeThou and the others shuddered at his antics and his irreverence, openly whispering that the man was so imbalanced that he was hanging onto reality by a razor's thinnest edge.

A five-year-old boy proved their undoing. Kalamatra, faced with the dying child, fought to master his emotions, struggling to bring a slight smile over the child's hollow, sunken cheekbones, but none of the doctor's antics could break the impenetrable walls imprisoning this particular boy. No matter what he tried, the youngster's silent, penetrating, glassy eyes revealed that he knew the severity of his illness. Awaiting death, shivering, the child huddled within his blankets. Day after day the oncologist pained over this boy. One afternoon while making rounds checking intravenous flows, Audrey saw Kalamatra quietly enter the ward and sit at the end of the boy's bed. With his burly hand, he grasped the boy's willowy fingers; for fifteen minutes they sat that way, the boy, with his eyes glazed, never giving the oncologist the slightest indication of a response. As Kalamatra left the ward, Audrey, waiting in the hall, stopped him. "I've applied and been accepted for a postdoctoral residency under your supervision commencing this July."

"What makes you think you can tolerate me?" the Greek sarcastically snapped.

She shook her head. "You're a marvelous doctor—the last couple of months have been illuminating. I've never been more enthused about medicine."

"Don't all pretty girls say that to their attending physicians?" The remark evidenced his total absence of social skills; as brilliant as he was as a doctor, he was equally inept in the social pleasantries of adult interaction.

"No need to be rude." Audrey bristled.

"Then why the announcement?"

Audrey shot back, "You certainly enjoy being difficult, don't you? Dr. Kalamatra, I wouldn't want to work with you if I didn't think your medical expertise was extraordinary. Let me set the record straight; you don't scare me. Intimidate me, yes. You're a brilliant doctor, but your bark is far worse than your bite. I'm choosing to work with you because, in spite of your unusual methods, I'm learning. Why do you need to be abrasive, why do you constantly fight with people, why do you need to break rules? It is a mystery, but I'm here to study medicine, not to analyze you!"

"Indeed you are feisty."

"What do you mean?" she snapped. "In the months we've worked together you've barely said two words to me . . ."

"American women are a curious lot. In the old country—"

"No doubt you're an authority on medicine, but your intuition regarding personal relations is wildly out of touch. You don't have a clue what I'm about." Audrey stomped out of his office.

The longer she worked alongside him, the more his inconsistencies baffled her. Dr. Kalamatra was a man of numerous sides. Like a chameleon, his colors often changed, within minutes the chief of pediatric oncology would vacillate between uninhibited buffoonery, a magician whose tricks were totally inept to a hard-driving, tireless diagnostician. Blood analyses, stool samples, tissue biopsies, extensive X-rays, radiation, chemotherapy . . . every detail, no matter how minute, any possible cure, however remote, was analyzed and re-analyzed. Kalamatra knew nothing of traditional work hours; he'd arrive before dawn and many evenings, late into the night, Audrey, when thoroughly exhausted, would leave him toiling at his desk. On numerous occasions she'd return at six a.m. only to find him still sitting at his desk, poring through thick individual files, tirelessly searching for clues.

Working together left her perplexed; during the countless hours they spent together nothing personal was ever discussed. An acknowledgment that either one of them had a life outside of the hospital was strictly taboo. Ferrington couldn't help but admire his drive, commitment, and brilliance, but she wondered how anyone could totally deny the existence of personal feelings. Who was this man? Was there anything else in his world other than his patients? What were his favorite foods? His hobbies? What about his past, his family? Except for a one-sentence explanation by Dr. Roberts, all other personal matters remained hidden in a cloud of obscurity; Audrey couldn't understand why he would permit a medical career to come with such a heavy obligation. Nevertheless, hour after hour he sat at his desk, constantly probing. Each patient presented a unique challenge, cancers never following an identical script. Was there something that could be done differently? Was there a piece of a puzzle missing? Could he possibly unearth anything to prolong a life? Frustrated, he'd summon Dr. Ferrington, demanding that she thoroughly review a particular patient's file and then the two would discuss the pros and cons of various treatments. Audrey, initially intimidated, became used to these grilling sessions and grew to relish their discussions. They became more frequent as a patient's condition worsened, but instead of being intimidated, becoming angry, and retreating, Dr. Ferrington swallowed her pride as she realized this was an opportunity to learn from an acknowledged master. Personal feelings were put aside; Audrey became a sponge, willingly absorbing Kalamatra's vast scientific and intuitive knowledge. Instinctively, she knew that years later today's diligence would be beneficial; Audrey Ferrington was determined to make a mark on her profession, and nothing would stop her from being a damn good physician.

Except for a bare-bones nightshift patrolling the ward, the two were left alone studying a case in the oncology library. It was past nine in the evening and Audrey hadn't intended to stay this late. Thirteen hours of consecutive duty had left her drained, desperately wanting to go to the gym and work up a sweat before going home and collapsing in front of the television. Perhaps good fortune would shine and the movie channel would have an old Tom Cruise favorite like *A Few Good Men* or *Top Gun*; she could snuggle up with a glass of merlot and a cigarette to momentarily minimize the tensions of the day. Upon grabbing her coat she noticed, across the room, Dr. Kalamatra's eyes directed on the oculars of a high-powered microscope.

"More slides on Glen Washburn?" Audrey asked.

Kalamatra nodded.

Audrey shook her head. For two hours that afternoon the two had scrutinized the Washburn case. A myriad of tests were administered and, after a prolonged discussion, they agreed that since the disease had metastasized, further intervention was hopeless.

"Why torture yourself, doctor, when all your looking, all your hoping, is not going to change the truth?"

"Cancer cells are venomous leaches, piranhas, voraciously consuming everything in their paths."

"And your spending all night here is going to halt that outcome?"

"Dr. Ferrington," Kalamatra's eyes never veered from the oculars, "perhaps we gave up too quickly."

"I resent that!" Ferrington lashed in retaliation. Her hands set firmly on her hips, she faced her superior. "You can criticize me for my lack of knowledge, but doctor," her nostrils flared in anger, "never insult me by insinuating that I don't care!"

"Stop with the threats," Kalamatra's voice showed no emotion. "And start reading from the chart. Just perhaps, with radical surgical intervention, while we might not be able to rid Washburn of the disease, we can prolong his childhood." Kalamatra set two identical massive skeletons outlining Glen Washburn's frame on the overhead projector. "Even disease-ridden bodies have some systems that still work. Dr. Ferrington, we're going to analyze that little boy inch by inch, appendage by appendage, to see what is and is not functioning." Almost three hours later, the two skeletons were dotted with information.

"So?" she asked, exasperated.

Deep in thought, Kalamatra kept staring. "Glen's mind remains sharp as a tack, the cancer's limited to the bone in the left leg, although traces of renegade cells are found in his groin. Most importantly, the boy wants to live. Tomorrow morning little Glen Washburn is going under the knife." Kalamatra pointed to the diseased skeleton. "Surgeons must remove as much of the left leg above the femur bone as possible, also the lymph system surrounding the groin. Chemotherapy will follow coupled with pumping intravenous antibiotics into his body."

"But the side effects, even for adults, can be devastating—diarrhea, cramping, nausea," Audrey questioned. "What price does one pay to preserve life?"

Kalamatra icily shot back, "Washburn might not be permanently cured, but hopefully, our intervention will allow him to experience his teenage years. Bottom line is the boy wants to live, he repeatedly asks if he'll be able to graduate high school; I wouldn't intervene if I didn't think that was possible."

It was almost two a.m. when they finished. The two entered the drab green hospital elevator without exchanging a word. Kalamatra pushed a button and the antique contraption clanged as it slowly lumbered toward the basement.

"God I'm hungry," Audrey blurted.

He shook his head, seemingly obvious that he hadn't eaten since eleven that morning.

"Yes, dinner." She smiled. "It's perfectly acceptable that even doctors deserve nourishment!"

"Are you inviting me?" Kalamatra incredulously asked.

"No, I just said I was hungry," Audrey said sharply. The doors swung open and she exited. Audrey steamed past the lone security guard. A steady drizzle fell, she cursed herself for forgetting her umbrella as she headed across the deserted parking lot towards her car.

A dirty, dented car pulled alongside her, the window creaked open, and a gruff voice yelled, "It isn't much, but a friend owns a diner on South Street. Join me!"

Not answering, she just followed.

A sign outside the Greek diner prominently proclaimed: *OPEN 24 HOURS*. An older woman dressed in black, her hair tied in a bun at the top of her head, looked up in amazement. "Are my eyes deceiving me?" She looked at Audrey in bewilderment. "Dr. Kalamatra is not dining alone?"

"We work together," Nicholas responded. Without waiting to be seated, the oncologist walked to his usual, secluded corner table.

A waitress, appearing behind the cafeteria doors, threw a menu at Audrey. She merely nodded at the doctor.

"What do you want?" the woefully frail woman with a haggard face barked.

"Any recommendations?" Audrey inquired.

"Don't bother asking him," the waitress interjected. "Man eats the same thing every time."

Audrey ordered a Greek salad and a lamb kabob.

The waitress turned.

"Wait," Dr. Ferrington yelled, "and a bottle of your best red wine."

"You would have taken quite a chance if you let him order." The waitress laughed at her own joke.

Thoroughly exhausted, Audrey leisurely sipped her wine. "The color red is about the only compliment I can give this drink." Although the wine was putrid, the alcohol served its purpose.

Finishing her first glass, she poured another watching as he devoured an appetizer of clams served over a bed of spaghetti.

"I don't like drinking alone," she noted as she filled his glass.

He took an obligatory sip.

"Another?"

He obliged.

Audrey smiled.

Preoccupied with his eating, Kalamatra didn't care that they sat in silence.

Audrey finally spoke. "We've worked side by side for months, and while I acknowledge that I immensely respect your work as a physician, I know nothing about you."

Kalamatra shrugged his shoulders. "What's there to know?"

Their brief conversation was interrupted when the waitress brought Audrey a salad and an eggplant parmigiana; at the same time she placed a plate consisting of broiled, almost charred, chicken breast, overcooked broccoli and a baked potato in front of Kalamatra. The waitress looked surprised to see the wine bottle empty. "Another?"

Audrey nodded.

Audrey lifted her glass. "Drink." Finally relaxing, she settled into her chair. "So tell me about you?"

A new bottle came uncorked. Nicholas shook his head but Audrey filled both glasses to the brim.

"A toast to Glen Washburn!"

They both drank.

"I don't often end up in Greek diners. Drink some more, it's good for you!"

Kalamatra mumbled, "I was born in Greece in a small town right outside Athens. I have a brother and sister, both much older. My mother worked as a teller in a bank, my father, a laborer on the docks, loaded and unloaded ships. Nothing out of the ordinary, we just lived." He sighed, obviously thinking he was finished.

"Go ahead," Audrey pressed. She lifted the wine bottle, refilling both of their glasses. Ferrington spoke with a combination of laughter and encouragement. "Here's to a man who has not forgotten his past!"

Nicholas continued, "Times were difficult, there were shortages, but somehow my father managed to keep food on the table. My brother and sister tried to work, but jobs were difficult to find. We scraped by, but just barely."

"It must have been difficult," Audrey interrupted.

The Greek muttered, "In my homeland the first-born was the golden boy, the prodigy. For me," Kal laughed, "there was never mention of work. All my family cared about was my education. At an early age my mother proudly said, 'Nicholas the doctor' because the sound of that brought a smile to her face. One day, before I was ten, my father came home excited; that day we packed our belongings and moved across town into a fancy home. No one dared ask Father how good fortune shined so brightly; but somehow, through my father's industrious manner, he was elevated to head purchaser of a newly formed shipping company. Mother proceeded to enroll me in one of the fanciest schools in Athens, Father opened up a bank account. I remember the celebration in the kitchen as he and my mother danced, their hands joined together, proudly holding their bank book overhead. In my early teens, summers were spent climbing in the Alps, winters on excursions to the Greek islands. I lived my mother's dream and attended medical school. My sister married a successful gold merchant and, within five years, had four children. My brother found a job as a butcher."

Kalamatra pushed his half-eaten dinner away.

"How did you end up here?" Audrey pressed as she nibbled on her salad.

Kalamatra sipped his wine. "The best and the worst occurred almost simultaneously. The completion of my medical school training brought the family joy; we celebrated late into the night. But it was that very week, a group of thugs broke into our home and removed our furniture. Mother cried, Father told us to keep quiet. After they left, Mother ran to the phone to call the police but Father tore the cord from the wall. A business misunderstanding, he explained. Tomorrow came and instead of the furniture reappearing, we packed our possessions and ended up boarding a steamer departing for America that very day.

Staying behind, my sister and my brother stood at the dock, waving goodbye. As the ship steamed into a gloomy gray Mediterranean sky, my father, sullen and withdrawn, sat in the rain, secluded at the rear of the vessel. Father permitted no questions; even to this day, the reason for our departure remains unclear." Kalamatra, his eye sockets accumulating moisture, spoke in a barely audible whisper. "Half-way across the Atlantic, the ship ran into a fierce storm. Waves, cresting at over twenty feet, tossed us about but still my father sat alone, facing the angry ocean. I remember going to him, begging him to come inside, but being the stubborn man he was, he sat shivering. Two days later, a persistent cough overtook his body; he spit up thick phlegm, but my father, despite my urging, stayed outside. The fourth day, under bright sunlight, I found him still on the deck, vomit coating his body. Antibiotics were administered, but being severely dehydrated, he needed intravenous solutions, but the ship had no such provisions. Two days later my father passed away; the captain said a few words and his body, wrapped in a blanket, was shoved overboard."

"And your mother?"

"Never the same. Seeing him disappear into the depths of the ocean, her lust for life sank with him. We lived together for three years in a small, one-bedroom apartment in Astoria, Queens, barely squeezing by on the pennies she received baking and on my small stipend from a nearby hospital emergency room. Mother rarely left the apartment, making no effort to start a new life in America. I completed my internship and then residency at a state hospital in Queens. Just as I was finishing my training in oncology, my mother got sick. At first it appeared nothing more than a severe case of the flu, but one day I came home to find her frighteningly pale. Pneumonia followed and, unwilling to summon the energy to fight the disease, she passed away."

"You were left alone?"

"I had my medicine." The doctor, raising his hand, signaled to the waitress for a check. The two bottles of wine took their toll, Audrey smiling as she watched Kalamatra clumsily exit the diner. Swaying, trying to regain his sense of equilibrium, he stumbled toward his car. Replacing the rain, a chilly wind whipped through the parking lot.

"Time to go home."

"Let's walk, the fresh air will do us both some good!"

"I don't often drink," he confessed.

"That's obvious," she changed the conversation. "Tell me, doctor, how did you learn to practice medicine the way you do?"

He shrugged his shoulders.

"Why be so eccentric? Do you secretly enjoy ruffling feathers?"

"Probe! Discover!" he slurred his words. "Investigate!"

Audrey laughed. "I was just teasing."

Not understanding, he didn't respond.

They could hear the whining of a diesel engine, a truck came streaming toward them, and, as the truck sped past, the massive wheels splashed into a puddle sending an errant spray of water into the air, the majority landing on Kalamatra's left pant leg. Returning to the now empty parking lot, Audrey chided, "I trust chivalry is not dead. The least you can do at this hour of the morning is follow me until I safely enter my apartment."

Audrey drove off; Kalamatra followed until she parked her car directly in front of her apartment. Kalamatra, pulling up behind, exited and walked her to the door.

"Your pants are still wet," she noted.

"They'll dry."

"Don't be silly, you'll catch a cold. Come inside, it'll take just a moment to throw your pants into the dryer; besides, a cup of hot coffee will do you good."

Thoroughly embarrassed, wearing Audrey's flannel robe, with shirt, shoes, and socks still on, he sat on her green couch as she poured cognac. Socially inept, never a person comfortable with casual nonsensical conversation, Kalamatra strained to find something to talk about while his pants dried. "Don't you need sleep?" The topic was safe; he knew that both of them had to be in the hospital by seven a.m. to do their rounds.

Audrey lit a candle.

He sat perplexed.

A smile spread across her face as she luxuriously inhaled a cigarette.

"I'm surprised," he said.

"Only behind closed doors."

Kalamatra, a man who prided himself on being in control, cursed himself for being in this situation. It was his personality, drive, authority, that motivated actions. Witnessing his over-sized feet crammed inside her fur-lined slippers, Ferrington laughed. Walking to the window, she slightly parted the blinds, the city street lights pouring through the opening. As Audrey bent over to open the window, her breasts, without the support of a bra, fell forward, pushing against her robe. "Why?"

"Why what?" he shook his head in disgust, from the confusion of the question and the utter embarrassment of the moment.

"No girlfriend waiting at home?" she inquired.

He shrugged his shoulders.

"You were married, tragically scarred, I suppose? Did your wife leave you?"

"No!"

"Come on, there must be a past horror story of a relationship turned sour . . ." she paused, then sipped from her drink. "Does it come as a great surprise that a woman could find you attractive?"

"Save it for the movies," he snapped.

It was Audrey who laughed.

She then walked over and lightly kissed his forehead.

"Why?"

"Because I felt like it!" She paused. "Look, doctor, I'm not a baby; situations like this don't embarrass me. I do what I want, when I want!"

Desperately, his eyes searched for the door. As Audrey lifted the cognac bottle and refilled their glasses. "Come on Kal, loosen up . . . take a few chances. What do you expect, a coquettish, submissive female?"

He didn't respond.

"Add a little zest to your life. Each morning, does a mechanical robot wind you up? You march, bark, incessantly work; but I've asked myself, there must be someone hidden beneath your suit of armor, a person who has feelings, emotions, passions." Audrey laughed. "Kal, I give you credit, if you weren't a great doctor, you'd be an Academy Award-winning deadpan actor. It took two bottles of wine and half a bottle of cognac to dent your armor."

"My pants?" was all he said.

"You are indeed a pill." A mischievous grin spread across her face.

"I have to leave."

She cut him off, mockingly adding, "Why do men insist on making a spontaneous moment so confusing? Ever since I met you, you baffle as well as amuse me." Her fingers gracefully undid the knot holding her robe together; she walked toward him and her terrycloth robe fell open, her hands slowly encircled his hips.

The remainder of the night was a blur. At its most basic, a bullfight, two figures pushing each other into physical realms thought unimaginable. Audrey proved a tiger in bed, playing, tantalizing him into a series of shuddering physical climaxes. Volcanoes erupted; momentarily he'd rest, but her teasing would summon him to resume his charge. The venue constantly changed; the floor, couch, bedroom, bathroom, repeatedly he thought he was finished only to rediscover an unexpected reservoir of energy. Never knowing what she'd do next, Audrey vacillated between meek and submissive to dominating, holding his arms down, whispering erotic fantasies into his ear. Her lovemaking followed no script—in one breath she was tender and caring, in the next, demanding he perform to her satisfaction. As the pinkish hues of the early morning light filtered through the parted Venetian blinds, Dr. Ferrington fell asleep. Although exhausted, Kalamatra's eyes refused to close. Seizing the opportunity, he slipped out of bed, looking at his pants, now dry, the price for waiting unleashed pounds of pent-up pressure.

17. Another Day at the Hospital

The next day found them going about their professional business, never once alluding to the previous night. She sensed he wanted to talk, but she made sure an opportunity didn't present itself. He kept looking at Audrey, trying to get a reading from her stoic eyes. Ever the dutiful resident, Ferrington revealed nothing, staying focused on her allotted rounds. Minus his usual sparkle, he went about his magic routine.

Two days later they met in the doctors' lounge, it was barely past six in the morning, and chance found them alone. Slipping on her laboratory coat, she bent down and leafed through her locker. Locating her stethoscope, she stood poised, prepared to work.

Kalamatra stood by the door, his arms barricading the opening. "Didn't it mean anything to you?" he questioned.

"What?"

"You're kidding me," he blurted. "Two nights ago?"

Ferrington responded, "We'll be late, it will upset the children."

His jaw tightened.

"Perhaps I'm old-fashioned," Kalamatra volunteered, "But, in case you don't remember,"—his words were laced with sarcasm—"we slept together. That meant something, didn't it?"

"That was two nights ago, it lasted for a couple of hours," Audrey clinically assessed. "Frankly, our getting together took me by surprise. Dr. Kalamatra, it makes no sense to blow our little liaison out of proportion. Clearly, it was impulsive on both our parts. We had a rough day on the ward, tensions needed to be released." Audrey forced a laugh. "Perhaps it was the second bottle of red wine; just think of my disappointment when I returned home and realized I forgot to save the label."

"You're kidding," was all he could muster.

"Yes, we did it. But frankly, it makes no sense to make our liaison anything more than it was—an impulsive act. Our getting together doesn't change the fact that I'm engaged and plan to marry. I'm not interested in another long-term relationship; one is sufficient."

He stood stupefied.

"Dr. Kalamatra, you and I are opposites—you're at the apex of your medical career while I'm a raw neophyte. You're sixteen years older than me. I'm at an age when it's okay to experiment before I marry; your life is cast in concrete, consumed by medicine. I still think I can have everything, including a personal life. Deal with our brief encounter for what it was; our emotions got the better of us!"

Curiosity prompted her, alcohol lessened their inhibitions, Audrey taking pride that her female charms could still pry open doors. The proud Greek stormed out of the room. For the next couple of weeks, although she sensed her supervisor was uncomfortable, Ferrington steered their relationship to safe ground—medicine. Hour after hour they worked side by side; he needed an explanation but none was forthcoming. Even though it was before six in the morning, the hospital corridor was cluttered, as Audrey, dodging nurses, stretchers, orderlies, made her way to the oncology laboratory. She stopped abruptly when Dr. Reginald Roberts grabbed her arm. Startled, she stared at the hospital director. The slight, balding man removed his glasses, leaned over, and lightly kissed her cheek. "Word has circulated that congratulations are in order!"

"How did you know?" Audrey, taken by surprise, hesitated, afraid that the hospital director heard about the impending Everest expedition before she had a chance to submit a formal request for leave.

"You're marrying into quite a family, certainly one of the most influential in Pennsylvania. W.A. is a pillar of his generation, a fierce lion in a country of tame animals; hard-driving, industrious, a man who doesn't comprehend the meaning of no. Our country was originally built around people who possessed that dogged type of inexhaustible spirit; more of that is needed today." The medical director awaited Ferrington's response.

Audrey smiled. "Thank you. W.A. deserves credit for what he's achieved." Not wanting to prolong this discussion, she turned and began walking down the corridor.

Roberts' raspy voice caused her to halt. "Dr. Ferrington, did you know that in my youth I, too, was a climber?"

Audrey, her back turned, stood frozen.

Roberts continued. "We also have mountains in West Virginia, obviously nothing that would compare to the Himalayas but, from a child's eyes, any first hike, even a hill, is a major obstacle."

She turned in fear. "How did you hear?"

"Quite by accident. This morning, in the car on my way to work, at the end of the early morning radio newscast," Roberts continued, "there's a lady who keeps us common folk abreast as to the whereabouts of the rich and famous. All she could talk about was Philip Hornsby's engagement party, spiced by a surprise announcement of an impending Everest trip."

Audrey shuddered. "Dr. Roberts, before I accept, I plan to ask your permission. I would never have given an affirmative answer regarding my availability, certainly not before consulting you."

"It did cross my mind that a public announcement was a bit presumptuous."

"Philip wants me to accompany him. He wants me to request a four month leave of absence; my inclusion on this expedition depends upon your decision. If you object, I'll cancel the trip. No way is a mountain climb worth jeopardizing my medical career. And, besides, the intended trip is still only in the exploratory stages, details are still in their infancy so, until I became convinced the trip is actually going to take place, I thought it was unnecessary to burden you."

"There's only one small problem." Roberts hesitated. "Hospital protocol necessitates you ask your immediate superior; that, in your case, is Dr. Kalamatra. While ultimately I have the final say there's no sense in unnecessarily ruffling feathers. Talk to him, I can't see why he'd object. I remember him once telling me, back in Greece, in his youth, he summered in the Alps." Dr. Roberts then excused himself and hurried down the hall.

Audrey, dressed in her hospital whites, waited as Dr. Kalamatra, standing behind his cluttered, unkempt office, leafed through a thick stack of laboratory reports. His face muscles taut, furrows chiseled under his deep-set eyes, he studied a laboratory report. "Bring me the most recent blood tests on Anna Youngley." The doctor's voice was terse. He could see Dr. Ferrington's blank gaze. She had no idea who he was talking about.

"Third bed to the right. She's the thirteen-year-old girl with the icy demeanor."

"Of course, I remember, I just forgot her name—the one who never smiles." Audrey hesitated. "I have the feeling she thinks you're funny but just won't let herself show it. There's a softness in her eyes; what perplexes me is that upon visual exam she appears healthy, the only visible abnormality is that her pupils have a yellowish pale."

"And if these recent blood slides are correct, Anna has a reason to frown. Her white corpuscles are dangerously low—leukemia wreaking havoc on her body. She maybe has a couple months left, not much more. Why her? I ask myself . . . so delicate. . . so afraid . . . robbed of a life when it is only just beginning."

Ferrington handed Dr. Kalamatra Anna's leukocyte and hermaphrodite studies. Kalamatra, sliding the pathology dissections in a viewfinder, glanced through the oculars then slammed the report on the table. His eyes moist, he grabbed his magic wand, slid a cape over his bushy brows, and headed toward the stainless steel doors of the ward. Ferrington couldn't help but notice that the chief of the pediatric oncology ward, as he went through his magician's routine, was noticeably strained, demonstrating none of the spontaneity or zest that usually marked a performance. On this particular day, Kalamatra's tricks were dull and lifeless, the children's accompanying laughter even sounded forced. Audrey kept looking at Anna Youngley; even as the doctors swirled down the corridor, Anna showed not a trace of emotion as her eyes stared straight ahead. Audrey paid scant attention to Kalamatra's antics, preoccupied with analyzing Youngley's condition. A thin film of moisture covered Anna's corneas; a pale yellow paste shielded the whiteness. Kalamatra, prancing up and down the corridor, abruptly turned and stood beside Anna's bed. His hands, fumbling inside his cape, clumsily produced a straw pigeon. Anna, stone-faced, apparently didn't notice. Ferrington intervened and placed a magic wand to Anna's forehead, inserted her hands into a pair of black gloves, and a multicolored scarf mysteriously sprouted from her finger-tips. Before leaving the girl to examine the giggling boy in the next bed, Audrey bent down and lightly kissed Anna's forehead, the girl's face breaking into a faint smile. The locomotive turned into a horse, the caboose into a rider, and, as Audrey jumped onto Kalamatra's back, she gave him a mock kick in his imagi-nary stirrups to prod him along as the two exited through the door. The children clambered for more; even Anna raised her hands, imploring the magicians to return.

Alone in the drab green corridor he shouted, "Dr. Ferrington, you were so bad," Kalamatra beamed, "that, in spite of yourself, you were wonderful."

Audrey slipped off her costume. "Did you see Anna?"

"I did."

"She actually smiled!" Spontaneously her arms hugged him in delight.

"I've been at my wits end at how to enter her world; ever since Anna's been on this ward, she never speaks, pretends not to hear, never laughs, but, Dr. Ferrington," a broad smile spread across his face, "somehow, through your improvisation, you broke down barriers I couldn't penetrate. Dr. Ferrington," Kalamatra wrapped his arms around her, "while your magical ability is far worse than mine, I do believe you're getting a feel for medicine." His bellowing laughter filled the corridor.

After they finished their morning rounds, physicians entered his cluttered office to assess cases. The hour hand reached noon; usually the eccentric doctor would take out a brown bag, and, so as not to lose valuable time, munch on his sandwich as he con-tinued to pour through his reports but this day proved different. The oncologist informed Dr. Ferrington that lunch was in order.

Protocol told her not to protest. Eating in the crowded basement cafeteria found Kalamatra conversing in animated tones; he spoke to Audrey of his native Greece, his parents' immigration to Philadelphia, his longing to return to his homeland as the conversation, disjointed but spirited, flowed from subject to subject. Kalamatra confided his excitement at her inclusion in the day's magical show. His hands then waved, clumsily demonstrating a new trick. Shaking her head, she watched as he bumbled. Tomato stains soon spotted his white hospital coat; although he was making a mess of himself, his exuberance infiltrated the lunch room. A man who seldom talked now bantered so rapidly she could hardly utter a word. Punctuated by self-conscious laughter, Audrey listened as Kalamatra wove in tales of his youth. As they left the cafeteria, Kalamatra turned toward his office; Audrey obediently followed.

"Dr. Kalamatra, lunch didn't provide the right opportunity, but there is an issue I need to talk to you about."

"Private?"

"Yes."

They entered his office. "Sit down. Go ahead!"

Audrey couldn't help thinking that the state of his office was a perfect reflection of the man—pasta stained his bushy mustache, hair disheveled, yet an infectious grin warmed the gutted lines beneath his eyes. She started in an innocuous manner. "Dr. Roberts tells me you were once a mountain climber."

"Far back," Kalamatra laughed, "in my youth."

Audrey continued. "I don't know if you're aware that my fiancé, Philip Hornsby, is co-leader of an American expedition that plans to tackle Mount Everest this fall."

Shocked, Kalamatra sank back into his chair. He hardly heard Audrey as she described the unscaled wall, the team's makeup, the great challenge, the once-in-a-lifetime opportunity.

"You said you're planning to get married?" he uttered.

"You knew that."

"I heard rumors . . . but, I thought . . ."

"After the trip," she added matter-of-factly, "plans are set!"

"Oh I see." His voice was distant.

"Dr. Kalamatra, I know you're busy, but Philip has invited me to join the expedition as part of the medical support team. One problem exists," Audrey paused, her hand brushing her hair back, "my inclusion would mean I'd need a four-month leave of absence. I've already taken the liberty and spoken to Dr. Roberts; he has no problems with my request, except that you, as my attending supervisor, grant your formal approval. It'll only be for a a couple months, but the trip is so important to Philip we're postponing our marriage until our return."

Kalamatra turned toward his bookshelf and, with his back facing Audrey, raised his left hand. Violently his hand crashed downward, pounding a stack of books to the floor. "Where is your commitment to medicine? Obviously I made a mistake telling you that you had the possibility of becoming a good doctor when you're requesting a sabbatical even before finishing your residency. Frankly, I've never heard of anything more ludicrous! Perhaps because you're a woman," he sneered, "you never intended to seriously pursue a career. What an immense waste of training when you'll marry, have children, then practice medicine when it doesn't interfere with child rearing."

"I have every intention of maintaining a full-time career."

The Greek's voice turned bitter. "Let me tell you that I, too, would love to climb. There are many things I'd like to do but a responsibility, an obligation to patients, creates a barrier."

Audrey was stupefied by the enormity of his attack. "You don't understand, I'm not leaving medicine, I'm only requesting a temporary postponement."

"Must I remind you that you've taken an oath to care for others, yet you utter words of a selfish girl."

Ferrington's anger burst out. "I have a right to a full life, being a doctor doesn't make me a droid. Caged in this city for over half a decade, I crave wide open spaces; why would a couple months sabbatical make such a big difference?"

Kalamatra interrupted. "And what will happen to your patients? Are their conditions supposed to go into hibernation while their attending physician prances around the globe?"

"Again you're overreacting," she shot back. "Other residents are available, patients will be well attended. Besides, a couple months delay in the start of a fifth-year career can hardly be translated to mean a lack of dedication."

"Either you're a doctor or an imposter."

Despising his preaching and his arrogance, Audrey, unloaded. "Let me tell you, Mr. Demigod, that perhaps it is you, more so than me, who needs a break. This ward, the patients, they'll exist, maybe not quite as well, but the hospital wouldn't cease operation if the great Dr. Kalamatra wasn't here. No one is indispensable, including you!"

"How dare you talk to me that way!"

Twenty-four hours did nothing to calm his rage. Seething, Nicholas barged into the hospital director's office. "I don't approve. Her plan is folly. Why allow her to be an exception?"

"Through the grapevine I understand that you didn't know that Dr. Ferrington is engaged to someone special," Roberts countered.

Agitation gutted the lines under Kalamatra's deeply recessed eyes, the Greek's boiling frustration evident by his clenched fists.

"Doesn't the name Hornsby mean anything?" the hospital chief chided.

"What does that have to do with it?" Kalamatra pressed. "In my mind, the issue is simple: How can a hospital director be manipulated by a resident who fool-heartedly puts mountain climbing ahead of her medical training?”

“Don’t you read a newspaper or watch television?” Roberts inquired.

“What relevance does that have?”

The hospital director rubbed his chin. “Medicine alone does not run this institution, we exist on financing. For your information, Dr. Ferrington is marrying the heir to the Hornsby Foundation. Philip’s father, W.A., is the single largest private benefactor of this hospital. Nicholas, you’re grossly overreacting, and, like it or not, the world exists by trading favors. In return for his years of generosity, we are simply reciprocating.” Roberts slipped off his bifocals. “Kal, I know you well enough to realize you’re not simply protesting a leave of absence. I’d say,” he hesitated before confronting his associate of over a dozen years, “that you’re suffering from a good case of plain old-fashioned jealousy.”

“Over her?” Kalamatra’s hands were riveted to his hips.

“Come now,” Roberts laughed, “in case you haven’t noticed, Dr. Ferrington is both beautiful and bright. In my time, when a woman like that came along, she created a fuss. I’m sure times aren’t that different, but let me tell you, Kal, as a friend, it’s unfortunate that you’re a bit too old for that colt. Nevertheless, it’s certainly refreshing to see that a woman can stir up dormant hormones. I’ve long thought you needed a diversion from your medicine to balance your life; but next time, choose someone more available.”

18. *Always a Business Deal*

Father and son were engrossed in a conference when W.A.'s secretary opened the door. "Pardon me, but a William Marshall is returning your call."

"The file," W.A. insisted. A thick folder labeled *W. Marshall, Executive Director, International Explorers Club*, was handed to him.

Philip instructed the secretary. "Transfer the call to the conference monitor."

Before speaking, the elder Hornsby glanced through the documents, and his trademark bravado initiated the conversation. "William, how good to hear your voice. It's been years since our days together at Dartmouth. I remember you—tall, with glasses, you were a member of the outing club. If my memory serves me correctly, you were in a class a year behind me."

"W.A.!" Marshall responded. "At your tender age, I'm surprised at the clarity of your memory."

"Over the years, I've followed your career with interest."

Marshall laughed. "And I, yours. Apparently the investment business has treated you well."

W.A. openly poked fun at himself. "All a man can ask for is three meals a day and a roof over his head." W.A. then turned serious. "Is your family still involved in Shane Steel?" William Marshall had no idea W.A. was merely reading from the file placed before him; the truth was he didn't remember William Marshall, but whenever he spoke with anyone from whom he wanted to extract a favor, his research department provided a detailed dossier. A cover page listed potential hooks, avenues to pursue to produce a common bond. Over the years W.A. possessed an uncanny ability to twist biographical information to his advantage.

Marshall took the bait. "Shortly after college, United Technologies purchased controlling interest in Shane Steel, and our family retained involvement as part of the deal. My father stayed on as president for ten years, then retired. Shortly thereafter, I left to oversee family philanthropic interests. For the past twenty years, I've chaired the International Explorers Club."

"Did you marry Sally Weeks?"

"Do you remember her?"

"Certainly! Does she join you on trips?"

"Never had any interest!"

"Do you travel?"

"My last major expedition was back in seventy-four in the Patagonia range on the tip of South America. In recent years persistent bursitis of the hip has forced me exclusively into administrative work. W.A., my exploring days are over; besides administrative responsibilities keep me plenty busy."

"Do give the missus my best." While W.A. didn't have the vaguest memory of William Marshall, he did remember Sally Weeks—a chubby, blond Minnesota matron who attended neighboring Colby Junior College. The men joked she was good for nurturing, but little else. She religiously attended every college mixer, always standing alone, hoping someone would at least talk to her, if not ask her to dance. No one, to W.A.'s knowledge had a physical relationship with Sally—the ensuing embarrassment would have been too much to endure.

"William, I'm calling for a purpose." The pleasantries hopefully served their purpose. "About two months ago, a Professor Birdwein from Colorado came to visit you. Do you recall?"

Marshall hesitated. "What was it concerning?"

"He wanted your organization to sanction an upcoming expedition."

"Vaguely rings a bell, but hundreds of initial proposals pass before me every month. A major part of my responsibility, as diplomatically as possible, is to selectively eliminate endeavors that don't fall within the club's guidelines."

Birdwein came to you with a proposal to pioneer a new route up Everest; does that refresh your memory?"

"Almost ten percent of the requests we receive involve Everest!"

W.A. pressed the hold button, musing to his son, "Your partner must have made some impression!"

"Speak louder," Marshall urged.

"Don't you keep records?" W.A. pressed. Exploiting a weakness was one of his favorite devices as forcing people to act out of their own ineptitude lessens their clout.

"Of course I do," Marshall hemmed.

"Have your secretary refresh your memory; tell her to look up Harry Birdwein, it would be in a recent file."

"You're as bossy as you were in college," William retorted.

Hornsby laughed. "Occasionally I still bark. Now, about those records."

"Hold on." Within five minutes he returned. "You're right. Six weeks ago the professor requested formal board approval for an attempt on Everest's southwest wall. My notes indicate that while group members possessed an excellent climbing record, their objective was both too dangerous and had little scientific appeal. The meeting ended with me telling him not to return."

"William, let me get to the point."

"I was waiting," Marshall interrupted. "I certainly didn't think your call was purely social."

"Years ago, your organization sponsored some of my son's excursions."

"And wisely so. Philip was a magnificent climber."

"Philip wants another crack at Everest."

"Old friend, if I could help, I would; but there's no sense in mincing words. W.A., Nepalese bureaucracy makes it virtually impossible to secure a permit. Our organization has no influence in attaining either of the two slots, pre- or post-monsoon, that are available each year. Waiting time to obtain a permit now ranges anywhere from seven to ten years so what you're asking is not within my purview."

W.A. smiled, his prey trapped; William Marshall, hook, line and sinker, swallowed the bait.

W.A. then launched his offensive. "Did you know that Harry Birdwein has already obtained a permit for this autumn?"

"His expedition will never leave the drawing board," Marshall retorted.

"What if I told you that Philip is joining forces with him—would that change anything? Furthermore, I thought you'd be interested in the names of companies and organizations who already pledged support on the condition that Philip is named deputy leader. Just yesterday the chairman of the Philadelphia Explorer Club called to say that this expedition would be their major undertaking for the year; similar positions have been taken by the Green Mountain Mountaineering Association and the Rocky Mountain Alpine Society; United Supplies has promised to provide full provisions; Simu-Tex pledged protective outer gear; Ryder Boots will supply footwear; tents, and ropes and technical gear provided by Alpine Adventures. But William, to be recognized worldwide, this expedition must carry your organization's official stamp of approval."

Marshall countered, "They don't have the resources."

W.A. interceded. "If you're worried about the finances, I'll personally ensure the group's stability. As far as arranging and paying for publicity, it'll all be handled. Your club will not have to lay out a penny." A long pause ensued. "William, now is the time to align yourself with this courageous venture. Video crews will provide instant communications; ongoing progress of the expedition will be continuously broadcast back to the States; merely log onto the internet and there will be streaming live visuals, people will be glued to computers as Americans can take pride as a brave group of climbers tackles and conquers one of the last remaining, supposedly impenetrable, barriers of the natural world."

"W.A., your enthusiasm is contagious."

"William, as a note of my sincerity and my deep-seeded belief in the aims of your organization, after your club grants its approval, I'll send a check made out to your organization—no strings attached; use the money as you see fit!"

"I can't promise anything."

"Just do your best for the Green & White!"

19. The International Explorers Club

Philip Hornsby's schedule for the month of March didn't contain a sufficient number of hours. Time was spent lining up support for the expedition, numerous personal calls were necessary; and, in the case of major benefactors, selected personal visits were mandatory. The additional responsibilities of a blossoming political career required numerous public appearances. Complicating matters, these commitments had to be sandwiched between his typically hectic business schedule. Fortunately, Audrey was also preoccupied, both being pragmatists, neither voiced a strong objection to their limited time together; both knew their time would come. Their present endeavors would solidify careers; and, like a fine-aged wine, when time permitted, they'd savor their sweet rewards.

Much to W.A.'s surprise, Marshall's assistance was painfully slow in developing. It was two weeks after W.A.'s personal call before Marshall showed the first inkling of reconsidering by writing a personal letter re-inviting Harry Birdwein to Washington to address the club's executive committee. W.A.

promised that Philip would accompany Harry and when the committee asked probing questions, Philip would answer.

Waiting in the rear seat of a chauffeur-driven car at the Washington International Airport, Harry, arriving on schedule, secured his bags and he and Philip drove to the headquarters of the International Explorers Club. Small talk wasn't necessary, both knew the importance of the upcoming meeting; their chance of success hinged on the committee's endorsement. Upon entering the Gothic hall, a secretary instructed them to wait in a cavernous, dimly lit reception room. Philip stood and glanced at the bookends of the numerous chrome-encased copies of vintage explorers magazines while Harry, pacing the floor, nervously fingered a thick file covering details of the proposed trip, the botanist spent his every waking hour of the prior fourteen days assembling this two-hundred-page report. Included were detailed biographical sketches of the lead climbers, a pictorial essay of the route, proposed campsites, as well as a section precisely detailing bottled oxygen usage. Even a schedule of required caloric and liquid intake to be consumed at specific altitudes was included.

"So many dreams rest on their decision." Harry pondered, "If the Society formally backs us, within weeks we'll be on our way." The professor paused. "Peter and Clayton are presently sitting in my house in Boulder awaiting the outcome of this meeting." An uncomfortable silence ensued before Harry continued. "Philip, no matter what happens, before we go any further, I must confess that initially none of us were overjoyed about having you as a participant, I had to convince Peter and Clayton to give you a try. But since deciding to join us, if it was not for your input, we'd never get a chance."

Philip responded, "Harry, factually answer questions. No fanfare, no emotion, no euphoria, be cold and detached. This group respects professionalism; they will not be emotionally swayed by a wide-eyed, exuberant, romantic dreamer. Where necessary, I'll intercede."

Fifteen minutes tediously wore by until the plank oak doors creaked open. William Marshall motioned them inside. Marshall pointed to the podium, nodding to Philip to start. But instead, Harry Birdwein nervously took his place behind the speakers platform. Philip Hornsby, appearing surprisingly relaxed, sat in a seat directly next to the speaker's right. Marshall, glaring at Philip, obviously disappointed that Hornsby wasn't delivering the presentation, began the questioning. Harry Birdwein fumbled, sentences broken, thoughts fragmented. The meticulously crafted, scientific approach unraveled as Harry couldn't help injecting the wonderment of such a venture, the challenge, the necessary daring. As the meeting lengthened, board members' questions became evermore precise, while Harry's responses became evermore glowing and romantic. Questions were raised regarding evacuation procedures, rescue preparations, and supply chains. As the meeting entered its second hour, Harry responded by sinking even deeper into a morass of tangled replies.

Marshall shook his head. "What I'm hearing is you're proposing the three lead climbers will bivouac for an entire night supported only by slings, on a nearly vertical wall at an altitude of over 26,000 feet."

Philip Hornsby, sensing the desperateness of the situation, stood. "Exposure and frostbite constitute a constant danger. Steps will be taken to ensure the transfer of warm blood from the body's core. Scientists have developed pre-packaged hot packs to put on the climbers' chests and backs, especially over the sternum and heart. A cotton cloth, folded a number of times, will be soaked on its inner surface with hot water from a Thermos then wrapped inside a climber's thermal underwear.

Never can a warming solution be placed directly against a bare chest or abdomen as it could cause burns or irritations."

"As I was previously having trouble getting particulars from Professor Birdwein," William Marshall nodded, "it is indeed gratifying to listen to your responses."

"Perhaps he didn't understand your questions," Philip retorted.

"Mr. Hornsby," another member of the board challenged, "if an accident occurs on the mountain, and if the victim's body core temperature is dangerously low, what other steps could be taken?"

Hornsby answered with assurance. "Give the victim hot sweet drinks. Do not, under any circumstances, administer subcutaneous or intramuscular injections."

"Frostbite?" the challenger pressed.

Philip countered, "Frostbite occurs in three stages: first degree—white cold extremities become hard and numb; second, blister formation, and third, usually after a couple days or weeks, necrotic black tissue develops. Often it's difficult to determine the extent of frostbite, whether superficial or deep, but the treatment remains the same—increasing a patient's vasodilation helps blood to more readily flow. Rapid rewarming is extremely painful and, if done too quickly, can result in acidification of the tissue and irreversible injury." Philip, sensing he had established command, added, "A touch of alcohol might even help."

Hands on hip, his wavy hair brushed to the side, Philip then spoke extemporaneously for the next forty-five minutes. The committee members sat transfixed, marveling at his mastery of the facts. "State-of-the-art equipment will be at our disposal. An extensively equipped field hospital will be erected at Base Camp under the direction of Dr. Audrey Ferrington."

William Marshall went directly to the jugular. "Please address the most sensitive issue."

"Which is?" Philip queried.

"The one that perplexes us—safety procedures on the wall."

Philip interrupted. "Let's be coldly realistic. A certain degree of risk is inevitable and I, as one of the three lead climbers, acknowledge there is an element of chance which can't be avoided."

For the next half-hour, Philip handled the most grueling inquiries with skill and confidence. He combated criticism with precision, turned doubters into believers, and, if a question was unreasonable or baiting, Philip maneuvered the questioner into an embarrassing situation of having to respond to his own unanswerable question. Philip's vast skills as an orator, silencing even the most persnickety board members, proved invaluable. After the questioning ceased, and to a round of cordial applause, Marshall thanked Harry and Philip for their presentation and asked them to wait while the panel deliberated. Fifteen minutes later, the door swung open and, wishing to be the first to offer congratulations, William Marshall thrust his hand forward.

20. Everyone Wants to Join

From despair to the starting gate, the next weeks saw a flurry of activity, all positive. The botanist felt rejuvenated, a dream almost abandoned now only weeks off. Once W.A.'s publicist selectively leaked word of the upcoming expedition, a flood of dossiers of people who wanted to join the climb poured in. Journeying to the world's pinnacle drew people like a magnet; Everest's mystique knew no bounds, climbers from every walk of life wanted to be included. Although the hour was late and the embers of a dwindling fire dull red, Harry, Peter, and Clayton sat studying résumés piled before them. "Since Dr. Ferrington will be joining us, I have no clue why we want to even consider a second physician, but Morley insists we have another doctor's name available." As they leafed through dossiers, almost all applying physicians were in their late twenties, many specialized in emergency medicine and accomplished climbers. Harry smiled then chuckled, shaking his head in disbelief. "Greek, age forty, previous experience, twenty years ago. The doctor notes that in his youth he spent a couple of summers hiking."

"And?" Peter questioned.

"For the last twenty years, the applicant admits he has not had time to climb, joined no expeditions, done absolutely nothing. A footnote indicates that his time has been preoccupied directing a pediatric oncology ward at the University of Pennsylvania Hospital." Harry Birdwein grabbed the rubber stamp and marked *reject* over Nicholas Batiste Kalamatra's application.

21. Jealousy Rages

She did everything possible not to be cornered by the Greek, but when he barged in front of her locker she had no choice but to deal with her supervisor.

"I'm going to Everest with you!" Kalamatra blurted.

"Birdwein definitely said no," Audrey was emphatic.

"Then go with me—just the two of us!"

She stood, astonished, shaking her head. "I have plans, commitments . . ."

"All you're doing is joining a well-oiled army. You're a mere appendage hanging on the coattails of Hornsby's power and money."

"And you're about the most obstinate, opinionated man I have ever met. Your naïveté baffles me, you have no idea of the enormity of planning an Everest assault."

Kalamatra snapped, "I'll climb Everest; alone, if necessary, one foot in front of the other until I reach the summit! No fanfare, without a publicist snapping my picture every inch of the way!"

"Nicholas, you are one stubborn, foolish man. Let me confess; I made a horrible mistake sleeping with you. Why can't you accept that it was pure happenstance, the mood struck me, we fucked, we got up, it was over." Audrey glared in anger. "I'm marrying Philip!"

Nicholas struck back. "I'm a bit old-fashioned, but, for me, emotions were involved, there were feelings; I guess I'm a pre-historic monster and don't know the rules of a modern-day liaison. A night together, as much sex as one can cram into a short period, then thank you ma'am, no baggage allowed, don't bother me again!"

"That's not entirely true; for a brief moment we shared something special."

Kalamatra cynically laughed as he unleashed further venom. "Good fortune has shone on the great Dr. Ferrington. Your future is secure. You'll become the perfect doctor, live in the big white house in the suburbs, fancy cars, maids, gardeners, butlers, raise two children with the help of a nanny."

"Enough!" Audrey stormed off.

22. *The Good Old Boys*

Philip, after accepting the post of deputy leader, treated Harry, as the weeks wore on, with surprising dignity. He went through the perfunctory daily ritual of calling Birdwein, reviewing the day's objectives and keeping the expedition leader informed of significant progress. In what had previously been a bureaucratic death march, energized by Philip's vigor and clout, the expedition was breathing life as doors opened. Sponsors, so hard to previously pin down, now waited in line. A myriad of bureaucratic hassles, once cumbersome, faded into oblivion. Previous roadblocks turned into paved highways and, instead of causing jealousy, Philip's administrative abilities deepened Harry Birdwein's respect.

Three weeks remained before the scheduled departure date when a fax arrived from Austin Morley: "Nepalese Minister of Home Affairs plans major sendoff." Sitting at his desk, he kept staring at his uncle's communication, his dream now only days off. The phone rang, it was Philip. Harry listened, shocked, as Hornsby explained, the prestigious International Explorers' Club was extending an invitation to Professor Harry Birdwein to be their monthly keynote speaker. The news left the botanist speechless, he needed to fly to New York City the next morning where he would address an assembly of the most respected and recognized explorers in the country.

Philip and Audrey were at the airport to greet him. With the scheduled speech only a couple hours away, they chose to go directly to the International Explorers' Club and dine afterward. Entering the main chamber, Harry marveled at the stately surroundings—worn, maroon leather covered the one hundred intricately carved chairs; six massive chandeliers, ornate and stately, glittered overhead. Harry's attention was captured by a wild boar's head that hung over a well-oiled mahogany mantle. Every detail of the club exuded a culture reminiscent of Teddy Roosevelt, an era of seasoned adventurers; stuffed otters, blue-tailed foxes, and lynx sat atop coffee tables. Established nearly a hundred years ago as a retreat for gentlemen after a day's outing, the club evolved into a sanctuary for moneyed men who fantasized about the sporting life. Statues of men whose names were synonymous with the group's rich heritage lined the walls.

As was customary, Tyrone Louis, a dignified Black man nearing his eightieth year, stood at the door coaxing members to part with their martinis and take a seat inside. Exactly as their ancestors did a century ago, William Standhope and Alexander Blackwell, the two elder statesmen of the club, slowly moved toward their appointed positions in the first row. Tyrone escorted Philip and Audrey to chairs in the front row, next to the club's current president, William Marshall. Carrying herself with an air of dignity, the tilt of her head exuding vitality, Ferrington, wearing a soft gray wool suit, eased into her seat. The men seated in the front rows openly gasped.

"Absolutely beautiful. Why did I object to having women amongst us for all those years?" Randolph said patronizingly.

In a beige cashmere turtleneck, a loose scarf, a brown suede sports coat and wool pleated slacks, Hornsby, dressed far more casual than most, let his ease and confidence illuminate his inner strength. During the cocktail hour, with Audrey latched on his arm, Philip took immense pleasure as the club's elders came and addressed him. As climbing leader and the acknowledged strength guaranteeing the economic stability of the expedition, he both demanded and received his due respect. Philip knew it was only a matter of time before his portrait would be framed on a wall, he already possessed the attributes and achievements to warrant inclusion, but this trip would serve as a coup-de-grâce, the trip would present him with an opportunity to make a mark so worthy his profile would be cast in stone.

Estes McCovey, an unlit pipe dangling from his mouth, took his traditional place as master of ceremonies. "Distinguished audience, tonight we have the distinct honor to have as our guest Professor Harry Birdwein of Boulder, Colorado. Professor Birdwein is the leader of the International Explorers Club's officially sanctioned American Spring Expedition, which will attempt Everest's previously unscaled southwest wall. Tonight, accompanying Professor Birdwein, is Mr. Philip Hornsby, the summit assault leader, and Dr. Audrey Ferrington, the head of the medical team."

Philip stood to a round of polite applause. Audrey, coaxed by Philip, raised her hand.

McCovey continued. "Professor Birdwein's accomplishments are many: A highly successful plant physiologist at the University of Colorado who, many years ago, attained the rank of full professor. Dr. Birdwein was also a celebrated member of one of the first successful winter assaults of Mount McKinley. Before reaching his thirtieth birthday, he was credited with solo ascents of the highest fifty peaks in western United States. In connection with this upcoming expedition, Professor Birdwein recently returned from a surveillance mission in the Solu Khumbu region of Nepal with his sons, Peter Birdwein and Clayton Johnson. Ladies and gentlemen, Professor Harry Birdwein."

Audrey surveyed the expedition leader, for a man nearing his fiftieth birthday, Harry's pronounced barrel chest filled the room. Even though he dressed the role of a country bumpkin, there was something about the burly resonance of his raspy voice that brought her comfort. A purity in his eyes radiated as he spoke of his beloved Everest. In a world of confusion and veneer, she found Harry's simplicity surprisingly refreshing; Birdwein possessed a quality that unmistakably reminded her of her own father. The professor started by politely thanking all those who assisted in launching the expedition. After that laborious introduction, Harry traced the origins of the expedition. In the midst of a sentence, the back doors opened and Nicholas Batiste Kalamatra entered the auditorium. The intruder propped himself in a chair in the back row, tipping the rim of his cap at the curious stares of those seated in front, and then appearing relaxed, Kalamatra clasped his hands behind his head. Harry, having no idea who this late-comer was, never deviated from his prepared text. "Technical advances have made what was previously impossible now within our realm." The expedition leader continued by extolling the need to subordinate personal goals in order to meet team objectives. McCovey, sensing the termination of Birdwein's remarks, began clapping. The elder statesman of the club then stood alongside Birdwein and asked if there were any questions. Hands were raised.

"How many climbers will reach the summit?" Covington inquired.

"The assault team is composed of three climbers."

"If all goes well, will others reach the summit?" Mr. Blackwell pressed.

Philip stood. "No. Our efforts will be solely centered on the rock face. After reaching the summit, we're evacuating the mountain."

"How do you plan to transport the necessary equipment to the mountain?" Blackwell queried.

"Three hundred and fifty sherpas have been hired," Philip answered.

"And the arrangements . . . the necessary permits?" the questioner pressed.

"Details have been coordinated through the auspices of Austin Morley of the Machapuchare Trekking Company." Philip eyed the crowd. "All necessary permits are already on file in Kathmandu in the Office of Home Panchayat Affairs."

The oldest member of the club, William Randolph raised his hand. "I . . ."

"Yes?" Philip urged.

"Will you . . ." Randolph stumbled, his words garbled. Hands shot up to protect him, but Randolph stumbled upon his train of thought. "Use oxygen?"

"Six hundred cylinders, each weighing four pounds, are already in Nepal. Units will have a three-valve delivery system. These newly designed canisters were recently weather tested in extreme frigid conditions on the Ruth amphitheater on the flanks of Mount McKinley and performed to perfection."

Kalamatra's hand shot up from the rear of the room.

"Yes?" Philip acknowledged the questioner.

"How can I join?"

Audrey, recognizing the voice, cringed.

"So sorry," Philip openly snickered at the questioner's gall, "participation is by invitation only, this expedition is not appropriate for amateurs."

"Then I qualify. In my youth, I climbed in the Alps."

Hornsby stood, peering over heads in the audience, trying to identify a face to the questions.

"Love the out-of-doors, just hard to find the time," the voice yelled over the crowd's murmur.

"Am I talking to a club member?" Philip whispered to the club's chairman.

William Marshall, sensing a confrontation, stood and terminated the questioning. "Naturally, we'd all like to go on such an exciting expedition. But since we're running a bit short of time, I thank Professor Birdwein and Mr. Hornsby for their most stimulating discussion." After a polite round of applause, the audience was asked to retire to the grand ballroom for cocktails with their guests. A crowd of enthusiastic questioners gathered around the lectern; Harry, Philip, and Audrey stayed to answer questions. Audrey, seeing the oncologist march down the aisle, scowled as she stopped him a half dozen feet from her fiancé, "What are you doing here?"

"Dr. Ferrington, you look stunning. How stupid of me to become so accustomed to seeing you in your hospital whites. Indeed," his eyes glanced up and down her body, "this represents a marked improvement!"

"Try to behave," she whispered.

"You're not exactly one to talk," he sniped.

"I'm here with Philip."

"I've never had the pleasure. No better time than now." Pushing her aside, Kalamatra cornered the expedition leaders. "My name is Nicholas Batiste Kalamatra, I'm here to volunteer my services. My application was rejected, but I'm confident that was an oversight that can be corrected."

Harry Birdwein spoke in a whisper. "I do remember reading your application."

"And?"

"Your qualifications didn't warrant inclusion."

"You're making a mistake!" Kalamatra barked. Terseness in his words prompted those within hearing range to halt and listen.

Birdwein addressed Kalamatra. "We'll do fine without you."

"I said I'm going!" Nicholas insisted.

"Well, bravo," Mr. Randolph, captured by Kalamatra's zeal, inappropriately laughed as he slapped Kalamatra on the back.

"Harry," Philip Hornsby's face tightened, "I feel some responsibility to deal with this gentleman since I'm familiar with the name. Correct me, but doesn't my fiancée work under your supervision?"

"She did."

"Then, for her sake, I'll be polite." Philip Hornsby's smile camouflaged his mounting irritation. "All members of the expedition have been screened, obviously you're enthusiastic but our objective far surpasses your technical abilities."

Philip then walked away, turning his attention to a gentleman waiting to ask a question.

As Hornsby departed, Kalamatra grabbed Harry Birdwein's arm. "I've arranged for a leave of absence from the hospital; the dates of the trip fit my schedule."

"As I informed you previously, we're fully staffed. Besides, you haven't conducted research into pulmonary edema, frostbite, or associated high altitude disorders. Further, you have no experience at altitudes over twenty thousand feet. Add that to the fact that you haven't climbed in years."

Nicholas emphatically stated, "I repeat, I want to be included."

"The answer is an unequivocal no!"

As Audrey stood by Philip, her arms encircling his sculpted shoulder, the inklings of a plan fueled by envy and jealousy took form. At that moment, a decision was made—alone he would tackle Everest.

23. They Are Off

D r. Ferrington was forced to miss the gala bon voyage party held in the Expedition's honor in the ballroom of the Waldorf Astoria in New York City. Turmoil surrounding Dr. Kalamatra's unexpected leave of absence, combined with her impending sabbatical, prompted Dr. Roberts to keep assigning duties to Dr. Ferrington. The hospital director reasoned that halting midway through a residency was enough of a concession, so, saving face, Ferrington was put on rotation the night of the party. Audrey didn't have the audacity to plead with Dr. Roberts to excuse her, nor would she allow Philip to use his influence to intercede, so she spent her final evening in America as an attending physician. Activity was light, a few minor bruises, a broken leg, but the predominant hours were spent playing cards and leafing through magazines.

At noon the following day, the scene at the British Airways terminal at Kennedy International Airport was chaotic. Photographers, reporters, and television cameramen pushed and shoved for footage and quotes from the departing team. Harry Birdwein, after introducing his sons, stood behind a barrage of microphones and delivered a brief statement, thanking all for helping. Philip stepped to the microphone and thanked W.A. for his efforts. Audrey Ferrington, the team's only woman, purposely stayed in the background. Amidst cheering and excitement, with knapsacks bulging with equipment, the entourage was shepherded into a private waiting room before starting the first leg of their odyssey by boarding a fourteen-hour flight to New Delhi, India.

Kalamatra, five days later, caught the early morning train from Philadelphia to New York City. Upon arriving at Pennsylvania Station, he crammed his two backpacks into a taxi cab and, forty-five minutes later, was deposited at the international departure ramp of the JFK terminal. Without fanfare, pomp or ceremony, he stood in line, checked his knapsacks, then shoved his carry-ons through security before boarding a jetliner with a ticket, NY-London-New Delhi-Kathmandu. Stuffing his gear under his seat he sat sandwiched in a middle row in the economy section of a packed plane.

24. The Ceremonial Trek

Thoroughly exhausted, the climbing expedition waited in the steaming, crowded New Delhi airport for their baggage to clear customs and be loaded onto a connecting Royal Nepalese aircraft for the continuation of their interminably long journey. Harry Birdwein, monitoring the transfer of the voluminous gear, hassling with bureaucratic representatives, positioned himself inside the roped-off customs area. Pacing the floor, his patience thinning, Birdwein looked aghast when an airline employee informed him that a hefty financial penalty would be levied for the massive amount of excess baggage that lay strewn before them. An argument ensued; the officer listened then left. Twenty minutes later he returned and informed the expedition director that his pleas were fruitless and they would be charged accordingly. Philip interceded. After fifteen minutes of bargaining, with a bribe stuffed into an outstretched palm, the very same bureaucrat who insisted they pay excessive baggage charges now graciously, with a wide smile painted across his face, allowed the entourage, and all of the baggage, to board the next plane. Temperatures pushed beyond one hundred degrees as members of the expedition crammed into a stifling, antiquated turboprop airplane. After an hour delay on the tarmac, the plane taxied down the runway for its final destination—Kathmandu, Nepal.

Austin Morley waited to greet them in the Nepalese Airport. Minutes after entering the terminal, Morley arranged for the expedition members to be ushered into a private airport lounge for afternoon tea. An overhead fan provided scant relief to the oppressive heat. Audrey stood by the window and watched as customs officials opened boxes.

"Pay them off!" Philip insisted.

Meeting the climbing group at the airport, Austin Morley explained, "The start of your expedition will be delayed five to six days. I regret the inconvenience, but the king of Nepal, when informed of the magnitude of this group's intended mission, has organized a formal parade to be held in your honor."

"Ridiculous," Harry protested.

Morley responded, "A reoccurrence of a recent rash of insurrections will be minimized if your march has the king's personal stamp of approval. Sherpas are fiercely loyal, their support is crucial."

Philip stoically handled the news. "A parade in our honor will provide film footage that can be utilized to our advantage."

Peter Birdwein voiced his dissent, "What's the logic of holding a parade prior to successfully completing our mission?"

Morley interjected, "Parade or no parade, you'd still have to wait. A shipment of medical supplies coming from a pharmaceutical company in San Francisco inadvertently ended up misdirected during a transfer. The missing boxes were traced to Anchorage, Alaska, the goods are already in transit."

Harry Birdwein turned to the group. "Typical of my uncle to turn waiting to our advantage. Tonight we're opening champagne and toasting Austin Morley for a job well done. A few more gray hairs, but still as crusty as ever. Damned if you're not the same cagey Scotsman I remember. Glad to see the years haven't tarnished your ingenuity."

Outside the terminal fierce-looking Sikhs, wearing their hair in turbans, sat in the driver's seats of waiting taxis. Waiting for Philip while the gear was sorted, Audrey crammed into the backseat of a small car for the twenty-minute ride to their headquarters at the Yak & Yeti Hotel. Close to thirty minutes passed sitting behind the foul-smelling bearded driver. Sweat coated her forehead, a cotton t-shirt and light pants were soon stained in perspiration. Philip, Harry, and Austin Morley stayed behind to supervise the loading of the equipment. No matter how tired they were, Philip was adamant that each time their prized possessions were moved, vigilance was necessary to prevent pilferage. Under a broiling sun, mound after mound of baggage was roped into human-pedaled tricycles called rickshaws. After an interminable wait, Philip appeared.

"Why?" she asked.

"Any missing piece of equipment could spell disaster; all details must be in order." Neither driver nor passengers exchanged a word as the bearded Sikh, continuously honking the car's horn, threaded the cab through the congested streets.

After dinner, the members of the high altitude assault team were summoned for a meeting, Audrey excluded. Philip, arriving last, took his allotted seat directly across from Harry. The elder Birdwein launched into a presentation that included charts, graphs, and computer printouts. As the meeting dragged on, a slow-burning kerosene lamp left a fine grayish residue over the ten-foot plank table. Adding to the congestion, ventilation in the cramped quarters was non-existent. Every fifteen minutes, a Nepalese youth, with a slight build and matted hair, entered offering pungent fermented tea and *kussi*, a Nepalese cookie. Austin Morley would have preferred *chang*, a locally brewed beer, but, until the meeting was adjourned, Philip strictly forbade the consumption of any alcoholic beverages.

"How many sherpas are available?" Hornsby directed his question at Morley.

"Three hundred and forty-seven porters have been recruited to carry from Lamsangu to Everest Base Camp. Thirty-six high altitude sherpas are prepared to navigate the treacherous Solu Khumbu ice field. Twelve comprise a high altitude team; six sherpas in the party have gone as high as 26,000 feet. Two sherpas, Ang Nia and Pemba, have summited. If any route other than the yellow rock band is chosen, an additional eight are capable of staying by your side."

"Who's the sidar?" Philip asked.

Hornsby listened while Morley explained the difficulties in choosing a head guide, or sidar, for the excursion. "Four have previously led expeditions—Pemba, Jungbar, Ang Nia, and Anbar." Morley continued, "But I suggest you defer making a choice until you reach Everest Base Camp. Postpone a decision, keep everybody on edge, it will serve your interests. The entire operation, once you leave Kathmandu, must be self-sustaining as there are no supplies enroute." The expedition coordinator reported that six and a half tons of food, five tons of mountaineering hardware, two and a half tons of communications apparatus, eight hundred pounds of oxygen cylinders and regulators, one hundred and fifty pounds of medicines, must be transported on human backs over the one hundred and sixty miles of dirt paths before reaching Everest Base Camp. He then shared a chart detailing an analysis of the decreased weight load each sherpa would carry as the days progressed. Each porter would start shouldering one hundred twenty-one-pound loads, but by the time the expedition reached Base Camp, all would carry packs weighing slightly over ninety pounds. Once reaching Base Camp, all but forty-eight porters would be released, leaving the remaining sherpas to shoulder an average of seventy pounds until Camp II was established. After that, the eight high altitude sherpas would haul loads of sixty pounds to the base of the yellow band." Taking pride in working out the precise details, the Scotsman finished, "A Himalayan assault is akin to a complex military invasion; if the troops are properly deployed, only then is there a chance for success!"

Hornsby grilled Morley, "In the event it becomes necessary, are more sherpas available?"

"Impossible!" Austin volleyed. "I've scoured the land; every available body has been recruited. Spring is planting season; women and children have been left behind to toil the fields."

"A dozen additional porters would provide a comfort zone," Philip pressed.

"Forget it!" Morley snapped. "Already there are too many mouths to feed."

Clayton questioned Philip. "Since it will be difficult preparing a campsite for a group of this magnitude, how about allowing Harry, Peter, and I to forge ahead?"

"We're marching together." Philip Hornsby was adamant. "I promised the Society film coverage, if we're spread out all over the wilderness, filming will be impossible."

Austin Morley interjected, "Don't underestimate the difficulty of the upcoming march, between twelve and sixteen days of hard pushing remain before establishing base camp. Take time to acclimate; spend a minimum of a day at Namche Bazaar, and another at the Tengboche Monastery."

Four nights passed and Phillip never touched his fiancée. Night after night Philip fell asleep slumped at a desk in their room, a pencil in his hand, so tired he could no longer compute the exact number of oxygen canisters needed. Hornsby's self-imposed distance was a far cry from what she imagined, her partner's fanatical devotion to making sure every detail was correct left no time for her.

Six interminably long days intervened until their formal sendoff. At breakfast on the morning of the king's send-off parade, Austin Morley addressed the assault team. "It makes no difference if you don't understand; wave, be polite, the Nepalese society has its unique customs." Within the hour, expedition members took their positions in line as Nepalese, numbering in the thousands—men, women, goats, cows, teens, chickens, toddlers, babies, dogs, cats—lined the path, as the parade honoring the American climbers inched toward the Swayambhu Monkey Temple. At the very front of the procession, an elderly monk, regally dressed in a flowing robe, had an ornately carved brass breastplate prominently displayed on his chest. Surrounding this esteemed elder was a host of young children around the monk waving elaborately decorated prayer flags. Next in line, a hundred women dressed in elegant robes with silver and turquoise jewelry dangling from ankles, waists, and necks. Atop their heads, the women carried straw baskets brimming with fruits and breads. Muscular, bare-chested guards followed with their razor-sharp swords, drawn and held overhead, glistening in the noon sunlight. Behind them, the queen of Nepal walked alone, a coterie of guards kept her highness a safe distance from the pressing throngs. A delicate white lace scarf shielded the queen's face; her jewelry, limited to a pear-sized diamond, was suspended from her neck by a chain of vibrant sapphires. As the graceful woman moved through the throngs, her outstretched hand, beckoning friendship, waved to the crowd. Nude, except for waistcoats, six muscular men followed, dragging a long handle attached to a wooden cage that contained an eight hundred pound Bengali tiger. Baring its teeth when onlookers threw food, the tiger growled, saliva pouring from its mouth as it tried to squeeze a paw through the cage's narrow opening.

Behind the fierce beast came a row of trumpeters, their horns blaring. Near the rear of the parade, a dozen elite guardsmen, their blue military uniforms adorned with fluffy white fringes on both shoulders, crisply marched forward. A wide gap followed before the king, next in the caravan, appeared. The royal monarch sat in an ornately decorated open wooden box, his platform hoisted by eight human mules. Small boys, running along both sides of the monarch's carriage, employed peacock feathers to fan the seated king as he was carried through the dusty streets. As the Nepalese ruler came into view, monks, lining the procession with their hands lifted, prayed to Buddha for the king's longevity. Seeing the monarch approach, the crowd obediently bowed, reverently praying for his highness's divine protection. Directly behind the king's carriage, the guests of honor marched in groups of two. Walking alongside the stoic expedition leader, Austin Morely raised his hand saluting those crowding the streets. Directly behind them marched Philip and Audrey, followed by Peter and Clayton. The team wore bright yellow hats with the insignia *A.E.E.* sewn in purple letters on the front, per Morley's edict. The entire team, except for Morley who sported his Scottish tunic, also wore short khaki pants with bright orange high-altitude rain jackets draped over their left shoulders. Filming this spectacle, a slew of cameramen ran through the crowd.

"Participation in a celebration before a climb is successful is absurd," Clayton spat as he kicked a hiking boot into the hard-packed dirt.

"Wave," Philip admonished Clayton and Peter, "and stop bitching. The two of you behave as if there's just you and a mountain. Stop being naïve, we need their support."

Bitterness rang in Clayton Johnson's voice. "Only Philip Hornsby, before anything's been accomplished, demands to be treated as a celebrity."

Audrey, intervening, inquired, "Where are we going?"

"To Swayambhu," said Austin Morley, "the holiest of the Nepalese temples."

"And I don't give a damn," Johnson erupted.

"Shut up and walk," said Philip, without a smile ever leaving his face, icily rebuked the rebellious Turk.

After a mile, the parade edged toward the outskirts of the city.

"How much farther?" Audrey questioned. The noonday sun was oppressively hot.

"A quarter of a mile directly up those steps." Morley pointed to a long row of stairs.

Dangling on tree limbs, overhanging the staircase, were numerous monkeys.

Morley explained. "It's their version of a church."

"A what?" Ferrington couldn't fathom what she was seeing.

"My dear," Austin Morley shot back, "don't act so surprised. Your Western customs are every bit as odd. The Nepalese don't exclusively corner the market for bizarre rituals. After all, you pray to a man nailed to a cross, newborn babies are dunked into frigid rivers, boys have the foreskin of their penises snipped. We're here to honor our hosts by paying homage to their gods." Ever so slowly, the procession climbed the stairs fronting the temple, as monkeys, chattering and dangling from adjoining trees, swung from branch to branch. The king, refusing to leave his chariot until he was atop the domed throne, held up the march as his servants grunted and groaned, hauling his rotund body up the hundred steps. After taking his allotted seat in a gilded chair on the podium, his royal highness clasped his hands overhead. Four young boys ran forward, fanning the king with elongated peacock feathers. Once the king was seated, the ceremony commenced.

An elder monk raised his hands and two younger monks, standing on either side of the altar, banged their mallets against the gold-leafed gongs signifying the American ambassador had come to the podium. A bald man addressed the crowd. "It is a great honor that within this magnificent kingdom lies the tallest mountain in the world. For many years, Nepal's borders were closed and these jewels were off-limits to outsiders. It is only through the generosity of his highness that men and women are now afforded an opportunity to test their acumen against the giants of the world. Let us hope," he continued, "oh Great King, your support will lend a note of good fortune. Under the able leadership of Harry Birdwein and Philip Hornsby, if anyone possesses the capability of being successful, this team proudly carries the banner as America's best."

In the far recesses of the crowd, a figure pushed forward through the congestion.

The American ambassador droned on. "Your blessing gives dreams an opportunity to be transferred into the realm of reality."

The French ambassador spoke next, offering his country's hope for a safe and successful mission. Once the diplomat was finished, an elderly Nepalese monk, shirtless, his thin gray beard dropping from his chin, held a silver mallet between his raised hands. His arms swung forward, the mallet striking the gold-leafed, oval gong. Chimes reverberated, the monk sinking to his knees, his head bowed in deference to a single emerald-green eye that dominated the overhanging stupa. Following his lead, the crowd sank to their knees, praying to the god housed within the protruding emerald eye.

The king, with his feather-waving entourage fanning him, then stood. Chanting in Nepalese, the monarch spoke in a barely audible whisper, pausing only long enough to allow an interpreter to translate his words into English. "From the eye of the great Buddha, I ask the almighty to shine brightly on our guests. One needs courage to scale the wall of the gods. Those who try to reach the top of the mighty Sagarmatha, let their spirit soar upward, their path illuminated by his divine guidance."

A commotion from the back of the crowd caused the king to momentarily pause. Glancing outward, annoyed that someone would have the audacity to cause a disturbance while he spoke, the king resumed his blessing. "It is with a spirit of utmost co-operation that the W.A. Hornsby Foundation has donated funds for the building of a new hospital facility in Kathmandu. In return, speaking for the people of Nepal, I pledge our country's cooperation."

As the intruder pressed forward, Hornsby, looking behind, shook his head in disbelief; the bushy brows were unmistakably those of Dr. Kalamatra, the man who begged for inclusion in the expedition, the same man they rejected. How dare the doctor who had been Audrey's supervisor have the audacity to travel halfway around the world to sabotage their effort? Philip nudged Audrey. "Look! Behind!" Audrey peered into the sea of faces. Suddenly her cheeks blanched, her knees nearly buckling as she saw Kalamatra thread his way through the crowd, his hand raised, waving in excitement, a self-satisfying smirk painted across his face.

Accompanied by a loud blast of trumpets, the king, upon finishing his remarks, was surrounded as human pall bearers crouched low to lift the monarch atop his waiting chariot. As he descended the hundred steps, monkeys dangled overhead. Occasionally, a monkey would apparently slip, fall a couple of feet, but somehow manage to grasp a lower branch before crashing into the wooden canopy. As gongs rhythmically clanged, with attendants grunting, the human mules carted the ruler down the winding stairs. The queen, walking alone directly behind her husband, was followed by the caged tiger. As members of the procession took their allotted positions, everyone in the crowd knelt, except the lone figure who pushed through the crowd.

"Wait here," Philip tersely instructed Audrey. He abruptly left the entourage, forcing his way through the milling congregation to confront the intruder. Their paths met.

"I'm going with you." Nicholas extended his hand. "I'm here to help."

"You are indeed persistent," Philip Hornsby glared, "Back in the States I gave you my answer; my response today is still the same—no!"

"Quit being so difficult," Kalamatra spat. "Make up a name for me, call me an auxiliary medical officer, but I'm tagging along."

Onlookers, overhearing their harsh exchange, backed away. As she neared them, Audrey pleaded.,"Nicholas, why?"

"Dr. Ferrington, what an unexpected pleasure," the maverick Greek physician gloated. "Arrived just this morning, delighted you haven't left, gives me a chance to start from the beginning."

"No means no!" The tiny arteries on Philip's forehead pulsated.

Audrey, trying to mediate, interrupted. "Philip, since he's already in Kathmandu, possibly reconsider; certainly, a second physician can be of use."

"Nothing would change my mind; the man's judgment is not to be trusted."

A devilish grin was painted across the Greek physician's face. "You haven't yet told me where you're staying." Nicholas turned to Audrey. "Perhaps the three of us can have dinner tonight?"

Philip emphatically retorted, "Not a chance."

Kalamatra was not deterred. "Save your rebukes, I didn't come halfway round the world to be rejected." At that precise moment, accompanied by a military guard, both fore and rear, the king's chariot passed before them. As the vast assembly bowed their heads in reverence, Kalamatra's voice could be heard. "Greeks have strong backs. There's no way you can tell me you can't use my services to haul goods through the Solu Khumbu ice field."

"You're a lunatic," Philip snapped.

"And you're an arrogant bastard. Besides, you've monopolized every available body. For me to go alone, I need a minimum of ten sherpas, you've given me no other choice . . ."

Philip spat, "You embarrass us!" Hornsby grabbed Audrey's hand and tried to push her away from the argumentative physician.

Kalamatra responded by grabbing Hornsby by the shirt.

"Take your hands off me," Philip lashed.

Confusion reigned, Audrey screamed, the two men scuffled, and, before punches were exchanged, the two wrestled each other to the ground. Arms pummeling each other did little harm as Audrey screamed, "Guards!" Within a minute, three policemen yanked the adversaries apart.

"That man attacked me." Hornsby pointed to an official badge displayed on his chest. "Look for yourselves!"

Kalamatra's eyes appealed to Audrey. "I . . ."

Hornsby, brushing dirt from his clothes, barked, "Don't just stand there," he screamed at the police, "take him away, the man assaulted me."

The police pinned Kalamatra's arms behind him.

"I did nothing," the doctor protested. "It was he . . ."

"Lock him up!" Philip extorted.

"Philip!" Audrey screamed. "For God's sake, you can't do that!"

Kalamatra, forcibly being led away, momentarily pulled free of a hand gagging his mouth. "Don't think you'll stop me!"

25. Battle of Egos

Philip Hornsby requested and received permission for a private audience with his royal highness hours before a state dinner the king was hosting in their honor. Profusely apologizing for the bizarre incident at the conclusion of the ceremony, Philip informed the monarch that the assailant had no affiliation with the trip. "Yes, he is American," Hornsby begrudgingly admitted, "but we, in the United States, have our share of crazy people."

The king responded, "As long as my guest was not offended."

Hornsby assured him that he was fine.

The king asked, "What do you want done with him?"

"Whatever is necessary to guarantee he doesn't hinder our progress."

"He will be detained!"

"As your majesty wishes. Again, my apologies." Hornsby left, satisfied their relationship was not impacted by the chaos of the day.

Sitting upright in their bed, Audrey punched the bedpost. "Why doesn't he grow up? What does he think he's proving? Philip, you've got to intercede; Kalamatra can't be left to rot in a foreign jail cell."

"Confinement might knock some sense into his thick skull."

"Tell the king to put him on a plane home. Deport him, but he can't be left in a dungeon."

Philip dispassionately responded, "The man earned his punishment. If I never hear the name Nicholas Batiste Kalamatra again, I'd be delighted. No way I'll tolerate some idiot sabotaging our mission."

"But imprisonment for ten days?" Audrey shuddered.

"Confinement will keep the buffoon out of trouble." Philip leaned over and blew out the candle, and unexpectedly his hand groped for Audrey. Ferrington, for one of the few times in their relationship, disregarded his advance. Philip then rolled onto his back and, within minutes, drifted to sleep.

Hour after hour she tossed. Frustrated, she dressed and, in the middle of the night, slipped unnoticed from the hotel. Taking out a street map of Kathmandu, it took her a half-hour of wandering through the winding streets to find her destination. A lone light burning in an office gave her hope Morley was still at work. She banged against the wooden door before it creaked open. "Philip would be furious if he knew I was here," Audrey began.

"Come in, shut the door." Austin Morley's desk was covered with voluminous stacks of material. "What happens behind these doors is our business, no one else's."

"Dr. Kalamatra baffles me . . ."

Austin Morley laughed. "He marches to the beat of a different drummer, that's for sure."

"All Kalamatra did was announce he was joining us. But jail, isn't that a bit harsh for arguing with Philip?"

"You're forgetting to mention the willingness to fight."

"Both were out of line." Audrey clarified.

Austin Morley's fingertips rubbed against his chin.

"Perhaps it's the doctor's hot temper, or his doggedness, but," Morley laughed, "he does have a quality I admire. The man doesn't know the meaning of no. In my profession, strong egos are run of the mill, but I cannot remember encountering anyone quite so pig-headed."

"Truthfully, I don't know what to make of him, but after we leave, do me a favor, get him out of that hell hole and see to it that he's put on a plane back to the United States."

26. *Persistence or Insanity*

The team was seated when the expedition planner entered the room. Whether it was Harry Birdwein, Philip Hornsby, or any of the other thousands of adventurers he had assisted, Austin Morley knew his place. It was his job to launch an expedition, but once supplied, individuals chased their own dreams. Austin Morley took everyone by surprise when he announced he was remaining in Kathmandu, explaining to the gathering that his contribution to their effort would be best served by manning his post at the Machapuchare Trekking Company. Morley explained it made no sense for the team's logistics coordinator to be in the field, saying that he'd be in daily radio contact and, if problems did arise, his location in Kathmandu would enable him to marshal the requisite resources.

Exact details of how he ended up locked in this godforsaken dungeon remained fuzzy. He vaguely remembered being pushed down a flight of stairs. A key was inserted into a lock, a wrought-iron door swung open before being slammed shut. As the guards departed, he was left alone to rot, caged in a windowless pit.

Pressing his face between the iron bars, Kalamatra screamed to be let out. Pacing the dirt floor, shivers rifled through his body. A ghastly scream echoed through the dank chamber, across the narrow dirt hall. A crazed inmate salivated while on his knees offering prayers to a small pile of stones. A man in the adjoining cell, his skin marred by inflamed boils, taunted the frightened Westerner by opening his toothless mouth and mocking him. A rat scurried beneath the iron grate into the doctor's cell, the vile creature disappearing into an open hole in the rear of the eight-foot by six-foot by eight-foot cell, the very same opening that was his toilet. Horrified that this intruder would return to bite him, Kalamatra backed away from the metal bars and lifted his feet onto a wooden platform. Trying to keep warm, he tucked himself in an embryonic position, but he kept shaking as there was no blanket, pillow or mattress, just a hard board. Philip Hornsby would pay; the bastard had no right to do this to him.

Nicholas lost count of the days . . . two . . . three . . . four . . . the routine inside the dungeon never varied: mid-morning, a fifteen-minute walk in the hallway, then herded back into his pen. Caged like a dog, he tried bribing the guards. Officers willingly took his belongings—wrist watch, shoes, comb—but never returned any favors. Fighting to avoid psychologically falling apart, he summoned every inch of his reserves; bars would not rob him of his spirit, but the fact remained, Nicholas Batiste Kalamatra was a forgotten man. Twice a day, the clanging of metal indicated the arrival of vile mush. Supervised by guards, two inmates nude from the waist up, pushed a flat wooden cart through a narrow aisle. Stopping at each doorway, the workers glopped a blob of this paste onto a filthy wooden plate and, before shoving the gruel in a slit between bars, the accompanying officers took a long pointed stick, forcing each prisoner to retreat to a far corner of his cell while his food was being shoved into his cage. On day five of his confinement he was desperate;

Nicholas held up his treasured gold necklace, a going away gift from his grandparents when he left Greece. Moving toward the iron gate, he dangled his prized possession. A spike jabbed his thigh, the stick's sharp tip slicing through his pants, leaving a ring of blood oozing onto his pants. The toothless guard, taking delight in this torment, laughed. Kalamatra, clutching his thigh, dangled his necklace again. The tip of the guard's stick quickly snatched the chain. "Please make sure he reads this," he whimpered. On his hands and knees, Kalamatra inched forward, the letter dropping onto the dirt as the guard jabbed the stick at him. Scrambling backward, he inadvertently stuck his hand into the open hole. Wet, urine-laced feces engulfed his right arm. Hysterical laughter erupted, the stench of the urinal, combined with the potato-like mush caused him to vomit.

"Water," he pleaded.

The menacing stick kept him in the remote corner; the note on the ground was untouched. Another day in this hell. Out of desperation, he shoved mush into his mouth. A single tin of water, doled out each morning, was nursed to last an entire day. Alone and deserted, he was told nothing, never informed of the charges against him, nor when he'd get out. He'd scribble a notch into the mud wall each morning to track the days; today began day seven of his confinement. That morning a commotion on the staircase forced him to take notice voices became louder as guards approached his cell. "Out!" they yelled.

Too weak to walk, the oncologist was pulled by his arms and dragged through a series of small openings. Fearing the worst, he asked questions, but his uncertainty ended when guards shoved him into a four foot by four foot cell, a holding area so small that sitting or lying down was impossible. After about an hour of enforced standing, the door swung open. An officer in a heavily starched khaki uniform said, "You are free to go."

"What?" Kalamatra couldn't believe the words.

The officer threw a note in his direction. Kalamatra recognized Audrey's writing.

I did all I could. Hornsby told them ten days, without him knowing I intervened on your behalf, pleading for a week. Leave the jail and proceed to the Yak & Yeti Hotel, see Mr. Achilla, the manager, in his safe there's a plane ticket for your return home. I'm sorry this happened. You shouldn't have come!

For two days Kalamatra lay in a room at the Yak & Yeti Hotel, Achilla tending to his needs. Incessantly, Kalamatra mumbled, but Mr. Achilla paid no attention to the crazed doctor's mutterings as he brought food, water, and medicine into his room. It wasn't until the third day, still too weak to walk, that he was able to sit upright in his bed. Whenever the balding Nepalese man entered the room, Kalamatra fired questions, demanding information regarding the progress of the Everest expedition. Achilla avoided these inquiries, informing the doctor that as soon as he felt strong enough to travel, Achilla would take him to the airport. After a fourth day of bed rest, Nicholas's strength sufficiently returned allowing him to sneak away from his hotel room. Barely strong enough to stand upright, Kalamatra flagged down a rickshaw driver and collapsed in the backseat of the human-powered taxi. The doctor's eyes struggled to stay open as a boy pedaled his ailing passenger through the congested streets. After twenty minutes, the rickshaw pulled up in front of a carved wooden sign that stated: *Machapuchare Trekking Company.*

Kalamatra barged inside. "I demand to meet with the director!"

A secretary, seated behind a rattan counter, icily responded, "Mr. Morley sees people only by appointment."

"Tell him Dr. Kalamatra is in his office." As he waited, the cluttered walls of the reception room grabbed his attention; thirty to forty enlarged pictures of mountain climbers standing atop summits were plastered all over the walls. Under each picture, a letter of appreciation addressed to the colonel was framed and displayed. Fifteen minutes passed until Colonel Morley stood by the door. The celebrated expedition organizer stared at the wobbling physician. "It's an honor to meet the individual who created such a stir. The least I can do is offer you tea." Austin Morley's words were deliberate, his British accent pronounced. "I was under the assumption you were detained."

"Until a few days ago. No sense wasting time, I have no choice but to enlist your cooperation because tomorrow I'm leaving on an expedition."

"Where are you going?"

"Everest Base Camp." Disbelieving the words, Morley rubbed his chin. "You are indeed one stubborn man. Doctor, Mr. Hornsby has made his position abundantly clear; you are persona non grata."

"I don't need Philip Hornsby's permission." A smile spread across Kalamatra's face. "Since I'm going alone, I need assistance in obtaining a trekking permit, gathering supplies and recruiting sherpas."

Morley moved his bifocals to the bridge of his nose, a smile spread across his face as he packed loose tobacco into a pipe's white marble oval bowl. "You'd make John Wayne proud, before me sits the reincarnation of a gun-toting Western cowboy. There's no sense wasting my time or yours; even if I wanted to, I couldn't help. Every available porter has been recruited for the American expedition, besides which Birdwein and Hornsby cleaned me out of equipment." The expedition planner pointed to the door.

"They say I'm crazy, don't they? That my judgment is impaired and I'm irresponsible, not to be trusted. Tell them to fly a kite. At my stage of life I make my own decisions. Over the last couple of months, my life has become unglued, so however undisciplined, however illogical, I'm going to Everest and no one is stopping me."

"Why?" was all Morley asked.

"I'm not sure," Kalamatra answered, "but believe me, I'm not the Machiavellian creature that Philip Hornsby portrays me to be. For a person who usually needs to know everything, I'm not sure where this journey is going."

In his line of work he encountered all types, but never had he met someone like Nicholas Batiste Kalamatra. Intuitively, Morley felt that the physician would not harm the expedition; anyway, having traveled halfway around the world, who was he to deny the doctor his opportunity? Besides, Kalamatra would never be a factor since he was so far behind. His secretary listened as the expedition planner barked instructions: "Tell Ang Nugal to bring me the maps of the Solu Khumbu region. Have Tensing go to the Office of Home Panchayat Affairs and obtain Dr. Kalamatra's hiking permit." Morley turned his attention to the topographical maps. "Beware of the Lamjura Pass," the colonel cautioned as he spread the maps across his desk, "you'll probably encounter snow in the higher elevations." His finger continued to trace the trail's route as it wound toward the world's highest summit.

"Everest, how quickly can it be reached?" Nicholas pressed.

"Twelve to sixteen days."

"When did the Everest expedition leave?"

"Seven days ago!"

"Can I catch them?"

"Not until Everest Base Camp," Morley cautioned. "Let me warn you, don't go too high too quickly. Discipline is essential;

proceed slowly. The body requires time to adjust to the debilitating effects of an oxygen-deprived atmosphere. Oxygen sickness strikes haphazardly, without a set pattern. I've known cases where victims at altitudes less than 10,000 feet have become incapacitated. Forget the summit towers above 29,000 feet, Base Camp sits perched at over 18,000 feet. You'll be venturing into a rarefied atmosphere where nobody can predict when and who will be affected."

"I'll go slowly," Nicholas assured Morley.

"They all say that."

"I'm different."

"You certainly are," Morley laughed.

Ignoring the sarcasm, Kalamatra said, "I need equipment, chocks, ice picks, crampons, ropes, whatever you can scrounge together."

Morley faced the Greek. "Technical equipment is only necessary if you insist on crossing the Solu Khumbu ice field. Be forewarned that the glacier is one of the most perilous parts of the journey. Appearing solid, the ice flow houses a labyrinth of crevices, walls collapse under the heat of the midday sun. Avalanches cascade down the ice field without warning."

"And sherpas? How many can you recruit? At what price?"

"The going rate is five dollars a day, U.S. currency. The Machapuchare Trekking Company receives a fifteen percent fee for services plus a one-time consulting fee. Before I hire guides, porters, and cooks, payments must be received in advance."

Kalamatra agreed. "I'll need a dozen sherpas, a sidar, and a cook."

"Doctor, you have a peculiar habit of selective hearing, at the present moment, not a single sherpa is available."

"How many sherpas accompanied the American expedition?"

"Three hundred and forty-seven!" Morley paused, "They wanted more, but that is what was available."

"Money is not a problem." The oncologist emptied a pocket of cash on the table.

Without responding, Morley walked outside. A couple minutes later he returned. "My attendant says he knows of a distant sixteen-year-old cousin named Unkel who grew up in Kunde, a village just north of Namche Bazaar. Unkel wanted to join the American Expedition, but arrived in Lamosangu three days late."

"One is hardly sufficient," Kalamatra assessed.

"It's the best I can do!"

A smile spread across Nicholas's face, "Then you're going to help me?"

"On one condition."

"Which is?"

"Promise me you will NOT interfere with the American expedition!"

Nicholas laughed. "How could a solitary individual halt a well-oiled machine?"

"Both Philip Hornsby and Harry Birdwein would have my hide," Austin Morley responded, "and don't tell him that Ferrington helped you. Be forewarned that except for a sixteen-year-old boy, you'll be on your own." He then explained, "Lamosangu, a couple hours' bus ride from Kathmandu, is the end of the road. In order to reach Everest Base Camp, the remaining one hundred plus miles must be completed on foot."

"When is the earliest I can leave?"

"Two days from now," Morley reported, "go to the city bus stop at six a.m. Gear, food, and the necessary trekking visas will be waiting for you. Upon your arrival at Lamsangu, sherpa Unkel will meet you."

"How can I thank you?"

"Don't embarrass me." Morley closed the door.

27. The Time Has Come

Every night a lone kerosene lamp burned in their tent. Since leaving Kathmandu, Philip Hornsby was crazed; poring over details, planning, reviewing and anticipating. Never tiring, his solitary figure sat alone, plotting food consumption, departure times, and intended routes. Philip Hornsby administered every task with zeal. But this wasn't what Audrey expected. She was missing their shared moments and the subsequent expressions of emotions. Five of the first six nights on the trail she slept alone as Philip, preoccupied with planning strategy, fell asleep exhausted, slumped over a makeshift desk in the expedition's headquarters. Philip attacked the mountain as if it was an intricate chess game, plotting each move, analyzing repercussions. Audrey couldn't help but marvel at Philip's preciseness, his ability to command, and his leadership. Indeed, this was Philip's time to shine, and while she had hoped for something different, she felt pride being a partner of a man of decision, an individual whose presence prompted respect. But nights sleeping alone left her frustrated and angry too.

As the first rays of dawn were making an appearance, Audrey slipped outside, and with a blanket draped over her shoulders, she watched as Pemba went from tent to tent waking an army of porters. Before her eyes the sleeping city was transformed into a maze of activity; fires were kindled and dense smoke billowed upward. Pemba, seeing Dr. Ferrington sitting alone, placed a kettle of hot steaming water and a tea bag in front of her. In the middle of the campsite a gigantic frying pan was suspended over a burning fire. A cook placed chicpates, a thin potato-like pancake, in boiling grease over dancing flames. A human chain of sherpas transported water to the campsite in huge, earthen jugs strapped atop skulls. For an hour, Ferrington sat transfixed as tents were dismantled, condensed, and packed. Equipment was stuffed into pouches, leather harnesses were tied across the girth of the Nepalese variety of an American mule—a scraggly, furry animal called a yak. Periodically, Pemba reported progress to Philip. Even with Hornsby's urgings, it took a minimum of two hours of daylight for the massive expedition to ready itself. While the makeshift village was being packed, various members of the team found an odd array of ways to occupy themselves. Harry studied topographical maps, trying to memorize the upcoming day's significant hurdles. Peter and Clayton paced in circles by the fire, demonstrating nonexistent patience. Philip slipped outside and approached Audrey, but instead of hugging Ferrington, he instructed her to conduct water purification tests. Audrey, without arguing, began analyzing chemical contents found in a jug of water. After breakfast, as packs were being strapped on sherpas' backs, Philip convened the climbing team for a morning briefing. This meeting, an obligatory requirement, consisted of Philip delivering a synopsis of what to expect in the upcoming day, announcing where they would be stopping for lunch, down to precise times for morning and afternoon breaks, ending by stating a location for that evening's campsite. After a synopsis of the flow of the day, Hornsby, in minute detail, cited potential problems, river crossings, mountain passes, and footbridges. Philip even included an analysis of mileage between destinations as well as points of interest worth noting. Smiles appeared on three faces when he announced Harry, Peter, and Clayton were to head the column, while stating that he, Pemba, and Audrey would push the expedition along from their perch at the rear of the chain. Following this formal presentation, before adjourning, Philip asked for questions, but none were forthcoming. Before adjourning, Philip reiterated that any deviations would not be tolerated.

28. A Glimpse of Chivalry

Peering at the long line of sherpas, Harry and his sons took their positions at the front. As an elongated snake of humanity slipped into the forest, and Audrey sat by the stream surrounded by vials of water and numerous chemicals. "I'm working on the experiment you ordered," she coldly stated.

"Still?" he asked incredulously.

"Forty-five additional minutes are needed to complete the water purification studies."

Philip, faced with no alternative, watched as the expedition disappeared, sitting impatiently as Audrey cultured vials analyzing bacterial content. Sensing Philip's growing annoyance at their extended delay, she purposely dallied with the experiment. This delay wasn't turning out as she had planned; secretly she had hoped stalling would provide a chance for them to be alone, talk, bond; but because Pemba stayed behind, a lack of privacy prevented intimacy.

Finishing, annoyed that they were so far behind, Philip sprung forward. Hornsby led, Pemba shadowed, and Audrey walked fifteen yards behind. Upon reaching the crest of each hill, Hornsby scanned the horizon looking for the village of Dharte Chantara, the planned launch site. By mid-morning, rests were no longer permitted, their pace quickening in an attempt to rendezvous with the expedition. Progress proved slow because a light drizzle made footing slippery as water was seeping into their boots. Far in the distance, fluffy clouds showed signs of re-emerging. At the summit of each hillside, the three eyed the distant Himalayas. But since the mountains were hundreds of miles to the north, their sharp ridges appeared as small bumps. Audrey repeatedly asked Pemba if the newest mountain to appear in the distant horizon was Everest, but the sherpa answered no. Perpetually trailing, she trudged onward. Audrey knew her sensuous charms could derail her fiancé, but she just needed to find the right moment.

After three hours on the trail, Audrey, feeling the strain of constantly trying to catch up, tripped on a root bisecting the trail. Twisting her right ankle, her leg buckled as she crumpled onto the rock strewn path. Pemba, hearing her muffled cry, backtracked. Fearing a swollen ankle would fuel Philip's wrath, Audrey slipped off her hiking boot. Pemba, seeing the ankle bulge, helplessly looked on. Hornsby returned and saw Ferrington sprawled on the ground. She apologized for her clumsiness, but, much to her surprise, Philip neither lost his temper nor seemed upset. "Accidents happen." A puffy mass bulged from her ankle. "Wiggle your toes." Audrey did as instructed. "Not broken, but the ankle needs to be wrapped." After taping the ankle, Philip helped her to her feet. "For a couple hours, maybe even a day, you'll need to minimize weight bearing." Gritting her teeth, she struggled to her feet. Telling them she'd keep up, she didn't protest when Pemba took her backpack. The march resumed, Philip re-establishing his lead, Pemba following, Audrey lagging behind. Wincing in pain, she shuffled her feet forward. Within fifteen minutes, the separation between the first and last trekker increased to over two hundred yards. Even with her ankle throbbing, Ferrington pushed forward. After forty-five minutes, the path intersected with a fast-moving river that zigzagged through a ravine. Rocks rising above the gurgling water provided a stone bridge across the waterway. Fearing another accident, Audrey eyed the passageway with fear and tried to summon the courage to forge ahead. Philip, reappearing, bounced across the rocks. Without asking, Hornsby reached down, hoisted Audrey on his back, and carried her across the slippery span.

"I was scared." Philip placed his finger across her lips after unlacing her hiking boot and slipping off her sock. A hematoma the size of a golf ball bulged from the posterior of her right ankle. Audrey tried to minimize the injury. "It looks far worse than it is . . ."

Philip, slipping one arm around Audrey's waist, carried her to the water's edge. Using a backpack as a pillow, he instructed her to lie back while immersing her bruised ankle into the frigid stream. "Cold will reduce the swelling," Philip laughed, "but how presumptuous of me. It seems ludicrous to have a layman prescribe treatment to a member of the medical team." Philip offered Audrey his canteen. "Drink, and there's no worry that the water's contaminated, I can personally vouch for the physician who did the testing." They both laughed.

Pemba watched from a distance. An hour passed as Audrey's swollen ankle dangled in the frigid water, her head nestled in Philip's lap, her sealed eyes indicating that she had surrendered to much-needed sleep. Philip instructed Pemba to depart and reunite with the main climbing party. "Tell Harry Birdwein that Audrey suffered a sprained ankle, it might be a day or two until we catch up."

29. A Parallel Trek

Kalamatra rendezvoused with Austin Morley at the bus depot at 5:30 in the morning. The expedition planner, true to his word, obtained gear and necessary permits. Before leaving Kathmandu, Morley informed the oncologist that a four-hour bus ride would bring him to Lamosangu; this small hamlet of a couple hundred people marked the end of the bumpy dirt road and the start of the hiking path into the Everest region. Before leaving, Morley cautioned the doctor to be careful; Kalamatra promised he would. As the driver of the multicolored bus honked his horn, Morley hoisted Kalamatra's two backpacks and tied them onto an outside overhead rack. Remaining odds and ends were crammed under the doctor's legs. A final passenger squeezed into the already overcrowded bus; the driver, keeping his hand on the horn, pressed through the crowd. Although his departure wasn't exactly a joyous send-off, the Greek was on his way.

Kalamatra worried that his gear would fall off the top of the bus as the vehicle wound through the tropical, terraced lands. Peasants, tilling the neighboring fields, stopped working to shield their eyes as clouds of dust billowed from the bus's non-existent exhaust system. Each pothole rattled the overcrowded vehicle as dust, seeping upward from underneath the dilapidated floorboards, mixed with the repulsive smell of dirty bodies. Inside, peasants engaged in a steady banter. Since he did not understand a word of Nepalese, Kalamatra didn't pay attention; his eyes remained riveted outside the dirty window, anxiously anticipating a first glimpse of the Himalayan giants. By the second hour, fellow passengers' eyes monitored his every move. Fleeting glances marked him an oddity; tongues circled tooth-less mouths, a woman seated directly across from him, with her goiter drooping down her neck, directly stared, her boldness unnerving. Shifting uncomfortably in his seat, their eyes met and it became a battle of wills; finally her yellowish eyes, stained beyond their years, relented and drifted away. Westerners were obviously a rarity on the Kodari Express, but Kalamatra assumed natives had seen others like him pass before them, others similarly armed with brightly colored mountain gear. Entering the third hour, the bus ride became interminable. Across the narrow aisle, and back one row, a baby whimpered. The child's mother, a heavyset woman, her face aged with dirt, offered a swollen, blackened nipple to the infant, but even that didn't help comfort the child; the baby continued wailing. Directly behind Nicholas sat a woefully thin woman, her lap piled high with trinkets and woven clothes. Throughout the entire ride, seemingly unaffected by the suffocating heat, this woman clutched the articles she'd purchased on her journey to Kathmandu. The farther they jour-neyed, the condition of the dirt road worsened, potholes forced the bus to grind to a crawl. Nicholas laughed at the oddity of the situation; this dilapidated vehicle would be his last contact with the twentieth century. After Lamsangu, the remainder of his journey into the sparsely populated back-country would be completed under human power. Unexpectedly, the bus ground to an abrupt stop. Kalamatra stood and saw sheep blocking the dirt road, the driver dealing with this roadblock by blasting the horn. Angry passengers opened windows and shouted at a small boy tending a herd, but their screams were for naught as additional sheep clogged the road. Forging a passageway by nudging the bus into the rear of the herd, the irate driver, while beeping his horn, inched the bus forward. Enraged passengers screamed at the boy who responded by shrugging his shoulders. Fifteen minutes passed and they moved fewer than fifty yards. Kalamatra laughed, the inconvenience caused by the convergence of two worlds going about their usual business amused him.

Three hours into the trip, at Dhulikhel, Kalamatra had his first glimpse of the Himalayas. Perhaps because the bus was tucked into the confines of a valley, with the peaks hundreds of miles in the distance, the mighty Himalayas did not appear nearly as awesome as expected; the snow-clad summits were mere dots. Hour four found him slumping in his seat, the blistering heat causing extensive perspiration to flow from his forehead, moisture collecting in pockets inside his clothing. Above the driver's seat a thermometer nudged past the ninety-degree mark, outside waves of heat rose from the terraced plains, an absence of trees allowing the sun's penetrating rays to bake the red earth. During the trip's final hour, an elderly man seated next to him nudged closer and closer, trying to claim additional room. Not parting with an inch of space, Kalamatra sat immobile, his mind racing. Was he here to conquer nature, to prove something to Audrey, to Hornsby, or himself? He felt conflicted about taking a leave from the hospital and worried how the children would cope with his absence. Who was there to make them smile? And what did Audrey mean to him? Why was he so infatuated? Indisputably, she triggered a reservoir of capped feelings. What possessed him to chance everything for this fool- hearted venture? His train of thought was broken when the greedy man seated next to him again attempted to claim additional space. Stopping the man from invading his space, Kalamatra poked his elbows into the man's ribs, and territorial rights were reestablished.

No sooner had he solved this problem when fellow passengers stood. Ever-watchful, instinctively distrusting, Kalamatra clasped his hands around his precious belongings. He questioned the woman behind him. "Lamosangu?" A response wasn't necessary as the bus pulled into the town. Fears surfaced upon reaching Lamosangu that someone would try to steal his knapsacks piled in the storage compartment on top of the bus. His two backpacks, each weighing over one hundred and twenty pounds, contained climbing ropes, ice picks, pitons, tents, a sleeping bag, medicines, and food. Would the assigned sherpa be waiting? How would he find him? Kalamatra would never be able to identify the sherpa; Nepalese faces melted together since all had pointed cheekbones and weathered lines accented by embedded grime. Ages were impossible to determine; the young looked old and the old ancient.

As the bus ground to a halt within the crowded marketplace, donkeys, goats and waiting families surrounded the departing passengers. Kalamatra took his place in the crowded aisle, shoving others as he grabbed his gear as it was thrown from the bus roof. Once his precious belongings were in his hands, he retreated to a deserted spot on the far side of the marketplace and watched as overloaded donkeys and yaks grunted and strained as cumbersome supply bags were strapped atop protruding ribs. Whatever was not placed on the rumps of animals was then hoisted onto human backs. Natives, transformed into beasts of burden, uttered not a single complaint as loads were strapped to every appendage, heads included. Clouds of dirt soon obscured Kalamatra's view; even though he wanted to witness more, Nicholas wouldn't chance leaving his gear unprotected as these provisions were his life-blood for the next six weeks. Impatiently, he awaited the appearance of the assigned sherpa. He wondered if his guide had been a member of a recent American expedition that scaled Ama Dablam. When he requested that his porter speak good English, Austin Morley didn't respond. Kalamatra relished the idea of nights spent seated by the campfire listening as the sherpa shared tales of previous expeditions. Ever since he made up his mind that he was going to Everest, Nicholas read book after book familiarizing himself with the sherpas. From his reading, he knew that any attempt on Everest without a seasoned guide was pure folly. Known for their ability to serve as high-altitude porters, the sherpas were indigenous to the Solu Khumbu region—the mountainous highlands that surround Everest. World-renowned for their mountain-climbing expertise, the sherpas possessed an uncanny ability to acclimate, with apparently little or no strain, to altitudes over 26,000 feet. It was a sherpa, Tenzing Norgay, who accompanied the New Zealander, Sir Edmund Hillary, in the initial conquest of Everest. Hillary even afforded Norgay the honor of being the first to stand atop the world's highest summit, a politically wise decision that helped keep Nepal's border open.

Anxious minutes passed while he sat waiting. A midday sun roasted the hard, packed dirt; but the sherpa did not appear. Kalamatra kept wondering if he could have made a mistake. Could he have misunderstood Colonel Morley? The details of the rendezvous sifted through his mind. Unkel, the assigned sherpa, was to meet him at the marketplace adjoining the bus. Why was his guide not here? The delay left him perplexed and agitated. A young boy approached, but Kalamatra paid little attention, in the wilderness it was commonplace for a Westerner to be the object of curious stares. But this particular adolescent was far bolder than others. "Stop staring!" Nicholas shouted. "And go away!"

Not put off by his threats, the boy paced back and forth, "Churot Katatcha nun." The youngster took yet another step toward the climber.

Kalamatra raised himself into a retaliatory position as the boy closed to an arm's distance.

"Unkel! Unkel!" the youngster muttered. Nicholas shook his head in disbelief, the adolescent confirming his identity by pulling out a telegram issued by Colonel Morley of the Machapuchare Trekking Company. Kalamatra cursed his ill fortune; where was the seasoned guide he had been promised? Where was the experience of age, the wisdom of previous mountain expeditions? Where was the leathered skin, the knowledgeable, penetrating eyes, the experienced leader into whose hands his life would be entrusted? Shabbily dressed in a worn, hole-ridden garment, a mere boy, no more than sixteen, stood before him. The oncologist expected a tower of strength, but instead got an adolescent. The youth's matted hair was cropped short beneath his frayed cap; his small frame was frail and underweight. Cursing his luck, the Greek watched as Unkel, readjusting straps, secured his small bundle atop one of the two backpacks. Within moments, the child indicated he was ready by pointing to the trail. Enraged, Kalamatra broke twigs between his fingertips, deliberating whether the odds were stacked against him and that there was no choice but to abandon the journey. Accompanied by a mere boy, any notion of seriously tackling Everest bordered on madness. Standing, he eyed the sherpa. Unkel put his hand on the slightly larger pack; Kalamatra leaned over and hoisted the massive load skyward so Unkel could slip into the shoulder pads. Muscles in the sherpa's face grew taut as he tightened the straps. Nicholas lifted his pack, surprised to find that Unkel redistributed the weight, adding the heavy climbing equipment to his own pack, thus decreasing the poundage the doctor had to carry.

Unkel began walking.

"Did I tell you to lead?" Kalamatra shouted.

The sherpa pointed to the trail.

Kalamatra pulled alongside the neophyte. He examined his supposed guide; the boy's hands were calloused, dirt embedded beneath his split fingernails, grime glued to pores in his face, an unpleasant film caked into his neck; if his eyes didn't convey a softness that demonstrated his adolescent years, Unkel could have passed for a man twice his age.

"Let's get this straight, you'll follow my directions!" The Greek was adamant that an order of command was to be clearly understood.

"Atcha!"

"Where are you from?"

"Taboche. Outside Pangboche, north of Namche Bazaar."

The name of the first town meant nothing but Kalamatra was certainly familiar with Namche Bazaar. This information was at least partially comforting; while he was only a boy, at least he was a sherpa.

"Where did you learn English?"

"Be a guide, must speak!"

"How old are you?"

"Sixteen."

"Ever been on a trek before?"

"Yes."

"Once?"

"No, three." The boy looked at Kalamatra. "Unkel lead?"

Nicholas granted him permission, figuring that when Unkel weakened, he would be in a position to assist.

After leaving the bus depot, the dirt trail rose gradually for nearly three miles to the small village of Perkoo. Shortly after Perkoo, the path sharply descended toward the Bhote Kosi River. Before journeying across the narrow rope bridge that spanned the fast-moving stream, Unkel paused. Kalamatra eyed the passageway. With each gust of wind the makeshift bridge swayed, its wooden planks precariously balancing only a few feet over the tumbling rapids. Summoning the courage to cross, Kalamatra, trying to breathe life into his lethargic body, stood by the river's edge and dunked his head into the cold stream. Even though the stream appeared crystal clear, Kalamatra did not allow himself the luxury of a thirst-quenching gulp as drinking untreated water ran a risk of contracting a debilitating parasite. Worried that he'd plunge headlong into the water, Kalamatra instructed Unkel to proceed. Nicholas stared in amazement. The sherpa bounced across the span, at times not even grasping the rope railings. Kalamatra hesitantly followed, his hands clutching the frayed ropes while his eyes peered between cracks in the rotted log at the current tumbling below. After forging the passage, Kalamatra plopped himself on the opposing shore, feeling thoroughly delighted.

By early afternoon, muscles the oncologist never knew existed rebelled. Although he wanted to quit for the day, Unkel, fifteen yards ahead, kept up a slow but methodical pace. Embarrassed but unwilling to be shamed by a mere boy, Kalamatra refused to ask for needed rests. By mid-afternoon, not a whisper or wind or a single cloud in the sky diffused the sun's intense heat, the sweltering temperatures and insufferable humidity forcing Nicholas to strip to shorts and boots. Doggedly he continued, always in Unkel's shadow. Sweat coated his body, grime sticking to his hairy chest. Adjusting his backpack, his shoulders felt as if they were hammered by nails. By late afternoon, the gap between them widened, stretching to almost a half-mile. He lost sight of the sherpa but was too tired to care; Nicholas put one foot ahead of the other. Up a hill, down a hill, up, down, despondently he eyed each rise in elevation. Sinking to his knees, breathing labored, thighs screaming with pain, the oncologist's eyes pleaded to close. Slumping to the ground, he crouched, shielding his face between raised knees. The oncologist struggled to his feet, each step requiring a monumental effort. Arriving at the next stream, the oncologist eyed logs and a thin railing spanning the turbulent current. Kalamatra watched in dismay as Unkel comfortably moved across the slippery timbers. Lacking any courage at the moment, he was reduced to creeping along the timbers on his hands and knees. The thoroughly exhausted doctor removed his pack before collapsing on velvet moss adjoining the riverbed on the other bank. "High," the sherpa pointed to a hill. "Campsite!"

"Stop! Finished for the day! I couldn't imagine a more perfect campsite, plenty of water, wood nearby, soft grass." Unkel remained glued to a knoll high on the adjoining hillside as Nicholas let his weary feet dangle in the stream. Basking in the delight of the moment, the doctor's eyes closed. Periodically glancing upward, he worried that Unkel might have deserted him. Sitting on the hillside, the sherpa urged him to come closer, but Nicholas refused to move. If Unkel wanted them to be together, it was the sherpa who would have to capitulate. Morley warned him in Kathmandu that disrespectful behavior amongst the sherpas was becoming increasingly common; so, at the onset, he was determined to set the tone. The doctor screamed, "We're camping here by this stream for the night." Kalamatra avoided mentioning that the hill looming directly in their path sealed his decision.

Repeatedly, Unkel pointed to the adjoining hillside but every bone in the physician's aching body cried for a much-needed rest. Disobeying orders, Unkel refused to leave the embankment. Nicholas yelled but the mutinous sherpa wouldn't budge. Perched on the hillside, Unkel erected a tent, and then pushed rocks together to form a fireplace before scavenging for wood. If his legs weren't throbbing so badly, Nicholas would have gone after the disobedient sherpa. As the last remnant of the sun was disappearing, the doctor lay slumped in the lush velvet moss. Although dusk brought no relief from the hot, humid temperature, he closed his eyes within minutes.

Upon awakening, hordes of gnats swarmed. Irritated by these tiny pests, Nicholas waved his hands while feverishly rubbing his eyes. As darkness settled, the air became thick with no-see-ums. Gnats crawled into his hair, invaded ears, darted into nostrils. Flinging his arms brought no relief. Finally, it dawned on him, for his first night on the trail he chose an insect hollow as his home. Stuffing gear into a backpack, he stumbled upward to join Unkel on higher ground.

Sleep proved impossible as endless scenarios flooded his mind. Tossing and thrashing, Kalamatra sat by the tent's opening, his face peering into the darkness. After years of inactivity, how could he challenge the world's highest peak when after only one day's march every bone in his body ached? A lack of experience would also certainly rear its head later on the mountain, when technical experience was necessary, and few lessons from his youth would suffice. Ludicrous is what it was, but Ferrington was no different, her experience was as limited as his. Neither would reach the summit; it was journeying together that would drive him forward.

A vague pinkish hue creeping across the eastern horizon rescued him. Soon as the sun's rays provided sufficient light to dismantle the tent, Kalamatra, exhausted but anxious to proceed, dislodged the tent stakes even though Unkel was still wrapped within his sleeping bag. The sherpa stared in bewilderment at the Westerner's bizarre antics. Although it was barely past five in the morning, Unkel crept from his bedding and reluctantly prepared a breakfast of biscuits and hot tea. After eating, Nicholas stood by the trail while Unkel packed the cooking utensils. The oncologist paced anxiously, driven to see Ferrington and the surprise in her eyes. They were not catching anyone if they didn't get moving. Annoyed at the sherpa's procrastination, Kalamatra's hands motioned for Unkel to lead. Displeased at the idea of being on the trail before the sun made its first appearance, Unkel squatted by the smoldering fire, holding his ground. Deciding he wasn't marching until the sun appeared, the sherpa propped himself against the stump of a hollow tree. Waving his arms, Kalamatra urged the sherpa to begin, but Unkel pointed to mist enveloping the river, a reminder that night still lingered. Battle lines were drawn, but short of manhandling him, there was no way Kalamatra could change the sherpa's mutinous stance. Hovering above the defiant adolescent, the oncologist paced back and forth. Since the American expedition had a multi-day head start, Nicholas reasoned that if they were to catch the main party, extreme measures would have to be taken. Nicholas's eyes pleaded with Unkel. Finally relenting, the sherpa rose to his feet and proceeded into the thick soup. Dense ground fog necessitated slowing their pace to a crawl, yet they forged ahead.

Kalamatra's instincts proved correct; an hour after commencing the march, a blazing sun burnt through the fog revealing a deep turquoise-blue sky. As their pace accelerated, Nicholas felt rejuvenated. During the entire morning, Kalamatra remained a couple of yards behind Unkel, assured he could pass the sherpa at will. By mid-morning, without the doctor uttering a complaint, the two reached the small hamlet of Nihalley. Kalamatra felt that while retuning his body was a necessity, a hiatus between his youth scampering hillsides in Greece, and years spent forging a sedentary medical career could be overcome. He envisioned himself as an old warrior; battle gear needed a couple days of physical retooling. What he presently lacked in muscle tone and endurance he made up for in unbridled enthusiasm, the word *no* never entering his vocabulary.

By noon Unkel stopped and loosened the straps of his pack. "Here, lunch, family in hut have chang." A wide grin formed around the sherpa's pointed cheekbones. "It good."

"What?" Nicholas had no idea what Unkel was talking about.

"Chang?"

Unkel explained, as best as Kalamatra could tell, that chang, a locally-brewed delicacy, was a combination of hot-buttered rum and fermented beer.

"Me go chang."

Nicholas replied, "Water with iodine pills will do!"

The sherpa deposited his pack by a rock and, canteen in hand, entered a nearby hut. While waiting, Kalamatra stripped off his backpack and sprawled against the flat side of a rock, the shade of an overhanging laurel providing relief from a beating sun. Perspiration dripped from his body, rest providing an opportunity to figure a way to catch up with the Everest expedition. Even at the breakneck speed they were traveling, they could make up three, maybe four days, but if they stayed on the same path there was no way they would catch the climbing party. Examining the topographical maps, his eyes focused on a vast desert stretching hundreds of miles to the south. A plan emerged; traversing across the flat plains of the Terai was faster than pounding up and down repetitive foothills. Besides which, either route, whether through the Terai or the foothills, would deposit him at the entrance to the Solu Khumbu region. Both had drawbacks; trekking through the foothills was far longer, while venturing across the desert would prove hot. Weighing alternatives, a decision wouldn't have to be made until they reached Yarsa. At this small village, still a couple of days ahead, the path divided; he would either stay on the conventional traveled northern route or leave the mountains and skirt across the upper extremity of the desert.

While musing over this plan, Unkel returned, a broad smile painted across his face. Beaming, his body swaying, Kalamatra assumed that Unkel had not only located the chang, but indulged himself with a liberal sampling.

"Remove that flannel shirt," Kalamatra barked.

"I fine." A sheepish grin spread across the adolescent's grime-encrusted face.

"It's too damn hot to be wearing so many clothes."

"Find chang."

"Take off that shirt!"

"No."

Kalamatra shrugged. "Wear the shirt if you want, but don't sit near me." A stench emanating from a corpse was mild in comparison to the sherpa's pungent odor; was it a native rule that circles of dirt must permanently stain necks?

"Want drink?" Unkel shoved a jug of chang toward him.

"No!" Nicholas spat.

"Chang!" There was urgency in the sherpa's voice as he thrust a half-filled canteen toward Nicholas. Kalamatra relented, but after one gulp of the vile liquid he spit out the putrid mixture. Returning the canteen, the sherpa drained the remaining contents.

While they didn't constitute what veteran mountaineers would consider a well-oiled expedition, and no prominent organization was sponsoring their journey, no business concerns donated equipment, nor were commercial endorsements plastered on clothing, Nicholas Batiste Kalamatra felt success was theirs for the offering. Even though he remained cautiously suspicious, he felt an odd warmth for his sixteen-year-old companion; fate thrust them together, the two would defy conventional wisdom.

That night Kalamatra let Unkel choose the campsite. Chatter and banter accompanied their dinner. Unkel, struggling with his limited English, told him of his family background, his desire to one day attend school, and an ambition to read and write. As the night turned cold, stars glittered overhead, yet both stayed by the fireplace. Alternately, both threw twigs into the smoldering embers, watching as wooden sticks burst into multi-colored flames. Nicholas entertained the sherpa with magic tricks; Unkel's eyes gleamed in delight, just like kids in the hospital.

The next morning a vicious wind tore through the trees strewing debris across the trail. Under normal circumstances they would have rested for the day, inclement weather forcing a postponement, but Kalamatra wouldn't hear of a delay. Marching through low fog, their trek resembled a roller coaster—up, down, up, down; the trail meandering through thickets of rhododendrons only to plunge back into valleys. Late afternoon, well past a reasonable time to quit for the day, found them still on the trail. A small consolation was that at sunset, the sun made its first appearance as a northern breeze stirred through tree branches. Unkel led, but the trail, cluttered by tangled rhododendron stems, hampered the sherpa's progress. Unkel knew not to complain as the sun descended across the western horizon. Forced to use a machete to cut through the strangling underbrush, whenever the sherpa paused to clear the trail, Kalamatra's weakening body propped against a rock. Each rest period seemed like a fleeting moment, the trek disintegrating into a series of breaks in which a prone position was the Greek's favorite. Unkel backtracked to where the doctor was slumped on the ground; as enthusiasm fueled the doctor to stand, his body rebelled and within minutes he was on his back. Willing himself to his feet and refusing to give up, the Greek doctor pushed on. Staying fifteen yards in front, the sherpa continuously waited. After each break, Unkel resumed marching, his mechanized gait never varying. In a burst of energy, Kalamatra tried to pull closer.

Head down, arms pumping, and heart pounding, he narrowed the gap to five yards before plowing into the sherpa's back.

"Keep going," he burst! "Don't for a moment think I'm giving up!"

"Look there!" Unkel pointed.

Seventy yards up the trail at the apex of the hill, an elderly, meticulously coiffed Japanese man sat in a portable chair eating a sandwich, a napkin spread across his lap. A hand employed a rhododendron leaf as a fan to temper the late afternoon heat. The doctor went ballistic. After a couple days of trekking, how could this man have ventured this distance? Fifteen feet from where the Japanese man sat, Nicholas halted. Sweat dripped from the oncologist's brow; his legs trembled; every bone in his body ached. Yet unmistakably, before him sat an old man dressed in an open-collared silk shirt, sagging brown knee pants, a burnt orange bandana around his neck, a camera by his side. As Kalamatra drew near, the man offered him half of his sandwich.

Nicholas moved closer.

"Less wind now, bad earlier today," the man said.

"How long have you been here?" Kalamatra interrogated. How was it possible, with no roads, no access other than human power? How could this elderly gentleman have ventured to this point? What was especially galling, while sweat and dirt coated Kalamatra's arms and neck, the Japanese man's pale yellow, silk shirt revealed not even the slightest wrinkle. Gritting his teeth, Nicholas tried to contain his seething rage.

"Are you part of the American expedition?"

Nicholas hesitated. "When did you last see them?"

"Three, four, maybe five days ago."

"You're traveling alone?" Nicholas inquired.

"Five porters accompany me. Earlier today they went to Nihalley for a couple of hours." The gentleman's precise diction bespoke his refinement. The elderly Japanese man explained he lived in Kyoto, was widowed for the past eight years, and before retiring, made his living manufacturing fabric for export to foreign countries. Hobbies included daily walks and collecting miniature railroad cars.

"Why did you come here?" Nicholas wondered aloud.

A proud smile spread across his face as he shared his dream of seeing Everest before his death. "In five miles the trail rises abruptly, a small Buddhist shrine sits on the crest of the hill, there, without binoculars, you can see Everest." Wishing Kalamatra a safe journey, he said he'd pray for him. Kalamatra tightened the ties on his gear and departed. At the top of the next hill, he turned and watched as five Nepalese men, surrounding the Japanese gentleman, lifted him onto a wooden platform and, employed as human mules, hauled him down the trail.

30. Harry's Win

Ferrington feared her injury would inflame Hornsby, but her fiancé's response took her by surprise. Audrey stayed on Philip's shoulders the entire afternoon. Although hardly speaking a word, she relished that her injury produced a silver lining; the two would, out of necessity, have a night alone—an evening she'd make sure they'd remember. After depositing his fiancée on the ground, Hornsby—cook, companion, medic—set up a campsite.

"Whether you're a U.S. Senator or I'm a physician with a large medical practice, promise me there will be time for us."

Shaking his head he said, "Here? Now? Ferrington, there's a more appropriate time and place. Our time will come . . ." He wasn't able to finish the words before Audrey slipped off her shirt. It took coaxing and cajoling, but her efforts proved successful. Her part of their partnership was to pry open doors. Ferrington accepted that nobody ended up with a perfect life, but she never thought of herself as a nobody—she wanted it all. For the first time since she left Kathmandu they both went to sleep satisfied.

By five a.m., at the first hint of light, she was perched on Philip's shoulders again. By ten a.m., at Dharti Chantara, the two caught the main party as they were finishing packing their campsite. Porters looked in bewilderment as Philip, with Audrey strapped atop his shoulders, trudged between bundles being roped together. Sherpas applauded Hornsby's heroic effort. Entering the morning briefing, Philip reported that with another day's rest Ferrington would be fine after twisting her ankle. Before the procession left, he instructed Harry, "Stop for the night immediately before the Lamjura Pass. Under no circumstances," Hornsby made it clear, "attempt to reach the top." The meeting ended and four hundred figures took their assigned places. Harry Birdwein's stout figure proudly in the lead.

With his sons flanking him, Harry Birdwein relished pioneering the route. By mid-morning, a combination of heat and humidity obliterated the endless line of marchers as the procession wound its way from hillside to valley to hillside. Not a whisper of wind sifted through branches, and even with a temperature soaring past one hundred degrees, nothing was going to stop the lead climbers. After a brief lunch, Harry Birdwein was the first on his feet, focused on keeping the entourage moving. Four hours of daylight remained when the caravan reached the Lamjura Pass. Birdwein eyed the steady incline to the top of the pass as clouds, momentarily parting, revealed a deep blue sky. Bathed in afternoon sunlight, the razor-sharp mountains shimmered in the distance. Given these ideal circumstances, Harry instructed Clayton and Peter that it was senseless to stop. Standing at the base of the hillside, waiting as the entourage plowed onward, neither Harry, Peter, nor Clayton gave credence to Philip's earlier stern warnings to set up campsites before the pass. Clayton Johnson and Peter Birdwein greeted the decision to proceed by slapped their father on the back. As they scaled the Lamjura Pass, clouds lifted. After two hours of marching, Harry was the first to triumphantly reach the top. Delight emanated from his eyes as columns of sherpas joined them. Removing his pack, Harry felt a euphoric surge that comes from besting a day's expectations; he and his sons slapping hands for a job well done. That night the mood at the campsite was joyous; the sherpas, liberally indulging in chang, sat around the fire listening as Harry and his sons sang a terrible rendition of "Home on the Range."

31. Dissent

Trekking by moonlight, Hornsby and Ferrington rejoined the main party early the next morning. Waiting for the expedition members to convene for their usual morning briefing, Philip barely touched his food. Conversation was nonexistent as Hornsby sat fuming that his orders weren't followed. Although the expedition successfully navigated the Lamjura Pass, he shared no joy at their accomplishment; spontaneous decisions courted problems.

Clayton broke the awkward silence. "Base Camp should be established within a week."

Philip angrily glared at Clayton. "Before we begin, let's set the record straight. Harry, you had no business pushing ahead!"

"An opportunity presented itself," Clayton interceded.

Peter also came to his father's defense. "Our action pushed us ahead an entire day."

"That is not the point," Philip retorted.

Clayton interjected, "You getting annoyed doesn't minimize our accomplishments."

Philip confronted Harry. "From now on when we agree on a destination, you and your cowboy sons abide by set plans."

"Philip," Johnson exclaimed, "Now that things are being said in the open, I'm sick of you and your asinine rules; mandatory lunch stops in native huts, endless planning, needless over-regimentation. Take your rules and cram them!"

Philip retorted, "Stop being naïve! We're here to succeed." He faced the Birdweins with glaring disdain. Clayton rose and left the tent. By the time the meeting was adjourned, Harry and Peter were both thoroughly chastised. They left the gathering in silence.

An hour later, the expedition departed; only Ferrington and Philip remained behind. Audrey rested all day; by early evening, her ankle felt better. Standing, feeling no pain, she grabbed Philip's hand and cajoled him to leave his work and join her. Proving she was fit to rejoin the march, although limping, she led him toward a riverbank. The gurgling sound of a nearby stream broke their silence. Venturing into the thick underbrush, Audrey tried to locate the stream's source and Philip reluctantly followed. A little more than twenty yards off the path, Audrey stumbled upon a fast flowing stream. Removing her shirt, she liberally doused icy water over her face, shoulders, and between her breasts. Waving her arms, she encouraged Philip to join her, but Hornsby stood, arms staunchly crossed, hands riveted to his hips.

"Come on, loosen up," Ferrington chided. "I owe you one," she teased, "it's not every man who would carry me." She removed the rest of her clothes and ventured ankle-deep into the stream. Splashing the glacial water onto her body, the frigid water ignited a spark of life. She mused over the novelty of the situation—mud caking her neck, fingernails hidden under a coat of grime, a dense six days' growth of hair bristling on her legs. Impulsively, she turned and dove headlong into the stream.

Wiping water from her face, she coaxed Phillip. "Join me, even our great leader is entitled to a little relaxation." Teasingly she splashed water, her breasts breaking free from the stream as droplets of water danced down her shoulders.

"I need to get back to the campsite, there's still work to do."

"Philip, stop being so damn serious. Besides," she held her hand towards him, "if you choose to remain dirty, that's your business, but nothing could be more urgent at this moment than helping clean me."

As he removed his clothes and inched into the frigid river, her eyes feasted on his muscle-bound body. She splashed water over him, the numbing coldness forced both to quickly lather and shampoo. After cleaning, both shivering, they nestled into the moss beside the river's bank, the sounds of their laughter could be heard over the gurgling stream. Audrey teased Philip with her visions of his being the intrepid vagabond, the Jack London of the twentieth century, the fearless warrior. With moonlight glistening off the supple curves of her sculpted hips, she playfully leaned over and began nibbling on his neck.

"You are one beautiful woman," Philip admired, "I almost . . .

"Forgot?" Audrey looked at him seductively. He sat beside her as her hands kneaded his muscles, fingers massaging his scalp and neck. Audrey, her legs straddling him, playfully added, "Come on, hero, smile. Believe me, I knew I wasn't marrying a frivolous man, but I have a small contribution to add to our relationship." She nibbled on his ear. "It's called fun!"

32. Chasing Passion

Two more days of arduous trekking brought them no closer to catching the American expedition. Each time Nicholas struggled to reach the crest of the next hill, the trail wound down into another valley to face yet another hill. Valleys, all bowl-shaped, were nestled within bellies of protective mountains; all had similar rows of thatched huts crowded within small clearings on the valley floor. No matter how steep the incline, Kalamatra marveled at how local tribespeople cultivated every inch of available ground. Somehow, these resourceful people converted lands native to broad-leaved evergreens into rows containing rice, potato, and barley. Even without the benefit of modern mechanization, the peasants ingeniously created an efficient system of reservoirs, as terraces lining the hillsides trapped afternoon showers. This strange landscape was a far cry from the massive glaciers and towering peaks that he imagined would accompany his journey. Stunted alpine shrubs, yaks clinging to steep terrain, vertical, razor-sharp rock walls, and snow-capped peaks were nowhere to be seen.

By the morning of day four on the trail, ever hopeful of gaining ground, the doctor quickened the pace. But his renewed efforts brought little reward. Doggedly staying on the dusty trail, instead of trekking the usual five to six hours, Unkel and Kalamatra pushed ahead upwards of ten to twelve hours a day, but their efforts did not produce any sign of the American expedition. Refusing to accept that their lead was too large, they trekked while the sun set and sweat coated their bodies. Unkel no longer had to coax the doctor. Kalamatra refused to quit until darkness made farther passage impossible.

As Unkel prepared dinner, the oncologist, eyes glued to topographical maps, formulated a plan. In order to catch the Americans, drastic measures would have to be taken; it felt necessary to venture off the established trail and journey into the Terai, an expansive desert spreading south of the Himalayan foothills. While the heat would be oppressive, this route could cut days from their trip. Tomorrow, upon reaching Yarsa, if they headed due south and walked across the northern boundary of the Terai, they could return to the trail many miles past the Lamjura Pass and either be ahead, within eyesight, or, at worst, no more than a day or two behind the American caravan.

"Unkel, we are not going over the pass at Yarsa." Kalamatra's eyes remained riveted to the topographical maps.

Unkel's eyebrows lifted, a line of surprise etched across the bridge of his nose. "Quit? Go back?"

"Absolutely not!" Nicholas chuckled.

Confused, Unkel countered, "but trail goes . . ."

"There is another route. See for yourself!" Kalamatra spread topographical maps on the dusty path.

"One trail!" Unkel pointed to dotted lines on the map. "Go mountains!"

"We'll never catch them; this route will save time!"

Unkel shook his head. "No go!" Grains of dust nervously sifted through Unkel's willowy fingers.

"Perhaps you don't understand." Nicholas stood, towering above the sherpa. "I'm not asking you; I'm telling you!" Nicholas, irritated at Unkel's balking, chided the sherpa. "You're afraid, aren't you?"

"Wet in high land before Terai . . ."

"Is it the Terai or the surrounding swamps that scare you?"

"Both." The directness of the sherpa's answer surprised Kalamatra. Suddenly, he understood Unkel's apprehension. Renowned as a mountain tribe, sherpas were afraid to leave familiar terrain.

Unkel nervously broke sticks while feeding the fire. "Dust, much heat . . ."

"We will wake early, trek from five-thirty until ten in the morning, take a long rest for lunch, then, after four in the afternoon, resume marching." Ending the conversation, Nicholas stuffed the topographical map into his backpack. Excited by this change in plans and delighted that a respite from these hills was in sight, he ate every drop of the gruel on his plate, then entered the tent. His thoughts turned to Audrey, of holding her, of winning her love. Damned if he wasn't going to see if their momentary fling could be kindled, transformed, expanded. The woman had flair and vitality, and he possessed a reservoir of pent-up feelings clamoring to be shared. Years of walling himself off were suddenly crumbling; he was no longer voluntarily taking a path of isolation. Wooing her found him heading for Everest; laughter erupted; someone else's obsession was his folly, the thought of setting a foot on Everest's yellow band or even crossing the dreaded Solo Khumbu ice field sent shivers down his spine. Scaling a rock face was an absurdity; the only reason he was in this wilderness was to pursue a woman who ignited a flame inside of him and nothing would prevent him from exploring his feelings. Maybe their relationship would grow, maybe not, but for sure, nothing ventured, nothing gained.

33. Tradition and Culture

Her diagnosis was correct; within two days, her ankle sufficiently healed. As Philip and Audrey joined the main party, Hornsby assumed control. All details were monitored. The expedition pushing forward at a snail's pace was in accord with her fiancée's plans. His remedy for there being a constant irritant was to put the Birdweins in the front, a position from which their bitching couldn't be heard.

Early mornings proved the most taxing for Peter and Clayton. Up before daybreak, dressed and ready to proceed, the two paced waiting as the massive arsenal was fed, packs secured, and tents dismantled. Two to three hours of valuable daylight were wasted before an inch was gained. Adding fuel to the fire, Philip's ultra-conservative objectives for the day infuriated them. Each afternoon the expedition would come to a grinding halt while hours of daylight still remained. But what galled Peter and Clayton the most was Philip's edict that to capture the authenticity of their journey all members of the high-altitude climbing party needed to eat lunch in a native hut along the path.

Harry Birdwein sensed a confrontation was in the making; the next day his prophecy proved true. Shortly before noon, upon arriving at the designated lunch stop, while other team members took off packs and entered the hut, Peter and Clayton defiantly paced outside. The sun was intense, air crisp, but the morning pace, dismally slow, found them waiting more than walking. Brimming with energy, Clayton snapped, "We're not going inside!"

Peter faced his father. "These lunches are done so Philip will have abundant photographs for background material for a documentary capturing the lifestyle of these nomads."

"Hornsby says it is a necessary tradition, otherwise we risk alienating the local inhabitants." Their dad's retort lacked conviction.

"Harry," Peter glared, "if you go inside today, that's your choice, but we're not joining you. Both of us are sick of Hornsby's dictatorial ways."

Choosing not to comment, Philip took note of Peter and Clayton's absence from lunch. While waiting to be served, Philip whispered to Harry that it was his responsibility that two young maverick climbers cooperate with team rules. Birdwein nodded but didn't leave the hut. Harry eyed his hosts squatting beside the open hearth; the family's ages spanned generations. A fifty-year-old grandmother, who looked ninety, had a three-month-old infant in her lap while tending an open fire, beside her a half-dozen of the infant's brothers and sisters played on the packed dirt floor. A robust, pudgy-faced woman, presumably the mother, squatted over the flames, her fingers slicing potatoes into sizzling grease. Preparing lunch was a family affair; two of the adolescent girls repeatedly beat the boiled potatoes into a smooth, thick consistency while a younger brother slapped the leather-like chicpates against flattened rocks. The smallest of the children, a toddler, fed dead branches into the flames as the mother flipped the flattened potatoes into the vat. Philip and Audrey waited for their food as two cameramen, scampering inside the hut, filmed this supposedly quaint lunch.

"Chicpates," Pemba looked directly at Harry. "How many?" Not answering, his eyes remained glued to the muscular forearm of the woman stirring the thick potato mush. Black smoke surrounded her as smoke billowed toward the hut's ceiling. Shrugging his shoulders, the expedition's co-leader edged closer to the wooden staircase, expecting, hoping, that at any moment Peter and Clayton would join the group. Staring through slats of the second story to the ground floor he watched as yaks, chickens, and donkeys milled together. As the grandmother dished globs of food into hardened clay bowls, Harry sat perplexed, wondering why an open hearth sat squarely in the middle of a second-story room that had no chimney. Overhead smoldering wood produced black smoke that clung to wooden ceiling beams. Instead of having an exhaust system to funnel billowing smoke out the thatched roof, smoke accumulated in ever-thickening layers until gradually drifting downward toward three small window openings. Coughing, Harry stayed as low as possible as smoke drifted toward the floor. Leave, stay, bolt, a battle raged inside his head. Peering through the cracks in the mud wall, Harry gazed at the neighboring forest. Books about Everest glamorized living with native families; the march to the mountain was an opportunity to experience natives' lives, share their food and lodging, enjoy their simplicity. No mention was made of the filth, the ever-present chance of contracting cholera, diphtheria, or hepatitis. Reports filtering back to the West emphasized the spiritual calmness of the Nepalese people. Birdwein supposed he'd probably only remember what he'd romanticize; already he could envision himself glorifying these abhorrent surroundings, describing the dirt as colorful, the choking smoke as authentic, and, on the ground dirt floor, dried animal feces as a small price to pay to be part of a working farm. But at that moment, he longed for his sons and their special camaraderie. A decision was made; he stood abruptly and descended the wooden staircase; if the price of success included alienating his sons, that tariff was unacceptable.

Standing outside, he gazed upward. Eyeing the surrounding granite walls, he detected a slight movement in a rock overhang rising due east of the hut. Staring as sunlight reflected off the wall, he couldn't believe what he was seeing . . . about two thirds of the way up the five hundred foot cliff Peter and Clayton clawed upwards. Glancing downward, they saw Harry's solitary figure, their father's hand waved, motioning to them to continue. Upstairs word spread, climbers on the wall; lunch halted as spectators scampered outside to gawk. Within minutes, the audience below was composed not only of Harry, but hundreds of porters, sherpas, as well as Ferrington and Hornsby. Philip, his pursed lips registering his indignation, watched with his eyes riveted to binoculars. Clayton and Peter chose to free-climb rather than hammer safety bolts into the wall. Their fingertips adhered to minute granite sleeves while toes located footholds no larger than half dollars. Even though the wall was lined with minute fissures, it was mere child's play to these two accomplished climbers. Within minutes, the exhibition ended when both men sat atop the rock. Perched together, arms draping over each other's shoulders, the climbers' laughter echoed down the mountainside.

Once off the face, Philip confronted the two. "That was a foolish stunt! Either of you could have been hurt and an injury would have jeopardized the entire mission."

"Philip," Audrey tried to mediate, "nothing happened!"

"To begin with, their place was inside, with us! They know the rule."

Peter turned and faced Philip. "Unless I'm wrong, my father is the co-leader of this expedition."

Philip turned and confronted Harry. "Did you give them permission?"

"No." Birdwein answered.

Philip shot back. "Harry, if you're going to lead, then lead! Stop acting like a scared puppy wagging his tail between his legs. Don't be afraid to confront your sons for fear it might bruise their fragile egos." Philip turned and marched off. Left together, Harry, Clayton, and Peter spontaneously laughed. Not a word was exchanged during dinner that evening.

34. *Doubt or Love*

In the middle of the night Audrey threw on clothes and left the tent. Intermittent rain and dense fog hung over the campsite as she positioned herself beside command headquarters. With rain seeping inside her jacket, water puddling around her boots, for the better part of a half-hour she stood outside the doorway. Through the transparent orange nylon walls, she watched Philip; she desperately wanted to talk, to understand him, to be held, but unable to summon the courage to confront her fiancé, she walked across the campsite and took refuge in a barn. Chickens, scurrying between her legs, nudged between her feet. She tried to coax the animals outside, but they too sought protection against the rain. An hour passed as Audrey sat huddled, peering into the pelting rain. She couldn't fathom what on earth could cause Philip to work all night, but there he sat, hour after hour squatting over a table, pen in hand, a kerosene lamp providing scant illumination as he calculated and recalculated the necessary trips to stock the mountain. Her mind kept replaying the day's altercation, the tension at dinner unbearable as the Birdwein clan and Philip didn't exchange a single word. But what irked her the most was the sting behind his stern words. She kept wondering, who exactly was she marrying? Did she love him? Like him? Was Philip capable of love? Even though their relationship wasn't perfect, she found comfort in his immense strength, his accomplishments, his mind, his drive to succeed, and their lifestyle. But should or could there be more? Doubts prompted her to burst into Philip's tent. "We must talk!"

"You're up late." He adjusted his bifocals.

She stood shivering.

"What time is it?" he asked.

"Late enough that yours is the only light on."

"Why are you here?"

Audrey blurted, "The argument today, why did you humiliate Harry in front of his sons?"

"He was indecisive."

"Ease the tension. Send Clayton and Peter ahead. Let them forge a route through the ice flow."

"At an appropriate time." Hornsby refolded the maps before him. "Right now, they need to be reprimanded and reminded who is in charge."

35. A Curse

After the first sign of morning light, Nicholas sprang into the lead. The two hours required to reach Yarsa passed quickly. Reaching the outskirts of the village, the trail split; the wider, more traveled northern route spiraled into the mountains, while a seldom-used narrow path meandered southward, first passing through marshlands then abruptly descending into the desert. He anticipated that if they walked steadily, they would reach the outskirts of the Terai by nightfall. Unkel shook his head in disgust as Kalamatra charged down the narrow debris-strewn path. Reluctantly the sherpa followed.

The late afternoon sky was filled with color as billowing clouds collided with the lavenders of the departing sun. Abrupt changes became evident in the landscape surrounding the trail—hollies and bayberries now lined the path replacing the more prevalent laurels and oaks of the higher regions. Rhododendrons, so plentiful on the established route, were no longer traveling companions. Hour after hour slipped by, but energized that his innovative plan would reap its rewards, Kalamatra plowed forward. Behind him, head down, eyes glued to his threadbare sneakers, his cheekbones taut, the sherpa trailed. It was past eight in the evening when the effects of the sweltering humidity, combined with nearly fifteen hours on the trail, took their toll on the oncologist. Oppressive heat forced him to remove his shirt; his breathing became labored. Clad in boots and khaki shorts, he pressed on as hot, heavy, still air congested the path. Perspiration covered every inch of his body, yet he doggedly persisted. Unkel, despite the merciless heat, refused to shed a single article of clothing. Rest stops became more frequent, but conversation between the two remained nonexistent. Ever since Nicholas had chosen this trail, Unkel lagged behind, showing his displeasure by shuffling his feet across the baked red clay. Sensing a need to reassure him, Nicholas took out a topographical map and pointed to the area where they would rejoin the more established route. Unkel, registering his annoyance, refused to look. His icy demeanor raised doubts over the feasibility of this route; yet Nicholas was committed. There was no turning back; if they were to catch the expedition, this was their only hope. Stopping only because it became impossible to see the trail, Unkel erected the tent, then set about preparing a dinner of rice and dehydrated mixed vegetables. Guzzling water, Kalamatra offered his canteen to Unkel, but the sherpa refused. The oncologist gazed back up the trail, distant mountains mere toothpicks dotting the horizon. Unkel pointed to the food. Instead of entering the tent, Kalamatra remained under the alders, falling asleep fully clothed.

He awoke past midnight, the air frightfully still, not even a whisper of a breeze breaking the suffocating heat. Unkel, assuming that Kalamatra planned to stay outside, placed a sleeping bag next to his feet. Perspiration bathed the doctor's aching body, he craved a shower, a hot bath, but instead he curled into a fetal position. A cramp knifed through the doctor's left calf muscle; wincing in agony, he dragged himself into the tent.

Unkel, pushing his toes forward, unknotted the spasm in his leg. Once the cramp disappeared, Unkel's eyes closed. Fumbling through his backpack, Nicholas located a harmonica at the bottom of a side pouch. The instrument, wrapped in its original cellophane case, still bore the insignia of a music store in West Philadelphia. Since his musical ability could best be described as a combination of minimal and miserable, what possessed him to cart this harmonica halfway around the world remained a mystery. But, unable to sleep, he came up with a plan to occupy the endless hours of darkness. Aided only by a sliver of moonlight and a flashlight, Nicholas, harmonica in hand, left the nylon structure and ventured outside. A potpourri of strange, unidentifiable sounds became traveling companions. Half expecting to confront some heinous nocturnal creature, he trudged down the trail until he came upon the crest of an embankment; from the brim of this hillside, he heard the gurgling sounds of a dribbling stream. Peering below, Nicholas could barely make out a pool of still water. He went to explore, grabbing vines to break his fall as he scampered down the hillside. Edging to within arm's reach of the still pool, he ripped off his clothes and then dove in. After a couple of minutes, he pulled himself back on the river's edge. Shielded behind a clump of rocks, he located a relatively dry spot and built a rock fireplace. Employing a Swiss army knife as a miniature ax, he cut a dozen crisp, dry wood shavings and by match number four, ignited a small fire. Heaping wood shavings onto the blaze, flames jumped into the air. Buoyed by the fire, his mood became light and carefree. Depositing the harmonica wrapper into the fire, he put the instrument to his mouth and started making noise, not music. Employing branches as make-shift drumsticks, Kalamatra beat on a hollow log while sucking the night air through the harmonica. A small cylindrical rock caught his fancy; intermittently, he switched from the wood sticks and began banging stones against boulders while blowing through the harmonica. A half hour passed, maybe an hour, as Nicholas banged and grunted. Losing track of time, he played until the fire petered out.

At the first sign of light, Kalamatra, fully dressed, stuffed his gear into his pack. Propping himself to a seated position, the sherpa readied himself. Sensing Kalamatra's impatience, Unkel slipped into his sneakers, exited the tent, and started preparing breakfast. Nicholas, peering through the transparent walls of the orange tent, watched as the sherpa struck match after match, but dew made igniting the damp twigs difficult. Unkel persevered until thick smoke emerged. A couple of minutes later, a biscuit, bowl of porridge, raisins, and a cup of steaming hot tea was placed before him. Unkel's self-imposed silence stained the air as the two ate. Kalamatra, choosing not to further antagonize the adolescent, couldn't understand the sherpa's reluctance. The day's march promised to be comparatively easy; after passing through a marsh, they would descend a steep hillside before reaching the arid plains of the Terai.

Even before the sun peeked over the eastern plains, Nicholas, ten yards in front, plodded ahead on an almost nonexistent trail. Unkel stayed close behind Nicholas's heels as stagnant, heavy air clung to the baked earth. Oppressive humidity caused perspiration to puddle in their underwear. With each step, the temperature seemingly increased another degree, yet the two descended toward the desert floor. Repeatedly, Nicholas was forced to wait as Unkel, frequently pausing, mopped sweat dripping into his eyes. By mid-morning, in order to gain some needed relief from the suffocating heat, Kalamatra removed his shirt and, wearing only khaki shorts, boots, and socks, doggedly placed one foot in front of the other. Their pace slowed; five minutes of rest was followed by marching fifteen minutes. By ten in the morning, thickening heat caused both to falter, rests becoming longer than time spent on the trail. By midday, dense ground fog filled gaps between them. Kalamatra hoped the sun would burn through the clouds, but instead of the weather clearing, fog thickened. Sweat, like a river pounding through a constricted canyon, streamed down his neck. The temperature soared to well over one hundred degrees, yet both plodded along without exchanging a word. By late afternoon they came upon a final hillside protecting the northern boundary of the Terai. As far as the eye could see, a dense marsh spread across this last section of higher elevation.

"You lead," he instructed the sherpa.

The sherpa's feet squished into the soggy moss. Kalamatra followed. "How much farther?" The sherpa didn't turn around, and Nicholas' words were garbled by squishing mud as the two ventured into the bog. As Kalamatra struggled to keep up, sweltering heat caused him to become disoriented; he swore he heard gurgling sounds, and imagined bathing in a cool river, icy cold water flowing over beds of smooth rocks and pools of crystal clear water deep enough to immerse his body. But dreams of nude bathing soon turned into nightmares; instead of intersecting a frigid mountain stream, the two plodded through swampy marshlands. A grayish film puddled atop the water's surface, swarms of miniscule insects dancing on putrid pools proved an ideal breeding ground for mosquitoes. For a solid hour, the two wove their way through the marsh. On numerous occasions, Unkel, in the lead, halted, peering into dense fog banks. Conditions deteriorated; any semblance of a path disappeared as the sherpa's weaving mirrored his indecisiveness. Kalamatra, too tired to register a complaint, meekly followed. Pesky mosquitoes wreaked havoc; swarms of insects hovered over their heads, bombarding their arms, neck, and ears. Nicholas, in desperation, resorted to slipping on full-length pants, a long-sleeved shirt, and, employing two bandanas, except for small slits where his eyes remained visible, covered his face.

This coat of armor temporarily held the nasty creatures at bay, but it did nothing to halt the constant whine of the pests' onslaught. Foamy white fog slid between them. With each succeeding footstep, water squished in their boots. Peering back, past footprints were inundated with pools of water. The doctor yelled at Unkel to keep going, but bewildered Unkel didn't move. Hands on hips, chin bowed, Kalamatra feared the worst. "We're lost, aren't we?"

Unkel said nothing but his glazed eyes and pale skin confirmed Kalamatra's suspicion. The sherpa had no idea where they were heading. Unkel began shaking, expecting to be the recipient of the doctor's wrath. Instead of getting angry, the physician stared as numerous blotches of blood dotted the sherpa's neck where mosquitoes pierced his skin. Nicholas reached into his backpack, removed a first-aid kit then smeared vile smelling insect repellent over the sherpa's exposed skin. Even as the sherpa tried to pull away, Nicholas coated his palm with a large glop of the rancid lotion, then applied the repellent over Unkel's face and squirted oil into Unkel's hair. By the time Kalamatra finished applying the oil, the doctor's hands were blackened with grime.

Unkel stood mute, his glassy eyes staring into the fog. Trying to remain calm, the doctor questioned, "Will this heat lessen?"

"No."

"The fog?"

"No."

"The trail . . . where is the trail?"

The sherpa's head dropped, his shoulders sinking as he sank to his knees.

"How many more hours until we reach the Terai?" Kalamatra questioned. Lashing out was pointless, placing blame meaningless, all that mattered was to find a way out.

"Elders say," Unkel hesitated, his words garbled, ". . . cursed!"

Not hungry but needing food, Nicholas pried open a metal container of kippers. Warm oil rising to the top coated the sardine-like fish. After pouring rancid grease onto the soggy mush, he forced the contents into both of their mouths. Once finished, they sat silently as hordes of minute insects swarmed. After fifteen minutes, the insects' incessant buzzing compelled Nicholas to stand. The sherpa led; slowly they trudged onward. After progressing less than one hundred yards, Unkel halted as the trail dissolved into a sea of mud. Losing his balance, the doctor tumbled headfirst into the swamp. Distracted by the mud seeping under his shorts, he paid little attention to Unkel's errant path. Stops became more numerous, rest periods lengthened, but Nicholas, realizing the utter futility of getting angry, believed if he were patient, Unkel would forge through. Turning to face Nicholas, the sherpa's hands clasped over his face, protruding arteries and temples pulsated, hands trembled, Unkel's downcast eyes confirmed Kalamatra's suspicion, they were lost! Unkel sat cowering and pleading for forgiveness, both expecting and deserving a severe reprimand for his failure. Witnessing Unkel's collapse concerned Nicholas; Kalamatra had one concern—get them through!

Kalamatra surveyed the situation; if they followed a straight line due east, they would exit the marsh. Using a compass as a guide, he pulled Unkel to his feet. Before launching an assault, Nicholas unlaced his leather bootstraps attempting to prevent additional water from seeping inside, but he felt a sharp pinch on his right ankle. Kalamatra couldn't remember where he injured himself, but, from the stinging sensation, he either bruised or scraped the ankle against a rock. Feeling as if a splinter was lodged under his skin, Nicholas removed both the boot and clinging wet sock. Once the sock was off, he gagged, witnessing a half-dozen heinous black leeches burrowing into his ankle. Panicking, he grabbed a twig and tried to brush away the engorged creatures, but the suckers were tightly embedded into his skin. Jabbing at the leeches' tough leather-like exterior, he punctured the intruder's body; blood squirted, but the suckers did not release.

"Fire! Burn!" In the distance he heard Unkel's voice. Fighting to maintain composure, from his medical training he knew heat, if applied directly over the leech's incision, would cause the teeth to separate from the skin. Unable to tolerate viewing these creatures, his sock covered the leeches. Torrents of fear surfaced. How long would they be in the marsh? How many leeches lay in waiting? What infections might result? Steadying himself proved impossible, but their only alternative was to press on. Head down, following a compass heading east, he repeatedly crashed headfirst into mud. Muck coated his body as his hands clawed for anything solid. The pace brought clumsiness. With fog and water surrounding them, their muddied bodies crawled forward in the slime. Every twitch made the doctor fear another blood-sucking leech was burrowing under his skin. Kalamatra screamed, but Unkel did not respond. Fog, marsh, mosquitoes, and leeches blended together, tears streamed from his eyes, nausea swelled, and his legs felt as if they were pierced by thorns, and tacks riveted into their arms, but he refused to stop. Reaching solid land, he ripped off his clothes; vomit erupted upon seeing his body. Leeches were lodged under his arms, attached to his wrists, burrowed into his groin. Hands tore at the intruders, fingertips clawing against the leeches' tough hides.

"No!" Unkel yelled. "Fire!"

"Stay away!" The physician's bloodied hands wiped tears pouring from his eyes. Lying on the ground, blood mixed with a yellowish fluid oozed where leeches made incisions. Unkel, stooping over Kalamatra's sprawled body, witnessed horror in Kalamatra's eyes. The oncologist's hands tried to hide his face, but a leech was even burrowed in the separation between his fingers. Instinctively, Kalamatra tore at the leeches' armored skin, his fingertip pried beneath a pincer to dislodge the blood-sucking intruder. Horrified, the doctor watched as half of the leech's mouth surrendered its grip while the remainder of the creature, now separated from its body, tightened its grip. Blood camouflaged what was left of the dismembered leech, but to his horror, half the teeth remained embedded. Unkel removed what was left of Nicholas' pants, shirt, and underwear. Too exhausted to resist, the doctor lay with his hands shielding his eyes. As the sherpa's hands touched his body, each lump signaled another invader burrowing into his skin. The once proud physician collapsed in self-pity, the revulsion made him frantically tear at the leeches.

Stretching four ropes from adjoining bushes, Unkel tied the doctor's ankles and wrists. As tears streamed down his face, Kalamatra couldn't free himself as the sherpa ignited a small fire. After feeding an end of a stick into the flames, Unkel removed the burning twig, blew out the flame, and steadied his trembling hand before applying the red-hot ember against an intruder's body. Once scorched, the leech's head curled upward, the suckers prying open, the creature releasing its grip. Kalamatra screamed numerous times during this process when a smoldering twig inadvertently grazed his skin. Before he loosened the ropes, Unkel swabbed alcohol and betadine onto the wounds. The sherpa stripped. Kalamatra looked with revulsion at the thirty or more leeches that bore into the sherpa's dirt-smudged flesh. "Rope . . . tie Unkel!" Kalamatra did as instructed, the sherpa never once complaining as the doctor applied the red-hot ember of the twig over the burrowed invaders. Both collapsed.

A new day brought optimism; the swamp was behind them, one final, steep decline, and then, the desert. Once on the flat desert floor, the two struggled forward accompanied by an unrelenting sun beating on arid soil. Passage through the midday extreme heat of the Terai forced a change in strategy; on the trail from five-thirty in the morning until nine-thirty, then resuming from four in the afternoon until ten in the evening. Conversation was kept to a minimum; each peered at the distant mountains, both anxious to re-enter the foothills. Each night, although exhausted, Unkel tended to chores. Nicholas watched as the sherpa gathered sagebrush and ignited a fire. Within twenty minutes, dinner was ready. A kettle of steaming water boiled atop the flames, potatoes and salt lay on a knapsack. Nicholas wanted to say thanks, but fumbled trying to find the appropriate words. Before going to sleep, Nicholas checked each of their bodies for lingering damage caused by the leech ordeal; yellow pus oozed from an infected sore on the sherpa's left thigh, but except for that one nasty wound, no lesions were infected. As a precaution, the doctor reapplied Merthiolate over all of their wounds.

Kalamatra asked, "Tomorrow afternoon, meet main trail?"

The sherpa responded by pushing a potato toward Nicholas but it sat untouched. Unkel filled teacups with boiling water, then glopped teaspoons of sugar into the steaming mixture. Sipping tea, Kalamatra studied the topographical maps, hoping that tomorrow they'd exit the Terai. He guessed they could probably reach Jorsale by nightfall, if everything went well. Feeling revitalized, he turned to the sherpa. "Namaste," Kalamatra uttered a Nepalese salutation, "I'm not good with words . . . but, without you . . ."

"Job!" The sherpa, embarrassed at receiving a compliment, placed a finger over his lips indicating thanks was unnecessary.

The next morning the path finally wound toward the mountains. To the north, tails of clouds clung to the summits of distant snow-capped giants. Although their bodies screamed for rest, they plunged on. Unkel needed to reach familiar higher ground and the prospect of reaching the Tibetan trading center of Namche Bazaar tantalized Kalamatra. Knowing they were within a few days of this famous sherpa village propelled the physician forward; he wondered where he was in relation to the expedition. What was happening to Audrey? He knew she'd be surprised to see him. He didn't know exactly what either of them would say, but the reaction in her eyes would speak volumes.

The Terai behind, the two saw a peasant and a yak toiling on a hill as they entered the foothills. They slumped to the ground for a needed lunch break as soon as the main trail was within view. Unkel handed Nicholas cold potatoes and hard biscuits, stale crackers and a cup of chang. Kalamatra, after sterilizing water, refilled canteens three times. A smile spread across Kalamatra's face. "Where do you think we are in relation to the American expedition?"

"Man . . ." Unkel pointed.

"Ask him."

Unkel did as instructed, returning a few minutes later. "Expedition no pass!"

A huge smile spread across the oncologist's face thinking about the reaction a certain individual would have when she found a guest waiting to greet her at Namche Bazaar. Energy brimming, the oncologist bolted toward Everest.

36. *A Tale of Two Worlds*

Nine days into the march Audrey finally accepted that until the mountain was conquered personal conversations with her fiancé would be kept to a minimum. Although this upset her, she knew Philip's dedication to a team goal dwarfed personal needs at the moment. With responsibilities piled on his plate, Philip didn't have the time to waste on what he considered her enthusiasm, playfulness, and need for emotional fulfillment. Appropriate times at appropriate places; this trip was a temporary derailment, a once-in-a-lifetime chance for Philip to put his heart and soul into doing what no other human has ever accomplished. Audrey understood, but didn't share this view. Ferrington's thoughts drifted to her parents, the tenseness during their last meeting, their discomfort with the pomp, ceremony, and money of the Hornsbys. She thought of her youngest brother, a pang of sorrow that she was so much older she was missing his adolescence. She thought of Dr. Kalamatra, his brilliance, caring, unbridled vitality; yet his socially inappropriate behavior was an embarrassment. She thought of her life, soon to be Philip's wife, the prestige, power, and glamour. Her fiancé loved her and would stand by her, the man was rock solid. He carried her through the night, possessed the strength of a concrete pillar, yet his standoffishness was un-nerving. When Hornsby focused, nothing stood in his way. At the conclusion of this trip, she welcomed a return to normalcy, to re-establish mutual bonds. Instead of the confusion she was now grappling with, she craved stability. Within a couple of years, she wanted to start a family, build a medical practice, and make a difference in others' lives. Audrey knew this was not a place to make judgments as these were trying circumstances. This trip was Philip's final odyssey to sow the seeds of youth.

37. A Race . . . to Survival

Excited they were in front of the expedition, Unkel led throughout the morning trek and Kalamatra stayed pinned three yards behind. By mid-afternoon, under deteriorating skies, the two arrived at huts situated at the base of the steep wall protecting Namche Bazaar, the fabled sherpa trading center. Kalamatra insisted they walk a hundred yards upstream and erect their campsite at a spot adjoining the Dudh Kosi River. Directly across the narrow, swirling waterway stood an imposing wall, knowing that at the top sat the renowned sherpa village drove the oncologist crazy. In the fading afternoon light, Kalamatra scrutinized the wall. On the lowermost slope, Nicholas saw a trail crisscross between twisted, stunted evergreens. High above, clouds obscured his vision. Though the task of climbing this cliff in broad daylight would have been a sufficient challenge, the thought of ascending this wall in twilight was intoxicating. A voice inside screamed, *Dare the unknown, take chances!* Seeing Unkel set up the campsite he blurted out, "You don't understand me, do you?"

Unkel shrugged his shoulders.

"While we've had a few setbacks, while I've made a couple of miscalculations, at this moment, I've never felt more alive! I'm not worried about what will happen days, months, years from now. That blasted wall that looms in front of us is all I care about!"

Unkel didn't respond.

"I can just imagine what you'll say when you return home; I can just hear you complaining that bad luck had you trek with a half-crazy Westerner. Well, look at us!" Nicholas laughed. "A devoted sherpa and a crazy doctor on an expedition to the world's highest mountain." Nicholas babbled on. "And my infatuation with Dr. Ferrington, I don't know what it means. Maybe I've been alone too long, perhaps my dedication to medicine and patients have walled off reservoirs of feelings, but something about being with that lady derailed me. And this trip is crazy, absurd, idiotic, there's no logic, no reason! Am I properly prepared? Not the slightest. Do I care about standing atop a rock pile? I couldn't care less. Does scaling that yellow band interest me? Not in the least! Irrational, who cares! Audrey—a passing fancy, a crazy one night liaison or a deep-seated meaningful relationship?" The oncologist shrugged his shoulders. "Don't for a moment think I know what I'm doing. Through the luck of the draw, through no fault of your own, you got stuck on a journey with an incorrigible bastard who has an exuberance for life and about as much sense as a stubborn elephant!" Suddenly realizing the sherpa didn't comprehend a word, Kalamatra sauntered away, claiming a position on a neighboring boulder, his eyes glued to the towering wall. Thirty minutes passed as light rain filtered downward, yet he continued to sit and stare at the hillside protecting Namche Bazaar. Water slid down the exposed granite. In the dwindling light, the wall took on a foreboding aura as trees merged with shadows and bushes blended with rock outcroppings. Heavy dark clouds obliterated the summit, but gazing upward, his spirit, like pent-up oil spurting from a recently uncapped well, was ready to explode. Returning to the campsite as Unkel transported rocks from the riverbank to build a fireplace, Nicholas barked at the sherpa to stop.

Unkel eyed him. "No hungry?"

"We're going to Namche Bazaar now!"

The sherpa's mouth opened in disbelief.

"You heard me." Nicholas sprang off the rock and began dismantling the tent.

"Why?" Unkel's eyes glared. "Dark!" He looked upward. "Rain! High, snow!"

Kalamatra changed into his mountaineering parka, slipped into waterproof outer pants then laced his hiking boots. The sherpa, hands gripping his hips, head frozen, lips pursed, refused to budge as Nicholas stuffed the nylon tent into a pack then kicked apart rocks forming the fireplace. Within a couple of minutes, there was no evidence remaining that just moments before there had been a campsite.

Unkel held his ground. "No climb!" The sherpa eyed the overcast, blackening sky. "Hour late . . . weather . . .sleep . . . dark . . . morning . . . clear sky!"

The sherpa's reluctance forced the oncologist to lead.

A rapidly flowing river was his first obstacle; a narrow strip of logs spanning the Dudh Kosi served as a temporary bridge and, within minutes, the Greek crossed the river. In the waning light, as the trail steepened, Nicholas shimmied up steep stretches on his hands and knees. Legs tightened, breathing strained, shoulders ached, but he inched upward. A third of the way up the wall, visibility deteriorated when rain turned to snow, glazing the path with a slippery film. He wished Audrey was sharing this climb with him; no doubt she would smile when she heard about this exploit. Weariness mandated rests; initially breaks lasted just a couple minutes, barely enough time to ingest a cold potato and a glucose cracker, but as the sun set, short, choppy breaths forced prolonged halts. No matter how long he rested, he could never completely catch his breath. Adding insult, Unkel never needed to stop. Stumbling upward, the precise movements of the early march dissolved into a clumsy, awkward push. Joy, satisfaction, pleasure and triumph never entered his mind; instead, torture, pain and bone-chilling cold filled his aching body. As murky darkness enveloped the wall, snow, instead of relenting, intensified. Rests became more numerous; exhausted, he laid with his head nestled into his backpack, over-taxed muscles pulsating, eyes yearning to close. Raise a white flag and surrender? Romanticize all you want, except for Unkel, who was pouting, no one else was there to care.

Panic set in as darkness encroached. Gusts whipped snow in his face, mountain and snow blended into a maze of white. Searching for the trail, he kicked snow accumulating by his feet in frustration. Unable to find the trail, precious time was wasted. Faced with diminishing light, an aching body, buckets of descending snow, his own indecision, the oncologist stood immobilized. Waving for Unkel to pass him, the sherpa took the lead, but the pace, much to Kalamatra's annoyance, did not quicken. For agonizingly long minutes, the sherpa stood mute staring into the wind driven snow as the last of the lingering light disappeared into blackness. Only a few feet separated them, but tumbling snow prevented eye contact. As ice caked eyelids shut, fingers groped for Unkel. Stupidity left him with a mountaineer's most feared enemy—a dreaded white-out—a condition in which mountain and snow merge.

"Keep going!" a voice inside pleaded. Clumsily, the oncologist slipped and stumbled down an incline, his fall broken by a clump of dwarfed pines. Raising himself to his hands and knees, gasping for air, he fell back to the ground. Windblown snow, stinging his eyes, forced him to keep his face down. Thickening snow found its way under his goggles. His eyes searched, but hope of finding a path vanished as the storm grew in intensity; wind-driven pellets feeling like darts penetrated his body.

"Unkel!" The howling winds gobbled his words. "Please," he pleaded, "don't leave me! Unkel . . . Unkel . . . Unkel . . ." Tears froze on his eyelids. What he most dreaded came to fruition— he was alone. Desperately, he groped in the darkness for a sign of Unkel's footprint. Goggles were coated with a crusty film and a layer of ice coated the hairs on his exposed wrists. And a sting- ing numbness crept into his fingertips. Knowing survival meant movement, he tried, but standing proved impossible. The air was piercing cold; each breath felt as if a sledgehammer sliced his lungs. Rising to his knees proved exhausting; temples pounded while the backs of his eyes and cheekbones felt as if they had been sliced by an axe. Summoning what little reserves were left, he struggled to his feet, only to fall belly first into the snow. Tears rolled down his face, icing his lashes and freezing on his cheeks. Pain scissored his chest. Curled into an embryonic ball, his body was coated by a dusting of snow. Why hadn't he waited? Why was it so important for Audrey to find him holding court in the sherpa's climbing mecca, Namche Bazaar? Did he really believe Ferrington would think more of him? Would success on a trail affirm his manhood? Would she love him less if he admit- ted his vulnerabilities, confusions . . . his mind ran amok, what was he trying to prove, and to whom? Laughter erupted. What a silly game to play in such a remote place; this venture felt like the work of a madman. He tried to tell himself there was no joy in life without sinking one's soul and flesh into a dream, no rewards for half-baked involvement. He had left behind a world where passivity and docility were not only accepted but revered, where adventure and courage were interpreted as signs of im- maturity and flightiness. But, sitting huddled within his cocoon, even this Vince Lombardi pep talk did nothing to rejuvenate his freezing body. All he wanted was to retreat, thank Unkel, and hug Audrey. Instead, he laid alone, shivering as snow pelted downward.

He had no idea how long he was alone when an arm shook him. Barely hearing Unkel's voice screaming, the sherpa's hands scraped off inches of snow coating his body. Clasping his underarms, Unkel pulled him to his feet. Once standing, Kalamatra shook free. He held steady momentarily, but within seconds his rubbery legs collapsed as he crumpled back to the ground. Again, Unkel hoisted the doctor to his feet. Trying to strap the doctor to his back, the sherpa tied ropes around Nicholas, but before he could secure the oncologist, the doctor tumbled back into the snow. With his hands firmly gripping Nicholas's wrists, Unkel tried to drag the doctor's limp body up the path, but progress proved impossible.

Suddenly Unkel was gone. Each successive breath felt as if a boxer was mercilessly pounding his midsection while the referee refused to halt the onslaught. Abandoned, an hour, two, perhaps three passed. When he next awoke, he was covered by at least a half-dozen inches of snow. Strange voices towered above; he could hear Unkel yelling, but his mouth was frozen and Kalamatra's voice was inaudible. Blankets were wrapped around his shoulders as his body was hoisted into a cradle made of tree limbs and ropes secured his frozen carcass onto the wooden frame. Four, perhaps five, tribesmen grunted as he was dragged up the hill, his cries swallowed by a howling wind.

When he woke, Kalamatra was dry, and a roof was over his head. Coarse blankets were piled on his sleeping bag. Propping himself on his elbows, he saw hundreds of illuminated flickering lights, ornate wood carvings chiseled into an altar and gold-leaf lettering adorning the stucco walls of a Tibetan temple. A copper gong hung directly above the room's lone window; a monk squatted by the opening with a mallet clasped in his palms. Kalamatra had only fuzzy recollections of what happened; he and Unkel became separated . . . people dragged him . . . strange voices . . . getting sick . . . left alone . . . buried . . . voices from above . . . being pulled . . . Nicholas Batiste Kalamatra, the warrior, the man whose spirit knew no bounds, laid prisoner, encased within his sleeping bag. Unable to stand, sleep temporarily removed him from his misery. Silhouetted against the open window, the same monk held a copper goblet cupped within his hands. Chanting and rhythmically rocking back and forth, Nicholas begged the monk to bring him his backpack that contained glucose, but the monk didn't budge. Rising to his knees the room spun, forcing him to slump back onto the baked mud floor. Marshaling what little resources were left, Nicholas whimpered, "I need . . ." A deluge of tears cascaded down his face. Dragging himself toward the window, he noticed the monk's scraggly gray beard and wrinkles chiseled into the man's face. Covering his skinny body, the monk wore a threadbare brown canvas robe held together by ornate silver buttons. His feet were bare and calloused, dirt caked his toes. The monk's eyes remained riveted out the open window, staring at the distant mountains as his head bobbed rhythmically, paying no attention to the Westerner. The man's forearm grew taut as the mallet was raised overhead before descending against the gong, a sharp shrill vibrating throughout the room. Dizziness forced Nicholas to retreat to his bedroll, lying shamefully disabled on the sleeping bag.

The next time he opened his eyes the room was engulfed by sunlight. Kalamatra glanced toward the window as streams of sunlight shimmered against the copper gong; the oval mallet rested against the window, but the aged monk who held vigil over his body was missing. Was it just a figment of his imagination? Had an old man not sat and prayed all night? Where was Unkel? Why was he deserted? Too weak to crawl across the floor, he lay defenseless with a tortured psyche knowing he had been beaten, spirit and enthusiasm undermined by a failing body. Quitting was all that was left, he battled, but lost. A flood of "ifs" surfaced; if he hadn't taken ill, if he hadn't stupidly assaulted the wall, but he had only himself to blame. He'd committed a series of tactical blunders; all that was left was gaining enough strength to trek back to Kathmandu.

"Eat!" Nicholas could barely distinguish Unkel's slanted, high cheekbones as the sherpa squatted at the foot of his sleeping bag.

"Wet rag, water!"

"Eat!"

The sherpa pushed a bowl of mush toward him.

"Sick!" Propping him into a seated position, Unkel thrust a potato into Nicholas's palm, but sitting upright caused dizziness. The sherpa held a canteen to Kalamatra's parched lips, water dribbled down the doctor's neck, but the few drops that seeped into his mouth soothed a raw throat.

"Glucose," Nicholas begged.

Not understanding, Unkel shook his head.

"In the backpack," Kalamatra pleaded, "open the canteen, pour powder into water."

Anxious to help but confused, Unkel positioned himself by Nicholas's side.

"Medicine . . . in pack . . ."

As a precautionary measure before leaving Philadelphia, Kalamatra purchased glucose in case he needed instant energy. How ludicrous to be caught in this situation, the twenty feet separating him from his emergency kit might as well have been miles. Realizing the possible consequences of lapsing into a sleep from which he would not awaken, he begged for the glucose, but Unkel returned Nicholas's pleas with a blank stare. With trembling fingertips, the sherpa pushed a potato into the

Greek's mouth. Summoning what little energy he could muster, Kalamatra crawled toward the backpack. Within arm's reach of the backpack, Nicholas's hands flung gear until he located the glucose. Clutching his precious prize, Kalamatra crawled back to his sleeping bag, his hands never once lessening their grip on the plastic container. Ripping open the sack, he stuffed powder into his mouth and poured water from the canteen, forcing the mixture into his body. Even though the glucose would be more palatable dissolved, Nicholas couldn't chance waiting for the powder to dilute.

38. *An Unexpected Rendezvous*

Abandoning their usual place in the rear of the expedition, Audrey disliked being in the middle of the pack. Repeatedly, she urged Philip to trail behind, but Hornsby was adamant. "From this moment on," Philip reiterated, "surveillance is crucial." By midmorning, Clayton, Peter, and Harry closed to within view of the hillside protecting Namche Bazaar and as instructed, waited. Upon reaching the river, Philip ordered the lead climbers to launch an assault on the wall. On the steep hillside, a fear of dislodging loose rocks forced the marchers to keep wide separations. Waiting their turn on the face, Audrey sat alone as Philip, using binoculars, followed Harry, Peter, and Clayton's passage. This primitive highway fascinated Ferrington; she marveled that a three-foot path was the major supply line linking Tibet, Everest, and Namche Bazaar in the north to Kathmandu and the Terai in the south. Once the orange parkas of the advance party disappeared over the upper ridge, Hornsby, Audrey, and Pemba proceeded up the well-tramped artery. Halfway up the steep embankment, Audrey saw a lone nomad, weighted down with articles to barter, heading down the trail. Even though the climbing party numbered in the hundreds and the nomad was alone, climbers and sherpas stepped to the side. Philip yelled to Pemba to tell the man to step to the side, but the sidar said a man loaded with goods moving downward had a right to the trail. Philip fumed; this decision defied logic, simply because a few sacks were clasped to a nomad's back and tied atop his head, it made no sense that hundreds of porters were forced to wait.

Three hours of continuous marching brought Harry, Clayton, and Peter within view of the crest of the steep embankment that protected Namche Bazaar. Delighted they would reach their destination by mid-afternoon, the three leapfrogged upward, anxious to reach the legendary trading center. Situated in a naturally carved bowl, Namche Bazaar's approximately one hundred and fifty dwellings were arranged in a circular fashion on a sloping plateau, and, except for a small group of people gathered in the marketplace and an occasional movement of a child or yak threading through the narrow corridors, what they imagined would be a robust village appeared dormant.

Hours later Hornsby and Ferrington, nearing the town, heard a shrill voice from outside a monastery echo down the trail. Philip and Audrey quickened their pace until nearing the hut. Peter screamed, "Doctor, hurry! There's been an accident and the same crazy guy that was jailed in Kathmandu lies unconscious!" Letting Ferrington pass, sherpas and porters stood to the side of the trail. Upon entering the monastery, Audrey gasped seeing Nicholas's body lying unconscious, his ashen face drooped to the side. Harry, seeing the fright etched across Audrey's face, grabbed her arm and restrained her from running to the inert body.

"Looks worse than he is," the botanist pointed to the remnants of the bag of glucose.

"How long has he been here?"

Harry answered, "Tribesmen tell me that two nights ago, in a blinding blizzard, he was hauled up the hill!"

"How many are in his party?" Philip inquired.

Peter volunteered, "As far as we can ascertain, only one, a youngster accompanying him goes by the name of Unkel."

"How did he get in front of us?" Ferrington's response was a combination of wonderment and admiration. Suppressing her emotional reaction, her medical training took over. After probing Kalamatra's body, Audrey assessed, "No internal hemorrhaging, no broken bones, no dilation of the pupils, no evidence of a concussion. Since I can't X-ray his lungs, as a precaution he'll need antibiotics. Best I can tell he's severely dehydrated. Instruct his sherpa to keep his lips moist, force liquids into his body, four to five days of rest is mandatory before he'll be able to walk!"

Philip intervened. "Leave the sherpa with an emergency medical kit."

"Why?"

"Because we're leaving him behind."

"We're what?" Audrey blurted.

"No need to be sentimental. He is not part of our expedition, and I've run out of patience putting up with this lunatic's antics."

An hour passed as Unkel and Audrey worked on the Greek's unconscious body by cleaning cuts and wrapping his forehead with wet compresses. When their work finished, Audrey and Unkel sat by his side, but never once did Kalamatra regain consciousness. After finishing a team meeting to review tomorrow's objectives, Philip re-entered the monastery. "Audrey, leave him, nothing more can be done."

"I'm staying here," she whispered.

Philip exploded. "You're what? Ferrington, don't be ridiculous! You haven't traveled this far to sacrifice an opportunity to go to Everest to play nursemaid to a certified head case. Kalamatra's stupidity landed him here, he deserves his fate. As soon as he's strong enough, his sherpa will help him hobble his way back to Kathmandu, a bit worse for the voyage, but he'll survive!"

An hour later she left the monastery and sat alone eating dinner. Outside, in the center of the village was a joyous party attended by climbers and local inhabitants. Audrey, choosing to remain secluded, was surprised to see Philip leave his makeshift desk in command headquarters and join the festivities. The quiet village was suddenly alive, reaching Namche Bazaar proved a homecoming for the sherpas and signified the march was nearing its end for the Westerners; the assault would begin soon. Everyone, except for the expedition doctor, joined in the revelry as Country Western music blended with traditional sherpa folk songs. When Philip returned to their tent, Audrey felt a desperate need to talk about Kalamatra, but Hornsby quipped that the pest received his rightful fate. Audrey left their tent numerous times during the night to check on the oncologist. Every time she entered, the sixteen-year-old sherpa, Unkel, sat squatting by the doctor's unconscious body with a canteen in his hand. By the morning Ferrington was a wreck. Before leaving, she sat beside Kalamatra, draping wet rags on his forehead. "Promise me you won't leave him." Her final words were directed at the sherpa.

39. A Brief Celebration

A day of constant pounding and threading through valleys nestled between 20,000-foot mountains brought the expedition to the famed Tengboche Monastery, the last inhabitable hamlet before reaching Everest base camp. Seated beside a roaring campfire, Philip Hornsby held a cup filled with chang and proclaimed, "After two weeks of trekking, we're finally perched at Everest's doorstep, success is soon to be ours!" The entire entourage raised cups in unison, the mood light and carefree, conversations punctuated with laughter as abundant rounds of chang were poured. Frivolous jousting amongst climbers and sherpas permeated the tepid air. As coals burned to embers, voices became boisterous, ringing with horribly sung songs. As Harry snapped pictures, Philip even stood in the middle of Birdwein's sons, draping his arms around Peter and Clayton's shoulders. As the hour neared ten o'clock, Philip excused himself and retreated to the expedition's headquarters, explaining tomorrow's details still needed to be analyzed.

Except for a few minor problems, Hornsby felt that the trek to Everest had been rather uneventful. Porters occasionally bitched, but hadn't rebelled; his perpetual nuisance, Dr. Kalamatra, mysteriously reappeared, near death, at Namche Bazaar but fortuitously self-destructed. And although Harry Birdwein's decision making capabilities were clearly suspect, in name only was he the expedition leader. All expedition members knew it was Phillip's efforts that put them in a position for success. He was on guard. Although his rambunctious climbing partners had the potential to present problems, he didn't doubt that Peter Birdwein and Clayton Johnson were competent climbers. But both were far too impetuous and flighty. Strict discipline was now essential since they were within view of the Nuptse-Lhotse Wall that protected Everest's massive cylindrical cone. Hornsby was adamant, under his watchful eye, no one would make a stupid mistake.

His fiancée, Dr. Ferrington, was proving a far more perplexing problem, he simply didn't understand her. Philip saw life in black and white, while his companion was a maze of contradictions. Complications cloud issues; identify a task and then devise a plan. Ferrington's vacillations caused unnecessary confusion. One moment she wanted emotional support, love, sex, even eroticism, the next he would see her lurking in the darkness, waiting outside his tent, pensively watching. Since leaving Namche Bazaar, their conversations were kept to a minimum. Neither had any tolerance and Philip couldn't understand why she was upset leaving Kalamatra. How anyone could feel guilty for leaving the crazed doctor was beyond his comprehension.

That night they slept apart; he didn't care and she didn't protest. An organizational briefing the next morning was perfunctory as there was little to discuss. The route to base camp was straightforward. By the time the procession was set to march, darkened clouds were signs of a brewing storm. Gathering force, winds whipped at the fragile tent walls. Philip radioed Austin Morley that the storm would force them to remain stationary for the day. Clayton, annoyed at the delay, cursed their luck as Philip instructed the assembly that an extra day's delay made no difference as they were ahead of schedule. Besides, he explained, additional time to acclimate to the rarified atmosphere would be beneficial. At the conclusion of the briefing, everyone but Audrey exited. As Hornsby sat analyzing and plotting, Ferrington sat comatose in a corner. Her emotional instability driving him crazy, Philip broke the impasse. Ever so lightly he kissed her neck, standing behind her he brushed his arms along her shoulders, running his fingers down her forearm. "Why now?" she questioned as his hands explored her hips.

"It would do us both good if we made love." In a fluid motion he removed her sweater and an undershirt silhouetting her breasts.

"Philip, not now."

"You, of all people, saying no."

Tears welled in her eyes.

"Believe me, I'm not some ogre." His hand caressed her shoulder. "Lie down!" She did as told. Philip's powerful hands massaged her shoulders, arms, and back. Ever so slowly his hands kneaded her tired muscles, bringing life back into an aching body. With her eyes shut, in the distance she heard him, "You're a wild colt, full of energy, impetuous, daring, carefree. I'm just more reserved. When we get back to the states we'll share a wonderful life, the best of everything—fame, money, prestige, children." His hands massaged her back. "Understand, I concentrate on one event at a time—I don't tolerate distractions; months from now memories of this adventure will bind us together. Foundations are built from common bonds and success, now is a time to stay focused. Everything has its time and place; Audrey, I love your spirit, your competence and although it's presently hard for me to find time right now to enjoy it, your sexuality adds zest to our relationship. Lately, because I haven't been responding, don't take it personally. Presently, I'm preoccupied. But soon we'll be at a seaside resort in St. Tropez tearing off each other's clothes."

"I'm just . . ." re-buttoning her shirt she fought to find appropriate words, "just not in a proper frame of mind."

Instead of getting mad, he whispered, "I love you."

Sequestered by the entrance of their tent, Audrey lay encased in her sleeping bag as pellets of rain pounded the taut nylon. Blustery winds gusting more than sixty miles per hour battered the paper-thin nylon walls. Parting the door flap, swirling fog pushed inside. Peering outside there seemed little chance that the skies would clear, but the prospect of being cooped inside for an entire day was so unnerving, she strapped on rain gear and headed out. Philip, diligently working, shook his head in bewilderment, but said nothing as Ferrington ventured into the howling storm. Fifteen minutes later, she re-entered sopping wet, but Philip never asked why she left. After removing her clothes, she resumed squatting by the tent door with a sleeping bag draped around her. Frustration intensified; ever since leaving Namche Bazaar her emotions were a roller coaster spinning out of control, her world unraveling. Philip, unexpectedly becoming even more of an enigma by not only attempting to be understanding, but by supporting her and even trying to make love. During this trip their relationship, instead of solidifying, was turning into a tangled mess. Philip treated people as if they were robots; events unfolded according to a precise schedule and, as long as events proceeded smoothly, Philip Hornsby was content. Her fiancé took pride that thus far his expedition was reminiscent of the great marches of Mallory, Hillary, and Hunt, and, in the process, if a climber's feelings were occasionally trampled, the end result would be judged by its success. Perhaps she was wrong, but this trip wasn't turning out as imagined. She had expected them to share a special bond, enjoy the serenity of the mountains, and savor the exoticism of the people, but it didn't feel that way. Unable to sleep, she lay caged and confused. Philip was a chameleon, revealing a compassionate side she never knew existed. "Let's make love," she whispered.

"Moments ago I tried and you weren't interested."

"I'm in the mood now."

"As soon as I finish work."

"Screw that," she muttered under her breath.

An hour later, without touching her, Philip blew out the lantern and was asleep within minutes. Nothing made sense. What did she want? What would make her happy? What was it about the crazed lunatic doctor, Nicholas Batiste Kalamatra, that attracted her? No one could deny he left a trail of buffoonery, was a social misfit, clumsy, awkward in bed; then he chased her halfway around the world to this godforsaken wilderness. Yet whatever his omissions, she couldn't deny his passion. And then there was Philip, a man to be admired, but did she love him? Life with Philip was predictable; Hornsby dealt with emotions as if he was a scientist measuring precise portions for a chemistry experiment. Goals were dissected then squeezed into manageable compartments. Hornsby was opinionated, authoritative, an individual whose vast accomplishments gave credence to his finely crafted veneer, besides which, she mused, her fiancé was so goddamn handsome it was sinful. Perhaps it was the enormity of what he offered that proved so troublesome, what more could a woman want? Yet, huddled within her sleeping bag, she felt confused. Be realistic, she urged, nothing is perfect; certainly a pot-bellied lunatic oncologist was not a viable option. What initially attracted her was his brilliance, his inaccessibility, her mistake was becoming infatuated. Given his unstable psychological state, in retrospect, it was stupid to seduce him. But who could predict the degree of the doctor's emotional instability, his kookiness, his bizarre behavior? Why this man was chasing her halfway around the world remained a mystery, their relationship had been limited to a couple of hours in bed and their time spent practicing medicine. Yet, in a strange inexplicable way, the doctor's antics touched a chord. How was it possible that she could be attracted to two such opposite men at the same time? One knew nothing of social graces, followed no customs, and didn't care what others thought; the other was sophisticated, polished, and a paragon of social graces. Yet, both men shared an unremitting drive to succeed; the word "no" didn't enter either of their vocabularies. Both men were driven, one would sit atop the world and business community, the other would fight with all his energy so his beloved patients could live to see another day. Longing for the trip to be over, she needed time alone to sort out this tangled mess. Instead of being excited seeing Philip scale Everest's yellow rock band, the closer they neared their objective, her enthusiasm waned. As hard as she tried, she couldn't share the excitement that drove her companion to dangle from Everest's flanks.

40. Harry's Dream

The next morning Philip announced that Harry, Peter, and Clayton would lead. He barked, "One night along the trail, but once reaching Everest base camp do not attempt passage through the Solu Khumbu ice field until I arrive. Extreme caution is mandatory; navigating the ice flow and scaling the yellow band are the two most dangerous obstacles we will confront."

Feeling fit, with Clayton and Peter flanking him, Harry Birdwein was the first to leave the campsite. After an hour on the trail, pausing to wipe sweat dripping from his forehead, he watched as the sun broke free between the mountainous barrier, angular rays penetrating through ground fog hugging the valley. Plodding upward flanked by his sons, this was a moment to be remembered. As dew evaporating under the sun's onslaught steamed upward from rhododendron branches, Harry wished every detail could be indelibly carved into his memory. Nothing would derail him as they made their way to a final outpost of civilization, Periche, a small decaying monastery. After camping there for the night, only a day would separate them from a final push to Base Camp. As the afternoon lengthened, snow fell. A trail of footprints marked their passage. Harry's chest began aching; hoping to stabilize breathing, he lengthened rest stops. The elder Birdwein didn't object when his sons, seeing him exhausted, took his pack. In dwindling light, the three dragged themselves inside the weather-beaten doors and entered the dilapidated Pangboche monastery; support beams were split, boards either missing or in need of repair in the floor, dirt stained the mud-baked walls. Directly in the middle of the courtyard stood what little remained of a once regal stupa; the Buddha's eyes were missing and streaks of decaying reddish iron cast throughout the hollow indentations of the man-sized face. Fingers were severed, a crack penetrated the statue's shoulder, no gold-plated etching adorned the lower panels, no intricate artwork graced the figure; instead, what was left of the decaying stupa was propped atop rotting timbers. Suddenly three elderly monks, dressed in tattered robes, emerged from behind a decrepit mud wall. The monks walked across the courtyard, their robes, unlike at Tengboche, lacked brilliant colors. The three ignored the climbers' presence. Receiving no invitation to stay, exiting the courtyard, in a field adjoining the monastery, Harry and his sons erected a campsite. Too tired to eat, Harry crawled inside his sleeping bag but his eyes wouldn't close. Watching his sons sleep, Peter and Clayton were his life, his world. What else did he have? A sterile botanical laboratory? Soon, his sons would have their chance, but whose chance was it? Was this trip for him? For his sons? Would success draw them closer or was he using his boys as pawns to live out his dream? He knew his body, tired and weary, would never summit; but what was driving him to push his sons to tempt death, pushing limits beyond what was thought possible? Why was it so damn important to break barriers? Harry Birdwein wasn't a religious man. In truth, he never gave the issue much thought, but huddled in his sleeping

bag he prayed for a favor for a man whose prime had passed—
let his boys return home safely.

41. Cold Water Cure

The storm forced Ferrington and Hornsby to halt midway between Tengboche and Periche. After dinner the two retreated to their tent, consumed by different agendas. Philip lit a lantern and planned, while Audrey lay immobilized, a battle raging within. Have sex? Don't have sex? She didn't know what she wanted. A part of her screamed to reach out, another to hide.

In the middle of the night, Pemba crawled into their tent, waking Audrey. The sherpa spoke in a sheepish voice, "Tent . . . hole! Mud! Stay!"

Hornsby didn't protest.

As Pemba lay in a sleeping bag beside her, the sherpa's odor prevented her from sleeping. Revolted, the stench overpowering, she wanted to remove Pemba's clothes and wash the filthy garments in the river. Instead, she slipped from her sleeping bag, positioning her head near the tent's open flaps, gulping fresh air before it became polluted. Gazing outside as tumbling snow filtered through the swaying branches, her thoughts centered on the upcoming climb. The mountain would extract its toll, dreams shattered. Perhaps triumphs and glory, but at what cost? Intuitively, she felt that with Philip in command the expedition would succeed. Her fiancé emanated strength, unless an unexpected catastrophe occurred, his will would propel them to the top. Philip was so consumed with summiting, she was not part of the equation. She needed to be held and fulfilled; yet, a foul-smelling sherpa now lay between them. The next hour Audrey thrashed against the nylon walls, her thoughts consumed with Nicholas. She missed his exuberance, his vitality. Roadblocks didn't dampen his spirit, prison bars couldn't even break him. Compared to Philip's staid tunnel vision, the doctor's crabby spirit brought a smile to her face.

Slipping open her backpack, Audrey pulled a wool sweater and pants over her thermal underwear and wandered outside. The storm passed; overhead a plethora of glittering stars illuminated snow-laden treetops. Accompanied by shimmering moonlight, she wandered until reaching a river, watching as churning water cascaded over exposed rocks. Reflections from clouds sailing across the sky glimmered on the water's surface. A spray coated her pants, the dampness prompted her to build a fire. Grabbing a handful of twigs, she fed the flames. Grime coating her fingers was the identical color of the gray, withered bark of the dead twigs. Leaving the flames unattended, Audrey scampered up the hillside and re-entered the tent. Without waking Philip or Pemba, she grabbed a toilet kit and slid down the embankment to the smoldering embers. On a flat rock beside the pool, she arranged the contents of her pouch: a bar of soap, toothbrush and paste, and shampoo. Shedding clothes, gingerly her foot slipped into the glacial tributary, the piercing cold numbing. "Go ahead," she chided herself out loud, "Jump!" Instead, she entered the stream inch by inch. After hands splashed the icy water over her arms and shoulders, she dove headfirst. Grabbing the soap, she lathered her body, scrubbing multiple layers of encrusted dirt coating her skin. Climbing onto the face of a flat rock, she massaged a sweet-smelling shampoo into her scalp. Suds soon seeped down her neck and back. Rinsing away the soap, forgetting the cold, she jumped back into the river.

Revitalized, she reentered the tent and squeezed into Philip's sleeping bag. Nuzzling her neck into a crevice of his shoulder, one hand began massaging his chest, while another finger touched his lips.

Philip's eyes opened. "Your hair's wet!"

Audrey laughed as her hand drifted down his thigh. "I'm worried you've forgotten!"

"At this hour? Under these circumstances?" Philip eyed the sleeping sherpa.

Determined to break their impasse, Audrey slipped her body on top whispering, "Water is revitalizing!"

"Privacy," he protested.

Her fingers touched his lips, her playfulness working its desired results.

42. Base Camp

The next morning they were greeted by a crystal clear sky. Marching between the jaws of mountains protecting the Everest mastiff, Audrey and Philip trekked with a perpetual shadow, sunlight bathing only the summit's upper rims. Audrey pointed to precariously balanced fingers that appeared ready to topple, eyeing daggers of menacing ice that formed a canopy over the trail. Philip knew only too well that avalanches were mountaineers feared bed partners. As the snake-like entourage inched forward, Ferrington knew she was entering a world where she didn't belong. The path from Periche to Everest base camp left behind any remnants of green leafy trees and budding flowers; departing a planet of colors, the massive expedition entered a world of black and white. But what Ferrington found most troublesome was that her emotions and physical needs were classified as excess baggage.

Far up the trail, Harry Birdwein led, his sons close behind, their thoughts overshadowed by haunting growls as ice shifted within glaciers gouging the surrounding mountains. After leaving Periche, for four uninterrupted hours, the trio marched without words, into a remote section of earth seldom seen by human eyes. Their pace quickened as they rounded the Nuptse Wall, the three gazing in awe as Everest's massive expanse hogged the horizon. Bulging from Everest's breast, the jagged Solu Khumbu ice field scissored across the mountain's belly. Words needn't be spoken as safe passage across the glacier, even under the best circumstances, was in the hands of the gods.

By the time she trudged the final yards to Everest Base Camp, porters and sherpas were busy erecting tents and stone fireplaces. Ferrington looked at what was to be her home for the next six weeks; Everest Base Camp, set on rubble and loose rocks, lay atop a lateral moraine adjoining the Solu Khumbu Glacier. Distancing herself from the group, she sat atop a rock and watched as what was once rubble sprang a city; tents erected, gear piled high, medical supplies sorted, a radio antenna pointing skyward was hoisted up by fifty men. Everest's launching point would be her final destination, she did not harbor any aspiration of going higher; the taut, grim face of her companions spoke of a battle that wasn't hers. During the next couple weeks, she would be relegated to waiting at this godforsaken rock pile, spying through binoculars, praying that good fortune would shine on those above. Hesitantly, she eyed the adjoining glacier, relieved she wouldn't have to pass through this foreboding obstacle. An hour wore by as she peered at the colorless world; during the entire time she sat perched on the rock not a single bird frolicked overhead. Even though the sun set, work continued. Ferrington and Hornsby were the only two accorded the privacy of sharing a tent—a waste of energy as she sensed Philip would sleep in the command headquarters, her premonition proving correct. Late that night, Ferrington ventured outside and kindled a fire, piling twigs on the coals. Suddenly she heard footsteps, Harry Birdwein's face appearing in the flickering light.

"You scared me."

"I'm sorry. I saw you leave the tent," Harry hesitated. "I thought we could talk, the trip has been difficult for you, hasn't it?"

"Philip knows what he's doing."

"And," he patiently waited.

"I too have pride. Believe me, he spares no one from his dictatorial methods. Philip's so wrapped up in making this journey successful that any semblance of a personal relationship has been relegated to a back burner." Words flowed from her mouth. "Back in Philadelphia, when we originally planned the trip, we talked about having fun, exploring, getting away together, yet until we succeed, I'm nothing but a stranger."

For the next fifteen minutes the two sat by the fire feeding twigs into the flames. "I'm not much of a talker," Harry began. "Years after Peter's mother's death, I adopted Clayton. Perhaps I should have remarried, but I brought up both boys alone. Any free time we had, we traveled to the mountains. I didn't know much about what to say to young boys, so instead of talking, I kept them occupied fishing, swimming, and climbing."

"And?"

"Their upbringing wasn't conventional. Since mountain climbing was my passion, I assumed it would be theirs. When Morley presented me with an opportunity to scale Everest, the dreamer in me couldn't resist."

Audrey interrupted. "None of this makes sense to me. Manhood achieved by clawing up a granite face? You, Philip, Clayton, Peter, yours is a foreign battle, not mine. This trip has only added bushels of doubt to an already confused mind, if only I could reduce life's complexities to a 1,000-foot wall. If answers lay at clawing to the top, I'd queue in line to enroll, but for me, instead of clarification, my psyche is a jumbled mess."

"I might have bitten off more than I can chew. Initially, I conceived our attempt to be a small, lightweight expedition; it ended up being transformed into this clumsy caravan. My sons are disappointed, they both despise regimentation. But Clayton and Peter refuse to complain, they're afraid to hurt my feelings because both know how much this trip means to me. When Hornsby dogmatically issues orders, my sons won't even look me in the eye, that's how much they resent anyone barking orders at their father. The irony is now that we're here, we'll reach the top, but this trip has been hollow. I crave returning to the simplicity of climbing with only Peter and Clayton."

Audrey spoke in a whisper. "I, too, had hoped for something else."

The two then talked for the next hour, the muscles in Harry's face easing as he recounted memorable moments with his sons. "Two years ago, a storm forced us to bivouac for three days in the Canadian Rockies. Once in Alaska, on the Susitna River, we ran smack into a grizzly bear and her three cubs. A bald eagle once followed our descent through the Gunnison Canyon." When he spoke of his sons, a warmth spread across his face. A softness, well protected, lay beneath his rough, calloused exterior. "Nothing needs to be this regimented." Feeling uneasy that he had revealed too much, Harry returned to the campsite.

43. *The Climb*

The day after the miniature city was erected, porters being released were paid five dollars per day for their previous two-week service. All that remained from a crew of over three hundred and fifty porters were, under Pemba's leadership, forty sherpas. Ten were designated as high-altitude porters, while the remaining thirty were assigned the treacherous duty of pushing a supply train through the feared Solu Khumbu ice field. Philip raised the pay for the remaining sherpas—seven dollars per day for those navigating through the glacier, ten dollars for those stocking campsites, and for anyone who reached the base of the yellow rock band, as an added incentive, a twenty-dollar bonus.

As expedition members crowded into the command tent, Audrey wished she hadn't attended the evening meeting.

"I don't care one damn for your blasted plan," Clayton Johnson said, glaring at Philip.

Peter said ,shaking his head in disbelief, "So, you're proposing that Harry, Clayton, and I pioneer a route through the ice field; then, stretch fixed ropes between camps I and IV."

"Exactly," Philip answered. "Safety first, fixed ropes need to be hammered to the base of the yellow band. Within five days, if the weather holds, you'll be at 26,000 feet."

"And end up exhausted!" Clayton lashed back.

"Once established, retreat to base camp. Before we launch an attack on the rock band, you'll have time to recover."

"And what will you be doing while we're working?" Clayton spat.

"Coordinating!"

"This is BS!" Johnson stood, hands on hips. "You're staying put at base camp while we do the dirty business of establishing a route up the mountain. Harry, say something!" Clayton barked. "Our original plan never called for you to go that high, you're being pressed into action because his Lord Highness desires to sit playing general!"

Peter snapped, "Since my father is the official leader, you climb and have Harry coordinate!"

"Clayton, that's enough," Harry interceded. "Bickering doesn't help! Reaching the top mandates working together; preparations are a complicated business and since Philip has experience coordinating an expedition, let him stay. Besides," Harry's calming voice intervened, "don't classify me a has-been. Might not be as sharp as I once was, but I'm up to the challenge of pioneering a route through the ice field and establishing campsites." The elder Birdwein's bravado astonished his sons; in these strange surroundings, their father became rejuvenated.

"Besides which," Philip added, "so long as he acclimates to the altitude when we attempt the wall, my plan calls for Harry to be positioned at the base of the rock in case we encounter troubles. There's nobody I'd rather count on. And, let's be clear, once we set foot on the wall, I'm the lead climber!"

44. *An Unlikely Couple*

Wishing he could lessen the pain, Unkel helplessly sat by the doctor's side listening to Kalamatra's groans. Whenever his mouth opened, Unkel stuffed white powder between the doctor's parched lips. Continuously, he draped the Greek's forehead in wet compresses, but never once did the delirious doctor regain consciousness. Days passed with no change. Finally, after four days of lying inert, Kalamatra, drenched in sweat, awoke. Opening his eyes, Unkel was asleep just feet from him, a ragged blanket covering the sherpa's body. Afraid that he'd lapse back into sleep, the oncologist stuffed additional glucose into his mouth. Crawling back to his sleeping bag, waiting for the powder to take effect, he watched Unkel sleep. Nicholas fought an impulse to wake the sherpa and thank him, but instead let Unkel get some well-deserved rest. Even though events of the last couple of days were sketchy, the sherpa, now curled beneath a frayed brown blanket, stayed by his side, his loyalty unquestioned. Unkel's care nursed him through a crisis of his own making, the doctor smiled, how unlikely that the two of them would end up as partners; and while his judgment as a mountaineer was not only untrustworthy, but stupid, the sherpa had an uncanny way of circumventing Kalamatra's mistakes and righting a teetering ship. How ironic that a boy who he'd originally mistrusted was the one who had kept them going. Although only sixteen, the sherpa possessed the cunning of a seasoned guide; dangers lurking in these rugged mountains did not scare him. Lithe and agile, possessing wiry arms and muscular legs, Unkel had an instinct for survival. Never complaining and always shouldering the brunt of the workload, tasks were done efficiently, without fanfare, and adversity never derailed him. Nicholas smiled, a more unlikely team would be difficult to imagine; yet he and Unkel were partners and, in an odd way, complemented each other. Calm and methodical, Unkel balanced Kalamatra's impatience and volatility with tolerance and imperturbability. When healthy, the oncologist took pride at his drive, but his zest was also his Achilles heel—repeatedly, he bound forward until he cracked. But when he self-destructed, Unkel picked up the pieces. While Kalamatra played hunches, teasing the unknown or impulsively plunged, Unkel found escape routes to extinguish the mess Nicholas left in his wake. The sherpa had little desire to barge into the lead, but when Kalamatra's direction faltered, Unkel took command.

Although weak, Kalamatra slipped on hiking boots. Before reaching the monastery's door, his legs wobbled. Slumping to the floor, three brown eggs lay less than an arm's length from Unkel's sleeping bag. Kalamatra looked in wonderment. How was that possible? Eggs . . . Kalamatra hadn't seen an egg since they left Lamosangu. The physician chuckled. Those fragile, brown oval eggs nestled in the ruts of a baked earth floor were a testament to the sherpa's resourcefulness; how Unkel located an egg at 48,000 feet left him bewildered. After cracking the shells, he poured the contents down his throat. An hour wore by until his strength returned, broken egg splinters and an empty bag of glucose beside him. Afraid that standing would make him disoriented, he remained still. Once again, he stared at Unkel. Nicholas shuddered at the thought of where he might be if it weren't for his loyal companion. Unkel's perpetual heroics no longer seemed out of the ordinary. Together, they comprised a well-balanced team; Kalamatra brimming with energy, while Unkel was armed with the necessary cement to keep loose ends together. Somehow they had persevered, a precocious sixteen-year-old sherpa and an impetuous hell-bent Philadelphian.

At sunlight, Nicholas crawled outside. After being confined inside the musty temple for days, the glaring sun momentarily blinded him making footing unsteady. This was not exactly a triumphant entrance to this famous Himalayan village. Muscles were sore, and his legs felt like buckling and filth coated his body. No flags were flying, people were not crowding the streets to greet the intrepid climber, no progress reports were wired back to Kathmandu, no one in America awaited a morning blog to keep up with the latest bulletins chronicling his progress, yet the word *surrender* was not in his vocabulary. Wandering toward the marketplace, expecting to find barrels full of rice, barley, eggs, salt, and fresh fruits for sale, instead, what he saw were wooden crates loaded with potatoes and salt. Shopkeepers didn't pay attention to the shabbily dressed Westerner. Intruding on an ongoing conversation between two merchants, Kalamatra inquired if he could purchase additional supplies, but his efforts fell on deaf ears as the men, apparently neither understanding his words nor his gestures, returned to their bartering. Taking out his wallet, Kalamatra displayed a handful of rupees indicating he was more than willing to pay, but even if a shopkeeper understood his requests, from the appearance of the barren shelves, except for potatoes of every conceivable size, shape, and color, and abundant sacks of salt, there was nothing else to purchase. Dejected, he retraced his steps through the dirt streets until returning back to the monastery. As he passed through the wooden door, Unkel rolled over and with eyes only slightly parted, stole a glance toward the corner of the room where Kalamatra had been for the past days. The vacant spot concerned him, and he sprang from his sleeping bag. As Unkel laced his boots, the doctor spoke. "I'm up and I've been out!"

"White lady doctor, part of big expedition, here . . . four days ago. Tell Unkel, wet rags on forehead . . . drink and powder."

"Unkel, I've made mistakes . . ." Gathering his gear, he told Unkel he'd wait outside.

A few minutes later Unkel appeared, sneakers untied, belongings haphazardly thrown together. "Have you eaten?" Kalamatra inquired.

"No."

"I've saved an egg."

"It for you." The physician walked toward Unkel and, cupping his hands in respect, offered the traditional Nepalese salutation: "Namaste."

"Duty!" Unkel protested.

"You saved me."

Embarrassed, the sherpa kicked the dirt.

"Sometimes it doesn't show . . ." Unkel looked uncomfortable, but Kalamatra continued, "but without you . . ."

A smile spread across Unkel's face.

Kalamatra, hoisting gear onto his back, tightened straps as he readied himself. Turning to Unkel, he instructed the sherpa to lead. Unkel began heading toward the path descending to Jorsale and the Dudh Kosi river basin. "Airstrip on cow pasture at Lukka, a couple times a week supply plane lands then returns to Kathmandu!"

"Wait!" Kalamatra yelled.

Unkel turned. "Go slow!"

Kalamatra grabbed him. "You're heading in the wrong direction."

"No, this path," the sherpa pointed.

"But we're not retreating," Kalamatra pressed.

Unkel slumped to the ground. Not allowing the sherpa time to protest, Kalamatra turned and headed toward Everest Base Camp.

"High . . . sick . . . potatoes . . ."

Kalamatra ignored Unkel's protests. After walking fifteen yards, Nicholas glanced over his shoulder. The sherpa stood frozen, disbelief etched into the furrows lining his face, Unkel's astonishment only fueling Kalamatra's enthusiasm.

The day's walk proved slow. After six hours of trekking, interrupted by numerous rests, Unkel erected their tent in the middle of the trail, under dwindling light. Kalamatra, after a dinner of cold potatoes, hard biscuits, and hot tea, sat outside, maps outstretched, gazing proudly over the miles covered since leaving Kathmandu. Now, he simply needed to follow the path to Everest Base Camp, meet with Audrey, win her over, then go home.

45. Rice Rituals

"Philip, get up!" Audrey exclaimed, "Trouble's brewing!"

"Ferrington, the sun's not even up, go back to sleep!"

"Look!" She grabbed his arm.

"What's gotten into you?" Anger marked Philip's voice. Parting the front flap on their tent allowed a blustery wind to barge inside. Eyes squinting into darkness, Philip stared as the high-altitude sherpas, their bodies swaying in unison, arms locked together by clasping elbows, squatted in a semi-circle around a roaring fire. Hornsby explained, "Tradition is that before the sherpas attempt to cross the Solu Khumbu ice field, praying to their god for safe passage, they only pass if omens smile. Sherpas are afraid of the massive ice flow, many accidents and deaths there, it's paradoxical, but the higher sherpas go on the mountain, the better they perform."

Audrey, peering at an embankment adjoining the lateral moraine of the Solu Khumbu glacier, pointed to a series of stone pillars silhouetted in the moonlight.

"Graves," Philip explained. "Nepalese call them *chortens*. The six closest are the remains of sherpas who died accompanying a Japanese expedition."

The two sat silently by the tent's entrance and watched as sherpas hoisted a twenty-five-foot wooden pole into the night air. Decorated with prayer flags and sacred ornaments, multi-colored streamers waved in the tepid night breeze. Ang Nia, leading the assembled sherpas in prayer, stood near the fire, his hands outstretched. The chanting ceased as Ang Nia removed a maroon velvet shield covering four gold-encrusted goblets containing sacred rice given by the head monk at the Tengboche monastery. One by one, the sherpas, with heads bowed, marched beneath the prayer flag before grounding kernels into scalps. Ang Nia then covered the goblet with a decorative cloth. The reigning high priest of the sherpas motioned for all to rise and, with hands pointed skyward, fingers extended, heads bowed, Buddha's emissary begged that good luck from the heavens shine upon them.

Pemba whispered, "If god smile, no accidents; if god angry, sherpas no carry!"

Removing the cloth covering, Ang Nia's hand placed hand carved dice into a goblet, the chanting increased as the dice were tossed into the fire. With his forearm covering his arm, Ang Nia fell to the ground.

Hornsby confronted Pemba. "Why silence?"

"Yellow smoke! No good!"

"That's absurd," Philip retorted. "No way this expedition is going to sit stalled for an entire day!" Hornsby pushed Pemba toward the fallen Ang Nia. "Go back and persuade them. Tell them the expedition leader will sweeten their prayer tree. If nothing works, dispatch a sherpa to Tengboche to pick up additional sacred rice from the head monk." Pemba returned, bribery was not helping. A day would be lost until another batch of sacred rice arrived; even additional money or a promise that the Everest expedition parkas would be given to the sherpas as a gift after the climb was successful would not change their minds.

All day Ferrington knew to leave Philip alone. Hornsby fumed but there was no amount of money that could counter a religious custom, so he had to wait. Late that afternoon, the dispatched sherpa returned. Again that night, they watched Ang Nia roll the dice. Green smoke puffed skyward, God bestowing his blessing that the sherpas forge a safe passageway through the ice corridor. Audrey was surprised that climbers, sherpas, and porters prepared to cross the Solu Khumbu ice field at midnight, but Philip explained that the ice was more solid than under a midday sun. Moonlight glistened as the group departed. Philip Hornsby was busy checking packs, ensuring each of the sherpas carried his assigned weight. While this process continued, Harry stood in front of the ice field, his eyes trained on the twisted labyrinth, Peter and Clayton at his side, as sherpas took positions behind the lead climbers. When Philip signaled, Harry, a flashlight strapped onto his forehead, started upward. Avoiding ominous overhangs, the botanist advanced; Peter and Clayton stayed close at his heels, but never once would their father relinquish the lead. An hour into the march a thunderous boom reverberated from high above; the ground shook, towers of ice scissored down the mountain. The sherpas cowered and stood frozen, but Harry, realizing the avalanche was sufficiently too far away to present danger, pressed forward. Two hours into the climb, the feared sun made its first appearance: heat melting the ice, weakening stability. Hands on hips, perspiration flowing from under his protective sun goggles, ever onward Harry pushed ahead, opening a lead stretching over a hundred yards.

By seven in the morning the pressure of being the lead climber took its toll, the botanist's breathing labored and pace slowed. Upper arms ached, chest tightened, each breath, due to the rapidly thinning atmosphere, causing a burning pain in his lungs. Both sons tried to lead, but their father snarled in defiance, this was his moment to shine. Sheer will propelling him, he insisted on finishing what he started. After seven hours of trekking, breaks became even more frequent; three steps, arms pumping forward, head down, chest expanding, contracting, expanding. Nearing the top of the passageway, an ice buttress shimmered outward. Harry's eyes searched for a route, but nothing appeared. Dizziness forced him to sit. Peter thrust a canteen into his hands; needing fluids, Harry drained the contents. Removing his goggles, his eyes examined the 200 feet that jutted outwards. During the ten-minute break, a layer of ice cemented the botanist's perspiring body to the surrounding ground. Dislodging his right boot, an ice chunk broke loose and, tumbling down the glacier, disappeared into a crevice. Behind, a line of sherpas clawed upward, the route up the ice flow appeared as if a spider spun an intricate web as numerous aluminum ladders spanned passageways. Fighting to break the inertia binding him to the ice, Harry raised himself to a standing position, retightened the crampons, then shoved his body forward. Four successive steps, a pause, three breaths, three more steps, another pause. His body tilting forward, the professor inched up the massive ice wall. All that remained before reaching the top was one final overhang, although his sons objected, he scissored his way up the wall. Seizing the corner of the overhang, he hoisted himself to the top. Pounding an anchor into the ice, he threw ropes down to his sons; within minutes an aluminum ladder hung from the wall and his boys joined him.

The next morning Harry continued leading. He knew too well that climbing a mountain Everest's size was like a giant game of leapfrog; set up a campsite, deposit food, canisters of oxygen, climbing equipment, then retreat. In successive days, camps II and III were stocked. Never in his wildest expectations did the botanist dare think he would be in the front, his youth recaptured. Even though every day spent in this death zone meant a lack of oxygen was systematically killing brain cells, to his amazement, he persisted, establishing campsite IV at 24,500 feet before scampering down. All that remained was to forge to 26,000 feet and establish a final campsite at the base of the yellow band. Desperately wanting to finish his job, four days exposed to an altitude of over 20,000 feet took its toll. At dinner, Harry felt nauseated, nerves and body eroding, he couldn't force food into his mouth. A voice inside screamed, "One more carry; dig deep, harness reserves, do it!" Seeing canisters of oxygen piled on Clayton and Peter's backpack, he fought an urge to plead with his sons to allow him to suck on much-needed oxygen, but that would violate Hornsby's plan, which called for the three lead climbers, when lying suspended for the night on the wall, to have supplementary oxygen available. Each climber needed a sufficient supply to provide a boost to get them to and off the summit. Perched at camp IV, night brought a bone-chilling cold; wrapped in a sleeping bag, as his sons sipped hot soup, their father coughed blood.

Sleep intervened and after waking, the botanist felt rejuvenated, headache gone and he no longer gulped to breathe. Initially, he struggled to figure out why, and then he saw two canisters of discarded oxygen lying beside his sleeping bag. "In the middle of the night," Clayton eyed his father, "you were gasping. Peter and I hooked you up to an oxygen canister, within minutes the growling within your lungs cleared."

"But the gas was meant for the rock wall!"

Peter spoke. "If Reinhold Messner made it to the top without supplemental oxygen, so can we. Since you're the one suffering from oxygen sickness, you use the gas."

Clayton continued, "The way Peter and I figure, with nine canisters left, you have sufficient oxygen to stay here and wait a couple of days before your gas runs out. By that time, the wall will be scaled and we'll be returning home!"

Laboring under a brilliant sun, with an oxygen mask secured to his face, Harry watched as his sons prepared to leave to set up a campsite at 26,000 feet at the base of the yellow band. "Stay here!" Clayton was emphatic. "Under no circumstances are you to move!"

Before the botanist had a chance to argue, his sons, technical gear draped over their shoulders, minus oxygen canisters, left their father shivering in a sleeping bag and headed upward to establish a final campsite at the base of the yellow rock wall. Sucking oxygen, Harry watched his sons claw upward. By early afternoon, feeling better, a decision was made; if his sons needed help he had no choice but to reach the final campsite; piling gear atop his backpack, he set off while Peter and Clayton reached the bottom of the yellow band. As a safety precaution, the two hammered fixed ropes into ice before excavating a campsite into the frozen tundra. Neither had the slightest idea that a half-mile below, in encroaching darkness, their father was in pursuit.

Without fanfare the botanist pushed on. Three steps . . . pause . . . two steps . . . pause. Tightness tore through his chest. Peering at the wall looming above, sunlight glistening off the vertical wall made detailed surveillance impossible, but a dangling fixed rope made the passageway clear. Concentrating on each step, after six hours, he closed to within 200 feet of the sheer wall. Peering at the granite sent shivers down his spine, the smooth rock showed no faults; only upon clawing on the wall would the yellow band unveil secrets. In the departing sunlight, a thin veil of perspiration steamed off the sheer granite face. Taking a last look at the wall, hoping that maybe . . . perhaps . . . another angle would reveal a fracture . . . a small ripple, surely, when Clayton, Peter, and Philip attempted the face a hidden sleeve would appear. Fighting to maintain his composure, the botanist fought to silence doubts. By late afternoon, a failing body combined with dwindling light turned progress into a snail's pace. Summoning what little energy he could muster, he used his ice pick to tunnel through the snow to excavate a hole large enough to protect his body from the wind's fury. Shivers, feeling like bullets spraying his body, tore into his extremities. A voice inside implored, *quit*, but knowing that climbing at night violated safety procedures, Harry crawled out of his hovel and kept going, scant illumination provided by a miner's light attached to his forehead. Hearing moans from below an hour later, Peter and Clayton hauled their father's almost frozen body into their tent. Harry's words were garbled as his sons scraped a layer of ice entombing their father's face. A mask was placed over his mouth; Clayton switched on an oxygen regulator to deliver maximum output. Once their father was wrapped in a bedroll, his sons slipped a clamp around their father's waist, tying him to the mountain. Since they only had one tent, the three slept piled on top of one another.

Harry Birdwein woke the next morning to an eerie silence, the nylon walls of the tent, instead of being stretched by the wind, listlessly drooped. Parting the front flap, he peered at hundreds of miles of blue sky, dotted by toothed giants. Breakfast over, he crawled outside. Much to his surprise, breathing, because of the constant flow of oxygen, came easier. Philip radioed Harry, "Camp IV . . . Come in . . . Window of opportunity; two, perhaps three days, the weather should hold."

"Hear you loud and clear," Harry responded. "Within the hour we will be heading down!"

Philip cut him off. "Luck shines! The mountain is Peter and Clayton's for the taking! When the weather shines, take advantage! Do what we came for, have your sons scale that blasted wall! Start now! Don't wait for me!"

A smile spread across his face as he watched his sons prepare. Pain, agony, discomfort were all forgotten, the trip was a culmination of dreams; questing, venturing, probing the unknown, now, his two sons beside him, the three were perched at a precipice where no person had ever before ventured, he was living his dream, daring the unknown, his sons about to set foot on a part of the planet previously off-limits to human beings. Existence was stripped to its bare essentials, gone were the accouterments of the Western world, nothing to buy or accumulate, money was useless. All that mattered was wind and weather; Harry savored the simplicity, succeed or fail, a mountain was what it was; nothing more, nothing less, just a massive conglomeration of rock and ice bulging, spiraling skyward.

46. *Triumph to Terror*

As Philip packed his gear to start upward, Ferrington sat perplexed, not believing what she'd heard. "You're not going to lead the assault team? Recognition, fame and notoriety is only associated with those who reach the summit."

Hornsby faced his fiancée. "Certainly I'd like to, but it's foolish not to take advantage of the weather."

Audrey faced Philip, shocked that her fiancé would settle for a back seat managerial role. "Are you sure this is what you want?"

"I'm heading up. That way both Harry and I will be positioned to help if necessary. Under my leadership, I have confidence this mission will succeed. The complexity of our expedition is what will bring the notoriety that my father desires."

Watching as Philip worked his way through the Solu Khumbu ice field, Audrey sat mesmerized; throughout this odyssey he had chosen paths that baffled her. Admiration filled her eyes as her fiancé made his way up and down ladders crisscrossing the Solu Khumbu glacier; she was marrying a man of immense inner strength. In her wildest imagination she couldn't believe he'd willingly settle for a support role, but to her amazement, his decision was made on what was best for the group.

Not a cloud dotted the sky as Peter and Clayton readied themselves to tackle the yellow band. They were dressed in orange parkas, ropes draped over shoulders, technical gear draped around their waists; pitons, dehydrated food, ace ax, metal bolts, a cagoule, and a miniature butane stove dangling from harnesses, words were unnecessary; nothing could capture their amazement and happiness that it would be just the two of them. Before leaving, Harry pushed the half-dozen remaining canisters of oxygen toward his sons. "Since I'm staying here, you'll need this more than me." Both refused.

The two were just finishing tying gear together when a radio transmission interrupted them. "Why are they waiting?" Philip spewed orders. "Harry, tell your two cowboy sons to get going. Have them climb eight hours, enough to go two-thirds up the wall. All along the plan necessitated that the lead climbers need to bivouac for a night dangling from a sling, those plans remain the same. Tomorrow they'll finish, scamper to the summit and by late tomorrow afternoon, repel down the face. You and I will be waiting at the bottom, then, if the weather holds, I'll make a solo ascent."

As they departed, Harry's massive arms, like a protective mama bear fawning over her newborn, reached out and embraced his sons. Scaling one hundred feet, Clayton and Peter checked a pulley system that would dangle from the wall, feeding extra rope and supplies upward.

Without talking, Peter in the lead, the two brothers hammered pitons into the wall. After fifty feet, Peter relinquished the lead, Clayton sharing the responsibility of pioneering a route. Johnson spotted a sleeve dissecting the face, small fist sized fissures providing sufficient handholds enabling him to shimmy upward. Peter took over again, but the next two hundred feet took close to two hours as the mountain scissored together, cracks sealed, the vertical wall glaring in defiance. Constantly switching leads, time in front became shorter and shorter, exhaustion taking its toll. After eight grueling hours, Birdwein's sons had ascended 700 feet of the 1,000-foot face. Neither spoke, both knew they were finished for the day; they knew what was ahead of them, tonight and tomorrow, as they would push danger to a new definition.

Clayton and Peter listened to their radios as their father urged, "Stay separated . . . rocks . . . fall . . . danger!" Twenty yards between them, the two spread across the face, hammering bolts into the rock before tying ropes to slings. Dangling thousands of feet in the air within makeshift homes, both lay encased in a hammock-like device. Cubicles proved so narrow that legs were unable to change position; but to survive the night, chores needed to be accomplished, food cooked, liquids boiled. Although neither had an appetite, both forced tea, bouillon cubes, and crackers into their mouths. Far below, Harry removed his oxygen mask to force freeze-dried meat into an empty stomach. "Clayton, Peter," Harry spoke into the radio transmitter but whistling winds snuffed out words. Removing his goggles, wind-driven snow pelted his eyes and lips. "Say something! Speak to me!" Tears flooded his eyes, a voice told him to evacuate the face and order his boys to retreat at the first hint of light. They pushed immortality to its very brink; he and his sons lay perched under a guillotine, an executioner stood poised.

Parched lips craving liquids, Harry removed his thermal gloves and tried to ignite a propane stove, but numb fingers wouldn't cooperate. Repeatedly, the botanist attempted to wiggle his toes, but felt nothing. Turning his oxygen regulator onto maximum capacity, Harry watched as bulging, thick, soupy black clouds enveloped below in a veil of darkness. Except for his bird's-eye perch, within a stone's throw of the world's highest point, nightfall blanketed the valley. Far to the west, winds shepherded fleecy clouds into a collision course with nameless 20,000 foot peaks. While the world slept, he sat transfixed, a private audience watching as clouds crawled upward along the Nuptse-Lhotse wall, leaving shimmering oranges and purples bathing summits. As these giants held court to a departing sun, he knew he didn't belong as undecipherable conversations echoed from peak to peak. In this supposed moment of triumph, anxiety overwhelmed him. Stripped of brashness, damnation of rules, annoyance at those who placed limits, everything dissolved into a muddled mess. Perched on this mountain with victory so near, all that remained was a shell of a man with frostbitten toes and a battered soul; he couldn't help but hear towering giants laugh at the seriousness he and his sons attached to reaching the top of this rock pile. Twice during the night, jettisoning empty oxygen canisters, the botanist eyed a multitude of stars illuminating the sky.

Morning arrived and there wasn't even a whisper of wind. Under a cloudless sky, a blazing sun danced over the ice fields. Far below, between camps II and III, Harry could see Philip's orange parka as he made his way up. His sons readied themselves, Everest's summit beckoning. In spite of Peter and Clayton's night dangling from a wall at over 26,000 feet, the botanist, with success almost theirs for the taking, couldn't possibly tell them to quit. If luck held, his boys would be standing on top of the world's highest summit by this afternoon.

Watching his sons prepare for their final assault, he was tortured by the question of why. Was this climb to satisfy his obsession? Were Peter and Clayton risking their lives so their father's fantasy would be fulfilled? A bizarre thought flooded his mind—what message would his sons leave at the summit? Would they thank Philip for his support? Would they romanticize about man's inexhaustible will? Would they feel an obligation to thank some god they didn't believe in? As a faint pinkish hue of sunlight peeked over the eastern horizon, a message would be delivered; his sons would finish, despite being battered and bruised, but these odysseys were over.

"Dad," he heard Clayton's voice echo from above, "have you eaten?"

"Not hungry!" Harry growled.

"That's not what I asked!" Johnson's command was emphatic.

Philip's binoculars were trained on the wall watching as Peter and Clayton scraped toward the summit. Hammering piton after piton into the wall, the two arrived directly under a final overhanging precipice. The rock's face appeared like velvet, not a crack or fissure evident. After a couple minutes of surveillance, Peter pointed to a slight fissure that dissected the wall directly under an ice serac; both knew they were breaking a cardinal rule of mountaineers, never pass beneath an unstable bridge, but these were not normal circumstances. Gulping oxygen, Harry watched as his sons shimmied up the final precipice. Within a half hour, the two hammered their way to just below a teetering, razor-sharp ridge separating them from the top of the wall. "Hold, you bastard!" Clayton whispered as he hammered a piton directly under an overhang.

The roar started as a growl. Rumbles intensified. Dislodged ice fragments rifled downward. Clasping his hands over his helmeted head, Clayton hugged his body close to the wall, but instead of subsiding, debris plummeted downward, the avalanche happening so quickly Clayton's screams were swallowed as the mountain erupted. As ice thundered downward, Peter watched in despair as his brother was engulfed in a furious stampede. Within minutes, the explosion ceased, the only reminder of the mountain's fury was a sky dotted with snowflakes filtering upward.

"Clayton . . . Clayton . . . Clayton!" Peter's screams echoed across the yellow rock face. "Speak to me . . ."

Clayton's hand perched from the sling, a clenched fist indicating he survived the mountain's fury, his body hugging the wall.

"Hold tight! I'll get you off," his brother screamed.

Just as Peter started shimmying across the face, the mountain erupted again, ice daggers rifling downward. As debris plummeted, Clayton's screams were lost in the guttural roar. After the explosion ended, Peter repeatedly screamed Clayton's name but there was no response. When the snow crystals settled, Peter saw his brother's body hanging from the wall, arms and legs dangling downward, chin drooped against his chest.

Peter yelled, "Say something, anything," but the unconscious body dangled in a sling swaying against the wall, there was no response. A lone rope, a frayed umbilical cord to survival, tenuously held his brother onto the mountain.

Peter radioed Philip. "Get up here! Hurry! Bring extra ropes, without assistance, there's no way I can get Clayton off the wall."

After reaching a distraught Harry, Philip scribbled diagrams and computed weight capabilities. A couple of minutes later he radioed Peter. "Position yourself fifteen yards above and to the opposite side of your brother. I'll scale the other side. After creating a triangle, we'll pound extra pitons into the rock for additional support and then thread a rescue rope between us and Clayton. Once secure, we'll cut the current rope that binds Clayton to the mountain, momentarily he'll plunge; all we can do is pray the new rope will support the three of us."

Audrey, monitoring the radio, interjected, "Why risk more lives when you don't even know if Clayton's alive?"

"An unwritten code."

"Unless there's a sign of life, leave him."

"No way!" Hornsby barked.

Within minutes, Hornsby started up the wall with coils of yellow rope draped over his body. Philip, aided by existing fixed ropes, reached Peter and Clayton in less than four hours. Johnson's eyes were frozen open, fissures scissored into Clayton's lips. A gust of wind shoved the unconscious body from the rock and Clayton's head rotated before slamming against the blood-soaked wall.

Across the rock face Peter yelled, "Remember Colorado! Rocky Mountain National Park! Fresh trout!" The encouragement in Peter's voice faltered as his brother's eyes remained frozen open. Once a safety rope was secured into clips, Philip took out a knife severing Clayton from the umbilical cord binding him to the mountain. Slicing away, the rope popped; momentarily Clayton's limp body spiraled downward, the safety rope arresting his fall. The next three hours Philip and Peter lowered Clayton off the mountain, but he never uttered a word.

Looking upward through binoculars, seeing dots being lowered, Ferrington banged on the radio transmitter, trying to reach either Hornsby or Harry, but her efforts produced only silence. The wall was finally evacuated slightly past midday. Anxiously, Audrey watched a line of climbers head down. Sequestered on a rock, she listened as a rhythmical death chant spewed from the mouths of mourning sherpas as the funeral procession bearing Clayton Johnson thread its way down Everest's flanks toward the Solu Khumbu ice field. The body, wrapped in a Tibetan rug, tied to a makeshift stretcher, was dragged by a team of sherpas. Peter, tears frozen on his face, walked directly behind his brother's body, Harry's arms draped over his son's shoulders. Every few steps the botanist reached out and touched the corpse. Upon reaching the Solu Khumbu glacier, hours passed as Clayton's body bag was hoisted up and down aluminum ladders. Seven sherpas alternated hoisting Johnson's remains over shoulders, passing the inert figure over cavernous holes slicing through the ice field. Behind the body trudged Harry and Peter, grief chiseled into their faces. The sound of men preparing for the arrival of a slain comrade reverberated throughout the campsite as sherpas erected a cairn, a funeral pillar of loose rocks stacked skyward honoring the dead. By late afternoon, with fifty yards left to reach base camp, Peter and Harry hoisted Clayton's body onto their shoulders. Tears poured down their faces as the two threaded their way through the assembled sherpas before placing the body on top of the funeral pyre.

Philip announced that at sunrise Clayton's body would be burned, declaring the remains to be spread as one with the mountain. At sunset, refusing to move, Harry and Peter squatted next to Clayton's body. Before the evening meeting commenced, climbers and sherpas formed a single line, walking alongside the rock rubble to pay respects. After all but Peter and Harry departed, eyeing the moon's reflection shimmering off the distant rock face, the two collapsed, unabashedly wailing with grief. Dreams disintegrated into a nightmare; Everest was to have been their special bond, although danger existed, they never really contemplated death. "Live life to its fullest" was a Birdwein family trademark; and, while all three knew that climbing courted risks, each gambled willingly with their immortality. Perhaps it was a chance to experience life at its rawest that drove them to challenge the world's most formidable obstacles, but where was justice for those who summoned the courage to dare. Neither could understand why God would take away the strongest and bravest—a person who pushed the human spirit to arenas thought unimaginable. Overcome by grief, their cries rifled through the frigid night air as the two were left to cope with a world devoid of a son and brother.

A labyrinth of early morning colors painted the sky as Harry and Peter hoisted Clayton's draped body onto a funeral pillar.

Anguished cries filled the air as Pemba ignited the bonfire, the Tibetan robes encasing Clayton's body billowing into flames. By midmorning, once the fire turned to smoke, all joined for an obligatory morning meeting. Philip started, "Everest struck back. Numerous cairns ringing base camp are a stark reminder of the mountain's disdain for intruders who claw at its side. Only if an expedition is lucky, and many are not, do all return. It is naïve not to worry that someone might die, death is often an ugly companion for those trying to scale Everest." Philip's next sentence shocked everyone. "No matter what happened, we're not abandoning our objective."

Audrey, her mouth wide open, couldn't believe what she was hearing.

Hornsby continued, "We haven't journeyed halfway around the globe to leave defeated. Since the accident, I've analyzed manpower; ample supplies and equipment remain, there are sufficient reserves for a final push for one climber." As Philip explained his plan, Audrey sat numb, even as the pungent smell of a man's charred remains mixed with smoldering embers, her fiancé was beckoning the mountain to unleash more of its rage.

"Philip, come to your senses."

"Dr. Ferrington, I'm finishing what we started."

Why Philip was returning to the mountain defied logic, yet all afternoon she watched in silence as he packed gear. At dinner, Hornsby confronted Harry and Peter. "Because of your prolonged exposure to the altitude, the plan is for both of you to stay at base camp and rest for the next three days, all ten high-altitude sherpas will assist by going to the base of the yellow band. By that time, I'll be halfway up the yellow band, and if I need help, you'll both have recuperated; but I'm not expecting to need either of you!"

Backpack crammed full, Philip, leading with his small entourage behind him, started across the glacier. The remainder of the night, with a sleeping bag draped over her shoulder, Audrey sat outside the tent monitoring progress. Climbing with the aid of a full moon, she watched as the lead figure would disappear behind a dagger of protruding ice and then, minutes later, Hornsby would reappear and scale a ladder fronting yet another ice buttress. Moving with cat-like precision, in what normally takes four to five hours, Hornsby passed the midpoint mark in less than two.

47. *Love Tests All Limits*

Nothing could hold the Greek back. Aided by moonlight shimmering off toothed giants, Kalamatra estimated that before noon they'd reach Everest base camp, eager to witness the shock registered on Ferrington's face when he arrived. The prospect of reuniting with the Everest expedition produced a flood of emotions, a game of one-upmanship added zest to their rivalry. He and Philip were polar opposites, neither could tolerate the other, yet he felt no animosity toward the botanist and his sons, if anything, he felt an odd camaraderie with them. If positions were reversed, he too would have excluded an unwelcome outsider.

His feelings toward the pesky Ferrington were a garbled mess. Only time would tell, questions had to be settled; was their passionate night together nothing more than a friction rub? No matter how perfect Audrey and Philip appeared, their relationship was missing soul. And his own feelings? Rage? Love? Jealousy? Passion? Nothing short of seeing her would provide answers. As the sun peeked over the horizon, Kalamatra and Unkel turned the corner of the Nuptse-Lhotse Wall;

approximately two miles up the valley, Unkel pointed to a grouping of orange and green tents at base camp. Realizing they were so close motivated them to quicken their pace.

Upon entering base camp, the sherpas that remained stood in awe and spontaneously clapped as the eccentric Westerner clasped his hands, greeting the porters with the traditional Nepalese salutation. "Namaste!" As applause grew, Nicholas appeared embarrassed, yet it was obvious that his antics, mistakes, and subsequent escapes had transformed him into a folk myth.

Seeing him, Audrey ran from her tent and threw her arms around his neck. "Clayton's dead!" He stood shaken as Ferrington described the accident.

"And Philip?"

She pointed to a miniscule figure high on the ice fields. "He won't quit! Says he's going to solo his way to the top of the yellow band."

Neither spoke, they simply stared at each other. Kalamatra stood dumbfounded; hold her or kiss her, he wasn't sure. But neither was she. She had never encountered anyone as unusual as Nicholas Batiste Kalamatra, and suddenly she felt nothing but admiration for his daring courage. Ferrington stood frozen, how was it possible that she could have such strong feelings for two men who were so different? Philip presented a carefully crafted veneer to the world, while the Greek knew nothing of inhibitions. Even their views of climbing were polar opposites; reaching the pinnacle of the world, Everest's summit, held no special hidden meaning for the Greek and meant everything to Phillip.

Her indecision was brought to an abrupt end as an explosion high on the Solu Khumbu ice field was so intense the ground below them shook. Wires anchoring tents snapped. Boxes of supplies, neatly stacked, splattered over the tundra. A minute later, another rumble, this time even more violent, further splintered the glacier apart. Walls tumbled. Shouts of fear echoed from those scampering downward off the ice field. As the ground settled 1,000 feet above, those at base camp could see minute figures gathered on a bulging crest of an ice buttress frantically waving their arms.

Audrey stood trembling. "What are they saying?"

"Mountain swallows people. Hole opens, shuts." Anbar interpreted.

Audrey yelled into the receiver, "Philip, say something, anything!"

Pemba made radio contact. "Accident … Accident … Leader and two sherpas disappear into black hole. Hear nothing!"

As muffled cries filtered downward, a frantic waving of sherpas' arms made her fear the worst. Her world had spun out of control; Clayton was dead, Philip was missing, and Kalamatra suddenly appeared. How did she become trapped as an unwilling participant with a mountain that had extracted its pound of flesh and was now demanding more? It made her sick. Logic and reason were distant memories; collapsing ice walls mirrored an inner psyche gone amuck.

"Help! Must have help!" Pemba pleaded.

"Unkel, grab extra coils of rope, we're going up!" Kalamatra announced. Even though their hands were wrapped in bandages, Harry and Peter strapped backpacks on their shoulders. Carting rescue gear over their shoulders, Kalamatra, Unkel, Harry, and Peter headed up the ice field leaving Audrey in tears. Once the rescue party was a third of the way up the ice flow, Ferrington strapped on crampons.

Progress for the rescuers was slow as the path up the glacier was strewn with rocks and boulder-sized chunks of twisted blue ice. Burdened with leading, Kalamatra inched upwards, the oncologist's hand accidentally brushing against an ice tentacle, the dagger splintering apart and plunging into a bottomless abyss.

Safe passage was forgotten, all aware that the ice flow might, at any moment, splinter apart. After three grueling hours, showing the debilitating effects of leading, the Greek deposited a reel of rescue rope on the side of the trail, knowing that Unkel would strap this additional weight onto his backpack. Scaling a final ice wall, Kalamatra approached the accident. Seeing the rescuer, Pemba ran to greet him, grief chiseled into the furrows of the sherpa's face. "No sign . . . no voice!" Pemba shook his head as a dozen sherpas knelt by an open abyss, their eyes staring into a black, cavernous hole.

An hour later, joining the rescue team, Audrey scampered to the accident site. "Where's Philip? When was he last seen?" the doctor pressed.

"When avalanche hit," Pemba reported. "Hornsby in lead, Ang Nia and Junga behind. Roar, mountain torn apart; screams, then nothing." Pemba pointed to the bottomless hole.

Nicholas inched to the lip of the crevice, "Hornsby!" Deep within the dark recesses his voice ricocheted, "Hornsby . . . Hornsby . . . Hornsby . . ." On hands and knees, Harry and Peter peered into the narrow four-foot-wide bottomless hole. A minute later they crawled away from the crevice, the botanist spoke, "No choice; someone has to be lowered!" Harry eyed the bandages on his and Peter's hands. "And it can't be either of us!"

"It's futile," Kalamatra assessed.

"You can't just leave them!" Audrey blurted. Wailing, Ferrington crawled to the edge of the abyss. From bad to worse to catastrophic to unimaginable, between sobs she screamed Philip's name into the bottomless hole. Inconsolable, no one dared go near her. Watching as the climbing party prepared to evacuate, Ferrington, perched at the edge of the abyss, screamed, "Sounds . . . far below . . . they are faint! Someone's still alive!" All crawled to the lip, there was no mistake, a guttural cry echoed from below. "One of us," Harry assessed, "must . . ." He looked at Kalamatra.

"I'm not going! The bastard doesn't deserve it! His own words sealed his destiny. There are chances one takes."

"There's no alternative, a rope will be strapped on your harness, Peter and I will secure you from the surface."

"You can't be serious?" Nicholas stared into the abyss. "Me enter that black hole?"

The botanist barked orders. "As you're lowered, shimmy your feet and hands against the walls, use your bottom to support your body. The surface opening appears narrow, but once in the hole, crevices will abound. You'll need this," Peter adjusted a coal miner's flashlight over Kalamatra's climbing helmet, then tied an emergency medical kit and extra coils of rope onto the doctor's backpack.

Crawling to the edge of the jagged opening, the Greek stared at the protruding ice tentacles splintering the four foot wide toothed cavity, the tomb sealed in darkness. Legs trembling, Nicholas inched into the hole.

"Once you find a body," Harry ordered, "tug twice on the rope and we'll pull the injured out."

"And if they're . . . dead?"

"Leave them."

"And me?"

"As soon as an injured climber reaches the surface, the rope will be funneled back."

"How can you be sure you'll relocate me?"

"We can't . . ."

Edging his body into the crevice, after descending one hundred feet, the oncologist peered up, a lone speck of light shone through the surface's narrow opening. A miner's flashlight provided minimal illumination, vision limited only to what lay directly ahead. Tethered to a rope, engulfed in darkness, shivering, the Greek was alone. Feet, searching for support, bumped against a protruding ice tentacle, the broken splinter cascaded downward. Dangling from the wall, the rope twisted as he was further lowered into the blackness.

"Kala . . . Kala . . . matra . . ."

Audrey's voice echoed throughout the chamber. "Keep go . . . ing . . . ing . . ."

An ice slab supporting his feet broke. Clutching hands to his chest, Nicholas eyed the hellish chamber. Intricate tunnels funneled into mammoth openings, menacing rows of stalactites stood poised, precariously balanced, ready to decapitate him. "Enough! Get me out!"

"Keep . . . keep . . . on . . . on . . . on . . ." he heard Audrey plead, "going . . . going . . ."

Fearful of venturing where footing was unknown, afraid to chance tumbling thousands of feet, Kalamatra peered into the darkness. "Retreat! Advance! Give up!" Repeatedly he yelled, but no answer. Sliding behind an overhanging ice tower, huddled between rocks he berated himself, "Give me a chance to quit!" But, despite his pleading, inch by inch, the taut rope lowered him ever deeper. Every breath caused a dull ache to slice through his lungs, bitter cold irritated his throat; attempting to warm incoming air, Kalamatra placed a wool sock over his mouth. A blood vessel in his eye burst, vision momentarily blurred, a layer of ice formed over the wool sock protecting his mouth. Logic screamed at him to retreat, yet he kept going.

"Philip," he weakly screamed, "answer me!" Floodgates of doubt erupted; what if he couldn't find a route back up the crevice? Impetuous, yes, but a hero, no, this was no way to die. He feared the worst, finding anybody alive was remote, yet repeatedly, without conviction, he yelled for Philip but heard nothing. How could he be so foolish? The irony of sacrificing his life for a man who he disdained made no sense, yet this rescue was some sort of unquestioned rite of manhood; valor calls, do your duty, but as he squeezed his body through a narrow opening ever deeper into a grave of his own making, this misguided rescue attempt was voluntarily committing suicide. His death would linger, arms and legs were numb, body to follow. "Philip . . . Philip . . . Philip . . ." Covering his nose and mouth with a bandana, leaving eyes protected by goggles, Kalamatra screamed, "Hornsby, answer me," but all he heard was his voice bounce from wall to wall.

"No . . . use . . . use . . ." he protested.

"Ma booo . . . ." the words were faint.

"Further down . . . to the left . . . ." Nicholas screamed at the surface. Lowered further, his feet struck an ice bridge. Gingerly applying his weight, the shelf held. Sinking to his hands and knees, he crawled toward the sound. "Say something!"

"Ah . . . tah!"

As his light searched for the source of the sound, the doctor shimmied across an ice bridge. Inching across the thin artery, directly below an anguished voice gasped for breath, "Om ba." Reaching the bodies, vomit rushed to his throat as he witnessed daggers of ice impaling the two sherpas. The closest, Ang Nia lay inert, blood frozen in pools beside the lifeless body, ice tentacles piercing his rib cage, thigh, and neck.

"Ke . . . ta," Junga weakly mumbled. Kalamatra crawled toward the sherpa, the porter's head was thrown to a side, an ice tentacle scissored into his left shoulder. Yanking the tentacle free and using his hand to apply pressure over the exposed wound, he tried to stop the blood from gushing from the opening. Junga gasped for breath. Nicholas administered mouth to mouth resuscitation, pushing air into the sherpa's collapsed chest cavity, only to suck out mouthfuls of blood. Muscles in the sherpa's arms and legs involuntarily twitched; suddenly Junga's palms opened, his fingers became listless. Kalamatra violently shook the sherpa, but Junga's glazed corneas remained open, but frozen. Nicholas had no time to grieve as garbled words, faint and weak, came from an opening below the shelf. Leaving the two corpses Nicholas inched towards the source of the sound. Below him was the outline of a body curled into an embryonic ball, the victim's left hand clutched within his belly. Kalamatra's flashlight circled Philip's body; Hornsby's face was ashen, lips parched, bluish green eyes sunk deep within his forehead. He touched Philip's shoulder ever so slightly, but even slight pressure made Hornsby moan. Piled beside Philip's left hand, two flesh-colored stems, each approximately three or four inches in length protruded from the snow.

"Keep them!" Hornsby gasped, "Fill a plastic bag with ice shavings."

"Why?"

"Fingers . . . to sew back on!"

Locked deep within the ice vault, both men wept. Kalamatra, forcing Philip's injured hand open, poured medication over the severed wound then applied a tourniquet to stop the bleeding before stuffing Philip's severed fingers, packed in ice, inside the expedition leader's pocket. Disregarding Hornsby's cries, for close to an hour he tugged, in vain, pulling the moaning climber upwards through the constricted corridors but, never seeing a minute glimmer of light filtering downward.

"It's no use. Leave me. Save yourself." Hornsby's guttural moans prevented him from saying anything else. As Kalamatra tied his only rope into Hornsby's harness, the oncologist cursed his luck; this was the ultimate irony, when it was his time for retribution, he was the one being left behind. "As soon as I tug, those on top are going to haul you out of this hole." Oblivious to Philip's screams, Nicholas jerked the rope and Hornsby, curled in a fetal position, clutching his injured hand into his torso, was inched upward from the ice mantle. Afraid to waste what little illumination remained of the weakening battery, as Hornsby's figure disappeared, Kalamatra switched off his flashlight. Arms wrapped around his torso he squatted, shivering in darkness. Every time Hornsby's body bumped the wall, Philip's moans reverberated throughout the cavernous walls. Left alone in the blackened abyss, realizing chances of a rope relocating him were slim, as the minutes wore on, fear left him desperate. If the tables were turned, if he was trapped, he was confident Hornsby would have abandoned him. Shivers swept through his body. Eyes closed. He awoke hearing faint words echoing from wall to wall. "Kala . . . Kala . . . matra!" Shining his flashlight toward the sound, there was no rope. Hands, nearly frozen, groped for an umbilical cord to survive but found nothing. Trying to stand, he crumpled back to the ice; thighs, toes and hands were useless. Tears froze on his cheeks as a bone-chilling cold rifled through his extremities, a voice inside screamed, *It's over*, but his eyes refused to close.

An hour passed, maybe more, before he thought he heard a voice, "Unkel come . . . come . . . come." Then nothing! Was it imagined? Does a mind play devilish tricks before succumbing? Minutes later, he again thought he heard the sherpa's voice bounce from wall to wall inside the ice cavity, but Nicholas' chattering teeth didn't permit a response. "Nic . . . Nic . . . Nic . . . " High above, Unkel slithered between jutting ice slabs. "Matra . . . matra . . . matra . . .," the sherpa's voice spiraled within the crevice's narrow corridors.

"Unkel . . ." he whispered, but his voice was swallowed within a labyrinth of intersecting tunnels. The sherpa, edging downward, trying to catch his breath, propped his body onto an ice mantle, but a frozen lip gave way and he somersaulted downward. Plummeting twenty feet, Unkel came to an abrupt halt when the jagged end of a sharp rock severed his left pants leg shattering a bone between his knee and ankle. Dismissing the pain, the sherpa kept going until stumbling upon the doctor. Kalamatra, coated with a film of ice, lay frozen, head listlessly drooped to a side, eyes glazed, a glassy film caking bloodshot corneas. Demanding recognition, Unkel slapped Nicholas's cheeks. He jerked the oncologist to his feet, but trying to make the doctor stand under his own power proved impossible. Shivering uncontrollably, tinges of blue appearing beneath his fingernails, Kalamatra's chattering teeth forced Unkel to remove his down jacket and wrap it around the Greek. The sherpa clipped his rope, their lone lifeline to survival, into Nicholas's harness. Kalamatra's lips, frozen together, prevented him from protesting. One would remain behind, probably forever. The sherpa jerked on the rope twice before Kalamatra's frozen body was inched toward the surface. Kalamatra's eyes pleaded with Unkel, but the sherpa never hesitated.

Nearing the opening, Pemba's hands reached into the crevice and pulled the doctor over the protruding lip. As his frozen body was dragged from the opening, trailing heels left ruts in the snow. Minutes later the rope was thrown back into the crevice in the hope of finding Unkel. Time after time the rope was fed into a different hole; time after time Harry and Peter's efforts produced nothing, but neither would give up.

Sealed in an ice tomb, Unkel sat crunched in a ball. An ice axe, preventing mobility, was strapped onto his mangled leg, but even the slightest movement caused him to cry in agony. A small consolation was the pain from his broken leg was lessened by bone-chilling cold. As he lay freezing to death there was no remorse, no feeling sorry, he had done what was expected, nothing more, nothing less, his eyes would close knowing he brought honor to his family.

Unkel was only semi-conscious when a descending rope hit his shoulder. Instinct made him clip an end into his harness. Tugging on the rope, he was hoisted upward, each time the sherpa's injured leg brushed the wall, screams echoed. Once reaching the surface, Ferrington, seeing the sherpa wince, removed his left sneaker and rolled up his pant leg, the shin swollen to the size of a grapefruit. X-rays were unnecessary, the femur had shattered. "Oh . . . *ma bujhdina*," Unkel moaned.

"Take these pills," Audrey ordered. After using a ski pole to prevent Unkel's broken leg from moving, Audrey stuffed additional painkillers into the sherpa's mouth.

The injured were wrapped in blankets and placed within feet of each other. Nicholas, too numb to talk, heard Dr. Ferrington's assessment: "X-rays will confirm what's obvious. The sherpa's leg is broken, a non-displaced fracture. Three weeks of no weight bearing, followed by two months in a walking cast. So long as he's careful, he'll heal. As far as the doctor is concerned, it will take a couple of days, but, with proper rewarming, Kalamatra will recover. But it's Hornsby's injury taht necessitates an immediate response, in order to prevent infection, a surgeon must immediately sever the index and middle fingers above the knuckle."

Harry faced Ferrington. "Soon as we drag them to base camp, you're operating!"

"But I have no surgical training!"

The botanist fired back. "They're your words . . . either the stumps are sutured or gangrene will set in."

Ferrington radioed Morley in Kathmandu. "Hornsby's hurt! Need immediate transport. Contact Royal Nepalese Air, send a helicopter to Everest base camp. Do you read me?"

"Are others injured?"

"Two sherpas, Junga and Ang Nia are dead, Unkel's leg is broken!"

Morley responded, "If the weather holds, a copter will be at base camp tomorrow morning."

"No! Today!" Audrey implored. She stared into Philip's dilated eyes, "Hornsby's condition is critical!"

"Afternoon clouds . . . limited visibility . . .can't be done!"

Philip, delirious, didn't respond when Audrey screamed his name. Philip, Kalamatra, and Unkel were hauled down the Solu Khumbu ice field.

Upon reaching base camp, Harry and Peter transformed the supply tent into an operating room. A kettle of water soon boiled on top of a propane stove. Wrapped in blankets, semi-conscious, moaning, Philip was tied onto a makeshift operating table. Ferrington was acutely aware that the procedure needed to be done in a hospital, under proper anesthesia, by a trained surgeon. Intravenous antibiotics were required, blood transfusions available, but the price of inaction portended a disaster; time was not an ally, unless she acted immediately, Philip would either lose the entire arm or die of blood poisoning. Removing a scalpel from the boiling water, Harry placed the instrument into her hand. "Cut!"

Ferrington jabbed a syringe of morphine into Philip's thigh, the painkillers rendering her fiancé unconscious. Tying his torso and legs to the stretcher proved unnecessary. Scalpel in hand, she began sawing, chunks of skin and bone soon lay on the table.

Pemba held Hornsby's severed fingers in the air. "Want?"

"Take them away!" she barked. Fifty-five minutes later what was left of the hand was wrapped in gauze. Audrey, wringing wet, sat shaking on a stool as Hornsby was carted into a separate tent. Trembling, holding a bloodied knife, Peter Birdwein tried to comfort the distraught doctor, but all he could do was hold her as her arms thrashed against his chest.

Changing compresses, wiping foreheads, forcing liquids into parched throats, Ferrington checked on her patients throughout the night. Philip never regained consciousness, and in an adjoining tent Kalamatra lay motionless next to Unkel. The sherpa, although wincing in pain, every hour crawled on hands and one leg to place hot compresses against Kalamatra's chest and stomach.

The remainder of the night Audrey sat by the fire, her mind playing tricks. In an adjoining tent two men lay unconscious; nothing made sense. Traits about Kalamatra both repelled and fascinated her; she had no idea what the future would hold. Would their relationship evolve, grow, fall flat on its face? The only certainty was that, with him, life was exhilarating. Perhaps they might mesh; she would bring love, guide and teach him, nourish him; while he would push, but to where? The man was unpredictable, brash, opinionated, obstinate, the pendulum would swing in directions she'd never control. Throughout the climb Hornsby had been a pillar of strength; Philip represented solidarity, decisions made during the march only deepened her respect for him. His leadership left no doubt, Hornsby was a man to be admired. She could balance her commitment to medicine, raise a family, have it all, but what did she want? As the second-guessing ripped through her psyche, searching for an answer added confusion; no decision could be made until she returned home.

48. Audrey's Choice

By mid-morning, a grinding hum could be heard as a helicopter advanced up the valley. Rotating blades, glistening in the sun, tilted slightly as the pilot landed the machine in a pile of rock rubble adjoining the glacier. Minutes later Hornsby's unconscious body, strapped on a stretcher, was hauled onboard.

"Room for one more," the pilot screamed.

Harry eyed Audrey. "Get in."

She shook her head.

The door slammed, the engine roared, blades swirled, and, within a minute, the helicopter disappeared. Why she stayed remained a mystery. For an hour she sat comatose in a corner of the Greek's tent, staring as Unkel sat vigil over Kalamatra's shivering body, forcing hot tea laced with glucose into the doctor's mouth. Unkel, disregarding the pain of his broken leg, sat glued by the doctor's side. Seeing pain etched into the sherpa's face, Ferrington offered, "I have medicine."

"Duty!"

Nothing she could say would change the sherpa's mind.

Nightfall arrived. Audrey, leaving her sleeping bag, crawled past the comatose Kalamatra and sat outside. Peter Birdwein, seeing Audrey alone, joined her. "Why didn't you leave when you had the chance?"

Audrey whispered, "I left the States thinking I was in love with Philip. He offered me a lifestyle straight out of the movies; elegant evenings, weekends in St. Tropez, Zermat, gala openings at opera houses, everything was neat and orderly, a coterie of people catering to our every need." Audrey paused. "And then the Greek barged into my life, the man's an embarrassment—awkward, brazen, socially inept."

"That doesn't answer why you didn't get into the helicopter."

"The least I can do is stay here and help."

49. *The Retreat*

Damage needing to be assessed, dreading what unveiling his toes and fingers would reveal, Unkel assisted Ferrington in slipping off Kalamatra's socks and mittens, but to her amazement amputation of either toes or fingertips would not be needed. By day three, Kalamatra's strength showed signs of returning; breathing stabilized, his body stopped shaking, color returned to his face. Unkel's broken leg showed no sign of infection, but the sherpa was limited to crawling, no weight bearing for weeks. Rest, followed by a cast, would be necessary, but an operation would not be needed. Mandatory rest was required before the remaining expedition members could start their journey back to civilization, but the crisis was over.

Waiting was torturous, all Ferrington wanted to do was return home, the trip leaving her with a maze of confusion and exhaustion. Nothing was clear; men and their twisted psyches, obsessions driving people to both risk and lose lives. Hours were spent staring at the surrounding toothed giants, their beauty meant nothing. Under the guise of adventure, the men in her life burdened themselves by shouldering saddlebags filled with errant dreams; Philip convinced that scaling a barren rock stood for something, Kalamatra chasing emotions, Clayton sacrificing his life. Facing the mountains, cursing men, their immaturity, their fragile egos, confusion was her bed partner.

Day four after the accident Kalamatra's eyes opened. Dragging him out of the tent, Ferrington perched him against a protruding rock. Not a word was exchanged as billowing clouds blocking the sunlight skidded across the sky. The jury remained deadlocked, either the fog would lift and the day would clear or they'd be caught in a storm. No matter the outcome, Ferrington made up her mind, even if snow descended in buckets, the time spent in this hellhole was over; they were heading back to Kathmandu.

Poised to begin their retreat, everyone stood in line as Harry and Peter sat by Clayton's grave saying a final goodbye. Conversation was nonexistent as the two placed pebbles atop a rock pile. Using ropes to lash wood together, they inserted a wooden cross above the grave, Peter chiseling a nameplate inscribed *Clayton Johnson* adhered to a stanchion. Father and brother sat by the tomb as tears, like spring floods overflowing banks, cascaded down faces. Suddenly Harry snapped, his fingers tearing at the stones, trying to unearth his son's soul. Peter pulled his father away, his arm encircling him as the botanist sobbed. "Clayton lives; his spirit, zest for life, simplicity, nobody can take his memory away."

Leaving the carnage of Everest behind, Ferrington led the procession as they wound their way over the narrow trail leading to Namche Bazaar. In the middle of the pack, disdaining help, Kalamatra stumbled under his own power. Directly behind, his body lashed to a wooden stretcher, sherpas took turns dragging Unkel. At the end of the marchers, Harry and Peter Birdwein walked together. The retreat was painfully slow; Kalamatra's weakened state combined with Unkel's broken leg turned progress into a snail's pace. Threading down the dirt path, there was no joy, no laughter, just the monotonous plodding of a defeated army dragging their beleaguered remains. Ferrington couldn't fathom Unkel's tolerance for pain, being dragged down steep inclines his makeshift gurney repeatedly banged against rocks, but the sherpa never complained. Instead of the march weakening the Greek, perhaps it was a northern breeze that carried crisp air, but when Ferrington instructed everyone they were stopping for the day, Kalamatra could have kept going. That night after dinner, the Greek offered Audrey his hand, extending an invitation for Ferrington to join him in his tent. Instead she turned her back, the last thing Ferrington needed was an additional emotional complication.

Reaching Namche Bazaar, a destination that should have taken two days, took five. The prospects of leading her crew the one hundred and twenty plus miles on a dirt trail to Lamsangu was mercilessly avoided when Austin Morley reached her on the radio. "Further south, at Lukla, there's a dirt airstrip cut into a mountain. I've arranged, weather-permitting, two days from now for an eight-passenger aircraft to land midmorning and cart you and the climbing party back to Kathmandu." For the first time in nearly a month, a faint smile spread across her face.

Early on the morning of the rendezvous with the Royal Nepalese aircraft, the retreating party arrived at a dirt-covered cow pasture cut into the side of a mountain. An hour later the whine of an engine could be heard; the pilot, steering the craft into a valley below the cow pasture, suddenly zoomed upward, darting over the ridge. After landing, applying full brakes, the pilot brought the vintage aircraft to a stop within thirty yards of a granite wall. Wheeling the plane in a semicircle, dust swirling, not even turning off the engines, the climbing party crammed through the doors. Unkel's stretcher was the last to be shoved inside the thirty-year-old twin otter's fuselage before the pilot applied full power and the antique craft lumbered down the dirt runway.

Arriving in Kathmandu, they went directly to the Yak & Yeti Hotel. Kalamatra told the reception clerk he and Dr. Ferrington needed just one room, the Greek's invitation was silenced when Ferrington, a separate key in hand, headed up the staircase. alone

A letter from Philip was waiting on her bed.

You did everything you could to save my fingers. Since home, two additional operations have been necessary, but the severed fingers were useless. But I'm a fighter; doctors tell me that within six months I'll be playing tennis well enough to give you a battle. Notify me with your travel plans, can't wait to see you. I love you!

The next morning Ferrington announced, "After breakfast I'm leaving."

Kalamatra couldn't believe what he was hearing. "You're what?"

"Morley's arranged that until he's recuperated, Unkel will stay in Kathmandu and work with him.

"We're traveling separately?" Kalamatra inquired.

"I need to be alone," Audrey quipped right back.

Entering the Kathmandu airport, Ferrington was besieged by reporters.

"How did you feel operating on someone you love?"

"Was he conscious?"

"Without proper supplies, how did you cope?"

"Have you been trained in surgery?"

As questions were fired, Ferrington's comments were minimal, relief coming only when the plane's doors were sealed shut.

Passing by a newsstand at London's Heathrow airport, Audrey stood in shock. W.A. Hornsby, the master of publicity, struck again; his son's attempt at trying to save Clayton transformed Philip into a hero; his subsequent accident a valiant attempt to finish what the botanist's son started. Leafing through the periodical, she started seeing Philip's picture, a caption reading: "American Expedition Fails—One Climber Perishes, Two sherpas Dead." Picking up another magazine, an enclosed story was highlighted on the cover page. "Fiancée of Senatorial Hopeful Performs Surgery on Mate." Covering an entire page was a photograph of her loading Philip into a helicopter. Pictures filled page after page; a photograph even captured Philip emerging from the cavernous hole, his mangled hand wrapped in bandages. The article concluded announcing that within the month, Philip would make a definite decision of whether or not he intended to run for Pennsylvania's vacated senatorial seat, public opinion polls indicating widespread support.

50. Home Sweet Home

Clearing US customs, she saw Philip waiting. Minutes later they were in the back of a limousine heading for his townhouse in Philadelphia, Philip assuming they were spending the night together.

"Your hand?" she inquired.

A small bandage covered the wound. "The marvels of modern medicine. Only the best for a Hornsby; Dad had the world's most renowned hand surgeon flown in from Switzerland to perform the surgery, the two severed fingers were grafted at the joint, but the rest of the hand was saved and is functional."

"And your career?"

"Going forward as scheduled. When will you resume at the hospital?"

"Hopefully tomorrow."

Philip cautioned. "Perhaps a little rest is in order."

Audrey retorted, "Not a day goes by without haunting memories of what happened on that mountain!"

"Time . . ." Philip volunteered, "heals."

Audrey whispered, "I should never have gone."

"It's over, move forward."

As the car whisked past her apartment, Ferrington instructed the driver to turn around.

"Why?" Philip asked.

She was at a loss for words.

Philip was surprisingly understanding. His arm cradling her shoulder, his voice filled with warmth and tenderness. "Whatever you want."

Early the next morning, headlights were still shining on cars when she drove to the hospital. Being busy was the only way she could dull the memories; immersing herself in medicine, returning to responsibilities and time forces you to stop thinking about personal relationships. Pulling into the deserted parking lot, following protocol, she went directly to see Dr. Roberts, the hospital director. The austere silver-haired physician sat perplexed as, dispensing with formalities, Ferrington blurted out, "I've returned, a bit worse from the journey, but ready to start."

"Bulletins were posted outside of the cafeteria keeping us abreast of the expedition's progress. All of us are curious, there must be tales."

"It's over . . . just let me start."

"So soon?"

"But on one condition . . ."

"Explain."

"Move my rotation away from Dr. Kalamatra."

Roberts' bifocals edged to the bridge of his nose. "Dr. Ferrington, studying medicine is not akin to musical chairs. Medical decisions are separate from personal issues; since you have started a residency in pediatric oncology, as long as Dr. Kalamatra serves as chief of that department, upon his return from Kathmandu you will work under his supervision. Coincidentally, he called yesterday, and within a week he'll be back." The hospital director adjusted his bifocals. "Ferrington, I appreciate you coming in today, but you are not starting for another ten days. You're less than forty hours from being off a plane, for your sake, for the patients' best interest, and, as a friend, take time off." The doctor pointed to the door.

51. Confusion

Entering the Hornsby Pavilion, a guard who recognized Dr. Ferrington whisked her onto a private elevator to the penthouse floor. Lost in a sea of confusing thoughts, she stood in the metallic box not sure how she'd react. As soon as the elevator doors opened, a receptionist pointed. "No need to knock." Seeing her enter, Philip, smartly attired in a black pinstriped suit, stood. Why did her fiancé need to be so damned handsome? Motioning for Audrey to take a seat, Philip addressed his father. "This discussion can wait until later." W.A., seated on a black leather couch diagonally across from Philip, rose and much to his disdain, watched his offspring exit.

"Tonight, your choice of a restaurant."

"I . . ." Ferrington fumbled with her words, "dropped by for a brief hello . . .need to rush if I'm going to catch my plane."

"To?"

"A surprise visit to see my family."

After giving her a hug he insisted on driving her to the airport.

52. Seeking Answers

"Can you . . ."

"Speak up," her father interrupted. "We have a bad connection."

"Pick me up."

"If only . . . I'll just hop in my truck and drive across the country so we can have coffee. Nothing would please me more."

"Then get in the car."

Jonathan was speechless when she told him she was standing outside baggage pickup at the local airport. "And don't tell Mom, I can just imagine her face when I come bouncing through the door."

Perhaps it was due to cumulative fatigue, what happened on Everest, or a plane ride across half of the world, but the emotional and physical exhaustion caused Audrey to collapse on a nearby bench.

Within an hour of sitting around a kitchen table, laughter was conspicuously missing. Peppered with questions about the trip, Audrey answered with curt, non-descriptive answers. A well of emotions wanted to burst, but instead she excused herself and headed toward her childhood room. She hadn't ascended but a couple steps when her father's worries echoed up the hallway. "I'm not used to seeing my girl without her normal vitality."

Abigail tried to temper Jonathan's worries, "She's just tired. Audrey's a battler; once she returns to her medicine she'll be fine."

Not wanting to hear anything else, Ferrington closed the door behind her.

A couple days passed and much to her parents' consternation she remained uncommunicative; confusion etched on her face broadcasting to her parents she needed to be left alone. Lost in her thoughts, she was desperate to sort things out, weigh alternatives, pit minuses against pluses, stumble upon a sign . . . but nothing was forthcoming.

On Sunday morning, except for church services, nobody did much of anything. That morning Ferrington proved an exception; the sun was barely peeking over the horizon when she entered the family's barn and dusted off an old trail bike. A voice urged her to drag the bike outside; she remembered moments in high school when confused, she'd slide into the saddle and furiously pedal, clarity surfacing, sweating while riding through the miles of scrub brush surrounding her house. Hopping aboard the bike, she started pedaling . . . and pedaling . . . and pedaling . . . and except for being coated in sweat, two hours later she returned as confused as before she left.

Upon her return, her parents were waiting in the kitchen. Audrey, tight-lipped as a clam, didn't permit a conversation. "I'm going upstairs to throw my things into a bag. It's time to go back to work. If I'm going to catch the noon plane I need to hurry." The highways were nearly deserted as they headed to the airport, the car's radio station tuned to National Public Radio. A panel of political columnists discussing rising stars of the

Republican party naturally turned to Phillip. "You must be proud."

Their daughter didn't respond.

53. Returning to Two Worlds

Driving to work in complete darkness, Ferrington had no idea how she'd feel confronting the eccentric doctor, but neither theatrics nor intimidation would scare her off. Exiting the elevator leading to the pediatric oncology ward of the University of Pennsylvania Hospital, she scooted behind a two-way mirror and peeked inside. What startled her was every face from a couple months ago was now different. Suddenly the door at the far corridor swung open and Dr. Nicholas Baptiste Kalamatra, his once rosy cheeks now hollow, pranced down the aisle, his magician's routine triggering wide grins and boisterous laughter. Even before an act was completed the children screamed for an encore. "That trick's too easy! I know how you did that! Don't think you're fooling us!" Zest missing, straining to prance from one end of the corridor to the other, the Greek's routine lacked its usual vitality. Situated behind the nurse's station, Gladys steadfastly maintained her position, her beady eyes warning the children not to allow their enthusiasm to get out of control.

Not knowing what possessed her, Ferrington exited and darted into a room that contained the physicians' lockers. A moment later, joining the Greek, she sprang through the doors, a black robe flowing behind her. Whirling in a circle, her cape swirling, a giraffe mysteriously appeared from beneath her garment. A balloon-sized object metamorphosed into a dragonfly then transformed into a chicken and, finally, a multicolored cow. Changing outfits she peeled away the cape and threw on a train conductor's hat. Kalamatra's final act, a departing choo-choo train, found him playing the conductor, Audrey, the engineer. Energy returned to his voice as the Greek bellowed, "All aboard that's coming aboard. This is an express train; change for local stops." Arms pumping, the two headed out the door. As they departed, the children screamed for more, but the door swung shut. Putting a finger to her mouth, Gladys, the head nurse, reappeared and demanded order be restored, annoyance spewing from her eyes when the doors unexpectedly reopened and the two physicians appeared for a grand finale. Heaving coal into an imaginary locomotive engine, her arms began chugging; motivating her was a smile that spread across the face of a woefully thin girl who, summoning the energy to sit upright in her bed, clapped for the show to continue. The Greek blew one shrill blast from an oversized whistle and powder, resembling steam, puffed into the air as they moved toward the stainless steel doors leading to an antiseptic dull green corridor. Waving from an imaginary caboose, Audrey threw handfuls of glitter into the air as she exited behind the conductor. Even before Ferrington's trailing cape cleared the passageway, Gladys darted into the middle of the hallway, her stare silencing the children's giggles. Within minutes, the ward settled back into a perpetual state of waiting.

Suddenly they were alone. Stuffing their magician's outfits into lockers, slipping on laboratory coats, Ferrington refused to allow their eyes to meet. She wanted to scream, her fists tight-ened, the awkwardness of the moment demanding release. It had been almost two weeks since leaving him in Kathmandu and they had not talked. Acting like this meeting was just another "ho-hum" nothing out-of-the-ordinary, he muttered, "I guess a time has come to learn some new tricks."

The remainder of the morning Audrey was busy. Medicines were prescribed, X-rays studied, chemotherapy regimens ordered and blood tests analyzed. Except for conversing about medical issues, the two physicians never exchanged a personal word. Immediately after lunch she attended a lecture by a visiting pro-fessor who presented a paper on experimental techniques of administering chemotherapy to adolescent patients afflicted with bone marrow leukemia. After the presentation, Ferrington scurried down the corridor and took a seat in an amphitheater of an operating room to witness a surgeon remove a malignant growth attached to the larynx of a five-year-old boy. Afternoon rounds then followed, Kalamatra's demeanor serious as the two examined patients.

After work, she returned to the deserted physicians' chang-ing room. A bouquet of red roses was pinned on her locker. A note read:

In celebration of your return to work.

Philip

P.S. There's a rumor circulating at the club that the Beales have hired a private tennis coach. Are you up to the challenge?

Instead of going home, she entered the expressway and drove in the direction of the rolling hills of Haverford Township. Pressing her foot against the car's accelerator the automobile sped through traffic. The blaring of horns, sirens, congestion disappeared as she escaped into a world alive with trees, bushes, and grass. Normally an hour trip, the ride to the country took less than forty-five minutes. Impulsively, Ferrington pulled off the highway and parked her car in a deserted lot adjoining a country park.

She walked alone. Although the sun was disappearing, the evening bringing a biting cold, she ventured farther into the woods, momentarily stopping beneath a row of towering oaks. A brisk wind forced her to button her overcoat, slip on gloves, and wrap a scarf around her face. Twigs lying on the ground captured her attention. Stooping to pick up remnants of fall, brittle sticks splintered into pieces. She questioned what she should do. She had no idea, but with darkness encroaching, she hurried back to her car. She craved clarity, a path to follow, but forks in the road left her perplexed.

Stopping on the way home, Ferrington walked into a diner, took a seat far in the back, ordered soup and half a sandwich, then sat and waited. Trying to occupy herself reading a newspaper, this diversion didn't work as a voice from within prompted her to take out a cellphone and dial Harry and Peter's home in Boulder, Colorado.

"Harry Birdwein."

"It's Audrey."

A pause ensued. "I recognize your voice."

"Peter?"

"He taught a climbing class today, he will be home soon."

"And you?"

"I'm teaching."

She asked, "Have you been in contact with Austin Morley?"

"Yes . . ."

"The sherpa, Unkel, what can you tell me?"

"Leg's healing fine, currently he's working as an assistant in Morley's office in Kathmandu." A pause ensued. "What about you?"

"Back at the hospital." A waitress came by and placed her soup on the table. "I just wanted to hear your voice. Tell Peter I was thinking of him. If either of you ever get to Philadelphia, a friend would be upset if you didn't visit!"

54. The Heart Knows

Exchanging her outerwear for a magician's cape, squashing a paper snake into one of three secret compartments in her sleeve, a pit gnawed in her stomach. Pondering what to do after work, she was a maze of tangled nerves; plans called for dinner with Philip at a small quaint French bistro, a time to reunite . . . for a man used to getting his way, since her arrival back in the States her fiancé had been remarkably patient.

Crammed into a closet that contained a one-way window so she could peer inside the drab hospital ward, she watched as nurse Gladys patrolled the corridor. The nurse's beady eyes intimidated children to peer blankly at paint chips peeling off an olive green ceiling. Dressed in her magician's outfit, the resident oncologist shoveled confetti into a secret compartment inside her cape. Suddenly a door leading from the opposite corridor swung open, Kalamatra's face painted as a clown, the black, white, and red rings unable to camouflage the hollowed depressed orbs gutting beneath his eyes. A weight loss of close to thirty pounds left the oncologist a shell of his former robust self, but an infectious smile burst with energy. Witnessing Kalamatra awkwardly fumble through his routine, Audrey wished she could disappear.

Labeling his tricks as magic pushed the word's definition past its extreme. Halfway through his routine, raising hands overhead was Audrey's signal to make an appearance. Cringing, she pushed the door ajar. The ensuing performance wouldn't have survived the first act of an off-off-Broadway show, Audrey so awkward she even fumbled trying to locate an elongated multicolored snake velcroed inside her cape. As children screamed, "You're not fooling us!" she nearly tore the cape's lining apart as her fingers tried to separate the snake from its hiding place.

After finishing their routine, for the remainder of the day, except for discussing cases, ordering medicine, prescribing regimes of chemotherapy, the two remained distant icebergs bobbing on a windswept angry sea. By five in the afternoon, after ten hours on her feet, Audrey sank in exhaustion by her locker. Peeking through a window she saw Philip in the back seat of W.A.'s black limo, the motor idling, waiting to pick her up. After slipping on jeans and a sweater, she buttoned her jacket, then threw an oversized scarf around her neck. Just as she exited into the parking lot, a car pulled alongside her and the wheels squealed to a halt. The driver's window was lowered, Kalamatra fumbled his words. "Tomatoes were plump, so I took a chance. It's nothing fancy, but I bought enough Italian bread and meatballs for two."

Audrey froze.

The time had arrived to make a choice. Conflict erupted. Opposites flooded her psyche. Stability versus spontaneity, passion versus predictability, a life with every material need met versus a future infused with doubt. At that moment, scaling a yellow band would have been easier. An internal magnet pulled her in opposite directions. And just like that, she abandoned logic and opted for spaghetti topped with red sauce.

About the Author

Bart Sobel grew up in Long Island, New York. His career followed two paths. Before starting his professorship at the University of North Carolina at Chapel Hill, he took a sabbatical and journeyed to Mount Everest. At UNC, Bart was recognized with the Nickolas Salgo undergraduate distinguished teaching award.

A second path led him to follow his father's footsteps as a summer camp director in New Hampshire. Bart spent seventy-two summers on the shores of Lake Winnipesaukee, forty years as a camp director. A highlight of that career was sitting around a campfire spinning stories. Thousands of youth were enthralled by his tales.

In retirement, two interests have been prominent: writing stories, and along with his wife, Lynda, traveling the world raising money for pediatric cancer by participating in marathons. Presently, Bart lives in New York City.